I0741387

ENYA'S SON

A Daughters of Ireland Novel

CINDY THOMSON

7th & Cherry Publishing

Pensacola, FL

FOR TOM

MY FE.
MY HEART.

Books by Cindy Thomson

Daughters of Ireland Series

Brigid of Ireland

Pages of Ireland

Enya's Son

Ellis Island Series

Grace's Pictures

Annie's Stories

Sofia's Tune

The Roots of Irish Wisdom, Learning From Ancient Voices

Three Finger: The Mordecai Brown Story,

co-authored with Scott Brown

Foreword

Dear Reader, start here. I know you want to get on with the story, so I'll be as brief as possible, but a little background on early sixth-century Ireland will add to your enjoyment of *Enya's Son*. More detailed explanations for the history buff can be found at the end in the Author's Notes.

If you've read the previous books in this series, you know that free women at this time in Ireland had more rights than those in other parts of civilization. They could own property, divorce, become warriors, make many decisions that were afforded to men. This did not mean, however, that traditional roles were not observed; they were, but the rights of all people were spelled out in a sophisticated set of laws referred to as the Brehon Laws. Men and women alike could divorce. As the story opens, Enya fears divorce because no reason had to be given, according to the laws, and a woman could only maintain her free status if she was connected to a family with some type of means.

Fostering one's children was a common practice of the time, although not usually done in the church. Columcille was exceptional in that case at that time.

Certain numbers were thought to bring blessings or curses, especially when one was the seventh son of a seventh son. I tweaked that in my story to include the fifth daughter of a fifth daughter. The ancient people were quite superstitious and such beliefs were commonplace even among the Christians.

Ancient Ireland was ruled by a somewhat chaotic system of kingship. The most powerful clans at the time of Enya's story were the Uí Néills in the north (Columcille's clan) and the Uí Néill's of the south. Uí Néill means Sons of Néill. The northern Uí Néills were possibly responsible for kidnapping Saint Patrick and bringing him to Ireland in the fourth century. There were many branches of the northern Uí Néills living in what today is Ulster and County Donegal. Columcille's father came from the Cenél Conaill. They also had control of parts of Northern Scotland—including Iona where Columcille eventually settled.

The concept of high king was a tenuous one. Battles were constantly waged. While the high king ruled from Tara in what today is County Leinster, his effectiveness on the island was questionable and at this time the northerners held the greatest wealth and power. A clan's territory was divided among lesser kings or subkings. Kingship was not inherited but elected. All the chiefs or subkings met to choose a high king. Likewise, the lesser kings were elected by the people: any free-born member of the clan, although we know only men were chosen. (If you're thinking of Queen Maeve, that story is thought to be myth and of an earlier time period.) The chosen king had to be from a noble (property-owning) family, free from deformity, and of legal age. What that age might have been is debatable.

The family Columcille's mother came from might have been known as the Mac Noes. There is some disagreement among scholars. I chose to make them a distant branch of the northern Uí Néills living in what is now County Fermanagh.

Some readers may not realize that at this time in Ireland priests could be and often were married and had children. The monasteries were the centers of learning and trade and while in other parts of Europe the church was more influential than the government (or was not distinct from the government) it wasn't that way in Ireland. In this story the villain hopes to make it that way.

Some parts of the story come from my imagination, and others from the ancient recorded stories about Saint Columba (Columcille.) For instance, when Columcille claims the "right of testimony," that is fictional. But when he senses angels in the clouds above Daire (Derry), that comes from the ancient books. If you have any questions about where history and fiction merge and diverge in *Enya's Son*, please feel free to contact me. Contact information can be found in the back of the book along with more information about my research.

Irish Gaelic names are problematic for English speakers, myself included. I have included a pronunciation guide and have also listed the ancient place names along with the current place names in the Author's Note for those interested. The map should also be helpful. Please be aware that place names have changed many times in Ireland as the language became more anglicized. For the most part I have used older versions of place names, but sometimes have altered them a bit for today's readers or chosen a version that was not the oldest. I have particularly done so with character names.

Now enjoy your trip to Ireland's (Éire) ancient past.

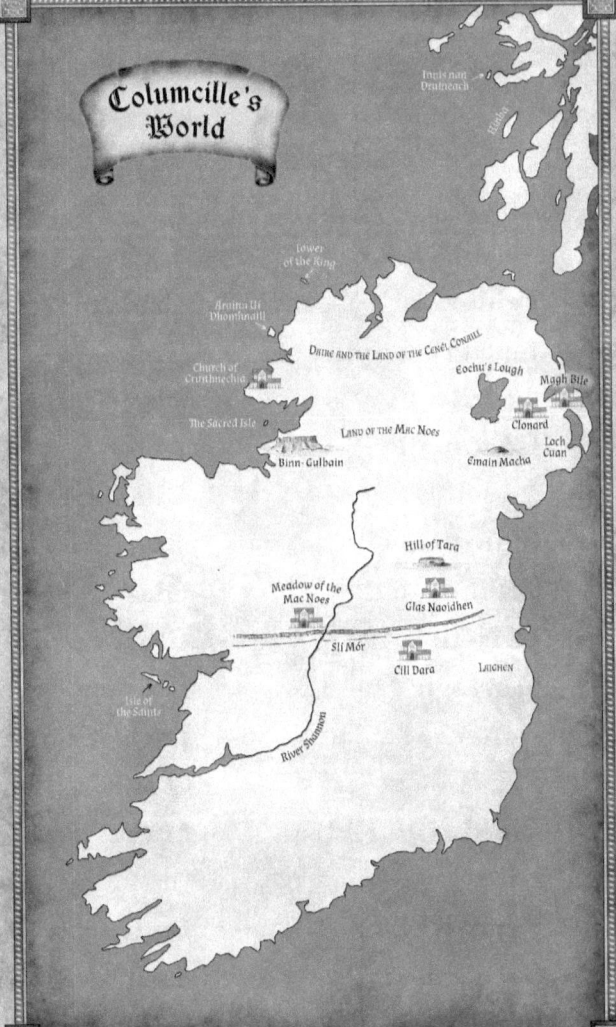

Columcille's World

Innis nan Druineach

Tower of the Ring

Aroina Ui Dhomhnaill

Church of Crunthnechie

Daire and the Land of the Cenél Conaill

Eochu's Lough

Magh Bile

The Sacred Isle

Land of the Mac Noes

Clonard

Loch Cuan

Binn-Gulbain

Emain Macha

Hill of Tara

Meadow of the Mac Noes

Glas Naoidhen

Slí Mór

Cill Dara

Luighen

Isle of the Saints

River Shannon

Pronunciation Guide
May vary in different regions of Ireland.

Enya: AWN-ya. This is the pronunciation I had in my head. However, EN-yeh, like the singer, is acceptable too. The traditional spelling for Columcille's mother is Eithne.

Feidheim: FY-elm. I used Fe for most of the story: FY

Columcille: Col-um-KILL

Crimthann: CREE-uh-fun

Uí Néill: E-nail

Murtagh: Mur-TA

Donnchad: DUN-a-kha

Ciarán: KEE-a-rawn

Kyna: KEE-na

Bairre: Barry

Cruithneachia: Krew-n-ha-na

Binn-Gulbain: Ben Bulben

Cill Dara: Kill-dar-ah

Glas Naoidhen: Glass-NEE-an

Laighen: LAY-n

Loch Cuan: Lock Q-an

Magh Bile: MA-villa

Innis nan Druineach: En-is na Drew-n-ich

Éire: AIR-uh

Mide: Mead

PART ONE

Chapter One

I am a woman who is deeply troubled.
—1 Samuel 1:15 NIV

Enya knew that at any moment he could pack her clothes in a bag and send her out the door. The ancient laws gave him the legal right to divorce her. Although he'd never mentioned such a thing, the possibility loomed over her head like a rain cloud, and she despised the power it gave him to reject her as much as she feared it. Her husband loved her, but was love enough?

Enya dipped a wooden stylus into a horn of black ink. One advantage she'd been granted was instruction. She'd learned to read and write in spite of—no, because of—the violence in her childhood. She had often tarried in the monastery when tempers flared at home. A respectful, obedient child, Enya had gained the favor of the monks who gladly shared with her the wonder of the world of language.

She would write a letter despite Fe's advice to stay away from the pagan ritual. If her husband did not find out, there could be no strife between them.

I am the fifth daughter of a fifth daughter. In the old ways, people believed this extraordinary, worthy of much praise and reverence because there are five kingdoms of Éire. A hand has five fingers and a foot has five toes. Furthermore, my name, Enya, begins with the fifth letter of the alphabet.

Some envy me because I am the daughter of the regional king Oran Mac Noe and have now married into a powerful clan. Being the fifth daughter of a fifth daughter, however, merits no honor for me because I bear a curse that boils down my bloodline. By some mystical touch that wings beyond the bounds of love and hate, this curse must end.

Enya paused to wipe the dampness from her eyes. When she lived with her father she hadn't known when the beatings would begin and had never prepared herself. Sometimes they came when he drank too much. Other times when the harvest was late. Often there had been nothing to prompt his anger that she could discern. "No charmed fifth daughter will cause my undoing!" he had shouted at her the day he made her stand beside his spear target. She had never planned to harm her father, only escape, but on that day she had taken up his thrown spear and aimed it back at him. After that she'd been sent away to marry.

Her father did not matter. Why tears betrayed her, she couldn't fathom. Taking a deep breath, she resumed writing.

An angry, hateful person my father was. Feidheim was granted permission to marry me simply to ensure peace between the clans. My older sisters all escaped the same way before me. Is it evil to desire escape? Some may say I was fated to marry into a royal family. Is that the blessing? They may believe so, but the only blessing is that my child would be in a fine position to become king of the Cenél Conaill, Feidheim's clan, a branch of the most mighty in all of Éire. I dare to think that this marriage could end my curse, never to be passed on. Perhaps those who listen to these pleas will grant my deepest hope.

Enya straightened in her chair and gazed through the window in front of her. The clan's

3

women trooped by with baskets of washing lashed to their hips and children bouncing at their heels. A sour taste formed on her lips. Dipping her tool into the ink pot, she focused on the parchment.

I am a failure. I am barren. I will produce no fifth daughter, nor first daughter or son. I am not blessed though I pray a thousand times a day for a child. I am like Sarah of the scriptures, a target of scorn and recipient of pity. But there is one difference: God told Sarah she would bear a child. She laughed. I would not laugh if God revealed such a thing to me, but my arms are cold and empty. The depths of my soul ache for a wee beating heart to press against my own. Young mothers avoid me, whisking their children away from my outstretched arms lest I pass some death curse onto them. I would curse no one, wish no one harm.

She paused again and then pressed the stylus more firmly to the parchment as she scrawled out her heart's desire.

I yearn for a child.

God, if he existed, would not hear the words of her heart. He had not thus far. So why not try the wee folk of the spiritual realm? She would wrap the vellum with a scarlet thread and tie it to

4

the fairy bush when no one was looking. Enya was desperate to conceive, frantic to put an end to the piercing looks of pity and distaste from the women in her husband's family and beyond. Her despair led her to hope some fertile magic might be sprinkled on her womb. Foolish, that. But she felt much better now that she had expressed herself in inky words.

"What are you doing, my sweet?" Feidheim called from the doorway.

She nearly knocked over the ink pot. He was never in the house so early in the day. Her body blocked his view of her writing. "Just mending, Fe." She shoved the vellum into her apron pocket and grabbed a bone needle she had tossed on the table earlier. The ink on her stained fingers began to soak through the folds of the apron. She bundled up the material and turned to greet him as though she had an ordinary pile of clothes in her hands.

Her husband grunted and plopped his large frame onto a stick-woven chair by the peat fire. "Lost the hog again."

"Again? Maybe he's wandered to the apple trees." She turned away and tossed her things into a basket. She began scrubbing her fingers in

5

the washbasin. Perhaps he would think she was preparing to help the cook. She wished she could tell him what she was doing, but he'd be angry. The unpredictable fury of men was something she always tried to avoid.

"'Tis likely he's up at Murtagh's barn. Thicker grass that's to the beast's liking there."

Enya squeezed her fingers together. The mention of Murtagh always brought the scourge of envy to her throat. Murtagh's daughter-in-law, Nola, had caught Fe's eye when they were younger. He had planned to marry her, but she was betrothed to one of the Murtagh clan before Fe was ready to take care of a wife. Fe himself had told Enya about it on their wedding night. He'd had too much ale and would never remember it now.

But Enya knew, and she also knew that Nola was as fertile as the rolling hills, bearing nearly one child every year since her marriage. Nola glared at Enya every time the two of them met at the well or at a feast in the king's castle, flittering her blonde eyelashes and smoothing her hands down her curvaceous hips. Enya had felt weak at those times and boyishly thin, not worthy of the love of her husband, and the memory of that feel-

6

ing forced its way into her consciousness at the most inopportune moments, especially during times of intimacy with her husband.

Squeezing what was now surely a blotted, messy letter into a tight ball, Enya tossed the vellum into the peat fire. "And you agree with the hog, don't you? 'Tis much more fertile at Murtagh's place than here at home." She brought her hand to her mouth to cover her sobs before she remembered her ink-stained fingers.

Fe bolted from his chair and took her into his arms. "Sweet, sweet. Believe what I've told you a thousand times. I love *you*, my Enya. You may not have a child, but you have me. Am I not enough for you, now?"

If only he could be enough. She buried her face in his shoulder and inhaled the scents of wet grass and horsehide. She had done nothing to deserve this gentle, loving man's affection. He had been patient with her complaining. He'd been tolerant of her melancholy, but how long would he put up with her barrenness? She never could predict a man's changed mood.

Enya hoped she was not fated to pass on the curse even while she feared she surely was. She could do better with her child than her father had with all his children, and she must. If her mother had lived she might have protected Enya and her siblings and taught the sons to be honorable men. The weight of living under an oppressive man had surely been what weakened her heart and sent her to an early grave.

They clung to each other for several heart-beats before Fe finally pulled back. "I've got to see to the hog. Would you like to come with me?"

And face that woman's scoffing stares? She couldn't. Enya shook her head and stared at the hearthstones.

Fe gripped her hands and raised them to look closer. "Been writing, have you?" He clicked his tongue and narrowed his eyes. The pagan festival was approaching when folks would breathe their wishes and desires onto strips of cloth, or write them down if they knew how, and tie them to the branches of a bush. He knew it as well as she.

She spoke before thinking. "Nay, I've been mending is all."

He turned to the fire and glanced at the wad of burning vellum and then lifted her chin up-ward toward his piercing green eyes. "That's all right now. Listen. 'Tis the Sabbath tomorrow. Time we went to Cruithneachia's church and prayed for God to answer your request for a child."

She stared out the open door while contemplating an answer.

He interrupted her thoughts. "I know it seems odd to you, this Christian faith brought to us by Father Patrick of long ago. But it is truth to believe in Jesu."

"I know you believe, my husband. And as your wife I will follow what you think best."

He sighed. "That is not what I want, Enya. I want you to see what I see, feel the love of Jesu I feel. 'Tis more than the ritual and observances you witnessed at that monastery near where you grew up. Such things have purpose, but I want you to know that God is close, teaching, disciplining, and nurturing."

She studied his ruddy face, his handsome cheekbones, his silky beard. What if the God he believed in would listen to him? What if the two of them praying in front of the church's altar could get this God's attention and convince him to grant the child they both wanted? The gods of the woods, the Christian God—she would appeal to all. "Very well. We will go. Now you run along

9

and see about the hog and I'll check with the cook to see how the meal is coming."

The women in Fe's clan always cooked together, choosing to divide and distribute both the work and the reward while the men functioned under ancient laws of hierarchy. Enya's husband owned cattle and grazing rights and had at least a hundred families paying him rent to live on his land. As a nobleman of the highest standing, nearly a decade older than Enya, Fe had the experience and wisdom that the people seemed to trust.

The reigning King Donall, a cousin to Fe, was aged. A successor would be chosen when the king died or suffered a physical or mental flaw that rendered him imperfect. At that time any clansman owning property could be chosen by a majority vote, and no one garnered as much respect from the people as her Fe. However, a man's age was important to this clan. They desired a king young enough to rule for several decades, as the current king had.

As nice as Enya's home was, the castle offered many luxuries. She'd been inside only a handful of times. The place was always warmed by fire, draped in tapestries imported from distant lands, and smelled of roasted meats and fine wines. The castle was the possession of the reigning king. Fe might not be considered due to his age, but his son?

Lifting her hand, she shook her head. She'd imagined this far too often. She had no son.

Enya turned her focus back to gathering herbs hanging from the rafters. She placed them in a basket along with a few roots. Kyna, a servant old enough to be her grandmother but quite hearty, would do the real work. Even so, Enya enjoyed joining in whenever she could. With the meat and cream the others would bring, Kyna would prepare a wondrous meal. Fe would find thick, bubbling stew waiting when he returned with the hog, a symbol of the home's fruitfulness. Enya would see to it.

"Coming today?" Kyna asked. She wore a tidy linen apron with a matching cap, attire fitting a servant in an important household.

"I am indeed. We are to prepare a special meal today, Kyna." Enya admired the woman's name and preferred to use it instead of the formal title of Cook. Kyna meant love or affection. If God were to grant Enya a child, she would choose a descriptive name like Kyna rather than follow tradition. Enya had few memories of her mother, and her father was best forgotten. Likewise, Fe had no attachment to his parents who died young. They'd be free to give their children, should they have any, characteristic names.

Kyna held the door open for her. They made their way toward the smoky air of the outdoor kitchen. The other women politely greeted them, but as usual, Enya only locked eyes with one.

"Have ye some mint?" Gormley asked, lifting Enya's basket from her arms. Gormley, whose husband Brody was the clan's largest property owner after Fe, had a multitude of children, but unlike almost everyone else, she did not hold Enya's barrenness against her. She was as close a friend as someone like Enya could expect to have.

"I do have mint. And some turnips as well. Excellent with mutton, I believe." Enya approached the carcass sizzling on a pit over a smoldering fire and inhaled the thick aroma.

"Indeed. A fine Sunday meal."

Enya cocked her head. "Sunday? I will not wait. Fe will have a fine meal tonight."

"Tonight? Have you lost your mind, woman? 'Twill be no time for—"

Enya grabbed her arm. "Tonight. They'll be enough meat on the shoulder that's ready. You'll cut it off for me."

Gormley exchanged glances with Kyna and then placed her fists on her round hips. "While your husband is older than mine, he can still give you children. But I've told you before, woman. An ample meal has nothing to do with making it happen. If you want a child in your womb, make petitions at the fairy bush."

Enya ignored her as she carried her basket to approach the cooking fire. "We will be traveling tomorrow. I'll take our meal tonight."

Gormley stuck her fingers into Enya's basket and pulled out a bunch of dried leaves. She rubbed them between her palms and then released them over the cooking pot. "Where are you going?"

Enya winced. Her friend was always direct, insisting information come forth without delay. She could read Enya in an eye blink, so Enya had no choice but to reveal all. She waited until Kyna had mingled far into the crowd of women before she spoke. "Fe wants us to ask the Christian God for a child, so we are going to Cruithneachia's church to pray."

Gormley drew her slender fingers through her pale, curly hair. "Christians! Think they know more about the course of life than the ancient traditions tell us, don't they now."

"Don't be that way, Gormley. I've tried everything else."

"Are you telling me you believe the Christian God has superior power?" Her blue eyes grew wide.

"I *am* saying that." Enya hoped that pronouncement would help dissuade the doubts that often besieged her.

"Ah, well then. That's it. 'Twill work for you." She winked and began stirring the pot with a wooden paddle as though the matter had been settled.

Enya gripped her friend's arm. "Why would you say that?"

Gormley's expression soured. She nodded to direct one of her daughters to look after the babies frolicking on a mossy blanket just paces away. "Enya, you may have forgotten, but the rest of us have not." Her words were sharp. "You are a blessed daughter by birth."

Enya lowered herself to a log bench. "No one who knew my father would say so."

"Makes no difference. Your father did not direct the order of your birth. The gods decided. Fortune will smile on you." She sounded a bit irritated by what she was saying.

Enya groaned. "There's been no smiling thus far, I am afraid. With each season's passing, I know my time for motherhood is slipping away."

Gormley shook her nearly white curls. "Are you the keeper of the days now? Do the sun and moon obey your commands? Are you now the sundial for the gods?"

Enya breathed in the dewy air. She was not any more special than anyone else. Perhaps she was, however, more cursed. A raven drifted on the breeze high above their heads, calling out to those below. The bird wasted not a moment fretting over the future. The animals did not compare themselves to each other the way people did.

Pride, the human sin.

Gormley was right. Enya no more controlled the universe than the tiniest insect or greatest wild beast could. There was order to life, and while she did not feel it, could not detect its ebb and flow within her own body, it was there. God, Fe's God, must make everything right.

The curse of her clan, however, she tried not to think about. Ill-tempers, threats, assaults—she'd run far away from the plague of the Mac Noe clan. She dared not call it back by thinking too long about her birth family.

She turned to her friend and patted her milky white arm. The smell of cooking food and the murmurs of female conversation was comforting. "Thank you, dear friend. I will go, and I will accept whatever Fe's God has for me." The words grated like sand in her mouth. This practicing of what she would say to Fe did not sound convincing, even to her own ears. If only she could believe.

The next morning, she and Fe traveled through the glen and among the rock-scattered fields toward the hillside where the monastery lay.

Fe protectively clutched her arm as they bumped along in the horse-drawn chariot. "Do not be nervous, my sweet."

"Nervous? Is that what I am?"

"You've not been to church many times, but we will have to change that."

"Why? Does God not dwell outside those walls?"

The corners of Fe's mouth upturned as he kept his gaze on the uneven road ahead. "Ah, he does. But believers gathering together to pray? There's nothing else like it."

"They're praying all the time in the monastery. I witnessed it myself when I was schooled. They let me choose whether or not to attend the prayer times, and most often I could see no reason. I could talk to God in the woods as well as in the wee church. Regular hours announced by a clanging bell. I never understood it. Imagine, informing God 'tis time to pray."

Fe's face beamed with a full smile now. He enjoyed her teasing, and Enya adored their time alone together, away from the glares of the clan's women, and far from Nola. Out here, under the wispy clouds and among the rolling hills, with the smell of moist earth filling their lungs, it seemed as though her wishes might actually be within her grasp.

Chapter Two

O LORD Almighty, if you will only look upon your
servant's misery and remember me, and not forget
your servant but give her a son...
—1 Samuel 1:11 NIV

From a rise in the landscape Enya spotted the monastery with its low stone wall circling the few buildings like protective arms. Each corner of the monastery was marked with a high wooden cross. "To identify the area of sanctuary," Fe told her. "Once someone passes within the shadow of those crosses, he is safe, and no one can harm him."

Enya nodded. "In Fir-monach even a man who enters sanctuary has to stand trial if he's done something unlawful." She hadn't spoken much about her homeland, and Fe never asked, but she'd not been to this monastery before and wanted to know how the monks operated.

"Aye, 'tis the same in all the kingdoms, my sweet. The crosses are there to ensure there's no

19

error in judgment. Man, woman, and child can come to these crosses and know they will not be judged in haste."

Smoke rose from one of the larger buildings, the refectory she supposed. She kept her eyes on the central structure, the church, as they descended toward it. A distinct yeast smell rose on the air. They were tardy, too late for morning worship, but Fe said the priest would welcome them anyway. Enya hoped they would also share their bread.

"God will hear your prayers, Enya. God always hears." He drew her close as they trotted along the last few paces through some yews that Fe called a sacred grove before they reached the monastery gate. His touch was warm and reassuring. She hadn't appreciated him the way she should have after she'd discovered her body's refusal to produce a child. The years had pulled her from him as if she were a dying vine and he the wall that had supported her.

He lifted her chin to meet his gaze. "You are sad all the time, Enya. You barely eat anything at all. You don't smile." He paused and let the words lie between them. She was a disappointment, she knew. He rubbed his rough thumb across her cold cheek. "You will pray for a child today, but I will pray that you will be happy again, the carefree, beautiful Enya I know you can be once more."

She immediately fell in love all over again. Pity he was right, though. She could not smile, no matter how good she felt inside. She could not force herself. Love was not enough to give them the child they wanted.

Fe clambered down from the chariot and approached the gate where a small iron bell hung. He gave it few shakes before a brown-robed man shuffled up from somewhere beyond the monastery's perimeter walls. Enya observed them from her perch in the chariot. The monk was short in stature and standing in the shadow of her much taller husband. Arching the monk's smooth, white forehead was a tuft of gray hair that continued down to his shoulders in stringy, thin wisps. His brown eyes widened as Fe spoke. He tapped his fingers together for a moment as though trying to decide what to do, but then proceeded to swing the gate open wide. He spoke loud enough for Enya to hear. "I am Brother Malachi, in charge of such things. Leave your horse. We will attend to him. Go on to the church. Father Cruithneachia will greet you there. There is welcome here for you. Come, and peace be with you."

The man's short, sharp words suggested he found their unannounced arrival inconvenient.

Fe returned and helped her climb out of the rig. She checked to make sure her comb bag was still attached to her belt, and then followed him inside the gate and along a limestone path leading to the centrally located church. The building was rectangular with a thick thatched roof. "Why are there no windows?" Enya whispered to her husband.

"There's a lintel above the door. See there?" He pointed to the west side of the church where a wee window crowned a thick wooden door with an iron latch. The lintel would not let in much light.

"Must be quite dark in there. Why would God, who created the glory of the sun, choose to be worshipped in such a wee, dim space?"

He shushed her as they approached. Enya clung to his arm as a brisk wind threatened to knock her off her feet. When they were just a few paces from the door, it creaked open. An aged man stood on the threshold with his hands outstretched. "You're very welcome, Fe. I am pleased to meet your wife at last."

Fe thanked him and introduced Enya. "Might we pray, Father?"

"Of course. Come in, please."

When the door shut behind them, blocking out much of the daylight, Enya struggled to adjust her vision. Candles on the altar opposite the door flickered and led them forward. Gone were the familiar beliefs of common people like Gormley, closed out by the door. Enya wanted to believe as her husband did. When the two of them were alone, she could imagine Fe's God as all-powerful. But in this shadowy place with men she'd never met before, men who did not seem to want her there despite their words of welcome, doubts grew back like moss in the shade.

As they knelt before the candles and the rough-hewn cross gracing the altar, a wave of sadness washed over Enya larger and more devastating than she'd ever experienced before. If Fe's God was omnipotent, and if he did not wish to grant her a child, it could not happen. What could she do other than lay down her entire life, and the life of her hoped-for child, as a sacrifice to the one Fe called the One True God?

23

Her husband began offering his prayers using his usual soft tone. Enya had learned early on to stand up for herself when no one else would. She did not quiet her voice now. Her wails and pleas rose to the latticework ceiling. Tears streaked down her face. All the anguish she had experienced living with a tyrannical parent burst forth as she wondered if the true God might in fact be like her father. If she wanted a child, she had to submit to this God, as difficult as it might be, so her pleading turned to sobs.

A touch came to her shoulder. Fe, she thought.

"Woman. Have you come here to the house of the Lord drunk? 'Tis a disgrace before God."

She turned to find the priest glaring at her, eyebrows arched. Behind him Fe rose from his knees. Such a remark called forth a question of honor, whether the man who spoke it was a priest or not. She'd have to remedy this misunderstanding right away. "You have misjudged me, Father. I am praying." The volume of her voice boomed in a way that seemed to surprise even Fe, and he backed away. Enya lowered her tone and inclined her head toward the priest. "God hears prayers, aye?"

The rotund man lowered his chin. "He does. He will hear the prayers you offer up sincerely to him today, child."

"I am most definitely sincere." Her voice cracked with emotion.

The priest's eyes softened. "What is on your mind?"

She felt compelled to unload her burden. "I have great sorrow and I poured out my anguish to God. God has not opened my womb. I have no children, but I believe he can make me fruitful if he chooses. My husband brought me here because he knows how troubled I am."

The priest's previous irritation dissipated. He stared into her eyes with a look of pity. "God will grant your request. Go in peace."

His words were few, simple, but so earnest that Enya no longer had doubts, not about this. Only moments earlier she had promised God that if he allowed her to give birth, she would give the child wholly to him. And now with this priest, this man of God, reassuring her that God had heard, she believed. She knew what she must do.

The priest left, perhaps to pray as well.

Enya whispered to Fe. "If I made a promise here in this place, while God was speaking, I must surely keep it."

"You must. What was it?"

She bit her lip and then told her husband she'd promised to foster the child to the church. At first he appeared crestfallen. Then he took her hand. "Our child will become a king. What better place for him to learn wisdom? We shall tell the priest."

When the priest rose to his feet, they approached. Enya's voice did not falter. "I will bring the child I will bear to you. To serve God here in this place."

Suddenly a ray of sunlight burst through the door's lintel and cast a dusty light on the floor at their feet. The church with its dank and confining space had not kept out the glory of God after all. She vowed to remember that always. God would find her wherever she called out to him no matter how miserable and low she felt when she prayed.

The priest smiled, placed his fingers on her head. "Bless you, child."

Fe told the priest about the cloth they had brought as a gift to the monastery. Then he reached for Enya's hand and led her out of the church. He said nothing as they retrieved their chariot from the monastery stables and went on their way toward home.

An unfamiliar smile met her lips. She could not contain her joy. God would give her a son! She just knew it, although the priest had not said so precisely. Enya pushed away the fact that she would one day return her son to the priest. She'd think about that later. For now she knew she would no longer be barren. A baby would soon be born.

Finally, as the shadows of the hills covered them like blankets, Fe spoke. "You are well, my wife?"

"I am more than that. Let's stop at that house there." She pointed to a wee thatched cottage. "I am famished."

A man answered the door. It was growing dark, but the light from the cabin's turf fire cast a warm glow around him. Was that how the angels in heaven looked? Surrounded by God's glorious light? It was an imprudent thought. This man was a mere human. However, the veil between the worlds could sometimes be lowered just enough to allow a glimpse. Even the common folks thought so. She seemed to have had many glimpses on that day.

When Fe returned he beckoned her to dismount. "I'll take the chariot to their horse barn. The man says they have only a little stew, but we are welcome to it. I told him to keep it for his family. We have enough bread the brothers gave us for the night. We will sleep in the dairy. He said there is warm hay for a bed and milk aplenty."

She wanted to thank the man herself but the journey and her intense prayers had exhausted her and she longed for sleep. Besides, he had closed the door and she did not want to disrupt the family's evening routine. Enya trailed along behind her husband as he led the horse and the rig to a small structure built into the side of a hill. A boy, no more than eight summers old, was inside brushing a horse.

"Your father has permitted us to stay the night," Fe explained to the lad who seemed a bit startled by their presence.

The child nodded and went back to his work.

"A fine beast that is," Fe said while securing their horse to a post and throwing some hay into a trough. "Does he belong to you?"

"Not yet," the lad said, his earthy eyes round and bright. "One day, when I'm old enough, Da says he'll be mine. I'll plow a field with him, too."

Fe laughed. "'Tis the job of the oxen. You should save this one for the races."

"Do you think so?"

"I do."

Enya was touched by the affection her husband showed for the child. Fe's tenderness showed he was meant to be a father, even from afar, as would be the case when the time for fosterage came. But, surely, God would not require their child to be fostered away for long. He would return to them at the proper time and always be theirs.

Later that night, after she had eaten more than her share of the brown bread from their knapsack—Fe had insisted he wasn't hungry—Enya cuddled close to her husband. They shared a tenderness that had not passed so passionately between them since their wedding night.

Chapter Three

*For a man's ways are in full view of the LORD,
and he examines all his paths.*
—*Proverbs 5: 21 NIV*

At the next full moon, Enya was sure she was pregnant. Her stomach was still as flat as an oar, but she had never felt so calm and reassured her whole life. Fe was contented because he said his prayers had been answered. His wife was happy again. When another full moon arrived and Enya's monthly blood had failed to flow again, there was no doubt.

She stood outside and gazed at the white sphere in the night sky, patting her sometimes-queasy stomach. Fe had gone looking for the blasted hog again and she could hardly wait to share the news. Gormley had earlier warned her not to tell him what she suspected too soon. "Don't get his hopes dashed, dearie. One missed cycle 'tis not proof. But two, aye, tell him when you've missed two."

Enya paced between the two massive oaks outside the cottage door. What was taking so long? A wolf howled somewhere in the distance and the hound inside the house returned the call. She could go after Fe with the hound for protection. Fe had taken the chariot, so she'd have to walk, but only one way. She wrung her hands until they throbbed. She hated the thought of Fe being at Murtagh's so long, but going there herself was not appealing. She paused and stared up to the heavens again. This time, she could not be mocked. In fact, telling Fe in front of Murtagh's clan might be quite satisfying. She hurried inside to grab her cloak, a lantern, and the hound's rope.

Halfway across the hill separating Fe's land from the Murtagh homestead, Enya began to regret leaving her cozy fire. Imbolic, the festival marking the beginning of the light half of the year, had passed nearly a month ago but the weather still breathed the icy breath of winter. The moon lit up frosty fields that twinkled as though scattered with stars. The beauty of it was spoiled by a frigid wind that slapped and taunted her like a bad dream. The hound led on, undeterred.

When at last they reached the crest of the hill, Enya could see Murtagh's cabin, a furl of smoke puffing out from the roof. A scuffling sound in a grove of trees to her right sent the hound barking. A hog, her hog, crashed out into the moonlight. "There you are, you foolish animal." She removed the rope from the hound and slipped it over the hog's neck before it scampered away, dragging the leash behind. "We'll catch you easily now," she said. The dog darted into the woods. She whistled for him to come back, remembering that Fe never took the dog to hunt the runaway hog because the hound was trained to attack, not herd. There was a sound of snapping twigs and then the hound was back at her side.

The commotion brought a stream of people out of the house. "Who's there?" an elderly man's voice shouted.

"Enya," she called out. "I've found my hog."

"That so?"

A crowd of dark figures climbed slowly toward her. She held out her lantern, but could not discern if any of them was her husband. "Fe? Is Fe there?" She bobbed her lantern to and fro.

Whispers bounced between the figures until they reached her. Murtagh, his long beard woven neatly into two tight strands of snowy hair, motioned to the woods. "Out there looking for the hog, I believe. Have you seen him?" He directed the question to one of his children. Murtagh's sons looked so much alike, dark-haired, average height, bland eyes, that she didn't know them apart.

"Could be with Nola in the barn," one offered.

Enya's knees grew weak.

"What would he be doing ..." another son's voice trailed off.

A voice from the back of the crowd grunted and a portly man wearing a gray cap stepped forward. His eyes were glazed, the effect of too much ale. "She went there to check on the first-calf heifer." The man speaking was Nola's husband Tierney. "No one knows more about birthing than my Nola," he said, staggering to keep his balance.

Old man Murtagh turned to Enya and grinned. "Probably gone to help out." He extended his hand and flashed his son a look. "Come with me, Enya. The wife will fetch you some tea. My boy will find your husband."

Nola's husband lost his balance and landed on the frosty grass with a resounding thud. The group broke out in drunken laughter as they struggled to pull the man to his feet.

"Come, now," Murtagh offered again, clicking his tongue to direct the dog to follow.

What if Fe and that woman were having their own drunken romp in the barn? The son had already run off to warn them. Enya would become an even bigger target of their scorn and pity. No, she had to go herself and confront her husband. Did he think she was a fool?

Enya pivoted and rushed toward the barn, the shouts of the surprised old man calling out behind her. When she reached the barn's double doors she lunged at one just as it pushed toward her, knocking her off her feet with such force that she landed on her back side.

"Whoa, now. Are you hurt?" The person speaking was washed in shadows, but she knew who it was.

"Fe, what are you doing in that barn? I demand to know." She crawled to her knees and retrieved her lantern that had been cast off beside her.

"Is that you, Enya?" He rushed to help her up.

She pushed him away. "Of course, 'tis me. I can see you were not expecting your wife." She could not control her shouting as images of her cruel father blurred her thoughts.

Fe grabbed her arm and brushed sticks and leaves away from her cloak. "True I was not. You have never come here before. Is something the matter?"

She bit her lip, trying to hold her tongue. His wrinkled face suggested that he was concerned, but perhaps he was just trying to cover his guilt. Despite first inhaling deeply, Enya spoke rapidly. "Come to have your way with the woman you loved in your youth, have you? And I have caught you!"

Fe's face paled in the lantern light as he tightened his grip on her arm. "You are speaking nonsense. Let's go before you humiliate yourself further."

"Me? I'm the one humiliating myself, is it?" She bit the insides of her cheeks until her gums throbbed.

He urged her toward the stables.

"What were you doing in there, Fe? Why do you not tell me if 'tis not what I said it was?"

"Helping deliver a calf." His words were short and pointed. He freed the horse and she followed them outside where the chariot waited under a hawthorn. He worked in silence to tie the animal to the rig.

Enya glanced around. No one had followed them, probably wishing to leave the quarreling couple be. She wandered a short distance away and held up her lantern to illuminate the path back to the barn. Muffled voices came from that direction and then a shout.

"She's come! The calf is alive."

Firelight bounced from torches as people scurried about.

She *had* embarrassed herself. Fe was helping a neighbor. Jealousy had loosened her tongue. She spun around.

Fe was already perched on the chariot.

She took a step toward him. "I'm sorry. 'Tis just that I was waiting for you because I had something to …" She remembered the hog. "Oh, Fe. I saw the hog. I almost caught him."

The sound of a barking dog made her turn back toward the barn. Murtagh climbed the hill toward them, the hound beside him.

Fe jumped from the chariot and whisked past her. "Many thanks, Murtagh." He took the dog and ordered him to sit. Enya felt even more goosey in the presence of their neighbor and this time she kept quiet.

The two men spoke briefly and then the old man lumbered back toward his family. Fe put the hound in the bed of the rig and climbed in to take up the reins. "We'll look for the hog tomorrow."

She dared not question him, not now. Who cared about the old hog anyway? They had enough wealth without him. Her throat burned, the old jealousy welling up again. Why had he always sought out that hog instead of letting him come back on his own if not to have an excuse to visit Nola? Hot tears burned her eyes. Hadn't he proven that he loved his wife? Why did she doubt so? As though two voices argued in her head, she blurted out her complaint. "Why are you not concerned about the hog now when so many other times you have gone in eager search of him?"

"Not now, Enya. I am in no good mood."

She sucked in a breath. She truly wanted to know. "Please tell me the truth, Fe." She blinked back tears and whispered. "You have always been in love with her."

The rig came to a jerking halt, sending the hound scuttling from side to side. He howled in protest. "Silence!" Fe shouted at the beast. His anger made her shiver. Fe gripped her shoulders with both hands and stared at her. "There has never been another woman for me. Can you not see that I was helping Colin deliver a calf? Have you not noticed that he has been helping me with the harvest? That's what neighbors do, Enya!"

Her breath caught. She never intended to make him angry, but now that she had, what would he do? She wiggled free from his grasp, and was relieved when he did not try to grab her again. "You could hire your help."

"I could, but 'tis not my way. You may be content to gossip with the cooks and spend time alone in the cottage, but I am not. I visit awhile, help where I can. And I do not want that meddlesome hog to root through Murtagh's wife's vegetable garden. They have a lot of mouths to feed."

Enya swallowed hard. "Did you say 'twas Colin you were helping in the barn?"

"I did."

"Not Nola?"

He shook his head and turned away. "Nay, I did not see Nola the whole evening."

"But Tierney said she was there because she knew all about birthing."

"You can believe that sloth if you wish. He has no idea of the toil going on in that barn. He's not labored a day in his life. That's why Nola works so hard. Her husband only knows the color of the ale in his cup."

"So she was not there," she said more to herself than him.

"She wasn't." Fe carefully put one arm around her and slapped the reigns with his other. "Has your happiness left already, Enya? Is there to be nothing between us besides this unfounded jealousy?"

She took a long, slow breath and stared off into the deep darkness that the setting moon had cast on them. The curse of her family was what was between them. She'd always feared it would come back in some manner. She leaned against

39

his chest and listened to his rapid heartbeat. "Please forgive me, Fe. I was so wrong."

His breathing slowed and they rode in silence, listening to the clopping of the horse's hoofs. She lifted her head. "Fe?"

He smiled at her. "Feisty as you are, I still love you more than life itself."

"Fe, there is something that will come between us soon."

His brow creased.

"Oh, nothing that will separate us. You've not divorced me yet."

He exhaled slowly. "I will never divorce you. Have I not just said that I love you more than life itself?"

"Aye. And I love you."

"Then what could it be?"

"Something that will be right here and grow so large you won't be able to put your arms around me."

"Enya!" He abruptly stopped the chariot again. "A baby?"

His face was so alight that she laughed out loud, tipping her head up toward the cloud-covered stars. "'Tis so."

He jumped from the chariot and lifted her down. Scooping her up in his arms he twirled around and shouted to the sky. "A baby! Praise the God who listens and answers our prayers!"

As glorious a moment as she'd ever experienced.

On the ride home, however, Enya could not forget that she had come from a long line of angry men. Perhaps giving birth to a girl would ensure this evil would not be passed on. But she'd felt strongly when the priest spoke to her that she would have a son, so the possibility that her child could carry the curse loomed large in her mind.

Chapter Four

An angel of the Lord appeared to his mother in dreams, bringing to her, as he stood by her, a certain robe of extraordinary beauty ... After a short time he asked it back, and took it out of her hands. —
The Life of St. Columba by St. Adamnán

While Enya had servants to do the washing, supervising gave her an excuse to talk with her friend. Gormley had servants as well, but did her own washing. Enya found her sitting near the stream, scrubbing garments with a rock.

"Having a winter baby, are you?" Gormley asked.

"I suppose I am." Enya hadn't thought about the prospect of birthing a child during the dark half of the year. Her friend, believing as she did in wood sprites and fairies, would fear such a thing, and now that it was brought to her attention, Enya had another thing to be concerned about.

Gormley smiled but did not take her focus off her work. "Well, I suppose since you've wanted for a child so long, and your God has seen fit to grant it, 'twill not be a scourge."

"What a thing to say." Weak-kneed, Enya pushed up from the patch of spring wildflowers she had been sitting in and wrapped her arms protectively around her belly.

"Oh, don't get all in a dither, Enya. You know as well as I do that this child will not be your only one."

"I know no such thing."

Gormley let out a heavy sigh as she tossed a wad of wet clothing into a basket. "Well, I know it. If you're to have one child, you're to have five, maybe more."

"Whatever magical thing you believe about this child I'm carrying, please keep it to yourself."

Gormley clicked her tongue as she lifted her basket of washing to her hip. "'Tis no denying a prophecy from a believer of your God, is there?" She started to march off.

"Wait." Enya joined her on the path back to her house. "What prophecy?"

Gormley continued walking. "A man, said he was a priest. Nay, a monk or something from

43

Cruithneachia's monastery. Stopped here a day or two ago on his way to somewhere. Came by my house for a meal."

Enya struggled to keep up. The man she described might have been the odd fellow who had welcomed Enya and her husband when they went to pray at the church. She wanted to know. "Tell me more, Gormley. You've not seen the man before?"

Gormley glanced away. "A stranger he was to me. I've not been to that fine monastery as you have." She turned to go.

"Please, Gormley, I want to know more."

"Fine. But I've chores to do." Her tone suggested resentment of Enya's wealthy position. Gormley was better off than most. What had caused this attitude?

"I'll help you."

"I thought you weren't interested in what others say about your baby." She narrowed her eyes at Enya.

"I'm sorry. You'll forgive me? 'Tis just that I want my baby to be healthy. I'm afraid to think about anything else."

Gormley paused and smiled. "'Tis every woman's fear that the birthing will go badly. But you need not worry, woman."

Enya took one handle of the basket to lighten Gormley's load. "Describe this man to me. I want to know if I've seen him before."

They continued up the path. The violet heads of the periwinkle were in bloom, a sure sign of spring. A light mist began to fall, freshening the air with the moist scent of new life.

"Let me think," Gormley said.

Enya kept silent, taking in the signs of the earth's reawakening on the island referred to by the name of a goddess, Éire. Why couldn't her baby be born in the spring when nature sings its annual welcome song? Why had God chosen the dimness of winter to bring forth this new life? She shook her head. Gormley's superstitions had gotten to her.

Her friend's voice brought her back to their conversation. "He was gray, dull eyes, a wee bit fat. Can't remember his name, sorry."

That description could fit a number of monks.

"Why was he talking about my baby?"

"He said a woman from our clan had visited several months ago. He was just making conversation, I think. But then I told him about you and about how you had prayed to his God for a child. He remembered you then, you and Fe. Said he had let you in after morning prayers so that you could go to the church." She paused to sigh heavily. "I think he thought you uncouth to come at such a time. What do those monks know? Do they think the rest of us plan our days by the ringing of bells?"

"I don't know, but I remember him all right. He welcomed us, true, but did seem a wee bit put out. Odd for a monk. They are supposed to be the most hospitable of all of us." She remembered his name: Malachi.

"What's supposed to be is rarely what is, woman." Gormley's cottage was in sight. They slowed down to lengthen the time they had to talk together. "Odd, you say? I suppose he was. Especially when he said that he knew you were a fifth daughter. I didn't think Christians cared about such things."

Enya's chest began to ache. How could he know this? "Tell me what he said about the baby."

"Are you sure you want me to continue, Enya? I'm sorry I mentioned it. What does it all matter?

Truly someone like you should have no worries. These things are no more important than badger trails."

Her life had been nothing to envy, not before now, anyway. "Please continue."

Gormley waved her hand over her head. "He's probably a bit mad, don't you know. Those monks rarely speak. They eat only bread, drink only water, and are awakened all night long for prayer. Makes them behave strangely. We should give it no heed."

She decided not to point out that if the monks ate only bread and water, this one would not be a wee bit fat, as she had said. The visit should not be dismissed so easily. "Tell me."

Gormley's children spotted her and began to stream out from the house like buzzards circling prey. Gormley let out a sigh, observing her gathering brood. The children would soon put an end to their private conversation. "He just said that a woman with a birth omen like yours would hear from one spirit or the other. And if she heard from a bad spirit it would mean the death of the baby, but like I said. He's an odd bird. Pay it no mind."

Enya's stomach rolled as though the land beneath her had liquefied. Gormley dropped her hold on the basket and slipped her arm around Enya's waist. "Come in for tea. 'Twas nonsense for sure and you'd do well to pay it no mind."

Later that night, when Enya was snug in bed beside her husband under a lambswool blanket, she told him about the prophecy.

"Well, that's one thing Gormley said that I agree with. The man was speaking rubbish. Do we not agree that God has blessed us? What God has ordained, no evil spirit can take away. Please, Enya, do not spoil your joy with such thoughts."

She let his words hang in the smoky air of their turf fire—warmed shelter. She wanted to believe him. When she was barren she had been sure that if God would give her a child she would desire nothing else. All would be bliss. But her worry and her pervasive jealousy had not departed. Perhaps she should have asked for more when she and Fe were praying in that forlorn church.

She pondered her lack of foresight as sleep engulfed her.

In her dreams she saw the man whose barn she and Fe had slept in on their way home from Cruithneachia's church. He appeared in the doorway of his cabin the way he had that night, with the glow of firelight surrounding him. But this time he stepped out of the house and the glow followed him. She had the distinct impression he was indeed an angel from God.

"I have a message for you from the Father Almighty," he said.

"Let me hear it."

He reached behind and brought forth a robe embroidered with flowers of red, gold, blue, and emerald. A more beautiful robe she had never seen. He approached and held it out to her. "Take it," he said.

Enya reached out and gathered the garment in her arms. It was softer than lambswool. She had just begun to admire it fully when he snatched it from her. He held it up to the night sky and let go. The robe drifted in the air above their heads and then it began to stretch and flow, doubling and tripling in size until she could no longer see its edges.

Enya pounded her fists on her chest. "Why give me such a precious gift and then take it away so soon?"

He glanced up at the robe and smiled. "Such a thing of beauty and honor cannot be contained by you, daughter of the earth. It must be cast free upon the wind to go to wondrous places where more souls will see its glory."

The robe seemed to take flight like a bird and soar over mountains and across a sea. Then a voice greater than the angel's boomed. "Woman, do not be afraid. You will give birth to a son who will bloom and flower like the embellishments on the robe. He will be revered as a prophet, destined to lead innumerable souls to heaven."

She thought about the glorious flowered embroidery on the cloak and knew it represented the beauty and innocence of a newborn child. When she imagined such a precious thing like the cloak being lifted out of her arms, she wept inconsolably.

The next day, and for many days after, Enya did not leave her house. She did not go with Kyna to the communal fire. She did not help Fe find wandering livestock. She only bathed when the servants brought water in for her in steaming caldrons. She might be with child, but she could still feel the ridicule of the women, and feared that Gormley might discern that indeed a spirit had visited her. Until she was sure it was a heavenly messenger who had spoken to her to remind her that she had dedicated her unborn child to the Lord, and not an evil spirit veiled as an angel and planning to kill her baby before its birth, she felt more secure waiting out the coming months within the white-washed walls of her shelter.

"Why have you confined yourself so?" Fe scolded one morning when she could not drag herself out of bed.

She should tell him about the dream, but feared speaking of it might give the message life, cause it to come true. Of course she would lose her son. He belonged to God. That was a bearable loss, however. Her child would not die. He would be safe. If she could be sure that was what the dream meant, she could rest easy. But if the dream was a foretelling that her child would not live, perhaps even not be born alive … her heart ached to think about it. What if there was something she could do? She sat up and braided her hair as she thought about the one man who probably had the answer.

"I want to go back to that monastery."

Fe sat on the edge of their straw mattress with his face drawn tight in worry. "Today? Why?"

She rubbed the bump in her belly. "It may seem foolhardy, but I think there is a monk there who knows what God has in store for our baby."

"You mean the one Gormley told you about? Didn't I tell you to pay that no mind? Listen, my sweet, we know we are to foster the child out. Our vow to God must not be broken, but God will not require our child for a long time. Why concern yourself now? I will tell you what you need to know about what is in store for our child." He leaned over and kissed her stomach. "He or she will grow strong and healthy and learn the ways of God. What more could we want?"

"I …" She considered lying, but in her heart she knew the truth was always best. "Fe, I had a dream many weeks ago. Remember that the monk Gormley told me about said that either a heavenly spirit or an evil one would speak to me? In the dream a spirit came to me. I want to know which it was. We must go back to the monastery, Fe. I think the answer can be found there."

His face showed that he didn't like this, and she was not surprised. Any talk of spiritual matters not pertaining to the church he attended had always sent Fe out into the fields or to the horse barn. So far as he was concerned, no spirits talked to people other than that of the One True God. And the way God spoke was in sunrises and rain showers, and in the earth's spring rebirth— natural things that were observable. And through the scriptures. He had already told her to dismiss the prophecy, but then she'd had this dream. How could she ignore it?

Fe shifted his linen mantle over his head and smoothed it down his chest. "I will not take you there for some kind of superstitious ritual, Enya."

That was the end of it. If she were going to talk to Brother Malachi, she would have to go without Fe's knowledge.

The next day Fe told her he was going back to Murtagh's place. "I know you would prefer I stay away, and I want to honor your wishes, Enya. They are building a trough to drain a bog between the boundaries. This would give both of us better grazing land for our cattle. I believe I should help out, but if you'd prefer I not—"

"Nay, you should go." She interrupted him with a shake of her head, realizing this was the chance she had been waiting for.

Fe pushed strands of hair away from her face and drew her thickening body to his chest. "Are you sure? All I want is for you to be happy."

She cocked her head to one side and pitched her voice to the lightest level she could manage. "Of course I'm sure. You should go. 'Tis important to be a good neighbor." And she meant that. Now that he had explained, she could not protest. Besides, she needed him to go.

"Indeed 'tis. If you need me, send the cook or my stable man. He is out in the hay field today."

"Do not worry about me. The baby isn't due for months and I'm feeling much better now that the time of sickness is past." For months she had wavered between bouts of nausea and hours of dark moodiness that worried her as much as anything could. But now she felt healthy again and full of energy. The only thing that disturbed her was the prophecy. She needed to clear that worry as soon as possible.

Fe rubbed his rough thumbs over her cheeks and kissed her nose. "I will be back before night-fall."

So would she.

Fe had taken their strongest horse, but they had another that would do. After telling the servants she had some grain to trade at the monastery for cloth, and explaining that she was surprising Fe with a new shirt using the plaid only the monks wove, Enya made her escape on the back of the mare with one saddlebag of trade oats strapped on each side. She could not ride quickly in her condition. By the time she reached the monastery she'd have to rush, get her information, and re-turn home before Fe missed her.

The monastery gate was locked. "Let me in!" Enya jingled the iron bell for the third time.

A young man, not a monk because of the absence of a tonsure, scrambled up to the iron bars and threw them open. "Please, lower your voice. The monks are praying."

She had been discourteous, but the sun was low and she had to return home. The jarring ride up the rocky slope and then back down had been necessarily protracted. "I'm in a hurry," she whispered, giving her horse's reins to the young man. "I must find one of the brothers."

"Which one?"

"She held out her arm. "He is about this tall, gray hair, portly."

The man sighed.

"I know that is not very descriptive. Middle aged. Oh, aye, his name is Malachi."

He cast her a sympathetic look. "What is your name? Perhaps I can ask around to find him."

She shook her head. "Where are they? I'll have a look for him."

"In prayer, like I said. I'm afraid they cannot be disturbed."

She bit her lip as she tried to figure out what to do. "What kind of monastery is this? I thought it was sanctuary. You know, once you pass the high crosses?" She tried to calm herself. "I am a woman in distress. I must find someone."

Two brown-robed men approached them. "What can we do for you, woman?" one asked.

The servant slipped away toward the barn with her horse.

"I'm looking for a monk here. I believe his name is Malachi and he spoke to someone about me recently when he passed through our village. He knows things about me such as the truth that I am the fifth daughter of a fifth daughter. You must know a monk by that name who recently traveled from here."

The brothers huddled together for a moment and then one of them departed. The remaining man lowered his hood, exposing large fawn-like eyes and a warm smile. "You must forgive us. It is our prayer time so I do not wish to disturb the abbot or the priest. You understand."

"I understand. I beg your forgiveness." She followed him to a small round building she was told was a guesthouse. "I cannot stay long. Do you think you can find this man for me straight away?"

He opened the door and motioned for her to step inside. "There is a fire here and a jar of tea.

You are most welcome to refresh yourself. The man you seek will come shortly." He abruptly turned, closing the door with a thud.

So they did know whom she sought.

Enya paced the room before warming her hands near the peat fire. A glance out the west-facing window told her she would have to leave soon even if it meant not speaking to the monk. Perhaps she should have gone to the church instead and searched out the priest she had met when she first came here. He might have been able to interpret her dream just as well.

Enya sipped the tea as the moments whisked by. She retrieved her cloak from a spike near the door and was just about to leave to collect her horse when the door creaked open. A man stood before her carrying a twig torch. "Ah, the fifth daughter."

"I suppose I am. And who are you to know that?"

The man entered and closed the door behind him. "I am your father."

Chapter Five

The wise woman builds her house, but with her own hands the foolish one tears hers down.
—*Proverbs 14:1 NIV*

"You're not my father. My father is in Firmonach. It has been some time since I've seen him, but you do not resemble the man at all."

"Oh, my dear." He seated himself on the stone wall surrounding the guesthouse bath and removed his sandals. To her surprise he turned toward the bath, which was filled with water, and plunged his feet in. "I am your spiritual father. Do you not know this? Is this not why you have sought me out?" He mumbled something about having been on a long journey and his feet aching.

A young boy entered the house with a bucket of steaming water and added it to the bath. The old monk sighed and leaned back on his wrists.

Enya glanced out the window again. "I have come because you know something about me. Did you not tell my friend I was a fifth daughter?" She did not wait for an answer. She would have to speak fast. Time was slipping away. "And you said something about a spirit visiting me. How do you know this?"

Malachi's eyes had been closed, but at those words his lids flickered open. "And has a spirit visited, then? That is why you've come?"

"Aye." She had no time to explain or wait for his explanation. "I will tell you my dream and I want you to tell me if my baby will die." The words felt like raw wool on her tongue.

He nodded and she sat beside him and told him the whole thing. "Please, Brother, I must get home before my husband misses me. Tell me what you know."

To her dismay, he sat silent. She shifted about, rearranging the folds in her skirt to indicate her impatience.

"Ah, the time has certainly come, and you are surely a blessed woman."

She grabbed his collar. "Will my baby die?"

He grinned, showing small, yellowed teeth. "He will die an old man."

She let out the breath she hadn't realized she was holding and then dropped her grip on the monk and moved toward the door. "Thank you. Truly, I am very grateful. But I must go."

He splashed about and wiggled off the edge of the bath, nearly slipping on the wet floor. "But you should know that your life will not be easy. The child, the man, will break your heart and cause you worry."

She paused with her hand on the door's latch. "That's what my mother said of me when she was alive. Perhaps 'tis the lot of all parents."

"I concur, woman, but few have endured more than you and your child shall. Do not forget this as you plan his future."

Such a statement should have been delivered with dread but a slight grin crossed his face.

Malachi tossed a wave toward her. "If you must, go. Go with the peace of God." He returned to the bath and plopped his large feet back in.

Enya hurried outside where she found the stable boy sweeping a walkway. "I must leave at once!"

The startled lad dropped his broom and ran off. Amused, and a bit surprised at the tone of her voice, she picked up the broom and propped it against a tree. The guesthouse door opened behind her.

"I must send you with a warning."

She sighed. Hadn't he just done so? She folded her hands in front of her and turned to face the monk.

His eyes bulged. The muscles in his neck tightened. "Heed my words, Enya of Mac Noe."

He knew her name and so much about her. Perhaps the Christian God had revealed these things to him. Malachi seemed to be otherworldly, which no doubt is why he seemed so odd to her.

Malachi cleared his throat before continuing, as though he really was conveying a spiritual message. "No matter that you now live with a new clan. Do not forget 'tis a great burden to be a fifth daughter."

He did not have to tell her that. She thanked him and rushed off to find her horse. A shiver ran from her spine to her neck. She had the good news she'd come for. Her baby would live and grow to manhood. If Fe were here, he would say to dismiss the old man's admonition as pure superstition. She put a hand to her beating heart as

63

she ran, telling herself that despite the monk's urgency, she must give it no heed.

The sun was setting by the time she arrived home. Kyna and Gormley met her as she trotted toward the barn. Kyna pushed a wooden stair step up to the horse and helped Enya wiggle down. "We were worried about you, running off like that with a babe in your womb. A pregnant woman on horseback. To think of it!" the cook said.

She'd been too bothered about having her dream interpreted to consider any physical discomfort. And now she had the prophecy. Both she and the baby would be fine.

Gormley gave Enya a delighted smile. "You've been on an adventure, have you?"

"I suppose I have. What brings you here? Shouldn't you be with your wee ones?"

"They are looked after. Your cook was asking around about you. I came to help."

Friends and neighbors. Like Fe and the Murtaghs. She was pleased to have a friend to help out. "You've had many babies, Gormley. You don't truly think I harmed the babe, do you?"

The woman smacked her lips before answering. "The babe's not too large yet, but I wouldn't be doing it again. I must go now." She gave Enya a peck on the cheek and hurried away.

"I won't," Enya called after her, rubbing her stomach. Everything felt fine.

Enya was just about to leave Kyna with the horse when she stopped her. "What would you like me to do with these?" She pointed at the still full knapsacks.

"Put it all back in the barrels. And don't mention this to anyone."

Enya entered the house and let her cloak slip to the floor. She pushed an apple crate up to the twig chair that Fe usually sat in, plopped herself down on the chair and propped up her feet. Her legs ached and her arms throbbed from the brisk horse ride. But she was happy. Her child would not die.

She closed her eyes and thought about her encounter with the odd Malachi. She wondered if there could be any other way he could have known about her birth order and the clan she was from. Something other than the power of his

God. There had been no time to ask. Perhaps he had been to her village when she was born. So many people were fascinated by a fifth daughter of a fifth daughter. It shouldn't surprise her if some folks had traveled to see it.

Fe bolted into the house, allowing the door to swing wildly on its hinges. "What's this I hear about you running off on the horse today? Woman, don't you know you could harm our baby with your foolishness?"

She *was* foolish to think the women would not have gossiped about her. Giving her husband a quick glance, she turned back toward the fire. "Please don't worry. I am fine and so is the baby. I shall not be riding the horse again, not before the baby comes."

Fe, normally a quiet man, began to shout loud enough to wake the dead. "Fine, are you? Well, you might not have been!" He urged her to her feet. "You went, didn't you? You went to see that monk after I advised against it!"

She stuttered, surprised that he had figured this out so quickly. "How? Why do you accuse me of this?"

He released her and paced. "Oh, Enya. Are we all daft now? 'Twas not hard to discover. The servants were bringing in the horse. I saw you lumber into the cottage right before me." He breathed in deeply and sighed. "I am afraid I lost my head. Are you sure you are all right, then?"

Everything would have been fine if she hadn't had to wait so long for that monk. She would make him understand. "Oh, Fe, I had to go. I had to find out what the man thought about my dream. He's a man of God." Albeit a superstitious man. "I prayed to no idols or fairies or other spirits. I thought you took me to the church because that is the proper place to turn when I'm distressed. I thought you'd be happy I did that instead of resorting to … Gormley's magic." She regretted naming her after she'd said it. She didn't want to lose a friend because of Fe's zealous concerns.

His eyes softened as he rubbed an open palm over his face. "'Tis not that you went to the church that troubles me."

She wrapped her arms around her husband's neck. "I told you, I am fine, and the babe's well. Brother Malachi said our baby would not die."

He looked at his feet. "I am happy for that, but there is more to this, Enya."

67

"What more could there be? I promise I will not go anywhere else before the baby comes. I'll get you some ale now. You'd be tired after working on that ditch all day."

He was dirty and needed a scrubbing. Now that she had embraced him, she needed one too. "I'll have a bath brought to the house. You'll feel better with a warm drink and a hot soak. I'll rub your shoulders. I'll—"

"Stop!" He pushed her hands away from him.

"What is it?"

This time he plopped down into the chair, looking defeated. "I told you not to go."

"Aye, you did. But I explained—"

He held his hand up to interrupt her. Enya let her shoulders droop. She'd done something terribly wrong, but what? She left the cottage and found a bevy of servants standing outside, eyes wide and mouths gaping. Pushing past them, she went to the kitchen and began filling a jar with honey mead. The weak drink would temper his displeasure. "Take this," she told the youngest servant boy. "Give it to Fe and heat a bath too. Tell him I will be along. I'm going to ..." She was unsure what to say. "Oh, just tell him I'm taking care of necessities."

Enya rushed past the lad, tears in her eyes. She strode the path to the well and back three times, praying and crying. She didn't like disappointing her husband. Why was she always risking an angry outburst? Hadn't she had enough of that in her birth clan?

Concern for the baby had driven her. Of course she had to have the dream interpreted. Fe should have taken her to the church instead of helping Murtagh. He really did seem to prefer being over there. Even if he wasn't involved with that Nola. Those women had mocked her for years before she became pregnant. Why had he not shunned them for her sake?

Her thoughts went on until a pain in her belly stopped her short. She gasped, frozen in place. "What's happening?" she shouted out loud.

Kyna was nearby and heard. She hurried to her side. "Are you in pain?"

All she could do was nod.

"Try to walk. We've got to get you back in the house."

Misery washed over her, nearly knocking her off her feet. Kyna held fast to her side as they moved. Others joined them but she didn't know whom or care. Her breath came in little puffs, making her feel like a beached salmon. After a few steps the pain subsided, allowing her to speak. "Fe. Go and get him."

There was a pause and then Kyna tried to urge her on again toward the well-worn green path to the house. "Fetch Fe!" Enya ordered, this time fully finding her voice.

"He's not there," Kyna said. "Left right after you did. C'mon, lass. We've got to take care of you and that babe."

"Nay. Send a messenger."

Someone took hold of her left arm. Enya felt faint and disoriented.

"Wait," Kyna ordered an unseen person. "We need to get her inside. We'll see how she is before we summon him."

Enya opened her mouth to protest. How dare the servant speak to her in that manner? But the words did not come. She felt her legs weaken and her head droop.

When Enya awoke she was in bed. The form of a woman hovered over her and then backed away.

Enya lifted herself on her elbows to see who it was. The woman had long, silver hair and a wrinkled, pale face. She wore a striped mantle of green and gray. Silver armbands matched her hair. She smelled like sage and thyme and just a light whiff of vinegar.

"Kyna?"

"I'm here."

Enya turned toward the sound to find her cook sitting on a stool, not a trace of worry on her face. "You've brought me the herbal healer? Fe would not like her being here."

The old woman backed away and busied herself jostling jars inside her hand baskets.

"Gormley asked her to come. It wasn't my place to turn her away. She says you're well. Only some indigestion. Look." Kyna held out a steaming jar. "She's made you some thyme tea. 'Twill calm you. Drink it."

Enya shook her head. "Where's my husband? Why didn't you send for him like I asked?"

"He'll be home soon. We didn't want to trouble him. Like I said, you'll be fine with some rest." She stood and placed the jar on her stool.

Enya reached out to stop Kyna from leaving. "Please, Fe must come home now." Her flailing arms sent the jar tumbling and the hot liquid splashed the cook's sandaled feet.

Kyna jumped back and gasped.

"I'm so sorry." Tears blurred Enya's vision as she tried to help Kyna. The healer urged her back down to her pillow.

"I'll clean up," the old woman said, dabbing at Kyna's legs with a bundle of cloth.

When her feet were dried, Kyna leaned over to whisper. "No harm done. Your husband is drinking with the Murtagh lads. Don't worry your head about him. He's as loyal to you as that hound." She pointed to the dog that had been brought in for the night.

"Kyna, you don't understand. I must have Fe here." Though she knew he was loyal, she felt lost without him when she was not feeling well.

"Plenty of time in the morning," the old healer woman insisted. "You must rest now for the sake of the baby."

She *was* tired. Her limbs had not yet recovered from the ride. "I'm sorry to have caused a fuss," she said, looking at both women.

The healer looped her baskets over her arms. "Do not give it another thought. Just be calm."

"I shall," Enya called out as the old woman bundled her head in a linen scarf and went out the door.

Enya settled down on the bed and closed her eyes.

Kyna leaned down and whispered. "We are not given a spirit of fear, my child. Remember those who love you and be at peace."

Enya drifted off to sleep, wrapped in the wisdom of Kyna's words.

There were a few more incidents of false labor in the following weeks. Along with that discomfort, Enya had come to anticipate Fe's absences, although she did not approve. Even though she tried not to show it, he must have known.

"Nothing to be concerned about. I love you truly," Fe would always say while pecking her cheek with kisses. "I'll stay if you'd rather."

She would feel guilty making him stay. She always told him to go on and then he'd wink and walk out the door.

One night she woke suddenly and reached across the mattress. Fe was not there. The house was quiet and she felt as though she had been sleeping for some time. An owl called out in the distance, and the hound whimpered in his sleep. The bed was cold. How could she help but be concerned?

Chapter   Six

There are three kinds of poor: poor by the will of
God, poor by one's own will, and poor even if one
owned the world.
—Old Irish proverb

Enya slept in bits and fits the whole night. When she awoke, she felt a little better physically, but still anxious. Fe had never stayed out all night. Why had Kyna told her not to worry?

She lifted her heavy body from the bed and washed in the basin. Drawing a bone comb through her dark locks, she wondered if she was so different from the northerners that they would never accept her. Perhaps her own husband had never fully thought of her as one of their own and that was why he preferred the company of others.

And this baby? He would be raised in the church, but the day would come when the kingdom would look to him as their king. She rubbed her stomach and the baby kicked. "You certainly are strong enough to take the crown for yourself.

I can tell that already. When you are king, no one will dare reject your mother."

He was half Fe's and raised out of sight of anyone from her birth clan. The prophetic dream had not mentioned her clan.

She brushed the wrinkles from her skirt as she laid it across the mattress. The monk, or seer, or whatever he was, had said life would not be easy. There was no mystery about that. Her life had always been a struggle having been raised by an ill-tempered man.

She dressed slowly, first tugging a too-tight linen dress over her belly and then topping it with a warm plaid mantle. She gathered the fabric at her shoulder with a large silver broach and rubbed the engraving with her index finger. It was the emblem of the clan, and she was part of it now whether anyone liked it or not. Her father made that clear when she left Fir-monach, though he hadn't needed to. This baby was of Fe's clan, not the one she came from. She would forget the story of her beginnings. Dressing like she belonged with the Sons of Néill helped not only to convince others, but also herself.

She straightened her shoulders and attempted to judge her appearance in a highly polished silver plate. She *was* worthy of respect. She would not cower and endure name calling. She would explain to Fe that his absence had embarrassed her and she could not endure it happening again. She was expecting a future king, after all.

When she turned to leave her sleeping chamber, she knocked her knees on the edge of the box bed. As out of balance as she was, she could not right herself and landed with a thud on her bottom. Sprawled and undignified—but otherwise unharmed—she considered the possibility that God himself had knocked her down because of her vanity and boasting.

Should anyone see her, big as a whale and just as graceful as one on dry land, she would be mortified. She crawled over to her mattress and rolled onto it. "Oh, dear God, why wouldn't Fe mock me as well?"

The door creaked and in walked Fe. She had blurted her prayer out loud, as she often did.

"I do not mock you, sweet Enya. I have never wanted to hurt you." Dim half-moons shadowed his eyes, but he seemed quite sober. He didn't say another word as he undressed, got into bed, and turned his back to her.

She opened her mouth, intending to ask how his staying out all night was not meant to hurt her, but changed her mind. Silence would better show that she belonged and make him want her there.

She ran the comb quickly through her hair again and left to find Gormley.

Outside, laborers concentrated on their work. Grooms cared for the horses. A few men scattered in the field like blackbirds, cleaning out the dead remains of the season's harvest. The smell of baking bread permeated the misty air. She must have slept late. Her growling stomach led her to the kitchen to search out some porridge.

"Sit right down." Kyna urged Enya toward a chair near a blackened cooking hearth. The woman worked quickly, scooping porridge into a clay jar and handing it to Enya before she returned to chopping turnips.

The meal slid easily down Enya's throat and warmed her luxuriously. She wondered if she would appreciate such simple pleasures when she was a busy mother tending an infant. For a moment her irritation with her husband slipped from her consciousness. Her pregnancy had been sending her emotions into a waterfall tumble.

"Don't judge him too harshly," Kyna said, breaking the silence.

"Have I said anything about my husband?" Enya licked the cream from her lips.

The cook shrugged her shoulders and turned to look at her.

Enya studied her servant who wore the plain garb of a slave and yet saw through Enya with the wisdom of someone with a much higher standing. Kyna knew her better than anyone in the clan. She had been at Enya's side almost continuously from the time Enya's father sent her north to marry into the rival clan ten summers ago. Enya had escaped a life of terror in which she never knew when her father's fists might find a soft spot under her eye or his boot meet her ribcage. She was safe now, at least from that.

Kyna brought her some tea. "I know I'm speaking out of turn, but I want to warn you against being hasty when it comes to the master of this house."

Being hasty had once saved her life when she confronted her father with a spear. "Are the women talking about me that way, Kyna?" A familiar hand of wariness rose to choke her, but she fought to speak despite it. "Is that what they say

79

behind my back, that I jump to hasty actions? That I'm impulsive?"

Kyna knelt before her and took Enya's hand. "Oh, dear one, you should not care about the gossiping women. Your husband, however? Don't you see that your strong ways are making your husband feel powerless? You must see that he feels as though he has control in his own house." She smiled wryly. "Even if he truly does not."

Enya's shoulders relaxed. She took a deep breath.

Kyna stood and patted Enya's hand. "'Tis no wonder, with none of your women folk here to teach you, and you having grown up around the monks, you've not learned these things."

"Thank you for telling me."

Kyna winked at her.

"I have been a wee disagreeable of late." She tried to measure the cook's reaction, to see if she agreed.

The woman only smiled and pointed inquisitively toward the door.

"I was going to see Gormley."

Kyna shook her head. "Do not confide in one who may betray you." She returned to chopping vegetables.

"Gormley? What do you mean?"

"I'll say no more."

"You don't like her?"

"'Tis not my place to like or dislike. I have said too much already."

Enya tried to persuade Kyna to say more, but soon gave up.

Enya rambled about the estate the rest of the day, not knowing what to do. It seemed everyone had information she didn't, and if she could not trust Gormley, the one woman in the clan who had shown her kindness, what should she do? She had always known Kyna to be truthful. She seldom spoke unless she had reason. Kyna was not a friend, precisely, someone to talk to hours on end, like Gormley, but the cook was steadfast and reliable. She had urged Enya to go to Fe, but Enya had not gone straight away, and now that she was home he was off tending the cattle.

Enya tried to busy herself sorting through the latest picked herbs and finally decided to take up her needle. Unsettling thoughts battered her. Should she sit idling by while others, even her servant, made decisions for her? Decisions that would ultimately affect her longed-for child? Nay, she would not. She would go see Gormley anyway and ask what the cook had meant. Gormley was always forthcoming. Enya, the perennial outsider, would get to the bottom of things the way she usually did—by her own efforts.

Enya tossed the mending she had been working on into a basket in the corner of the hearth room. Grabbing her cloak on her way out, she noticed that the baby had shifted downward in her womb. She could breathe more easily now, a sign the baby would be born soon. "Well, we'll just have to get to the bottom of this rumor before you get here, wee one," she said out loud.

When she opened the cabin door, a winter blast took her breath away. When had the weather grown so frigid? She pinched her cloak tightly under her chin and shut the door behind her. With the slamming of the wooden door a pain surged through her abdomen. She doubled over and let out a groan.

"What is it, my sweet? The baby?"

She hadn't noticed Fe. He seemed to appear unforeseen at times, like a shape-shifting druid. "Where? What?" Those were the only words she forced out words before her knees buckled.

Fe put an arm under her legs and drew her to his chest. He kicked the door back open and carried her inside.

"It … hurts … so much!"

"Quiet, now. Lie here." He placed her on the bed, but that was no comfort to her. She began to roll from side to side. "I'll get the midwife." His voice seemed to be swallowed up, like someone shouting from the depths of a cave.

"Get Kyna!" She blurted, surprising herself.

She must have passed out. Sometime later she noticed the room was dark and hot. Shadowy figures moved about. A pain washed over her and someone grabbed her wrists.

"Push!" several voices yelled.

She did, straining against the pressure until her legs went numb. When the contraction eased she collapsed onto a goose feather pillow. Sobs rose up, sounding so odd, like the way the old ones described the cries of a banshee, the fairy of death. Had she been dreaming? Enya grasped the neck of her linen undergarment when she realized that the wail had come from her own chest. She hadn't felt it rise up from within her, but rather the sound seemed disconnected, from afar. How was that possible? Someone dabbed at her forehead with a cool cloth.

"Rest now, child."

She rolled her head to one side to find Kyna praying, her lips moving silently.

A thump. Cool air. Someone opened the door. She understood. She had been in a house once as a woman was giving birth. Those present opened doors, uncovered windows, and popped lids from jars in the hope that these actions would cause the mother's womb to open as well. Now it was happening here. Enya's baby was not coming swiftly like he should.

Voices mumbled around her, but she couldn't make them out, didn't care to. The pain racked her like a storm beating a ship at sea. She closed her eyes and drew her shoulders in tight, guarding herself from the next wave of cramping.

"You must relax," Kyna whispered beside her. "The midwife says you are overwrought." She pressed on Enya's shoulders, forcing them away from her ears and down to her side. "'Tis better. You will see."

"Kyna," Enya whispered. "I know the baby won't die. The monk told me."

Little creases formed around Kyna's eyes as her smile reached them. "Of course not. Don't you be worrying about that now."

Her tone wasn't convincing, and with subsequent waves of pain and no appearance of the baby, doubt overtook Enya.

"She needs the bath." Gormley's voice rang out from somewhere in the darkness.

"Don't be foolish," Kyna said.

"Listen, old woman, we will let Enya decide. Don't be holding that cross over her head. She doesn't need that." Gormley's voice drew closer until her round face came into view, lit by torchlight. "Enya, dearie, would you like us to give you a fairy bath? You will feel much better and with the spirits' help the baby will just slip right on out."

85

Slip out? Aye, the baby had to come out. She nodded and quickly several hands lifted her from her bed.

Somewhere in the distance she heard a voice, Kyna's voice. "And in the house of Feidheim of the Cenél Conaill! Heaven forbid, Enya. Your husband will not soon forget this!"

It was fairy magic, Gormley's magic, and Enya was too weak to protest or so she told herself. As she smelled the herbs steeping she called out Kyna's name.

"Aye, dearie, I'm right here beside you."

"Where am I?"

"You are in my master's chair by the fire. They are preparing your bath. Please, Enya, do not do this. You know how he feels about this magic."

"Stop," she called weakly. "I do not want it."

Gormley moved toward Kyna, waving a dried shaft of grain at her. "You, old one. What do you know of our ways? You are as much of an outsider as she and your interference could send the child to the otherworld!" There was a snapping sound like a cord breaking.

Kyna's voice. "You may take my cross but you cannot remove our Lord from this house!"

86

"Nay," Enya whispered, feeling another wrenching wave building. "The baby will not die. He just won't come while you are here. You have to leave now, Gormley, you and all those you've brought."

The door slammed a few minutes later. "Who remains?" Enya asked. Her weak voice drew Kyna's face close.

"Only you, me, and the midwife. She said she would call for the physician if you want, but I think Fe already has him standing outside the door."

"Kyna? Can you give me a bath, one that does not call up fairy magic?"

"Ah, a bath with root of valerian," the midwife chimed in. "I have some in my bag."

The next few moments burst with commotion as the women retrieved the bathing basin, stoked the fire to boil water, and continued to try to ease Enya's pains by rubbing her belly with oil and stroking her forehead with damp cloths. By the time she plunged into the warm fragrant water, she was feeling much better. "Prayers," she whispered. "I must hear prayers."

Heavy footsteps. Someone else was there.

"I will pray with you, my sweet." Fe looked down at her bloated body in the basin and smiled. It was so good to see him now, and she was thankful he'd not been there earlier.

"Are you sure you want to be in here?" She squeaked, her voice barely obeying her.

"I am so proud of you." He bent down to whisper in her ear. "Please, let me stay and pray for our child."

The tone of his voice melted her heart. She had been so contrary that he felt he needed to beg. "Sure and pray with me, Fe. This is your house. This is your child … and I am your wife. I need you." Tears streamed down her face as he bent his head low and caressed her fingers in his rough hand. She could not focus on his words, he prayed too softly anyway, but as his breath touched her face she felt at peace. She had honored him in his house by sending her only friend Gormley out the door.

"Oh!" She wrenched her hand away from his and gripped the edges of the basin.

The midwife appeared on the opposite side. "I'm ready to catch the babe, dearie. You go right ahead and push."

Their son came forth in a bath of relaxing herbs blessed by the prayers of his father. Red and wrinkled. Healthy. They had earlier discussed what to name their child. He would have a unique name, one befitting the character he would need to escape the curse of his mother's lineage: his maternal grandfather's angry spirit. This child would be clever, bold, and fearless. Fe would announce the boy's name to the clan: Crimthann, which means fox.

Chapter Seven

I am under vows to you, O God; I will present my
thank offerings to you.

—*Psalm 56:12 NIV*

Enya ignored it like a field laborer oblivious to rain-laden gray skies. She knew the day must come, but she chose to put the thought as far from her consciousness as possible, relishing her days of mothering as any woman would. She cherished each gurgle, anticipated with pleasure each nightly feeding. So intense was her feeling for her child that Gormley began accusing her of excessive coddling.

"He's a future king," Enya said softly while they gathered spring herbs. The other women were not close enough to hear, but she would be careful lest they misunderstood.

"King of a monastery?" Gormley leaned her head back and bellowed too loudly for Enya's comfort. "You've lost your head, girl. Perhaps some nettle tea would improve your milk flow and settle your mind."

"Watch yourself," Kyna called as she gathered willow bark for the nasty tasting tea she believed eased the aching joints in her fingers. "'Tis not the same to go to the king's house as to come from it."

Kyna was trying to suggest that being in a royal bloodline was more important than not.

Gormley shook a nettle leaf in Kyna's direction and laughed again. "Bah. Foolish old woman spouting meaningless proverbs. The fairies know better. You should heed."

Kyna let the disagreement go.

Enya turned back to the patch of nettles and struggled to pluck the upper leaves without stinging herself, a chore most women left to the servants. Because the others thought her birthright was special, Enya sought to engage in menial tasks to show she was no hallowed daughter.

The clan's women best forget Enya's origins, as Enya wished to do. Unfortunately, Enya remained as twilight, trapped between the evening of her old life and the dawn of her new. She wished to force herself up from the murky waters of the past to embrace only the present.

Enya narrowed her gaze to concentrate on the task. Enya *could* pick nettles. She was perfectly capable. The more experienced harvesters gathered the herb quickly with little effort, but she could figure it out. Her rag-wrapped hand soon tingled with dozens of prickles.

Little Crimthann snoozed, unaware of his mother's anxiety. Perhaps Kyna had been right about Gormley pretending to be a friend after all. Patting her child's bottom made Enya's fingers tingle uncomfortably, but she could not admit any sign of injury, physical or personal, not in front of Gormley and the others.

Enya straightened her back. "I'm finished for the day." She scooped up Crimthann, snuggling his head against her shoulder. Then she trudged off, leaving her basket of herbs behind.

She did not speak to Gormley after that. She dared not. God might turn his back on Enya if she gave Gormley and her ungodly ways any heed. Fe and Kyna had warned her away plenty of times.

Enya gazed up to the heavens. Mounds of white clouds skimmed over the cold-blue sky. She would obey because this God had great power. She would not risk him taking her son farther away than the monastery.

With new resolve, Enya decided that should her former friend ask after her, the cook would tell her Enya had chosen to keep to the cottage with the boy. He was her future, a ray of hope in her dark world. Why wouldn't she shelter him? She would show the women, show all the people of Fe's clan, and even her father. God had exalted her by blessing her with a divinely special child. No fairy magic could have brought her this. Only the God of Patrick had answered her prayer.

The months sped by. Crimthann began to crawl, then walk, then run with a toddle. Once Enya weaned him there would be no reason to keep him at home. He was talking with articulacy rare for a child his age. A baby no longer. Soon she would have to fulfill her vow and take the child to the priest.

"I am going to do it," she told Fe one evening when he brought it up. "I need to prepare him first." She noted her husband's narrow look. "I will, I tell you."

"When?"

"By the next full moon." There. She had said it. In truth, she was afraid not to keep her promise. For all she knew the Christian God might call down his wrath if she tarried any longer.

When the first sliver of the waxing moon blinked in the sky, Enya began to pack a traveling bag for her son. She marked the days with slashes carved on the cottage's wooden threshold.

"Where are we going, Mamaí?" Little Crimthann pushed a sandy curl from his eyes with his chubby fingers.

"You're a big lad, now, son. We are preparing to go to God's house. Not today, but later when the moon is full."

His eyes grew large as goose eggs. "What will we do there?"

She pulled the child onto her lap and nuzzled her face in his downy locks. "You, Crimthann, will serve God there and earn the respect of the Father and of all men."

"Noooo!" He threw himself to the floor.

She picked him up and put him in her lap. "Do not act so, son. This is not a punishment. This is a great honor not all wee lads receive."

He made himself taller, twisting his small body upward like a flower straining for the sun, suddenly proud. "Will you serve God with me?"

She kissed his cheek. "I will, from here."

He spun, launching himself from her lap. "From here?"

"You are privileged to be the priest's helper, Crimthann. I will visit, but I will stay here with your father. I will always be your mother."

Young as he was, the light of understanding washed over his face. His eyes watered, and she struggled to keep her composure.

"I want to serve God, Mamaí. And you will always be my mother." He flung his arms around her neck and she gulped back tears. He was strong. Stronger than she was, by the grace of God.

95

The awful day arrived. Enya had made Crimthann a special striped robe and helped him dress. Then they joined Fe in the chariot. A fine mist coated their eyes and moistened their cheeks, hiding any tears they might shed.

Enya did not blame God. Nay, he had given her this child, and she had been fully aware of what would happen the day she had promised to give the child back. But no one could deny that she was his mother. She would be permitted to visit and bring clothes. Somehow, some way, she would endure the separation because that was far better than to never have had him at all.

The horse lumbered up the hill toward the monastery as though it pulled a bier to a funeral. No one spoke. Beneath the folds of her apron, Enya fingered a woven rope cross tightly between her fingers. She planned to give it to her son at the moment of their parting. When they reached the monastery gates, she sucked in her breath. Fe helped her down, and she stood looking through the iron bars, staring at nothing in particular.

A gray head appeared on the other side, surprising her. Malachi, the one who had prophesied about her child's birth, grinned at her through the bars before unlatching them and swinging them wide. For a moment, she waivered, not sure if she could follow through with the plan that felt like abandonment.

"There is welcome for you here. Come in." He waved a chubby hand.

Crimthann clung to Enya's robe from behind, but she didn't turn to look at him. The three of them, still a family however differently it might now be defined, followed another monk sent to guide them down a stone-scattered walk to the church. She told herself she was not abandoning her son. She would see him regularly. There was no place safer than a monastery. God would protect him better than she could. Here, he would not be an outsider like she was, or treated like royalty befitting Fe's standing in the clan. To stay as strong as she knew he was, Crimthann needed this housing, this neutral dwelling place.

"The Father is expecting you," the monk said, glancing back at them.

"We're going to see God?" Crimthann whispered.

"The priest," Fe answered. "He is called Father and the monks are called brothers."

The boy nodded. He was such a clever lad. He would learn quickly.

97

The church stood before them whitewashed and glistening through the misty rain. Enya remembered that it would be dark inside, and she paused a moment as though she could gather the light of the outside world and cart it in with her.

The monk mumbled something about blessing the coming and going and then motioned them inside. Fe went first, ducking under the lintel. Crimthann followed, and she quickly joined them, not trusting that the monk would not bolt the door before she got inside.

The priest was before the altar on bent knees, his head bowed in silent prayer. The monk closed the door quietly and spoke in a hushed tone. "Sit there. The Father will be with you as soon as he completes his prayers."

Enya studied the man's face while her husband and son obediently lowered themselves onto a bench. She must have been staring because the monk repeated the invitation. "Please, good woman, rest yourself. 'Twon't be long." He flipped his chin upward, reminding her of a beached fish struggling to fling itself back to the sea.

She looked away and scooted in next to her son. They waited, hands folded, inhaling stale air tinged with the scent of burning candles. Enya's palms perspired and her stomach tightened. If they could go quickly she might keep her sanity. Why was the priest torturing them by making them wait?

Fe's eyes were shut and he mumbled an old blessing while patting Crimthann's hand. This was hard for him too.

The sound of Father Cruithneachia huffing to rise to his feet shifted her attention to the front of the church. He crossed himself, bowed his head and then turned toward them. Malachi appeared at the priest's side and whispered into his ear.

Enya and her family rose and waited for the priest to join them. When he drew near Enya spoke up. "I am the woman who stood before you years ago, Father. I prayed for a child. God has granted me my request, as you said he would, and I am here to return him to God."

Puzzlement crossed the priest's face.

Fe interrupted. "To put him into your service, Father."

"I see." The priest bent low to look at Crimthann. "Is he an obedient child?"

"The most loyal child in all of the kingdom," Enya said.

Malachi cleared his throat and the priest turned toward him. "He is the son of a fifth daughter of a fifth daughter," the brother said. "He certainly belongs here."

"What?" Enya glared at the man as her husband tugged on her arm. She tried to ignore Fe. "What has this to do with my son? What has it to do with me keeping my vow to God?"

"What vow?" Crimthann whined, clinging to his father.

"Please, Enya. Not now." Fe stared at her, his green eyes darkening.

She lowered her voice and spoke only to the priest. "If you will, Father. I have been given a gift. And as much as it pains me, I know the gift needs to be returned to the church. For a time," she said.

The priest nodded and dismissed Malachi, who seemed reluctant to go but finally bowed and departed.

"Please, sit down," the priest said.

When Enya regained her composure enough to breathe without her heart pounding in her ears, the priest spoke again. "I am getting old. I can use a young helper to assist me with the church duties. I will accept this fosterage if you will agree to visit him at Easter and Christmas and bring him the clothing he will need as he grows."

Fe and Enya looked at each other. "But Father," Fe finally said, "the monk who escorted us in already told us the terms of the fosterage."

Was the old man feeble-minded? Was it really wise to leave Crimthann in his care? Doubts pelted her like rocks flung from a slingshot. She reached for the old man's withered hand. "Perhaps there is a better way, something more convenient for you, in which God can use my son, Father Cruithneachia. I don't think Brother Malachi would be the best teacher. He told us earlier he was in charge."

As if understanding her uneasiness, the priest nodded. "Do not fear, daughter. Brother Malachi will not have charge of the child." He narrowed his blue eyes to gaze at her. "The brother may strut around like a cock that thinks he's in command of the barnyard. But he is not in charge, God is, and if the Almighty Father has asked you to put this child into my care, then I will honor that fully. You have my word that the child will receive the best care, the best education, and that

Brother Malachi will have nothing to do with either."

The Father's words were strangely comforting, and even Crimthann seemed at ease now. Fe reached across their son to slip his arm around Enya's shoulder and whisper into her ear. "The word of a priest, Enya. 'Tis no better assurance we could hope for."

She removed the rope cross from her pocket and pressed it into her son's hand. "I will always be your mother. Do not forget."

He gazed up, eyes round with wonder. "I promise, Mamaí. I will not forget."

She kissed his cheeks and then hurried from the church, praying fervently that she had not made a mistake.

They were positioned in the chariot about to pull away from the monastery when she spotted him, Brother Malachi, standing beside a holly tree. Fe didn't seem to notice and steered the horse on a path that would lead them right past the man. The monk lowered his hood as they passed and shouted, "Favored daughter, you will reap what you sow!"

She gripped her cloak tight to her throat as they whisked by.

"What did that mean?" Fe asked, shouting over the wind that was beating them with such force they had to press their bodies close to keep from being thrown out.

She remembered that he had claimed to be her spiritual father when she met him at the guesthouse. It made no sense then and now seemed eerie. "I don't know. I think he's quite mad."

"I trust the priest," Fe said. For some reason, he seemed to think that would reassure her.

They continued on as a storm built on the horizon. She remembered long ago leaving the church and stopping at a home, the place that seemed to be populated with angels. Crimthann had been conceived on that night, she believed. Everything had seemed perfect then, but she had chosen to ignore what it would mean to barter away her son. Now she could think of nothing else.

The rain, that had earlier in the day been a soft coating of mist, turned angry, driven by a strong gale. "There's a house up here," Fe said. "You remember?"

"I remember," she shouted. Whispering to herself, drowned out by the pelting rain, she added, "I will never forget it."

Now was not the time for regrets or reflection. The rain fell harder, transforming the trail into a muddy river. "I'll have to go through the woods," Fe yelled to her, "or else we'll get stuck. Tie yourself to the rig."

She felt behind them for the length of rope they always carried. Finding it, she tugged until she had it on her lap. Her fingers numbed and cramped but she finally managed to uncoil the rope. She tied one end to the hand grip and wrapped it around her waist. She started to use the rest to tie Fe to the rig, but he pushed her away.

"No time for that. Hang on!"

When they left the road, the chariot bumped wildly over tree roots while Fe attempted to slow the horse down. Black tree shadows lurked everywhere. She hoped the horse saw them. If the beast did not they might slam into one without warning.

"Shouldn't we walk?" she called out, spitting rainwater from her mouth.

"I've got to slow the horse down."

Fe had lost control. They were being dragged through a dark forest by a frightened animal.

"Untie your rope!" Fe ordered.

Her fingers were slippery. She could not loosen it.

"Untie it and jump!" he yelled again.

"I cannot."

He dropped the reins and began tugging at the rope but it was dark and with each bump they hit they had to focus their strength on regaining their balance. She glanced up. "Fe!" They were headed straight for a tree. He wouldn't leave her. They would both be crushed.

Suddenly the rig lurched, striking something hard that caused the chariot to stop abruptly. A sharp snap told her the horse had broken the reins. The force of the collision lifted the chariot bed and she plunged into the darkness. Almost immediately she was on the ground. "Roll to the side," Fe yelled.

She did just as the wooden chariot smashed to pieces beside her. She closed her eyes, realizing that she had just dodged death. *Praise God!*

105

"Fe? Fe?" She scrambled to her feet and jerked at her rope constraint until she wiggled free. Her hands guided over broken boards, taking on cuts and splinters. "Fe?"

A groan answered just paces away. Not being tied as she was, Fe had been thrown a distance away from the wreckage.

"Where are you? Are you hurt?"

"Over here. Not hurt." He groaned again.

Enya crawled her way over. Fe was lying face up. "Why don't you get up then, Feidheim of the Cenél Conaill?" It was dark. She couldn't tell if he was bleeding. She bent low to his ear. "'Tis no one here but me, husband, tell me where it hurts."

"My ankle. Nay, my leg. Get me a board from the rig and help me up."

She did as he said, and using the board to lean on and her shoulder to balance, he was able to limp along beside her through the forest.

She strained to see through the darkness. "What if we don't find the horse, Fe?"

"Not a lame-witted beast, that one. He'll be headed to the shelter of a barn. There's a house around here somewhere."

She peered through the dim forest but did not see any lights. "What direction?"

"I think …" he turned his head to one side. "Nay, I think this way …" he hesitated. "Get me over to that big tree. We can be shielded from the rain and think a moment."

It took much effort, but eventually they hobbled over to a massive oak and crawled under one of its lower branches. The roots of the tree rose out of the ground, creating a crevice that cradled them while the rain continued to pelt the earth.

She began to sob. "God is angry with me. I must have misunderstood. He does not want me to give up my son. Fe, we have to get him back."

He cradled her head under his chin. "God is not angry because you kept your promise. He might be miffed at me for taking you out in this weather."

"How were we to know such a bucketing was about to spring on us?"

Fe focused his attention on the rain. "Someone's out there."

A faint light bobbed to and fro. "Must be someone from the house," she said.

A voice called out. "Someone hurt, are you?"

"We're here," Fe answered.

The light rushed forward until a man stood holding a lantern to peer into their shelter. Rain dripped from the brim of his felt hat. "Ah, there you are. You'll come with me to the house. The wife and meself will get you dried out."

Once they entered the snug cottage, Fe asked how the man knew to come looking for them. "Did you find the horse, then? That creature looks out for himself, make no mistake."

The man shook his head of fluffy white hair. "No horse. 'Twas a monk from the monastery who came by. Brother Malachi. Said a couple might need shelter, should I find them. The wife was in a terrible fright, thinking about you out here in the dark, so I came looking."

Enya shook rain from her cloak. "Are you sure that was his name? Malachi?"

Fe gave her a piercing look, but she wanted to know.

"A little peculiar man, but insistent. Said 'twas his duty to look after you, but he lost the trail of your cart. Malachi was his name for sure."

The man's wife, a tiny woman wearing a thick, warm shawl spoke up. "I told him to get on back to the monastery before he was the one gone missing. Thank the wee folks you two made it here all fit."

"Thank the good Lord," Fe added.

Enya wasn't sure whom to thank. Or to fear. Just as soon as she could she was going back to make sure her son was well and Malachi was nowhere near him. Something was odd about the whole business. What if that monk had done something to spook their horse or even loosened the rigging? And perhaps he'd come back to see if his mischief had done what he'd hoped. She'd show him that a mother protects her children, no matter what.

Chapter Eight

My son, hear the instruction of thy father, and forsake not the law of thy mother.

—*Proverbs 1:10 KJV*

The next opportunity to leave came when Fe was out in the fields. The blacksmith delivered a new grate for the fireplace and mentioned he was on his way to deliver goods to the monastery.

"Shall I send word to the master?" Kyna asked.

"I can't wait to get his approval. The blacksmith must go now in order to arrive at his appointment time and he's agreed to take me. Don't mention it to Fe. I'll explain when I return."

Enya was determined to learn if the mysterious monk was a bad omen or just a crazy man to ignore. He was no spiritual father of hers, despite what he might choose to believe. She'd been foolish to allow him to worry her when he'd said so. Still, if the priest could not protect Crimthann from a looney monk, the bargain would be voided, at least to her mind. And she was the mother.

When she arrived, she did not encounter Malachi. The servant who met her after the blacksmith departed for the monks' workshop, a lad who had seen about twenty summers, led her to the church. He was pleasant and understood immediately that she'd come to check on the wellbeing of her son.

"The priest will be delighted to see you, mistress."

"Delighted? Are you quite sure?" She glanced beyond the stone path they followed and noticed well-kept gardens and tidy, round straw huts. The last time she was there she had been so aggrieved she'd not observed how very nice and clean the grounds were.

"Indeed. He told us to expect your visits to be frequent, at least in the first year, and we are honored to have you among us. We are kin through the fosterage of your son."

Well, this was not the greeting she had expected. Instead of feeling like an outsider, she'd been made to feel a part of their community. "Is Brother Malachi in residence?"

"I am sorry, he is not." The lad paused a few paces from the church door. "He is on an errand away from the monastery. Is there something I can do for you in his stead?"

"Nothing, thank you."

The young man looked surprised.

"You have been most kind. I cannot ask for more. May I wait inside?"

"Certainly. Take all the time you'd like for prayer. If the priest is not free to attend you when you are done, please come to the refectory. We will be happy to provide a meal for you while you wait."

"Thank you. And my son?"

"He is napping. I will bring him to you myself when he awakes."

"May I ask your name?"

His face seemed to glow as though she'd complimented him. "Michael. I am at your service."

Enya entered the dim church. The breeze stirred by the opening of the door sent the lit candles flickering. The shadowy figure of the priest bustled about the altar. She sat on a bench and lowered her head. *I know he is yours, Father*

God. But I beg of you, give me assurance that he will be safe here.

She allowed the silence to surround her as she breathed in the aroma of incense. She had sat in quiet before in her cottage when Fe was away and Kyna was working in the outdoor kitchen. Enya enjoyed solitude, but this was different. She felt a presence. Not the priest, who was surely still nearby. This presence was otherworldly, a breath that encircled her and touched her heart in a way no physical being could. She'd heard of folks sensing the company of fairies and pookas, but in all her visits to the sacred wells and fairy thorn bushes, she'd never felt this. It was as though all the ancestors in the grave, the good ones, lifted their spirits to hers and lovingly embraced her.

Some time later a comforting hand rested on her shoulder. She looked up into the face of the priest. He smiled. "What can I do for you, child?"

She wasn't sure what to say. She'd come to the monastery out of a sense of anger and indignation. Her outrage had vanished. But then, Malachi did not seem to be there. "Tell me about the one called Malachi. The monk who was here with you when we brought Crimthann."

The priest lowered himself onto a bench and turned to look at her. "It is my son you speak of."

"Your … son by birth, you mean?"

"He is." The priest wagged his head. "Malachi is meant to serve here with me. Such is his birthright, but I'm afraid he lacks my devotion to the One True God. I am working to persuade him. Fighting against the old ways, as I must." The smile returned to his face. "But your son? He radiates the Spirit of the Living God." The man sat straighter as he spoke of Crimthann.

Radiate? Like a risen sun? She did not know if that was favorable or regrettable. "I am afraid that I do not understand, Father."

The priest leaned closer, as if sharing a secret. "I entered the nursery one night. I suppose it was midnight, right before prayers. I wanted to see if the bells had disturbed him. What I saw amazed me. A light glowed around the cradle while your wee son slept, a smile on his face. 'Twas a sign that God is with that child. You are a blessed woman. I indeed am blessed to have him in my care."

She gently touched his arm. "Thank you for telling me, Father." Tears blurred her vision. She blinked hard and pulled her hand away. She had done the right thing by bringing her son there after all.

The priest held his hand over her head. "May God bless you, woman, with more children."

More children? She had never considered that God might favor her with more than one miracle.

"Let us go and refresh ourselves with some nourishment."

She rose and allowed him to lead her out of the church. But what about... "Father? What is your concern about your son? I mean, if I may ask, do you think he could cause ... uh, harm?"

The priest paused and rubbed a hand across the brim of his tonsure. "He is my son, my flesh and blood. I hope he will accept the God of Patrick in due time. I have raised him to be a considerate, noble man, albeit without the help of a mother." The thin line of his lips drooped. "My wife died in a horrible accident when the lad was ten summers old. But that was fifty seasons ago, perhaps longer. The memory of an old man does fade. The absence of one's memories is sometimes more blessing than curse."

He turned and urged her to walk on with him. "My son does not always make choices I approve of, but to my knowledge he has never committed an unforgiveable sin. He is at a mature age, and I am late in life, so he no longer has duties in the church. I rarely see him, and neither will Crimthann. Malachi keeps himself busy working in the distant orchards and at fairs where he sells cider and apples."

The light from the lintel fell upon the priest's face, confirming that the man was old. Very old. She would need assurance that if he died, her son's fosterage would not fall to Malachi.

They walked in silence to the eating hall. The feeling of peace and utter contentment rose up once more. And then, absolute joy when Crimthann came running into her arms. She pressed the boy's head to her neck. "I am always your mother. Never forget."

Later, she pleaded for a private conversation with the priest.

"I am sorry, mistress, but I must leave now. The attendants will see to you." His eyes drooped as he bowed out of the room.

Michael stood between her and the figure of the departing priest. "His age requires him to re-tire early."

She nodded. A faint sensation of what she needed floating away from her and out of her reach seemed overly familiar. How would she ever communicate with the man who was her son's foster father?

Only moments later one of the brothers told her it was time to put the boy to bed as well. She held Crimthann tight, his wee heartbeat pounding against her own.

"Do not make the parting difficult for him," the brother warned.

She kissed her son and then Michael escorted her to the gate where the blacksmith waited for her. "My son looks well," she told Michael. "I am grateful."

Michael smiled. "How long have you been here?"

The lad swung open the iron gates to lead her to the blacksmith's wagon. "Two Easters now."

"What can you tell me about the monk called Malachi?"

"I know he is the priest's son."

"This may sound like an odd question, but have you ever heard him insist that he is someone's spiritual father?"

"He tells everyone that. Pay him no mind." He glanced around, but there was no one to overhear them. The blacksmith had gone to fill his sheep bladder at the well. "I believe he thinks more of himself than he should."

"Are you afraid of the man?"

"God our Father tells us to fear not. 'The fear of man brings a snare: but whoever puts his trust in the Lord shall be safe.'" The young man glanced to his feet, then looked up and nodded to the horse. "You will find that your mount has been watered, fed, and brushed. Godspeed your journey, mistress."

"I am grateful." She pressed a bronze amulet into his palm. Fe would not miss this ornament. "If my son is ever in danger, from this Malachi or anyone else, or if God forbid the priest dies, bring news to me at once."

If her request surprised Michael, his expression did not show it. "I will, mistress. Your boy is well, you understand."

"I thank you. God bless you, Michael."

When she arrived back at her cottage, Fe was seated outside the door, his muscular arms folded across his chest. In her haste, she had not taken into account what her going without him might mean for the survival of her marriage.

Chapter Nine

Pulse of my heart, song of my soul, light of my night.
—Irish saying

She'd done it again, dashed off to the monastery without his knowledge. And now he was waiting for her in front of their cottage, both arms creased across his chest as he sat on the water barrel. Thoughts of him dismissing her, sending her back to her horrid clan, caved in as she accepted a servant's help getting down from the wagon seat. She stepped toward him, her hands trembling inside the folds of her garments. "Please, Fe, let me explain."

"No need." He rose, opened the cottage door, and then stood to the side to allow her to enter first.

A trickle of sweat ran down the back of her tunic. She removed her cloak slowly, the softness of the material scooting breathlessly from her shoulders. The peat fire glowing from the center of the room cast a shadow across Fe's chair.

She leaned against the bed when he closed the door.

"I suppose you've been to see our boy."

"I have." She watched as he sat by the fire and sipped from a jar.

"I know the blacksmith had business there today. I am happy you did not travel without help. Our son is well?"

"Indeed. They seem to be quite fond of him. The priest believes God is with the child."

"Of course God is with him, but I am pleased to hear the priest thinks so."

"Our son is blessed." She went to Fe and placed her hands on his shoulder, gently massaging. "You are not angry with me for going, husband?"

He set his jar down on the floor. "No reason to be. You should visit as much as you like. You *are* his mother. So long as the priest approves of your visits, you should go."

"He did not seem to mind."

"Good. The child is yet young. Perhaps later, when he is engaged in schooling and chores, there will not be much opportunity. I see no harm in it now."

"No harm indeed." Sucking in a breath, she wondered how to bring up what was troubling her without casting light on the fact that she'd gone off without notice. She moved into his line of vision. "Fe?" He pulled her onto his lap. She gazed into his bright eyes. Not sensing any bit of anger, she continued. "The priest is quite old. How do we know our son's fosterage will be completed?"

"He is in God's hands."

She could not argue. She had sensed it.

In the warmth of their closeness her unease dissipated. Fe nuzzled his face into her hair. "You must be exhausted after your travel," he said, caressing the side of her face with his thumb. "The laundress has put fresh linens on the bed. Let me show you."

They rose from the chair. Candles glowed from a shelf on the wall closest to the bed, casting their home in a romantic light she had not noticed earlier. He was wooing her like he had on their wedding night. She dared to break the spell. "You won't leave before I wake, will you?"

"I will not go out without first telling you. Never again, my sweet."

"Nor will I."

Much later Enya woke to the sounds of night creatures. Fe indeed still slept next to her. When she moved closer to him, he wrapped an arm around her. Kyna's advice came to mind, reminding her how she must tend carefully to her beloved's ego.

He did not wake despite moving toward her. When a couple has been married for many seasons, one can move in the bed without disturbing the other. Why did some long-married couples remain affectionate while others, like her parents, barely tolerate each other? She could not deny that she and Fe were closer than her parents had been. He loved her. He tenderly loved her. Even when the hog's escapades made him angry or a spring crop failed and he slammed doors and kicked over empty buckets in the garden, his fondness for her had never wavered. Not even her jealous outbursts threatened to destroy what he felt for her.

Enya turned toward the shuttered window. Fe did not have the curse her father had. She must keep reminding herself of that. He had not been born into it as she had. She prayed that the God Fe and his people believed in would kill the curse of anger, cause it to end with her and never reach her son. She must believe so.

She rolled back toward her husband. His breath fell on her bare shoulder. The words of the priest played in her mind. *May God bless you with more children.*

The next morning Fe refused his usual practice of breaking fast with the men in the meeting house and instead ate porridge and cream at the table board with Enya. He spoke about his plans for the day. "It has been decided to build a road to the shore. A good plan, as we will be needing to haul kelp to the new field. A great many crops will be grown now. Some think a better use would be grazing pasture, but there's plenty of room for our cattle as 'tis. More corn and barley will result from our efforts."

Crops, the weather … she didn't care what he talked about. All that mattered was he was here with her. She carried their empty plates to the washing bin.

"Enya, I did not know our cook is a Christian."

She shrugged as she poured water warmed from the fire over the dishes. "She is a good woman. This does not surprise me."

"I hadn't noticed it before, but when I observed her trading with that peculiar brother we met earlier, I noticed she wore a hammered tin cross around her neck."

She spun around, water dripping from her fingertips. "Which brother would that be?"

"'Twas surely that odd one we met at the monastery, but I don't want you worrying about him anymore. Still, I thought you should see this." He pushed away from the table board to reach for his boots. He pulled something out of one them. "The cook brought over some trinkets he left. I snatched this one. I suppose you know what it is."

The silver ring shone from his finger and her throat tightened. "Fe, where could he have gotten that, and why would Kyna take it?"

"I don't know that she would have realized the insignia is from the Mac Noe. I suppose the old monk obtained it in trade. I figured to have it melted down."

She nodded her head. "Perhaps I should get new servants."

"You are the mistress of this house, Enya. But don't tell me you blame Kyna for this."

"I … don't know. She was a servant in the Mac Noe household. She should have known."

After he left she paced the floor. Trade was common. The monk could have gotten the ring anywhere. Kyna may have thought it unnecessary to tell her. If Enya were the woman Fe wanted her to be she would not be troubled. She must trust her husband and trust God. But for Enya, everything she wanted to hold close floated like a feather on a breeze far above her head. She could not conceive until she relinquished her child. She could not make the women in the clan favor her. She could not have her child at home. Everything out of her control. Her chest ached.

She pounded a fist in her hand as she marched from the front door to the window on the back of the cottage looking out over the loch. How absurd to imagine her trusted cook and the mysterious monk would have conspired to drop a reminder of Enya's wicked ancestry onto her husband's finger.

A crane flapped his massive wings and glided toward the water. She reached out a hand and watched as the bird soared out of sight. Bringing her hand back to her chin, she wondered. Had she been thinking that dismissing the servants would help her regain control of her tightly knitted nest of protection?

Och! Quick judgments were a troublesome family trait perhaps no better than the anger curse. Throwing a scarf over her head, she rushed out the door. The wind tried to push her away from the barn. She shouted to the stable boy. "Have you seen my husband?"

He did not even try to yell against the wind. Not everyone had a voice as mighty as her own. He pointed to the wall behind the barn. The horse pasture. Fe must be readying his mount. He hadn't gone straight to the kitchen to fire their cook. Tears blurred her sight as she thought about dismissing her oldest companion, the one who had kept Gormley from unjustly influencing her. *Please, God, let me be in time!*

She spotted Fe's tall form reaching up to bridle a horse. She hurried toward him, rain pelting her face.

"Enya! What are you doing out here?" He rushed to her. Wrapping his arm tightly around her shoulders, he led her to the back door of the barn and inside.

She sputtered raindrops from her lips. "Please, Fe, tell me you have not fired the servants."

"What? Enya, you didn't ask me to do that."

"I didn't?"

"You mentioned that it crossed your mind is all. You shouldn't have come out in this weather. Mentioning such a thought to me has done no harm."

She cocked her head to one side.

He kissed her. "If I had dismissed the cook and the others, you'd have been miserable. A bit of time off the flame allows the sizzle to die down."

"Indeed. You must think me terribly hotheaded."

He drew her head to his chest. "I prefer you the way you are, my sweet. Who knows you better than I?"

"Who, indeed. I love you, Feidheim."

She could not revel in his embrace too long, however. A matter still remained. What if that monk knew the sight of one of her clan's belongings would send her reeling.

"May I have the ring you wear?"

He held up a hand. "This? Surely you may, but I cannot think why you'd want this clunky thing made for a man's finger." He took it off and handed it to her. "I was going to take it to the blacksmith. Would you like it made into a brooch?"

"Ah, perhaps I would. I will take it to him myself."

He kissed her and turned toward the open barn door. "The rain is letting up. You can get back to the house now and into some dry clothing." His lips met hers again and then he left.

She would not take the ring to the blacksmith just yet. She needed to speak to Kyna.

Chapter Ten

He who keeps his tongue, keeps his friends.
—Irish saying

Once the rain had ceased, Enya found Kyna tending the outdoor fire. The woman acknowledged her with a smile and then tossed a stick into the flames. Bits of black soot floated in the air like wee birds winging toward the sun. Enya's strength floated away too, and tears streaked down her face.

"What's wrong, child?" Kyna whisked her hands together, and then wiped them on her apron. She stretched out her arms.

Enya fell into them, crying for the thing she'd thought about doing. The last time she'd been this emotional she was—

She closed her eyes, not daring to image she could already be pregnant. Pulling the silver ring from her pocket, she held it out to the woman.

"What's this?" She took the piece and held it to the sky. "The trinket I gave your husband?"

"'Tis. You got it from the monk, he said."

"I did." She narrowed her eyes. "Why has this upset you so?"

Enya wiped her face with the back of her palm. "Please, let's walk."

They took the path near the woods where Enya knew they would not encounter any of the other women. "I am troubled, Kyna. You have been with me a long time. You must know the markings of my clan are on that ring."

"Your clan? I did not know. Perhaps I should have, but 'tis not a servant's business. I am sorry I did not recognize it. The monk, that peculiar man they call Brother Malachi, told me it should be returned. Said the monks received it in trade, but he knew it belonged in the household of Fe. I assumed it was from this clan. I regret taking it now."

Enya handed the ring to her.

Kyna's eyes widened as she accepted it and swept it into the depths of her apron pocket. She knew of the curse in Enya's clan, of course. It affected the men most. In the women it came out in the form of impatience and loud voices.

The cook fingered the cross around her neck. "It must have been happenstance that the ring came to us. That man could not know of where you came, could he?"

"It seems he does. He spoke of all that fifth daughter of a fifth daughter business when I met with him at the monastery. I thought at first he may have been given divine understanding. But now, just thinking about him sends chills right through me, Kyna."

Kyna put an arm around Enya and led her to a wee stone hut at the edge of the woods.

"Is this where you live?"

"'Tis. Would you mind coming inside? We'd not be overheard there."

They ducked through the low opening. Kyna lit a torch after closing the door. The single room came to life. Tidy, as Enya would have expected. A sleeping mat was rolled up near the fire pit. There were no cooking utensils because Kyna did not eat there, but there was something unexpected. A shelf on the west-facing wall held a clay jar. Sticking out of the top were two scrolls. Nearby sat an inkpot and stylus. Enya moved closer to examine them. "You can read, Kyna? And write?"

"A bit. I practice when I am not serving you and my master."

"Who taught you?"

The cook cleared her throat and unrolled the sleeping mat. "Please sit. I've nothing else to offer."

"This is fine, thank you."

The woman stirred the ashes in her fire pit. When a warm glow sparked, she joined Enya on the mat.

"You ask who taught me to read and write?"

Enya nodded.

"I learned from you."

"Me? I don't remember showing you."

The woman took Enya's hand. "One can learn quite a bit through observation. I have been with you since your tender age of new womanhood. You spent many hours every day writing, and you used to read to me. Remember?"

"I do. The Psalms. The old tales. I did not realize you were watching the words as I spoke them."

Kyna chuckled. "I understood much of it by the time you married."

"I am sorry we no longer read together. We will have to resume the practice, and if there is anything you don't comprehend, you must tell me. I would be happy to teach you."

"I would like that." Kyna frowned. "I missed the meaning of that ring, but most things I discern quite well."

"Tell me what it is you discern."

"People, mostly. And that is why we must have this chat, child. I know it is not my place to advise you, but I hope you will accept my guidance on this matter."

Enya scooted to look directly at Kyna. "What have you discerned about me? Do you think I am a woman with too sharp a tongue?"

She laughed and patted Enya's hand. "You are a spirited lass. That is the way God made you. You should not change, just…tap it down at times."

Enya let out a breath. "I am trying to take your advice about Fe."

"Is it working?"

"I believe so." She sighed. "I know he loves me."

"He does. Everyone sees it. Even the Murtaghs."

Shame heated Enya's face. She lowered her gaze. "I have had trouble believing so myself, but he shows me now, and I am working hard to let him know my love for him is just as unfathomable."

Kyna squeezed Enya's fingers and then released her hand. "As it should be. Now, about Gormley and the monk."

"Gormley? What has she to do with this?"

"She knows your clan and your birth order."

"She does. Many of the women here do."

"That may be true, but Gormley believes it has meaning. The others may repeat things, like gossips, but Gormley? She practices the fairy faith in a manner that shows deep devotion."

"Well, do not worry, my dear cook. You know I have decided not to converse with her. 'Tis what God would want. If she asks about me, only tell her that my duties are my focus. Have I not told you this already?"

"You have, but you must still be vigilant. She has not asked me about you directly. I do believe you show kindness to her, and to everyone. 'Tis the way of our Lord. Be kind, but do not confide in her as you once did. And most certainly do not take up her ways. I know I shouldn't speak this way, but I feel I must."

Enya patted her hand. "I know I have listened to her in the past, but now I will be avoiding her as much as I am able."

"I do not think she will allow you to put her aside."

"What do you mean?"

"You two were friends for a time. She may believe she has your confidence."

"I did trust her once. But then on the night of Crimthann's birth …"

Kyna nodded. "You were right to heed my warning that night. Your child deserved a blessing at his birth, and Gormley was determined to see that he did not get it."

"Why would you say that? The woman is too forward most times, and she is misguided in her faith, at least it seems so to me to now. But she wouldn't wish my child harm."

Kyna whispered as though mice might overhear, for they were the only creatures close by. "Her belief in the spirits of the woods is so strong she put your friendship aside long ago. She has other reasons for wanting to be close to you. Your unborn child that night, no matter the sex, could not be the fifth daughter of the fifth daughter. Even if she didn't wish the baby to die, she wanted the curse, rather than the blessing, to be given at his birth, and all your children who follow until the fifth daughter is born. To her mind, the presence of the fairyfolk where your husband did not wish them to be would bring about disaster."

"But why?" An old fear rose in Enya's mind because she had a son and in her family that alone had been enough for a curse.

"She believed it had to be." Kyna sputtered her lips. "Such superstitions I wish did not exist in this land."

Enya straightened her shoulders. "Well, she cannot hurt us. You know God is stronger."

"But God expects us to use the good sense he's given us. That is why, when you showed me the ring, and I recalled my encounter with that monk, I knew I must warn you."

"Brother Malachi? I still don't see what he has to do with Gormley."

"He is like Gormley, trusting unknown spirits, perhaps evil ones."

"But he is the priest's son."

"Faith in God our Father cannot be passed on in a bloodline, child. It must be grasped by the believer, and I fear Brother Malachi has chosen not to embrace our faith."

Enya and her cook had never spoken so open-ly before. Perhaps it was the quiet privacy of the woman's hut that had opened her mouth. They should have always confided this way.

Enya gazed at the fire as she contemplated what the woman said. She tapped a finger on the top of the woman's calloused hand. "I thank you for your concern. You need not worry so. The priest has assured me his son will have nothing to do with the upbringing of my son."

"And you trust in this declaration?"

She shrugged. "You know me too well. I paid a young servant named Michael to bring me word should Crimthann be in any danger."

"Indeed, Enya, you are a woman who takes action."

"Was I wrong?"

Kyna clucked her tongue. "I would have done the same. For now, continue to avoid crossing paths with Gormley. It was in her presence the monk presented the ring. I don't know if she knew what it was, but I feel it wise to inform you."

"I thank you, but tell me more. Why would the brother be visiting Gormley?"

"To trade. Gormley was interested in his silver."

"Silver? With all those mouths to feed? I thought she'd want his apples and cider. That is what the priest told me he trades."

"She believes the fairies like shiny objects. What I thought peculiar was that the exchange happened here and not at the monastery, but a servant's place is not to—"

Enya put a finger to the old woman's lips. "I no longer want you to obey the rules of a servant. We must always speak together like this. Promise me."

Kyna's eyes sparkled with appreciation.

When Enya readied to leave, Kyna embraced her and whispered in her ear. "You may be certain that I will make further inquiries of this lad Michael."

"Tomorrow we shall both go."

As Enya scurried toward her cottage, she considered that she should have been comforted by Kyna's plan to check on Michael's fidelity, but the way the old woman spat out his name made her shiver.

Chapter Eleven

*Be not wise in thine own eyes: fear the Lord, and
depart from evil.*
—Proverbs 3:7 KJV

The following day after Kyna prepared the noon meal for Enya and Fe, she donned her cloak and left the house.

"I must depart too," Enya said, kissing her husband on the forehead. "The weavers have some cloth for me to examine. I am making our son a new tunic and coat."

"Ah, the lad is growing like a river rush." He clung to her arm as she tried to move away. "Take heed that you do not dress him like Joseph of the Scriptures. His father made him such a colorful coat that his brothers were murderously jealous."

She smiled. "Two colors, then. Forest green and bog brown. Will that do?"

He nodded and kissed her hand. "You may find me in the turnip field today."

Her heart twittered. He'd wanted to halt any jealous notions before they began. She loved him for that. She bit her lip. How could she then not tell him where she was really going? Enya had to keep reminding herself that her actions were not going to make her husband unreasonably angry. She lowered herself back to her chair. "Fe, I must do something before I meet the weavers. That ring, the one Kyna brought you?"

"Making it into some jewelry, are you? I said 'tis proper for you to do so. Go on, now."

"But, I've changed my mind about that. I … want to know more about its appearance."

"Back to the monk?"

"Aye. 'Tis right to do so."

"As you wish, my love." He pushed his empty plate forward, rose, and kissed her again. "I cannot blather all morning. There's work to be done. Take our cook with you."

She tried to stop him as he headed for the door. "But Fe, I have not told you everything."

He grinned. "Don't have to, Enya. Have I not made it clear in all these years I do not expect you to grovel to your husband as others do?" He placed his hands gently on her shoulders and bent to look into her eyes. "A man wants respect

142

in his household, sure, but I have learned something else. 'Tis a bit you have taught me."

She shook her head. "But Fe——"

"Love is all we need. If we love each other, and our wee lad, as God above loves us all, everything else falls as it should. Don't you see? We don't need to be like the others. We have God on our side. I trust you. You trust me. We both trust God." He let out a breath. "Praise God in heaven that you do see that now. Makes life much easier for us both." He squeezed her shoulders and then left.

Easier indeed.

On her way to the barn to meet Kyna she turned toward the perimeter of the dwellings. She'd stick to the trees to avoid …

"Out for a stroll, are you?"

Gormley emerged from barn. "I myself was just seeing to my man's mare. Brody says she's got a weak hoof. Brought her some green grass since she can't yet leave the barn." A sprig of mistletoe dangled from her hand.

Surprised, Enya scrambled for something to say. "Oh, I hope she's better."

"She is." Gormley followed Enya's gaze to the plant in her hand. "I know how to care for these things." She tossed the sprig to the ground near the barn wall.

Enya knew that the pagans believed the plant cured all ills and used it in some ritual practices to summon the spirits.

"What are you up to? Following your servant Kyna?"

Oh, that woman. How did she manage to be exactly where she wasn't wanted? "Uh, I am. I'm to meet her, uh, I mean to say … we're foraging today." The lie stuck in her throat. Following Jesu's ways did not actually make life easier as Fe had asserted. It made untruths painful to tell. Gormley, a follower of the old ways, could not be allowed to meddle, however.

Gormley glanced over Enya's shoulder and lifted her chin. "There's a fairy hawthorn growing twenty paces just to the north of your path. You'll be wanting to avoid that."

"I, uh … I am not going that way." Enya paused. She wanted to pelt the woman with questions about the monk and the trading she'd done, but she remembered Kyna's warning. She needed to avoid Gormley, not some innocuous fairy bush. "I must be off now."

They said farewell. Enya's heart beat wildly as she wondered if Kyna might have left without her, feeling an urgency. Passing the fairy tree *would* lead her to a shorter route on the way to the barn. Most avoided that path for fear of disturbing the fairies and facing their wrath. Even Kyna would have taken the well-traveled route. There would be thorns and brambles along the short cut. She glanced down to her calf-leather shoes, imaging how she would explain to Fe the beating her feet would be taking.

A twinge pinched in her chest. She could not lie. No longer. As she picked her way toward the forbidden bush, she thought about the laugh they'd share when she told him how she'd hurried to the barn.

Ahead she spotted the hawthorn tree, magnificently twisting its many arms toward the sky. If wood creatures were real, they would surely choose to live here. Untouched by humans, the deep woods exuded serenity, something she thought she'd sensed somewhere before.

Ah! The church. The same emotion had washed over her there. God certainly was everywhere, but in the midst of quarreling, meddling folks, the Great Power of the Universe was hard to hear. She heard him now. *Move quickly toward Crimthann.*

Kyna was seated on a chariot, the horse readied. "Let's be on our way," Enya said.

As they neared the monastery gates Enya narrowed her eyes and studied the back side of the guesthouses. The only movement came from the few sheep grazing along the tree line. Sure enough, Michael came into view.

"Let's go over there and call to him. Will be much faster than having him summoned to the gate."

Kyna turned the rig. When they were close enough she handed the reins to Enya and wiggled down, calling softly to Michael. He waved and opened a back gate.

"You shall report to me, young man. I am the ears and eyes of my mistress," Kyna said.

She sounded fierce. Enya admired her loyalty. She had not come to judge that. Enya needed to hear what Kyna might miss.

"I have not concealed the fact that the priest's son is an odd bird," Michael said.

"Indeed, but there may be more to discover. I have come to advise you what to look out for."

He nodded.

146

Exactly what Enya would have said.

"My mistress's birth clan, they are a … disagreeable lot."

Disagreeable? Enya would have said more than that. Violent, cruel, beasts!

Michael lowered his hood as though he needed to attend closer to what the woman was saying. "I do not understand."

"I suppose not." Kyna began to pace, then stopped. She spit her words. "Have you ever witnessed a beating? A man bloodying a woman's face? And stood by helpless to end it? Have you ever seen a man tie a woman to a tree, observe her bleeding wrists, and then cringe as he whipped her?" Her voice elevated a moment until she seemed to realize they might be overheard. She whispered something Enya could not hear, but she did not need to.

She'd been there. Enya had been the one tied to the tree, naked and nauseous. She nearly fainted now remembering it. It was good Kyna had come. Enya would not have been able to relate the story that needed to be told to convince the young man.

Michael's voice caused Enya to lift her head. "I understand, dear woman. Malachi may not be

147

so brutal, but he is equally menacing. Conniving, he is. I am certain he is plotting something, but I know not what. I will certainly look out for the lad, but where Malachi is concerned there is little I can do. He is the priest's son."

Enya's foot stomped uncontrollably, sending an echo into the air.

Michael acknowledged her with a nod.

Kyna reached for his arm. "Now then, you know I was here in her behalf. We beseech you to help us, young man."

From his pocket he pulled the prize Enya had given him to spy for her and handed it back. When Kyna did not take it, he let it fall to the ground at her feet. "I will not abandon the promise I made to you, mistress," he said to Enya.

Kyna picked up the trinket and placed it carefully within the folds of her cloak. Then she held up the Mac Noe ring. "We would like to know more about how this came into the possession of the brothers."

Michael seemed to ponder this a moment. "I can keep it until someone from the Mac Noe comes to the monastery to trade and then make inquiries."

"You would not mind?" Enya asked.

He shook his head. "And as I said, I will keep my eye on Brother Malachi. Anything else I can do for you?"

Enya wanted more reassurance. "I hope I haven't irritated you. You will still be kind? To my boy?"

"There is no question of that." The priest appeared behind the lad. Enya had not heard his approach. "Everyone here treats my foster son with the utmost respect. Isn't that so, Michael?"

"That is so. I was just reassuring his mother." Michael bowed and departed.

Enya worried her fingers at the edges of her cloak. "I do not mean to worry so."

The priest placed a hand at her back as he led her away from the guesthouse and down the path toward the church with Kyna following. "Have you brought something for the child?"

"Oh, no. Not yet. But soon. I am visiting my weavers today to order new clothes."

He nodded as though that was the reply he had anticipated. "I have an assignment for you, my dear."

"An assignment?"

"A commission. A duty."

She glanced up. They were headed to the wee stone church. "I will pray, Father. So will my servant."

"That is good. God will help you endure the months ahead."

He said no more until they reached the door. He opened it but did not follow her inside. She turned to look at him.

"One year from today you may return."

"What?"

Enya heard Kyna gasp.

"'Tis for the best. I see that now. One cycle of the seasons. In the meantime, pray for your son, attend to your husband, go about your usual amusements and duties. I will care for the boy."

Her feet were frozen to the ground.

"Go on and pray. God will help you. You will see. You may not believe so now, but that is because you have not grown in the spiritual discipline of trust."

That word again. How could she trust if she could not witness the wellbeing of her son with her own eyes? "I do not think I can ..."

"Oh, you will. You must. I am not giving you a choice, my dear." He shut the door after Kyna entered.

Enya's tears flowed freely in that dim building, the place where God had answered her prayer for a child. She wept as she clung to Kyna.

Moments later the door creaked open. Michael stood blocking the sun with his body. As he stepped to one side, she felt a glow enter her, and with the assurance she'd experienced before but had too quickly forgotten, she knew she must leave her son to God's protection. She would do so because God required it, not the priest.

"You must go now. The brothers will be gathering for prayer soon."

"Have mercy, won't you?" She lifted her hands. "Even if you won't accept compensation. Come to my house after three full moons, please. I will have Crimthann's clothing ready for you to deliver. And you, if you'd be so kind, will bring news of him to me?"

He sighed. "Certainly. I don't like Malachi."

"Lead the way," Kyna said, holding tightly to Enya's arm.

He didn't move.

"You said we must hurry," Kyna said.

"We have a few moments yet. Come with me. Perhaps your mind can be put at ease."

They followed him as they wove their way behind some huts until they paused at the edge of a clearing. She spotted the back of her son's fair head as the priest sat on the opposite side of a table.

Michael whispered. "His lessons are held here when the sun shines. Better light. He is learning the alphabet."

"My son is learning letters?"

"If we move toward this cedar we will have a better look without being noticed."

In gratitude, she followed. They crouched in the tall grass. "Is that a cake on the table?"

"'Tis. If the lad correctly writes his letters on the top of the cake, he is permitted to eat it."

Laughter floated to her ears. The priest smiled down at Crimthann, seemingly praising his efforts. "My son seems to be enjoying learning."

"I assure you, he is. The priest is clever in his techniques. His foster son is growing into a capable scholar."

She stood, ready to leave. "Then I am as proud of him as a mother can be. Thank you for showing me this, Michael."

Chapter Twelve

Better is he in whom we trust, the king who has made us all, who will not leave me tonight without refuge.
—*From "Song of Trust," attributed to St. Columcille*

It was after the birth of her fifth child that Enya learned her firstborn son was soon to be moved. Michael, now a monk, arrived at her doorstep breathless. Fe, who now considered him a friend, urged him inside.

"Your son has a new name," Michael panted. "And he is moving to a new school."

"What's this?" Fe shooed the two children who were old enough to walk out the door. "Without my permission?"

Michael sat on the stool closest to the fire. Kyna brought him a jar of mead. "Oh, the old priest intends to ask you, but I suppose you will concur, will you not?"

"How far?" Enya asked. She could count on her two hands the times she had visited Crimthann. "With all these children now, I fear I'll rarely see the lad if he is too far a distance." She laid her newborn daughter in a cradle near the bed she and Fe shared. Picking up her toddler son, she wiped his nose and passed him on to Kyna. She wanted to hear this conversation.

Michael drank from his cup before answering. "Magh Bile, the community of Finnian. You've heard of it, Fe?"

"I have. Near Loch Cuan, is it?"

"Aye. The upper part. He's to study there. 'Tis quite an honor, and as you know, the priest is elderly and feeble. He has done all he can for the lad."

"Are there others to go with him?" Enya asked.

Michael glanced toward the door. "Others will go. A bit of a troupe. A bard, a few monks, a watchman." Michael stood and handed Fe a rolled up piece of parchment. "'Tis there, for your approval, Fe."

"Are you on this list, lad?"

"Indeed I am." He beamed. "I have been given an important responsibility to see that your son, who is certain to be a great leader, is safely guarded."

Fe slapped him on the back. "Good work, Michael. I do not know how you managed it, but you have justly served God and our son as Crimthann's guardian angel."

Enya swallowed hard. Fe would ask her what she thought as soon as the monk left. Conflicting thoughts sparred in her mind. She would not wait to voice them in private. "I am pleased, Michael, that you will continue to watch over Crimthann." She turned to her husband. "I would like him away from that peculiar Malachi, Fe."

"He's not caused harm," Michael put in. "Not in all these years."

She huffed. "Not real harm, I agree. But he … troubles me." She wondered how much to say in front of Michael. But he was, as Fe asserted, their son's watchman. "My cook." Enya glanced out the window where Kyna was showing the children how to care for the herb garden. Crimthann's only brother perched on her hip.

"What about her?" Michael gave her strange look.

"My servant knows how Malachi has been behaving. Perhaps one day he'll be successful at what he desires to accomplish."

"I am not sure what you mean." Michael glanced to Fe.

"What are you hinting at, love?" Fe put a hand to Enya's cheek.

"My past, you know. Oh, if I could leave it behind, but that sleeveen Malachi insinuates that he may one day drive the horrid lot of them to me. He travels, you know. He's always about." No matter how long she'd been away, this was always her nightmare, that one day her father would come after her and seek revenge for that day when she'd threatened him with his own spear.

Fe let his hand drop to her shoulder. "Are you saying that monk, the priest's son, has had dealings with your father and brothers in recent times?"

She breathed out, trying to release the tension in her chest. "Truly I don't know. He makes like he has. Remember the ring?"

Michael nodded. "As I have told you, I was never able to make a connection. No one from the Mac Noe has come to trade since that time."

157

"And yet, Malachi has come up with more goods bearing their emblem."

Michael lifted his cup toward Fe. "That is unusual."

Fe lifted Enya's chin with his index finger. "Oh, my sweet, Malachi could have gotten the goods from a clan that got them from the Mac Noe."

She shrugged. "Perhaps."

Fe returned to his chair and maneuvered it to look at Enya. She picked up the fussing baby and cradled her to her chest. This child was their third daughter. Enya had kept her offspring close, away from Gormley, who had been much too curious about the birth order of Enya and Fe's children. Kyna said Gormley often asked if Crimthann was to stay at the monastery. They kept news about their fostered son to themselves.

She and Kyna believed Gormley was patiently plotting with Malachi. But why? It was a puzzle Enya had not figured out. If Gormley believed in pagan prophecy—the fifth daughter of a fifth daughter would be the most blessed—then why was she so keen to know the welfare of the firstborn? Enya had better find out before her son departed for a new school.

"Enya, why do you concern yourself about that man? Our friend here says she's been no trouble."

"True." She sighed. "There might be no reason for worry now, if Malachi is separated from Crimthann." She sniffed. "However, I do not wish to be so far from my son."

Fe nodded. He loved the boy too. He turned to Michael. "A great honor you say?"

"A prodigious appointment for Columcille. That is what they are calling him now."

Fe's face grew red. "What? From fox, the meaning of the name we gave him, to dove? That is what they call him now? What is the reason for this new name?"

Enya closed her eyes. She feared she knew.

"The lad has a temper. 'Tis a fire controlled, but he is spirited."

Fe slapped his knee. "Like his mother. They both speak their minds. They are strong that way. 'Tis nothing to disapprove of. So why not call him bear or wolf? Dove of the Church? That is absurd."

Enya laid the baby down once more. "They mock our son."

Fe huffed. "Surely not, love. He is respected."

159

Michael, his hair the color of sodden fall leaves, wagged his tonsured head. "Other lads, you know how they can be. 'Twas all in jest. Your boy has no quietness in his voice, and his manner is not light and airy. They call him Colum as you might name a burly, muscular man Tadpole. The opposite shows humor, but do not fret, mistress. The name has come to be associated with him in a kind way, a sort of turning the joke on its head. The monks refer to him as Columcille, Dove of the Church."

Enya's face flamed. "The priest, he has allowed this?"

Michael smiled at her. "Try to see the wit in it, mistress. Your son loves the church with a pure devotion. So they were right to give him that title, no matter the initial reason. Do you see?"

She supposed she could accept this explanation. "Does Crimthann prefer the name?"

"He does. But you can ask him yourself tomorrow."

"Tomorrow?" She had only recently given birth. "I cannot travel yet."

The monk flashed his shy grin again. "I have permission to bring him here to spend two days with you. He is most eager to meet his youngest siblings and see his parents."

Her heart soared.

Enya was awake the next morning before the baby stirred. She dressed and left the cottage to watch the sunrise. Her excitement over seeing the son who had been separated from her kept her from sleeping. Giving up hope of rest, she decided to offer her thanksgiving to the One who brought light to the world every morning. A salmon blush crested the eastern hills as she wandered to the shore and breathed in the air of a new day. The darkness of the waves seemed to sing, reminding her that the Creator is present and powerful even though she couldn't see him, even when she was far from that church. May it be so, Enya thought, with Crimthann when he is home, away from his teachers.

She sat on the cool pebble shore. Kyna would come look for her if the baby woke. For now she would enjoy some solitude. She adored being a mother, relished the look on her husband's face when one of the wee ones snuggled in his lap. She would never take any of it for granted, but she needed this wee bit of quiet.

A few moments later she heard footsteps approaching from behind. Her peace was about to end. "Keeva, Meredit, why are you awake so early?" She turned to find not her daughters, but Michael and Crimthann. Before she could rise to her knees her boy had his arms wrapped around her neck.

"Mamaí, I am so happy to see you!"

"No more than I am to see you, my son." She lifted his head from her shoulder. "Let me look at you. My how you've grown since Easter last."

He chuckled, his laugh sounding so much like his father's. "I know you could not come at Christmas, because of the baby."

"That's right." Fe had insisted she not travel, claiming that her age made her more susceptible to harm during childbirth now. She'd had some difficulty with Egan and it had scared them both. Perhaps he had been right because with rest she'd had no trouble with the last pregnancy.

"I want to meet the new baby," Crimthann said, his excitement masked by the sound of the lapping water at her feet. "I want to see them all!"

She glanced to Michael. "So early?"

"The monks rise before dawn, mistress. I could not hold the lad back any longer."

Enya, Fe, and the children squeezed in as much fun and frolicking as they could over two days. Trips to the ocean shore to dig for clams, singing by the turf fire before bed, wandering in the hills to look for butterflies. Fe had never before taken so much time away from caring for his livestock and supervising the workers in the fields. Enya thought there could be no greater joy than this time they all spent together. Of course, there was no greater sorrow than when the time came for Crimthann to depart. But the lad was not melancholy in the least.

"The school has much to teach me, Da," he said as he allowed his father to straighten the shoulders of the new cloak Enya had made for him.

"Learn as much as you can, son. Gain all the wisdom made available to you, and obey your teachers."

Crimthann nodded. Enya was still struggling with the name change. Since he seemed quite satisfied with the name, as Michael had said he was, she was determined to try.

She caught Michael's eye and tipped her head. He followed her to the other side of the chariot. She whispered. "How long until he returns home?" She stammered. "I mean, for good."

Michael stared past her as she answered. "Well, three years until he reaches the age of accountability. He will be free to do as he wills then."

"What is this age?"

"There is a story in the scriptures about Jesu and his parents. They visited the temple in Jerusalem and when they left Jesu did not immediately return with them. He had made his own decision about how long to stay there. The monks believe that at about the same age Jesu was is when a student can decide for himself if he remains at the monastery or returns to his parents."

"Three years?"

Michael nodded.

When she peeked around the horse she saw that her husband was still instructing their son.

"He will want to come home. With all the training he'll be getting, the clan will see no finer king."

Michael smiled and his face lit up, causing her to ponder how a mere monk could possess such angelic-like radiance. "He is certain to embrace all that God has in store for him. The old priest has believed so since the moment he came to live at the monastery."

She remembered him telling her how special Crimthann was. She'd already known.

"You will watch over him, and make sure Brother Malachi comes nowhere near him?"

"This I can tell you: I will see that he is safe."

She kissed him on the cheek, thankful that her son had such a trustworthy guardian. If it was necessary for her heart to be broken once again, at least she knew Crimthann would be protected. She turned back to her son to say her good-byes, tears flowing down her cold cheeks.

PART TWO

Chapter Thirteen

You must is the father of I won't. —Irish proverb

Colum agreed that his mother should not be told. He watched as Michael fidgeted. His friend would have paced about had Colum's cell been large enough. Instead, Michael tapped the tips of his fingers together, cleared his throat, and stood. "I cannot approve of this approach," he said.

Fe, Colum's father, drew in a long breath. "You do not know my wife. She is prone to melancholy. Enya has barely been able to accept Crim—, rather, Colum's stay here. She does so under the assumption he will be returning to become our king. No one rules since old King Donall passed on. Ah, there are others who could be elected, but we'd once believed it would be our son and she has not given up the idea." He set his eyes on Colum.

"But Father, why do you both not understand the reason I must stay? There are books here and

167

the collection is growing. As we speak, our father Finnian is traveling to Rome and Tours to acquire copies to bring back. With these books we can possess the knowledge that the apostles had, men who walked the earth with Jesu. Can you imagine it?" He could not contain his excitement even though he knew his father could not possibly understand, having not lived as he had. "My teachers tell me I am learning Latin so well that one day I will become a scribe. That is a most vital occupation, Father. I must do this for our entire kingdom."

Fe grunted. "Is not being king a vital service to our people?"

"To be king is an honor certainly, but to read books, and to help others read them? There is no greater purpose for my life."

His father's expression drooped. "You could have had the best of everything. You have never even seen the opulence of the castle."

"I do not wish to be a disappointment to you, Father, but I do believe I have what I need."

The man forced a smile. "A disappointment, you could never be. I understand that God has had his hand on you from the day your mother pledged you to the church. Who am I to say that God is wrong about your vocation?"

Colum resisted the urge to embrace his father. He did not want to give the appearance of gloating. "Thank you."

Fe nodded.

Colum cleared his throat. "Since my mother sent me to the church, she should understand my decision, but I respect your wishes not to tell her I am not coming home, Father."

Fe inhaled deeply. Still, Michael seemed unconvinced. "The truth is always the best choice," he said.

"You have obviously never been married, Michael." Fe sighed. "There are things that have to be done or not done, as the case may be, to keep a wife contented. 'Tis a difficult balance, but we will not lie to her. We will tell Enya where Colum is at all times. We will just omit telling her he has chosen to give his life and service to the church permanently. For now, at least."

"I have given my life to Jesu," Colum said.

"There is no need to correct your father," Michael admonished.

Colum directed his annoyance at being chastised at the parchment he held by twisting it firmly in his hands. If Michael wished for him to control his anger—as the man was always insisting—why had he said that?

Fe stood. "Your mother and I are proud of you, son." He bowed his head, whispered a blessing Colum could only detect a few words of, and then left.

Michael quickly followed him out. They would talk about him outside, Colum believed, so he urged the door to his cell open a crack to listen.

"Pity they would not accept you, Fe," Michael said.

Fe chuckled. "'Tis true that I am old now, but even if I weren't, I have all I need without being king. I had thought my son … well, perhaps one day Egan will be chosen. We shall leave these things to Providence."

"Who will be king now?" Michael asked.

"Since Colum has reached the age of decision without returning to the clan, the council won't wait. Brody is the most likely to be elected. Young, intelligent. Among the property owners he is the logical choice. His character is without tarnish."

Michael rubbed his hand over his temple. "You don't say Gormley's husband will be king. He is not much younger than you, is he?"

A grunt of consent, and then Colum's father added, "I was older than most when I became a father, but you are correct that Brody is not so very young, not as you are. However, I hear he is willing. I am not. Remember, I am not speaking of the woman, only her husband."

Michael raised the pitch of his voice. "This is growing clearer. Don't you see it, man?"

"What?"

"Gormley's pagan ways, the fifth daughter business, it was all a distraction. Perhaps even an attempt to drive you and your wife to send your son to the church, away from it all."

"Well, I do acknowledge that she hoped my son would not take the kingship. Probably wanted the king to come from her own household. Despite being misguided, that woman has been harmless. Enya was wrong to worry so about that one."

A horse whinnied. Father was preparing to depart.

"No, wait," Michael called out. "Enya was right. When Gormley ceased to have any influence over Enya, she got someone to help her, someone who was also interested in seeing Brody be made king."

"What are you blathering about, Michael?"

The horse's hooves stomped and there was a bit of commotion before Michael continued. "Brother Malachi."

They spoke in hushed tones, requiring Colum to scoot through the door to hear, but in the darkness he would still be concealed.

"Whatever you do," Fe said, "don't let Enya know that man is here."

"I have followed your request these many years, and I have watched him. He has asked after Colum, tried in vain to stoke the boy's ire, but thus far has not caused any harm."

"You've done a fine job keeping watch. I must go now."

"Nay, you see? Malachi tries to torment Enya for the same purpose. Both he and Gormley want Brody to be king and not Colum. Since Colum is so young, there would be little chance for Brody to ever rule after your son."

"Why would the monk care who is king? Especially now that he lives way out here?"

"Because Brody is Malachi's cousin, a distant relation."

"Even so, man, what difference does it make? Brody shall be king. They will get what they desire."

"I am not yet sure, but there must be something more behind this. I have a suspicion Brody's accession will not be fruitful for your people. I intend to find out why."

Colum heard a slap of horseflesh and galloping hooves. He hurried back inside. Why did these people care who was king? The most important thing was to share the knowledge and saving grace of Jesu. Kingship was only about legal matters, land and cattle possession, and wars—temporary, earthly concerns. It was Colum, not this Brody, who was in the most influential position.

The next day Colum encountered Malachi at the well.

"Do you know what they say about you, lad?"

He could not imagine what this man was getting at, or why he sometimes annoyed him so. If he wanted his cousin to be king, he was about to get his wish. Perhaps now he'd leave Colum alone. "It matters not to me. I am about the

Lord's business on this day, as I am sure you are, brother."

The old man smacked his lips. As though he hadn't heard Colum's response, he continued. "I only want to offer you the kind consideration of informing you what is said when you aren't around. So that you may treat people properly, knowing full well what they think of you." He put a hand on Colum's shoulder. "Here, let me get that water for you while we talk."

The rules of the society required him to be respectful of his elders, no matter how much they might exasperate him. Colum handed his wooden bucket to Malachi.

"Just a few of the lads who associate with that novice Ciarán, I'm talking about. You know, Ciarán comes from your mother's clan. Oh, but you probably don't know that. Your mother doesn't talk about the Mac Noe, now does she?"

Colum didn't answer. It seemed clear to him that Malachi wasn't interested in a conversation, just a lecture. Ciarán had been a friend to Colum. They helped each other memorize psalms and repeat the abbot's rule. The fact that the two came from very different backgrounds hadn't mattered to either of them. Colum didn't care that his friend's father had been a common carpenter. Hadn't that also been the occupation of Jesu's earthly father? Ciarán was effervescent, and jovial, and had many friends. One of them had been the gossip, perhaps.

The older man grunted, tugging the bucket up from the well. "I hear the lads think you are pampered, being from the Cenél Conaill. Wealthy lad fed by silver forks. Still would be, they say, if his mamaí came to visit." He handed the full bucket to Colum.

Colum, feeling mightily insulted, flung the pail away, sending sloshing water to the ground. Dashing back toward his cell, he heard Malachi chuckle behind him. What was humorous about being treated so after working as hard, harder, than any of them? A lowly priest, not a king, had raised Colum. He'd eaten dry bread and gruel, not beef and cream. His bed had been hard, not stuffed with goose feathers. He was not pampered in the least. Never had been.

When he reached his cell he threw off the cloak his mother had sewn for him and replaced it with the plain brown garb the others wore. Gritting his teeth, he looked around. He snatched the straw-filled pillow from his bed, marched outside, approached the communal, smoldering peat fire and tossed it on top. Flames immediately lit, drawing the attention of the monks nearby. He ignored their stares and lifted a stone about the size of his head from a pile nearby. When he took it inside his cell, he placed it on his bed. A stone had been Jacob's pillow, the man from scripture who had fought an angel. And now Colum, no pampered infant, would use this as his pillow.

Enya eagerly awaited Fe's return. She had wanted to go along, but with the children it was not practical. Leaving them with Kyna wasn't possible anymore because of the dear woman's advancing age. The rambunctious lot would be too much for her, and Enya didn't trust anyone else. But in the summer months, they would all go if they needed to. Colum might come home before then, though, saving them the trouble.

She listened to the children's heavy breaths of sleep. As she banked the fire, she whispered a prayer of thanksgiving.

"For hearth and meat, I thank you, Jesu.

For warmth and children, I thank you, Jesu.

For the love of my husband, I thank you, Jesus.

Watch over this household until dawn."

She paused, smiled to herself, and added,

"For bringing Colum back to the home where he belongs, I thank you, Jesu."

Kyna entered the kitchen carrying water buckets. "Are you settled in for the night?"

"We are. Thank you, Kyna. Have you been reading the writings the monk brought by?" The monastery loaned the pages the scribes practiced on, and Enya had found them helpful in teaching Kyna to read with competence.

"I have. Thank you, mistress. 'Tis a great pleasure. With your permission I will take my leave now."

"Of course. We don't need anything else."

The cook paused, staring. "Are you not retiring?"

"Oh, I can't sleep, Kyna. I think Fe might be home soon."

"'Tis been … what now, sixteen days since he left? I would not expect him until the new moon."

"I know, but I can hardly endure the waiting, as anxious as I am. That would the perfect time for Colum to take his rightful place, don't you agree?"

Kyna hugged her before she left for her cottage.

Enya lifted her arms toward the ceiling. She had done her part. Her son's fosterage was over now that he had reached the age where the monks allowed him to choose to come home, and she would now be with him to guide him, feed him his favorite meals, see that his clothing was in good condition, listen to his hopes and dreams, and comfort him when he needed the loving arms of a mother, something he had been deprived of. But no more.

A few nights later Enya peeked at the sky before retiring. The waning moon now appeared as only a sliver in the inky sky.

Sometime before dawn she heard someone moving around near the hearth. Excitedly, she crawled out from under her covers. "Fe?"

"Aye, 'tis myself."

"And Crimthann? Come here, my boy."

"'Tis only myself, Enya. The lad is not … quite ready to depart."

178

She thought she detected a slight tremble in her husband's voice. She padded over to the hearth. Just a wee glow emerged from beneath the ashes. Fe stuck a reed into the embers and then lit a lantern with the resulting flame.

"Why has he not come?"

"There, there, my sweet. You know how lads are. He enjoys the company of his friends. When he … departs from that place, Michael will send word."

"But he will come home, aye? You do not think he will refuse us for the comfort a few friends."

"Patience, Enya. You know where he is."

"I do." She pulled her shawl over her chilly shoulders. "We shall all go visit him right after Beltane, and perhaps coax him to return with us. Even if he does not become king this season, he should be with his clan and watch their observances. Would you not agree?"

"What the lad should do may no longer be in our power to affect."

Her heart raced. "What do you mean?"

He patted her hand. "He is of the age to make his own decisions."

"So, you do think he'll choose his friends over us. There's a lass, is there?" Anger welled in her head. What had that church done? Taught her son that his birth family had no merit?

"There is not. And I do not believe that is what is on his mind. He is determined to serve the God of the heavens, my dear, and not man."

She allowed herself a smile. "Then he shall surely come home. 'Tis what God ordained since he was conceived. Before, even."

He pulled her into a reassuring hug.

With the time of Beltane approaching, Enya sent word to her son. When she received a reply, she sat alone in the barley field to read his letter.

Dearest Mother,

I shall not be returning home for the festival of Beltane. I shall not be near you at all for some time. If I were to be, I would certainly visit. You asked to visit me. Please delay. We are quite engaged at the moment. I am to be made deacon! I promise to write you a letter very soon and tell you all about it. Send my love to Father and the children.

Your son,
Columcille

Tears welled in her eyes. He was not coming. He did not want them to visit. She didn't know if she could bear it. Only observing him with her own eyes could quell the tempest growing within her. She bit her lip. He need not see her so long as she could see him. A plan began to formulate in her mind.

Chapter Fourteen

Fools are headstrong and do what they like; wise people take advice.
—*Proverbs 12:15 MSG*

"I do think 'tis a fine idea for you to have help with the children," Fe said. He tipped his head to one side. "And you want to go see our Crimthann, that is, Colum, and this might free you to do so."

He knew her so well. "I will not neglect any of the wee ones, Fe."

"Of course you would not. 'Tis a long journey to Loch Cuan, though. You should wait until I can go with you. Winter would be the best time. I won't be as busy then."

He was sensible, but that was too long to wait. She'd focus on one thing at a time. First, a new servant. "I will begin looking right away. There are several young girls in the clan just the right age to look after children."

"A sound plan. Do."

Gormley's oldest children were the proper age, perhaps even the correct temperament, but the riff between Enya and that woman still existed. Gormley had once wished Crimthann harm. Enya could not trust any of them.

Where the women gathered to begin the day's cooking would be the place to start. The smell of charred wood told her she was close. She paused beside some tall grasses to compose herself before greeting the women. A magpie pecked along the side of the path. When she stepped out, the bird took flight, exposing the full spread of its white-tipped wings. She watched it go, and soon after another followed. Enya drew in a breath. To see a single magpie was bad luck, but if you saw two the bad omen was mollified. She bit her lip, telling herself to stop believing such things.

She moved onward. She'd not been to the cooking fire much since her children were born. Before that, she'd been pitied and ignored. Entering this fold in peace and friendship, when she'd not prepared for either, seemed a foolish endeavor. Why had she not brought Kyna? Many times Enya caught herself pushing that old woman to the fringes of her life without even realizing it.

Please, Lord, help me to see the good in people. Help me to see you in them.

A few of the women and girls looked up when she entered the fold. One or two acknowledged her with a nod. She cleared her throat. "Peace be with all here."

A mumbling followed as they returned her blessing. That wasn't so bad. She picked up a knife to help with the least desirable task, skinning the bloodied lamb lying on the butchering table.

"You do not have to be here," Ciara, Gormley's eldest daughter said. She seemed to sneer.

Enya straightened her shoulders and got straight to work. "Perhaps not, but I want to help. I've always wanted to help. I've just been … pre-occupied."

Silence fell. She was the wife of a fine nobleman. Her son was to be king someday. She was a woman of wealth, although she'd never wanted to be. She only wanted to be a part of a family, a kinship. To have the others like her would be nice, but not entirely necessary. She only sought acceptance.

A woman near the fire began to chant.

"God, be in the fire." She tossed in a stick. "God, be in the cooking," she continued. The woman waved one arm in the air. "God, be in the gathering around the table."

It occurred to Enya that Gormley's pagan ways had been losing favor. Christianity was blanketing the clan, perhaps in part to Fe's efforts. That realization gave her confidence she'd hadn't had before when approaching the women.

"May Jesu bless our work here today," she said as she continued scraping.

"'Tis good to have you among us, my dear," the older woman at the fire said.

When Enya looked up to acknowledge this kindness, she spotted Gormley. Her face was drawn tight, her eyes dark pools of hate. True, they were no longer friends, but Enya could not image why the woman despised her so much. Gormley gathered her daughters and removed to a spot beyond the crowd.

"Don't mind her," the kind woman called out. "Since the lot of us have welcomed the God of Patrick, she has grown bitter. She may come around yet."

A young woman with a tangle of dark hair sniffed. "She believes once her husband becomes king, that will change."

Enya gasped. "Her husband? He won't be king, my son—"

The old woman stood, surprising Enya with her vigor. "Your son is not here, my dear. The clan must have a king. We can only hope that woman has little influence over her husband, because it seems he will indeed be king."

The young woman brushed her thick hair from her eyes and nodded her chin in Gormley's direction. "She has a surprise waiting, though. We'll not turn our backs on the One True God."

That one. That lass would be Enya's new maid.

Later that day the dark-haired lass, whose name Enya learned was Branna, came to the house to begin her duties. The new maid's name meant "a beauty with hair as dark as a raven," and it fit her perfectly. The young woman's tresses were a shade or two darker than her own. Enya might

186

have rather had a maid homelier and less attractive to the farmhands, but this lass's firm faith in the Christian God was most important. She would be a good influence on Enya and Fe's children, Fe would certainly approve, and perhaps she would even inspire Enya to trust God more completely. In any case, she was as different from Gormley as she could be, and that pleased Enya.

When she introduced Kyna to her, she saw tension fall from the woman's face. Enya had been asking too much of her cook and now her duties would be eased considerably. "She will be a blessing to us all," Enya said.

Branna went straight to Sheela's cradle, picked her up, and moved to where Egan played on the floor with the other girls. Enya and Kyna watched for a moment as the raven-hair girl engaged the children by moving wooden blocks along as though they were horses.

"I will depart in the morning," Enya whispered to Kyna. "Branna's sister has agreed to nurse the baby. You will oversee the lass? Make sure all is fine in my absence?"

"As you wish. You know you can always depend on me. But … are you certain, mistress? Forgive me for asking, but 'twill be an arduous journey. Your milk will dry up, but before that happens it will not be pleasant."

Some of the women in Fe's family routinely gave their babies over to wet nurses, but she never had. "You will tell me how to prepare for that?"

The woman nodded. "'Twill still be difficult traveling. Perhaps you should take one of the male servants with you."

Enya gently touched the old woman's hand. "I cannot. Everyone is needed for planting time. And I do not need to. God will be with me. I must see my oldest child with my own eyes. When I am convinced he is well, I can return in peace."

"At least take the dog. To chase away wolves."

"That I can do."

Kyna would not release her arm. "One more thing I must say."

Enya remembered her vow to listen more closely to the woman. "Aye, what is on your mind?"

"Step lightly. Your son … he likes where he is, doesn't he?"

"I suppose he does."

"Watch and listen. See what you can learn before asking him to come home."

"Well, I don't …" She hesitated, biting back her usual hasty, unthinking response. "I promise I will listen before I say anything."

Kyna squeezed her hand. "Listen long. I feel I must say this."

"Thank you."

The next day Fe rose before she did. As she packed her bag, they argued.

"I am taking the dog, Fe."

He parted his morning-messed hair away from his face. "Not good enough. A woman is not to travel alone. You know this."

She sucked her lip.

He continued. "Since you will not delay, I have arranged an escort."

"Who? No one can be spared from the fields, Fe."

"Aye, no workers. Ninnidh will go."

"But Fe, he is so old. I will be attending him, not the opposite."

When Fe looked at her, tiny wrinkles formed around his eyes. "Like I told you before, no able-bodied man is free to leave right now. He is wise,

Enya. I have told you before, he attended the late saint, Brigid, when she died."

"I know he is a devout Christian. I just don't think—"

Fe interrupted. "It is decided. For your own good. Unless you would like to change your mind about going now."

"Very well, but I must ask. Is there another reason you don't wish me to go?"

He lowered his gaze.

She was right. "Do not keep secrets from me, husband."

He let out a breath. "Michael. How is that lad is always right?"

"How do you mean?" She felt herself growing angry, but if she was to be granted this leave of the household, she must allow Fe to explain, even though he should have done so earlier.

"He told me I should speak the truth to you, Enya. Even when I do not believe the truth is what you need."

Fe, muscular and hearty, could not hide his softer side from her. And because of this, she could not stay angry with him for long. He drew her to his chest. "How can our son, so young, on-ly on the horizon of manhood, know what his future holds? What he says today may not be what he will do a year or two from now."

She breathed in his smell, damp from sleep. "He says he is not coming home at all, does he?"

"Aye, that is what he says. But Enya, who knows—"

"'Tis all right, Fe. I will be patient with him, I promise." She lifted her head to gaze at her love. He planted a long kiss on her lips. When they parted, she kept her arms at his waist. "I love you for trying to protect me, husband."

She felt the tension in his shoulders. "Is that all?" she asked.

"I shall miss you, my love." He kissed her again. "You will be careful?"

"I will. I just have to see him myself, as you did."

He nodded and released her. "Since he is not coming home to be king, another will be selected."

"Not you?"

"I do not wish it. I am old. 'Tis not in my nature."

"Then who?"

"Brody."

"What? No."

191

"Do not worry, my sweet. He will do well and my brother Brendan and I will advise him."

"But Gormley—"

He shook his head. "Is a woman. Don't worry about her. Her husband will lead."

"And he won't for long. He is not much younger than you, and like you said, our son does not yet know his way in the world."

Beltane passed and indeed Brody had been named king, but Enya was sure he only held the position until the more apt man arrived. After the festival Enya was more than eager to be off on her journey.

Once they were on their way, the dog tied to the side of a small cart to walk beside them, Enya wondered what she should say to her traveling companion. He wore an extremely faded green cloak with the hood pulled up, concealing his face. Long white strands of hair drifted out of the hood toward his shoulders. He steered the rig, which was pulled by one of Fe's finest horses, and said nothing. Perhaps he was mute. Or deaf. Or both.

"You know I am going to see my son."

He cleared his throat. "I am keen to meet this lad Columcille."

"You are? Because he is to one day become our king?"

"If you are referring to the ruler of the clan, no, I am not interested in that."

She thought that was rather rude. True, he was not from Fe's clan, but he must have some interest. Fe had told her the old man had been a traveling poet in his younger days and he still liked to wander. "Will you be going back to Eochu's Lough when we return? That is where you are from, is it not, Ninnidh?"

He looked at her for the first time. His eyes were rheumy, his face lined. "I am not from any one earthly place. The reason I look forward to meeting your son is because he is to become a great spiritual leader and his influence will be abundant and widespread."

She was suddenly transported to memories of the dream she'd had before her eldest son was born. "Are you a man of God? A priest or monk? A prophet, perhaps."

He tilted his head back and laughed, his hood falling from his head. "If you mean a child of

God, aye, I am that by the grace of Jesu. But I do not work for the church and have taken no vows. I don't need them. I am loyal to the One True God."

She didn't know what to say to get him to answer her question. She'd be blunt. She knew no other approach that had a chance of success. "How do you know this about my son? Before he was born, a monk told me something similar about Crimthann."

He chuckled again. "I would suggest you begin using his name, the one he now answers to, or your son may come to think of you as a stranger."

She nodded, giving him an urgent look.

"You ask how I know this? Some would say I know things because I have the status of poet." He exhaled. "A revered position on this island, but that matters not at all to me. Your son? He is a bard, as they say, although he only labors for the church. I believe him to be a poet, as am I. He has this within his heart. I know this because perhaps my greatest God-given gift is the ability to listen well and to make observations."

Enya's only source of information on the outside world came from the circle of women she usually avoided. Or from Fe, but her husband was not a gossip and shared little of what he heard. Michael had given them a bit of news about her son from time to time. Now she realized she had undervalued this old man sitting with her. He knew things because he traveled, and men spoke to men, not women so much. And yet, here she was in conversation with a poet. What a gift Fe had given her.

She squeezed her eyes tight. Ninnidh was correct. She needed to listen and observe, just as Kyna had suggested. May God quell her quick tongue.

He placed his gnarled hand on her shoulder and continued to steer with his other. "The acknowledgement of Columcille's distinction is widespread among poets. Soon the whole island will fathom it, and you, his mother, must be prepared."

Chapter Fifteen

For as churning cream produces butter, and as twisting the nose produces blood, so stirring up anger produces strife.
—Proverbs 30:33 NIV

Michael gave him a disapproving look. "Concentrate harder, Colum."

"I'm trying." Colum stared out at the blue water of the loch from atop the windswept hill where he and Michael routinely came to practice without interruption. "I think the Spirit hides from me."

"Indeed not. If you cannot discern God's presence it is because you are not listening. He is always here."

Colum gritted his teeth. He despised being judged this way. Drawing in a breath, he began to slow his rapid heartbeat. It was difficult at times to control his anger, but he could do it with prayer and fasting. He willed himself to remember what the apostle John had written. God must increase and he must decrease. After a few moments he felt calm again.

Colum and Michael sat still beside each other in the grass. They had found a clearing in the woods that allowed a good view of the water and the wide sky above. The clouds, luminous and alabaster, drifted like angels, at least to Colum's mind. On days like today the reflection of the clouds could be seen on the still surface of the water. Yes, this was better. He was looking, and seeing with his heart. Ah, angels. Guardians and messengers. Like Michael.

"Aye, see with more than your eyes, Colum."

Michael seemed to read his thoughts at times. Colum closed his eyes and thought about how without God he would not exist. Neither would the grass, the wind, the blue sea. God breathed it all into being. With each inhale, this truth became more and more evident. God *was* there.

And then he saw his mother, in his mind and yet as clear as if he were a bird in the air looking down on her. She was journeying with an elderly man, a poet by the look of his garb. They were coming to see him. He opened his eyes. "Why did I just see my mother, as if I were flying above the road?"

Michael clapped his hands. "Excellent. You can see only those people God grants for you to see."

Colum stared at his ink-stained fingers. "You mean to say God has given me the gift of visions?"

"It would seem so. And I thought it might be."

"She is coming to see me. Why? I wrote and told her not to come."

"I have not been told. Is she near?"

This time without closing his eyes, Colum saw her at the abbey's gate.

"Wait," Michael said. "Remember this one thing. God and your mother have an agreement. When she sent you to the church it was not only for you to grow spiritually, but also for her. She may not understand this now. Keep that in mind and be patient with her."

Colum hadn't thought of how the separation would benefit her as well. "I will be understanding. Thank you for telling me, Michael."

They rose and hurried to meet her in the refectory where guests were always taken. When they were reunited she covered him with kisses.

"Don't be cross with me, Mamaí. We have been very busy here."

"I believe it is time——"

Her traveling companion cut her off, extending his hand. "I am Ninnidh. A pleasure to meet you, young man."

"You are most welcome here, Ninnidh. My thanks for escorting my mother." He gave her his best mockingly scolding look. "'Twas a long journey, which she should not have made."

His mother wrinkled her round nose, as her blue eyes grew more intense. "Nonsense. I am no wilting flower. The trip was no trouble. You did not come home. I had to come see you, then."

Colum took her hand. "I am happy to see you. Let's sit, please. Tell me about the family."

While his mother chatted about the children, about his father's new horses, and about the man named Brody—whom she insisted at this past Beltane had only been given a temporary position of power—Colum did not tell her how much of it he already knew. Instead, he watched the elderly poet. The man frowned and seemed to be nudging Enya to stop her blathering. At last, she got the hint and sipped her tea.

When the bell rang for prayers Colum stood. "You may come, too, if you'd like."

His mother took his arm. The poet did not rise.

"Aren't you coming?" his mother asked the old man.

"I will collect the hound from the stables and go for a walk." He drew a small harp from his traveling bag and moved away toward the back door.

"He says you are a poet like him," Colum's mother whispered on the way to the church.

"He appears to be, but I am just a scribe."

"That is not what he believes. Son, I have known since before you were born that you were destined to do great things. Others sense this as well, although what great things seems to be disputable."

"I will leave it up to God, Mamaí."

"You have grown into a fine young man, Crim—uh, Colum. Perhaps you should find another name for me."

This surprised him. He had only been trying to please her. "Mam, then?"

She smiled and patted his arm.

200

The old poet met Enya and Colum outside the church at the conclusion of prayers.

"Walk with me."

It sounded like more of a direction than a question. She answered him, nonetheless, desperately trying to ignore her painful breasts. Even binding them as Kyna had shown her hadn't eased all of her discomfort. "I am tired from the journey, but a short stroll would be fine. Won't you join us, Colum?"

"I have some chores to attend to. Please, go on."

Sighing louder than she meant to, Enya longed to retire, drink some sage tea, and apply damp cabbage leaves to her breasts—to dry up her milk. She should have thought of this long before going on this journey. Her impulsive decisions always seemed to cause her one kind of pain or another.

She moved down the stone path with her elderly companion, thankful for the leisurely pace of his stroll. If he had wanted time alone to lecture her about her son, he gave no indication of it. He didn't speak. She took advantage of the solitude to observe some fowl amongst the salt marsh, white wisps sidling through green needle foliage.

Enya and Ninnidh paused near some round huts where she caught a glimpse of her son. "Oh, there he is." As she stepped in his direction, Ninnidh blocked her way.

"Observe," he said, nodding toward a bench.

He was right. She should not overwhelm her son lest he decide not to ever come home.

They sat and watched as the monks swept away leaves littering the path around their dwellings. They mumbled something in unison. "What are they saying?" she asked the old man.

"'Tis Latin, the language of the Roman church. I expect they are chanting psalms, from the Holy Scriptures."

She really did not know much about the world her son lived in. She continued to watch. And listen.

Activity swarmed all around. This place was more populated than the wee monastery where Colum had been fostered. Magh Bile was referred to as an abbey, the house of the abbot.

The banging of an anvil came from one direction. When she turned that way, she saw the smoke from the metalworkers' fire. Pivoting back toward the sweepers, two men caught her eye. They walked toward another building, carrying leather bags on their backs. Scrolls stuck out the top. They moved so quietly she almost hadn't noticed them. A soft distant clanging of bells drew her attention next. A few boys without tonsures tended some animals in a pasture just south of the monks' beehive shaped huts. Novices, Colum had explained earlier. They might become monks later, if they decide to take vows to God and the community. When she'd worshipped with Colum earlier, she had only thought about the religious training he was receiving, but this place was a fully functioning family, not unlike Fe's clan, if you did not take into consideration the psalms.

The working monks before her ceased their rhythmic intonations and dispersed in several directions. She hadn't seen where her son went, but for now she was content to wait. She was learning about the abbey. Ninnidh had been correct. She'd absorbed much by just watching. "Why do they speak words from the scriptures while they sweep?" she asked him.

"'Tis an occasion to pause in the midst of labor to turn one's heart to God. God invites us to do this wherever we find ourselves."

A lovely thought, that was. She'd long believed she didn't require a church building or a priest or bells or an altar in order to speak to the One True God. But belief does not equal practice. She'd not answered the invitation nearly enough. *Forgive me, Jesu.*

Enya felt as though she'd awakened from a long sleep. Here, so near to her son in this place of learning, she felt God's presence more than ever before. She said goodnight to the poet, who wandered away strumming his harp. She wanted to stay on the bench a wee bit longer and enjoy the peace encircling her. Her physical discomfort at times made her want to rush to the guesthouse, but then it would pass and she found herself able to relax. She was enjoying this pause in the day.

Sometime later a shadow crossed her legs. She jumped when she realized the low angle of the sun had not darkened her lap but rather the presence of a man had. She turned to face her visitor.

"Hello, woman. You have journeyed a long way." Brother Malachi scowled at her.

With a rush of heat inflaming her face, old fears crept in, destroying her peaceful contemplations. "Why are you here, brother? Have you not tormented me enough, spouting your prophecies? Must you continue? My son is now a man."

He snickered. "May I sit as well?"

She scooted to leave as great a space between them as possible.

"Your son has a guardian here, does he not?"

"Michael."

"Aye, Brother Michael. If you knew what he has put me through over the years, you would perhaps consider my warnings to you as advice, not torture, as you said."

"What do you want?" She gazed at the wrinkles swathing his face. This man had aged faster than anyone she knew.

Malachi smiled but his eyes drew a more sinister expression. "Brody is now king of the Cenél Conaill." He smacked his lips. "Surely you must know if I have such news all the way out here at Magh Bile Abbey."

"Why does this concern you?"

"I suppose you have been too busy raising children to pay heed. I am returning to my father's church. He has gathered with the ancestors, moved on to his great reward, as they say."

She detested his disrespectful, haughty tone.

"I will assume his duties. As you must know, the church has authority over the clan. This is becoming the way across the entire island. The people rely on the church for goods, education, even protection. The people there require my … guidance."

"What are you talking about? My son will still be king one day. I know how that distresses you." She would not give in to a tyrant. "You might as well stay here if you don't like it."

When he shook his head Enya noticed his tonsure was not well groomed. She might not know much, but she did know that as a member of the community, Malachi would have to follow the abbot's rules. Perhaps he would not be returning to Fe's clan as a monk. Perhaps he planned to leave the community and become some kind of nonreligious leader, and a true tyrant. If this was his plan, the man was truly deranged. She stood. "I remember well your prophecy. A man like yourself was given the prophecy of my son's birth only due to the grace of our benevolent God. If you recall, the vision proved my son would be king. Perhaps you have forgotten."

He was on his feet, glowering down on her. She didn't care that she was of short stature. Nor did it bother her that she was three decades or so younger than he. Wisdom does not always come with age and size does not imply superiority. "I do not believe we have any more to say to each other," she announced. Turning away, she paused, then glanced back. His expression had not changed. "One more thing, brother. Stay away from my son."

His expression softened. "I have not forgotten, my dear. That vision was precisely why I have followed your son. It is my duty, you understand. To see how the vision unfolds."

"You, brother, have no duties regarding my son. Your father himself told me so."

He drew in a long breath. "Ah, my father, God … rest … his soul."

The way he said that caused her skin to crawl. Perhaps the old priest had had some kind of calming influence on this wild man, and now he was gone.

Malachi held up a finger as he continued. "Colum, being the offspring of a fifth daughter of a fifth daughter, bears your family attribute of ill-timed ire, and watching you now proves it is just that. I may have nurtured his, let us say, unwise temper, and at times yours as well, I confess.

Mere child's play. The sin of wrath is not mine, but yours. It shall be seen as your undoing, and perhaps even that of your son's."

She could not despise a human being more. *Listen*. Aye, she would not let him be proven true, so she gave no reply.

"You cannot change what God has ordained to be in someone's nature. Ah, so, I must be going. My work is done here." He tapped his large fingertips together. "Now it is time I returned to take my rightful place. Your son has proven himself to be devout. A great scholar. He is firmly entrenched in the monasteries and has no interest in returning west to be king. Has he not told you?" He clicked his tongue. "Ah, poor woman. What a pity that you've been left ignorant. Allow me to enlighten you. Colum will not be king. Not today, not next season, not ever."

She watched him pace away toward the tallest building, the church. How had she allowed this to happen? She feared her son had inherited the curse of anger. Michael had not been able to assuage that. No one had. Not even God. She had thought the church would cure him rather than nurse the plague along, which was what that evil, badger-eyed, wrinkly old man had made sure of.

The bells for vespers rang. Colum would be making his way toward the church as well. She'd wait for him and tell him all about her encounter with that disgusting man. She peered at each hooded face as the men approached. Finally she spotted him. As she waited for him to get closer, she thought about what she must say. Malachi was a horrible man. He'd made a fool out of her. He'd manipulated Colum's appointment to that far away place. She didn't know that for certain, but he must have. They must see to Malachi's destruction in the clan.

Her son paused and knelt down on the path. There was a child beside him, perhaps a son of the abbot or of one of the abbey's workers. They were close enough for her to overhear.

"I know the lad makes you angry, son. I have been angry at others more times than I can remember."

"What do you do, then?" the boy asked. His wee hands were balled in fists at his hips.

"I do what we all must. I contemplate what the Holy Scriptures say. 'A gentle answer turns away wrath, but a harsh word stirs up anger.' Show the lad some kindness. Then you'll see."

The boy tugged on Colum's sleeve as he had resumed his walk to the church. "Will that help?"

"It has always helped for me. God is faithful. Let him be your guide."

Someone nudged her off the path. Michael. He whispered in her ear. "Do you see why they call your son the Dove of the Church?"

She did see. Living here had kept her son safe from the curse, not hurt him as she had thought. God *had* protected him. And with Malachi leaving Magh Bile Abbey, all would be well. If Colum returned with her, as she had been hoping … she could not say what might happen. One thing she knew, she would not fuel the spark of anger that ran in his blood. She could not be his "undoing" as the monk had predicted. She would watch Colum only from afar.

Chapter Sixteen

Alone with none but Thee, my God, I journey on my way. What need I fear when Thou art near, O King of night and day? —Attributed to St. Columcille

They spoke as though he was not in the room. Colum glanced from the abbot, a white-haired wizened old man, to Michael.

"He is still quite young," Michael was saying.

The abbot's eyes widened the way they always did when one of his students caught on to a concept he was teaching. "Precisely, so. The perfect age to learn from Gemmán, the aged master."

Colum would not be ignored, despite his young age. He was, after all, a deacon, and not a mere novice. "What kind of master is he, Father Abbot?"

The abbot glanced quickly at Colum and then back at Michael. "The master is deserving of the title, having lived a spiritual life even before his conversion. He was once a druid in the old ways,

211

now a Christian. Colum will learn much from him."

Michael put a finger to his chin as thought about this. "You have been speaking to the one named Ninnidh."

The abbot grunted. "The old poet is right, Michael. If Colum is to become a great leader to many, he needs to know the old ways, the old tales."

"I want to go," Colum said. He was more than ready to escape the jeers of the other lads who thought him privileged. And besides, this sounded intriguing.

Again, the abbot seemed to ignore him. At least Colum was not being reprimanded for interrupting. The abbot continued, "It is not as though the lad will be corrupted. If that were the case, I certainly—"

"No need to defend yourself, Father Abbot. It is decided, and I am sure his parents will see the wisdom in it." Michael stood, giving Colum an urgent look that said he was to rise as well.

Before they departed, Michael turned back to the old abbot. "The province of Laighen, you say?"

The white-haired man nodded. "Indeed."

"You don't say Brigid's Cill Dara?"

"Ah, the island's blessed saint, God rest her soul. I am not saying Cill Dara, but near there you will find the aged master. You will depart tonight, both of you."

They accepted the abbot's blessing before leaving. Once outside and away from the common buildings, Michael slowed his pace. "That was difficult for you."

"It was."

Michael was wise enough to allow enough silence for Colum to recite a psalm in his mind. Perhaps that was his friend's intent. A verse resounded from deep in his soul, convicting him to control his emotions. *Cease from anger, and forsake wrath; do not fret yourself to do evil.*

Moments later they were standing at Colum's contemplation spot atop the hill. "'Tis only a matter of accepting authority, Colum. You will learn."

"Did I not say I was willing to go?"

"Whether the move pleases you or not is of no consequence."

Colum closed his eyes. Whenever he was angry he had difficulty sensing God's presence. He did not wish that. Slowly his body began to relax. "God instructs the abbot."

"You know 'tis true," Michael said. "I will write a letter to your parents."

Colum thought about his family for the first time since learning of his impending transfer. His mother was not going to like this.

"Read it again." Enya waved her arm at her husband who was sitting in his chair by the fire with a letter from Michael in his hands.

"Would you like to read it for yourself, my love?"

Keeva, their oldest daughter, held out her arm and wiggled her fingers. "Let me try."

"Children, go outside with Branna while I speak with your father."

The servant herded them out, carrying the youngest on her hip. Enya had survived the weaning. Soon the child would take soft food and did not seem harmed by the experience. At times that made Enya sad, so she spent most of her waking hours with the baby while Branna tended to the others. But now she needed to speak with her husband alone.

"Are you sure he's to go to Laighen?" Enya asked.

Fe let the piece of parchment fall to the floor. "That is what it says. Michael is going with him, immediately, it says. I expect they are there by now."

"And he's learning from an aged master? That's what it says?"

Fe sighed heavily. "If you don't believe me, read it, wife."

"I believe you. Do you think this is a good thing?"

"I do."

"For how long, do you think?"

"The letter doesn't say, but this fellow Gemmán I suppose is a hermit, so we will not be visiting."

Her heart sank. She must go. The letter said near the monastery of Cill Dara. They would take her in long enough for her to find out what was going on. She decided to change the subject. Since the coronation of the new king, the monastery under Malachi's control was asserting itself in troublesome ways. "What do you think is going on with the church, Fe? Will Brody render himself below the priest? Because I don't think you and your brother should allow that."

Fe grunted as he rose from his chair. He retrieved the letter, rolled it, and placed it back in his traveling pouch. "I believe Malachi's influence is only in his own mind."

"Kyna does not think so."

He wrinkled his brow. "The cook?"

"She knows things, Fe. She says a criminal has been taken from the monastery where he claimed to have been granted sanctuary. And the man is Malachi's nephew."

He rubbed his chin. "Indeed a fellow who killed ten of Murtagh's sheep has been locked in a cell, but he is one of Malachi's kin? Would he be Brody's as well?"

"Ask Kyna, Fe. She knows things." Enya frowned. "And Malachi threatens to bring my relatives here to help him. My brother, probably. Fe, we can't have them here. Not around our children." Her voice rose. Sobs choked away her words.

He embraced her. "Now, now, my sweet. I will not allow anything to happen to you or our children. Send the cook out to the fields with my midday meal. I will speak to her about this."

"Thank you."

Later that evening Fe asked Enya to walk outside to the well with him. "I think 'tis best you go on a journey. I know you want to see our Colum."

"You … want me to go?"

"Malachi has already sent for your brother. And the Brehon. There is trouble brewing, so take Branna and the children with you. The nuns at Cill Dara will offer you hospitality."

"Kyna told you this?"

He nodded. "And Brendan confirmed what she said. We have held a council. The Cenél Conaill will not tolerate this. Brody does not seem to agree with his cousin, and yet he refuses to correct the new priest. The church, under the rule of a corrupt man, will not prevail here."

She wrapped her arms around his neck. "Please, my love, be careful."

He nodded again. His gazed never left the floor. "There may be war, so you must go. Malachi seems to be gathering allies from the south."

Fear rose from her gut and burned her throat. Colum must pray for his family.

217

Chapter Seventeen

The extent of your prayers should be until tears come.
—*St. Columcille*

With four children, a maid, a cook, a wet nurse with her two children, and two male servants, Enya's entourage moved slower than she would have liked. Between caring for the children and worrying over her husband, she had never felt so exhausted.

Kyna pointed to a cooking fire she was tending in the meadow where they rested on what the men said was the halfway point of their journey. "Please, mistress, sit for a respite. I will make you some elderberry tea with honey."

How the woman had clarity of mind to pack what they needed on the journey, Enya could not image. "Thank you, Kyna."

"Are you quite right, mistress?"

"I am not. There must be grave danger." She jumped to her feet. "Take the children on to Cill Dara, Kyna. You all go. I'm going back."

"You will not." Ruan, one of Fe's farmhands, approached the fire with the wolfhound at his side. Being away from their home had emboldened him.

"You should not have left my husband either, man. We will both go."

Kyna left her preparations at the fire and came to her, her eyes pleading. "Think about why we have come, dear one."

"To escape a threat. A threat that may be coming from my own people." Enya took the old woman's hands in hers. "I must be there. I am the bridge to making peace."

Kyna pinched her lips tight before responding. "Nay, mistress. You wanted to leave to see Colum. We all did."

Enya pulled away from the cook. Smoothing her hands down her tunic, she gathered her thoughts. "Well, at first, aye, 'tis true. But then Fe sent us away to—"

"That's it, isn't it?" Kyna held out both hands, imploring Enya to listen. "This was not your idea. It was forced on you, and you don't like it."

The accusation smacked Enya in the face with storm-like force. "I am concerned. Fe needs me. That is the only reason." She could hear the sounds of the children returning with Branna from washing clothes in a nearby creek. She lowered her voice. "I know Colum is safe. I do not know if Fe is."

The male servant grew mute, probably preferring to allow the women to work out the argument.

Kyna stepped back toward the fire to continue her work. "Well, there is nothing to be done tonight. We must prepare for sleep."

When all the children were settled under a covering held up by thick branches and sheltered by a massive oak tree, Enya tried to rest beside them. Wiggling wee ones allowed little sleep, and she missed the warmth of Fe's body next to her. There was nothing she could do to make sure he was safe. There was no way to know if any harm had come to him. She had felt this miserable once before, when she'd left her firstborn child with the priest many years ago. Helplessness was the great gray cloud she could not escape from.

Having no good options other than continuing on, the troupe finally arrived at the place the legendary Brigid founded decades earlier. A woman dressed in white met them at the monastery gates. "I am Dervil, abbess of Cill Dara. Welcome, travelers."

The men were directed to a separate area of the monastery. Enya and the other women and children followed the abbess. After rounding a wall of vegetation, they encountered a large fire burning in the center of a courtyard. A nun walked around the flames, tending it as though she feared it might go out. But with flames as long as a man's arm that did not seem to be an imminent possibility. Enya had never seen such a fire apart from feast days or Easter.

"Mamaí, look!" Keeva pointed at a line of women, nuns wearing hooded cloaks, dancing on the other side of the flames. Their thin arms exposed when they raised them high, they moved like graceful swans.

What kind of place had Fe sent them to? She nudged her daughter against her as Kyna did the same with Egan, who also did not seem able to take his eyes off the spectacle. Branna, carrying the other two children, leaned in to whisper. "I think we've entered a pagan household."

The abbess must have noticed them gawking. "'Tis a time of worship. Did not the scriptures say David danced before his Lord?"

Abbess Dervil escorted them to the women's guesthouse. Anxiety continued to creep up Enya's spine. After she put wee Sheela down for a nap, she took a stroll alone, wandering back to the common area. Near the well she spotted Michael. She hurried to meet him. "I am surprised to see you here."

He took a step backward. "As I am to see you."

"Walk with me," she said, motioning to a path shadowed by yew trees. "Why are you not with my son?"

"He is not far."

"I did not ask that question. You are his guardian. Why are you not with him?"

He drew in a breath, sounding like she did when she had to explain to Keeva or Meredit for the hundredth time why it was not proper to bathe in the cattle trough. "The aged master, he is a hermit. Do you know what this is, mistress?"

"Tell me."

"An anchorite for God. Some believe hermits are odd and dislike people, but it is their love for people that compels them to take up this life-style."

"You mean to be alone for long periods of time?"

"Alone with God, I mean."

She could not stop herself from looking upward in impatience.

"Mistress, a hermit goes off by himself for the express purpose to pray for all of us who, because of our daily need to work and provide the necessities of life, cannot spend every waking moment communing with God. Someone from the community supplies him food and drink while he is at the hermitage. It is a great service such men, and sometimes women like Brigid of old who established this place, do for us."

"Michael, I understand. But if that is true of this man called Gemmán, then why did the abbot send Colum to him? Won't my son interfere with this endeavor?"

"Well, because the aged master has spent most of his life as a hermit, he is not accustomed to having visitors. He is willing, as he sees it is God's will, to have an occasional student. But his quiet is not to be unduly disturbed. I am here during the day and bring food in the evening. Colum's tutorage is a rare and great honor. The master has agreed to teach Colum the old tales, things most bards have never heard, as a favor to the poet Ninnidh."

The old poet *had* expressed his belief that her son possessed the spirit of a bard. He'd disappeared after escorting her home from Magh Bile. Probably a bit of a hermit himself.

"You should be proud that your son was chosen for this."

"Of course I am, but you should be there too. Wouldn't it be advantageous for you both to learn?"

He shook his head. "The aged master is a sensitive man. He guards the old tales judiciously, as the druids do. I am not permitted to be there during the day, and you should know if you try to visit him, Gemmán may abandon the training, fearing an outsider will corrupt the stories."

"I would never—"

"Nonetheless, that is what would happen. You can trust that I am still looking after your son, although he is not the child you think him to be."

She felt offended. "I … I was coming to see Colum, aye, but my husband has sent me, and my children here. Have you not heard?"

Again he sighed. "I have been here a month. This life is all I know."

"Of course. Fe believes Malachi, who is the new priest at our church, is trying to usurp the clan's rule. He believes there may be war."

His expression changed. "But Malachi has no army." Michael squeezed his fingers into fists. "I told Fe there was something amiss. I should have been more vigilant."

She touched his arm. "Nay. 'Tis my fault and my birth clan he conspires with."

Michael fussed with the hem of his cloak. "I might be able to do something about this if I were not assigned here. Let me contemplate this." He motioned to a flat stone and sat down on it.

Enya lowered herself, too, feeling the cold surface seep through her clothing to her legs. Helpless again. How she hated it. They sat quietly, and she was reminded of Ninnidh's instruction to her to pause.

Suddenly, Michael straightened his shoulders. "I was wrong. I am truly in the right place to affect this. I will ask Columcille to implore our God to stop this conflict. You speak to the abbess and ask her to do the same."

She rubbed her palm over her face. "I appreciate your devoutness, Michael, and that of my son. But I am afraid it is the time for us to act. We can't just sit here."

Michael rose. "You do not understand. But do not worry. He sees it already."

He was right. She did not understand but before she could ask anything, he marched away. She should get back to the children, but they did have a maid, so instead she rushed off to follow him.

Keeping enough distance so he couldn't see her, Enya trailed Michael. He lingered to say something to a monk so she paused to admire the work of some weavers. Glancing back, she noted he was headed toward the half of the monastery that was reserved for men.

"Take this to the bishop, carefully now, love."

She turned around to see a nun handing a bundle of cloth to a young lass. The woman's face was wrinkled in worry, as though she didn't trust the courier.

"May I do it?" Enya asked.

The woman looked relieved. "Do you know where his cell is, love?"

Enya nodded.

"Deliver this to his housekeeper. They are expecting it."

Enya held out her arms to receive the material and then rushed off to find Michael. His stride was longer than hers, but she was determined. When he stopped to chat again, she tiptoed ahead, sure that he would be exiting the monastery somewhere at the south end and she could wait for him there.

When she spotted the gate she was looking for, she approached a monk who was feeding a kitten cream from a jar. "I am afraid I'm new here," she said. "Might you deliver these to the bishop for me? I am only a guest and don't know where I am."

"A guest?" The monk looked surprised as he set down the jar. "You should not have been engaged for such a task. I will be happy to take that."

Relieved, she handed over the bundle and scooted out the gate before anyone could question her. Michael did come out soon after. Keeping to the shadows of a grove of trees, she continued to follow him. When he reached a rocky outcrop, she rested to catch her breath behind a pine. Michael was right. Her son was now a man. She would convince him to come home, just temporarily, to aid his father. No one would willingly take her to this hermit's hideaway, and she did not want to risk Colum's ecclesiastical future, if that was what he'd chosen, by upsetting the old hermit. She had to resort to behaving like an army scout in order to see her son. She did not yet know how she'd do it. Perhaps whisper to him from the trees whenever he was alone. She'd figure something out.

Michael began to climb, and Enya followed. The scarcity of brush cover meant she would soon be exposed, but it couldn't be helped. They were too far away now for him to send her back.

Her foot slipped, sending pebbles bouncing down a bald section of the hill. She froze, sure she would receive a scolding. But if Michael saw her or sensed that someone followed him, he gave no indication.

When he stopped on a mossy ledge, he pushed his hair back from his face and straightened his tunic. He was preparing to greet the hermit, she thought, so she crawled beneath a bush to watch. A mouse squabbled at her, and she held her breath, pushing it away with the tip of her shoe. She looked back up just in time to see Michael slip inside a dark passageway between two rocks. She was about to follow when she heard voices. Scrambling back to her hiding place, she sent more pebbles tumbling. Her heart pounding, she forced herself to look up, sure the men would be scowling at her. A bearded man with pinkish skin peeking out beneath ragged sleeves stood talking to Michael. As weak as the master looked, his voice surprisingly boomed. "We must pray at once!"

Colum came out of the cave carrying a wax tablet. He looked briefly in her direction, and then back at Michael. "I have seen it," he said. He sat down on the ground and Michael joined him. The old master returned to the depths of his cave.

Michael and Colum spoke and then, without warning, Colum stood and hurled his tablet off the side of the mountain. He howled into the wind. "Nooooo!"

What had Michael said to him?

Then Colum stooped, picked up stones and threw them as hard as he could. Michael seemed to be pleading to him. Well, if this didn't upset the hermit, nothing she could do would. She marched toward them, calling her son's name.

Michael ran toward her, putting a finger to his lips. Too late, though, the hermit emerged and he and Colum returned to the cave.

"What is going on, Michael?"

"You should not have followed me."

"But I did. I want an explanation. What did you say to upset Colum?"

"It does not take much."

"What do you mean?"

He glanced back at the cave opening. "I do hope he has settled down or Gemmán will send him away." He shrugged. "He might anyway since he's seen you."

"Don't blame me for this. You said something to him."

"Stay here a moment." He went back in the cave. A few moments later he returned. "Gemmán says he understands. Colum is calmer now. Let us go back to the monastery. We will talk on the way."

"But"—she pointed to the black hole in the rock—"he is *my* son!"

Michael offered his hand. "Perhaps you can see him later."

On their descent Michael began telling her Colum had a temper.

231

"I know this. He has been cursed with my family scourge. Are you saying that all these years in the church, all this time parted from me, has made no difference?"

"There has been incredible value in his training. You must not question that. He is learning to control his anger."

"What was he angry about?"

When they got to the place of loose pebbles that had troubled her on the way up, Michael went ahead to assist her. Back on the trail again, he inhaled deeply before continuing. "I only told him that your clan might be in danger due to Malachi's interference. He wanted to return home, but I told him that was not possible. He tried to insist, but I—"

She interrupted. "Colum wants to come home? You must let him. You said he was a man capable of knowing his own mind."

"Not when he is in one of those tempers."

Now she was the angry one. "I'm going back to get him." To her surprise, Michael did not try to stop her. She rushed back to the cave as quickly as her sore calves could manage it. She stopped when she saw her son and the elderly master kneeling on the mossy ledge. They were praying,

232

their faces bent toward folded hands. She heard their voices, first one and then the other, alternating as though reading one of the priest's litanies.

She felt herself being pushed backward by an unseen force. She might have tumbled off the mountain if Michael hadn't at just that moment come up behind her. The wind began to swirl, encircling them more powerfully than a seaside gale. "What is happening?" she yelled into the air.

"The Spirit of God is here, mistress. 'Tis a wondrous thing!" Michael shouted.

"How?"

"By the faith of your son. He prays for his birth clan. God hears. Do you not feel it? Your husband is well."

She did sense something. It was both a troublesome and comforting sensation. In the midst of the whirlwind, she heard God's voice. Rarely had she ever been so certain of anything. *Go home now, Enya. All is well.*

That night Enya slept soundly, better than she had since the night her first child was conceived. At daybreak she, her children, and her servants left Cill Dara—a place of miracles, she now understood—and returned home. As soon as they

233

left the shadow of the high crosses, one magpie flew overhead. She shivered.

Just one.

Chapter Eighteen

If we wish to make any progress in the service of God we must begin every day of our life with new eagerness. We must keep ourselves in the presence of God as much as possible and have no other view or end in all our actions but the divine honor.
—*Saint Charles Borromeo*

Colum awoke on the floor of the hermit's cave, feeling a bit perplexed. He was sure his mother had been just outside, about to summon him home, but she had left without speaking to him. He raised himself up on his elbows. Even a stone pillow would be better than having none. His body ached from the weeks he had slept on the cold dirt, and yet, he felt his soul refreshed. He noted the hermit's absence. He never seemed to be able to rouse before the old man.

When he left the cave to relieve himself, he heard a magpie's mocking chatter. The sun lit the horizon with a golden hue. God was in this sanctuary, as he was everywhere, of course. It was the

235

angels he missed. He'd sensed heavenly watch-men all around him in Loch Cuan and in the west where he'd been born. One day he'd return to his homeland. Just not yet. His absence was needed for his mother's faith to grow.

When he returned to the cave, the hermit was there. "You have done well to learn the old tales, son. Your memory is as solid as mine. 'Tis time you departed for the next step in your spiritual journey."

Colum had thought so as well, but he didn't expect the master to release him so soon. "Where shall I go?"

"Ask your guardian."

Colum turned to find Michael making his way up the slope.

They left Cill Dara after eating roasted pork with apples soaked in honey at the refectory where Michael explained that they would be going to a large center of learning referred to as Clonard. Sundays brought feasts at Cill Dara not unlike the meals with his mother. Now, however, he needed to prepare himself for the more abstinent lifestyle of a scholarly monk. "Are you sure we cannot go north to the land's end instead? That is my favorite place on earth."

Michael loaded the pony cart with the help of the driver who would deliver them to their destination. "If you knew Clonard, you would not ask this question. Why do you wish to go north?"

"Angels."

Michael stepped back from the cart. "Truly?"

Colum laughed as he climbed aboard. "You told me to search with my heart and God would reveal what it is I should see, and I see angels, but mostly in the oak grove bordering the sea north of my birthplace. I want to go back there."

Michael climbed in after him, sat on a crate, and rubbed his eyes with his thumbs. "Patience. Your friends will be arriving at Clonard as well."

"Ciarán?"

"Aye, and a few other lads you are acquainted with. In addition to that good fortune, you will be attending a large school, perhaps as many as three thousand students, under the direction of Finnian of Clonard, a different man from your first teacher, but like him, this Finnian has traveled much, spread his wisdom broadly. He studied for a time in Gaul. He lived in Cymru a very long time. When he returned he founded other schools. He even spent time in Cill Dara. And then our God directed him to the River

Boyne where he will one day make his resurrection, and this has grown to be the great Clonard Abbey."

"He is greatly aged, then."

"He is. And wise. 'Tis a great honor, Colum."

"All those people with him? What will they teach us?"

Michael smiled. "You have just learned all the bard tales. Now you will learn the languages of the scriptures, and many more things. The abbess of Cill Dara, a friend of Finnian's, arranged for us to go there."

If this was the largest school with the best teachers, Colum did want to attend. He had learned much already, but there was more to know. Obviously, thousands others thought so as well.

The cart bumped along a rutted path through the farm fields, making conversation difficult. Clouds began to darken the sky. Anticipating a shower, Colum and Michael spread a blanket over the edges of the cart and held it over their heads like a tent. There was not much wind, just heavy drops of rain.

Colum wanted to know more about Clonard. "Will we have our own cells?"

"If you build them."

He would need to figure out how. "Are you staying with me?"

"Not this time. There is little for me to do there. I do not think you need me anymore."

Sadly, this was true. "What will you do?"

Even in the dim light under the blanket, Colum could see his friend's smile. "I shall await your return among the angels of Daire."

"Aye, that's where they are, near my parents. Ask the angels to come to Clonard. Not all. Some should stay to guard my family." Colum had no idea if one could ask an angel to do anything. They were sent by God, after all. But if anyone could speak to heavenly beings, it was Michael.

Michael did not answer but thrust a sheathed knife toward him. "This is not a peaceful place where you are going. The abbey should ward off any evil, but be prepared just the same."

"So you are leaving me just when I may face danger?" Colum was teasing and his friend found it funny.

"If you need angels here, Colum, God will send them. If you do not see them, you don't need them, or at least don't need to be aware."

Later, when they approached the abbey, Colum was amazed by its size. Rows of round cells, more than he could count, dotted the banks of the river. Dozens of monks, all dressed in dirt-brown robes, strolled while murmuring prayers. Others fished from a round hide-covered boat in the river. Many others milled about. It was not until they passed by a tall wooden cross and entered through iron gates that he saw the church, much larger than any he'd seen before, and another impressive building he was sure was the scriptorium. He could not wait to see the books.

When they exited the cart, a magpie landed on top of Colum's traveling bag. It twisted its head, looking at him, and then flew off.

"One for sorrow," the cart driver said, repeating an old superstition.

Chapter Nineteen

*One for sorrow, two for joy, three for a girl, four for
a boy, five for silver, six for gold, seven for a secret,
never to be told!*
—Nursery rhyme

Fe and Enya gazed at the fire Fe had built to
burn the brush he had cleared from his new-
est field. Life for the clan had gotten much more
complicated. "Malachi lost one battle when Brody refused to allow him to take over the castle,
but he's determined to have a war," Fe said.

But standing under the star-flecked sky, tending to common chores, made the threat seem far
away, at least to Enya. The sound of the cottage
door creaking open, made her turn around.
"Keeva, you should be in bed, darlin'."

"Let her come," Fe said, opening his arms.

Keeva rushed to him. "I missed you while we
were gone, Da."

He smothered her with kisses. "I'm pleased
you missed your home, my sweet lassie."

She turned toward the fenced in area on the south side of the cottage. "Oh, my herb garden."

"Oh, 'tis yours now, is it?"

"She is in charge of picking. Later, Kyna will teach her how to care for each plant," Enya said.

Fe tapped her on the nose. "That's my fine, my lassie."

Giggling, she turned toward the flames. "We saw a big fire at Cill Dara," she said. Wiggling down from her father's embrace, she stepped closer to the flames. Her pale face reflected the yellow heat. She lifted her arms and began to wiggle like a worm, moving and hopping back and forth. "I'm praising Jesu," she shouted.

Fe gave Enya a puzzled look. "'Tis true," she said. "The nuns do this, but with a wee bit more grace."

Fe turned back to watch his daughter. "Is it proper? I mean, what if she continues this dancing as she gets older?"

Enya put her arm around her husband's waist and nestled her cheek against his chest. "Well, at Cill Dara no men are allowed at the fire. We could implement that rule here, if we must. But just look at her, so joyful."

He agreed, chuckling. They sat on the verdant grass carpet where they could keep an eye on Keeva.

"Hopefully the activity will tire her out enough for sleep," Enya said. "That child does not sleep nearly enough."

"She should enjoy it while she can. You and the children and the servants must stay indoors."

She pulled away from his embrace to look at him. "Why?"

"For safety. I do not jest about this, Enya. Stray no farther than the dairy barn."

While she'd been away, her uncle, Ernán, had shown up, proclaiming devotion to the Cenél Conaill. Although Fe said had at first been suspicious, Ernán soon won him over because he was a defector from Enya's father's tyranny. A few days later his two sons joined him, and Fe had welcomed them into the protection of the clan, thankful for more help in the fields. Ernán's wife had died many years earlier giving birth to the youngest son. Enya had never seen any of them exhibit the curse of anger. Perhaps it had passed by this branch of the family. All the same, this reminder of her past prompted Enya to avoid her uncle whenever possible.

The following day, that proved not to be possible, as she had not seen him before entering the barn to fetch goat's milk for wee Sheela. He was working on a spancel with a sharp iron tool. He glanced up when the sunbeam from the open door hit his face. Shielding his eyes, he greeted her. "Bless you, Enya. Have you come to see my work?" He held up the implement.

She stared, surprised to find him there and dumfounded that he thought she'd want to inspect the care of the livestock.

He let the spancel fall to the dirt floor. "Now, now, lass. You've not said a word to your uncle. I know you left miffed, and who could blame you with the temper your da has. But don't you want to hear anything about the old home?" He cleared his throat. "I always thought someone should tell you just want happened to your mother when you were a wee lass."

Enya had tried not to think of her mother. Fe had replaced her birth family, and when the children came they were enough for her. She turned toward the goat pen, bucket in hand. If she had allowed Branna to get the milk when she offered, Enya could have avoided all this.

Her uncle continued. "Life was hard for her, but I'm sure you know that."

"I do not care to think about that life. I have a new family now, Uncle."

"Just the same, you should hear this, lass. Your mother never wanted to leave you."

Her knees buckled and she grasped a wooden beam to steady herself. "I know she had some kind of accident. I'm not sure I want to hear."

"She was gathering bird eggs at the shore near Ceann Ramhar, slipped and hit her head on the rocks. Her death was mercifully quick. I thought perhaps you had imagined something else, given the temperament of your father."

She nodded her thanks, not trusting her voice. Her mind brought her to that place where her mother had met her end. She could hear the waves crashing, smell the salt in the air, and feel the wind whipping her hair across her face. As a girl Enya had spent as much time out of the house and on that beach as she could manage. It had been her refuge. She had often gathered bird eggs, listening to the ocean waves, hearing the squawking of corncrakes. Enya had never slipped. Perhaps her father had been responsible.

"Are you all right, lass? Should I get your children's maid for you?"

"Nay, I am fine, thank you." Thinking about the call of birds reminded her she'd seen the omen of the magpie as she left Colum. *One for sorrow ...*

After the evening meal, she helped Kyna with the washing up while Branna readied the children for bed. "I do not understand my conflicting thoughts, Kyna. One moment I was experiencing the peace of God and believing that he would care for Colum, and the next I was fearing the magpie. I saw just the one."

"And then you got this sad news. I am so sorry, mistress."

"Did it mean anything? The omen?"

"Only if it was God sending you that message."

"Fe would say I was believing in the old ways, and that I should stop."

"What do you think?"

Exasperated, Enya tossed her washing rag into the tub of water. "'Tis so hard, this trusting what cannot be seen. And then I see something, this bird, and I immediately want to trust that." She burst into tears and dropped to the ground, embarrassed but unable to stop.

"Oh, there now, dear, bear up. 'Tis no shame in having earthly eyes that search out the proof of a thing."

She sniffed. "My firstborn son was taken away from me. How does a mother ever trust anyone after that?"

Kyna turned her back to return to the washing. "That is not so. He was not taken."

"Well, you know what I mean."

The old woman held her hands at her side, water dripping from her long fingers. Her shoulders lifted as she took a breath. "You cannot give something and then expect to have it back. It is in the giving that you receive, and if you do not give, you will not receive."

"What are you talking about?" Had the old woman's mind turned to moss?

Kyna turned around and brought her hands together in front of her chest. "The scriptures from the monastery say, 'Give, and it will be given to you.'"

So she deserved this. "There is another book in the scriptures that I suppose the monks haven't shared, but I've seen it. 'Tis about a man named

247

Job. He said, 'The Lord gives and the Lord takes away.'"

"But there is more …"

Enya didn't hear the rest of Kyna's argument because she rushed back into the house. Later she'd apologize for her rudeness, for the dear old woman did not deserve such treatment. But right now she could bear no more talking of God. He'd taken her mother. Was God to blame or was she? Enya had been too young to help but perhaps if she'd taken her father's wrath in place of her mother she'd still be alive.

Branna held a finger to her lips when Enya entered and whispered. "Just got the youngest to sleep, mistress."

Enya approached the small box bed where Meredit, Egan, and Sheela nestled together in sweet slumber. She bent down to kiss each downy head. "I will never leave you," she whispered.

When she turned away, Branna stood watching her, holding Keeva's hand. Enya approached her oldest daughter and kissed the top of her head. "Nor you, wee one."

The three of them moved to the hearth where mending awaited. Enya's anger abated a bit. Children had a way of softening every heart.

"Why are you sad, Mamaí?" Keeva wrinkled her small nose.

Enya pulled the girl onto her lap and nestled her face into Keeva's fair locks, silky as her father's. Only Colum resembled his mother, although not her small stature. "Regrets, my heart. Your mamaí has regrets."

The girl squirmed as she turned to look at her. "What is that, regrets? A sickness?"

Branna held her needle aloft over the material in her lap, as though she wanted an answer as well.

"'Tis, although you cannot catch it from me, so do not worry."

Keeva put her hand on Enya's forehead. "You do not seem to be ill. Shall we make you tea?"

Enya hugged her tight. "You are lovely to ask, Keeva. I will be fine." She scooted the girl off her lap. "But tea seems like an excellent idea. I will go get Kyna to join us."

Kyna was about to carry in the dishes when Enya met her outside. "Keeva, come help our Kyna, would you?"

The child scampered out and relieved Kyna of most of her load. Enya took the rest. "I am very—"

Kyna interrupted her. "No apologies needed, mistress. You have had a long day."

The women gathered inside, forming a half circle in front of the hearth.

"'Tis a soft day we're having," Branna said.

"That it is," Kyna agreed. "Moist enough to straighten curls."

Enya laughed. Her cook always said that whenever they were caught in mizzle, not a downpour, but enough rain to feel it seep into one's cloak. Enya studied the faces of those around her hearth. She had once longed to be accepted by the women in her clan, and now she had the friendships she once longed for right here in her very own cottage. May God forgive her for her past sins.

The door crashed open and Fe entered, followed by his brother Brendan, Ernán, and Ernán's sons.

Branna hurried to the children's bed, but they had not awakened.

"What is it?" Enya asked.

"You all must stay in the cottage tomorrow," Fe said, his face flushing. "There is to be a meeting with Brody and the Brehons. Malachi will not concede authority, believing the church has superiority."

Brendan huffed and picked up a jar from the window ledge.

"I will get some ale," Kyna said, ducking out toward the storage chamber.

"Sit, lads," Fe said, motioning to the table board and stools.

Keeva tugged on her father's tunic.

"Not now, sweet," he said. "Your da has things to work out."

"Regrets?" she asked.

Fe glanced at Enya. Enya shrugged and hurried the lassie to the side of the room where the others slept.

The sound of something hitting the side of the cottage made everyone jump. "What was that?" Enya asked, hugging Keeva to her chest.

"I will look," Ernán's eldest son said, taking a torch from the wall socket and lighting it from the fire.

He was gone only moments when sounds of a scuffle outside sent the other men scrambling. "Bolt the door," Fe called out as they rushed into the darkness.

251

Enya ran to the door and Branna helped her fasten the bolt. She could hear shouting outside, Brendan's voice. "Youse can't scare us, you rogues!"

"Open the door. Hurry!" Fe shouted.

They carried in Ernán's son who bled heavily from a head wound. The children bawled from their nest in the bed. Enya tipped her head in their direction and Branna went to them while she and Kyna cleared the table board. The men laid the lad there.

Enya reached for her cloak. "I'll go for the healer."

Fe gripped her wrist. "Nay. 'Tis not safe, Enya!" He turned to Kyna. "Can you help him?"

"I will try." She gathered clean cloth from the mending basket. "We must stop the bleeding."

Ernán paced the length of the cottage. "'Tis a battle already. I should have known it would come to this. Once Malachi latched onto the Mac Noe's thirst for blood, 'twould only be war. And my son!" He let out such a mournful groan Enya thought her heart would break in two.

By morning the lad was dead.

One for sorrow …

Enya observed the dead boy's brother, Rory, sharpening his spear by the fire. "I am sorry for this loss," she said.

The lad did not look up, but his face reddened. Her heart ached to see this formally composed lad now filled with hate.

"War is the way of men," Kyna said when they worked to freshen the bed linens. "Women hurt each other in more subtle ways, but men settle disputes in a manner that has horrific consequences. God bless that lad. He will never forget what was done to his brother."

Enya pounded a pillow with her fist. "Why must this happen? I had hoped to escape it when I came here."

"We both did, truly. There is another scripture I have been reading. 'Tis Jesu's own words: 'In this world, you will have trouble.'"

Enya sighed. "Is there no hope?"

Kyna sprinkled the children's bed with dried heather. "To help them sleep better." She winked. "Let me show you that scroll."

After settling the children with some small yarn balls and carved wooden toys, they left them with Branna and entered the small room where Enya kept her writing materials. Kyna lit a can-

253

dle and smoothed open a parchment against the polished surface of Enya's treasured writing desk. Perhaps Colum had inherited his love of words from his mother.

"Read this." Kyna tapped a gnarled finger in the middle of the writing.

"These things I have spoken unto you, that in me you might have peace. In the world ye shall have tribulation ..." Enya shook her head. "There is no escape."

"Read on, mistress."

"Be of good cheer; I have overcome the world."

Kyna put both her hands on Enya's shoulders. "There 'tis. Hope. We know not when or how, but we know Jesu will prevail."

A tear streamed down Enya's cheek. "I will dare to hope, Kyna. I will."

Enya returned to the fire. The boy still sharpened his weapon. His feet stood in a litter of wood shavings. Enya stepped around him to take the kettle off the fire.

"The others have left?" she asked him.

Holding the tip of the spear up to the firelight to inspect it, he nodded. "They have."

"Why are you not with them?"

The boy looked at her for the first time. He was probably about fourteen summers old, too young for such tragedy. And yet, many like him had lost family members to illnesses and accidents. However, this young man's brother was murdered, perhaps by one of his own clan. She prayed for words to make this better, but she knew there were none.

"My da says I am not needed at the Brehon council. Said I should be here in case you all need me."

"Oh, well, we are grateful." She wondered if she should share that scripture she and the cook had just read, but decided against it because he might not understand her intent.

The silence was too painful. Tea should help. She poured a mug for him, which he accepted with thanks. "Are you a man of faith?" she finally asked.

"I cannot have faith that anything good will happen. I am sorry, but 'tis true," he said.

"I understand." She truly did. "But all the same, I will pray to the One True God for healing of this …" What should she call it? "This conflict."

255

He held up his spear. "This is war." The hound whimpered.

The door slammed open and Ernán walked in. "Rory, bring the hound."

The lad glanced at Enya.

She stood and inclined her head toward the door. "Do not worry. There is no war right now, and perhaps the meeting with the Brehons will settle it."

The lad's face remained grim.

She patted him on the arm. "You should be at the men's council, Rory. Go along. Everyone here will be fine."

She prepared to bolt the door after they left, but hesitated. "Branna, I am going out. Do not open the door to anyone but those who live here."

"But mistress—"

Enya held up a hand. Looking around, she counted the children. "Where is Keeva?"

Branna put a hand on the door latch. "In the herb garden, I suppose. I warned her not to go."

"I send her back. You stay here."

Enya glanced at Meredit and Egan, who played with spinning tops their father had carved for them. So trusting. So innocent. She thought about the fairy thorn tree's spindly branches dripping with bits of torn cloth soaked with the hopes and fears of the people. Supplications that would never be heard because of the manner in which they were offered. "Branna, Kyna, please pray." She bent down to stroke the heads of her children. Seeming to sense her anxiety, their wee faces wrinkled. She kissed their cheeks.

Kyna came to her and urged her away. "What are you thinking, child? If the men thought it was unsafe to even wander about our own pastures, how can you go out?"

"They think it might become unsafe. Later. So you two pray, and I will go speak to whichever one of my clan Malachi has brought up to meet with the Brehons." She marched outside, her metal belt swinging hard against the door as she closed it.

Keeva looked up from behind the tall, silvery leaves of mugwort.

"Come along, darlin'."

Enya moved to see what the lassie was doing. She had an armful of stems.

"Cook says when the smoke fills the cabin it calms everyone. She said you would like it, Mamaí."

257

"That would be lovely. Take it inside now with whatever else you've gathered in your basket. Mind Branna, won't you? Mamaí has an errand."

The girl tilted her chin upward and gave Enya a smile. She had such a sweet, obedient nature, always wanting to help. Enya sent her off toward the cottage while she scrambled for the barn.

Although the sun was shining outside, the barn was dim. She sensed its emptiness immediately. The men had taken all the horses. She dropped to the straw floor, feeling despair creep up her throat. *Why, God, when I am finally able to help are there no horses?*

She heard a sound at the door. She turned to find Gormley holding the reins of her horse.

"I need to borrow her," Enya said, flinging herself up.

"We have just returned. She needs a rest. I'm afraid—"

"No, I must." She reached for the reins.

Gormley stepped back.

Enya held out her arms, pleading. "You cannot be any more pleased about what's happened as I am. Come, Gormley, Malachi has played your husband for a fool."

258

Gormley would not look at her, probably realizing Enya was right. Perhaps Gormley hadn't realized just how evil Malachi was.

"Malachi, your priest, will not surrender what he believes is an ecclesiastical right to govern."

Gormley's husband had not been the wise, strong king the clan needed, but Enya would not point that out just now. "He is no priest of mine. Just because someone claims to follow Jesu doesn't mean—" A thought startled her. "Gormley, where are you returning from that requires rest for your horse?"

A shadow appeared behind the woman. "They aren't here," a gruff voice said.

A few more gathered. Gormley stared at Enya as though she'd been caught cattle poaching.

A scream erupted from the house.

"What have you done?" Gormley asked the man blocking the barn entrance.

"Just what needed done to check the place."

Enya recognized the voice. Her brute of a brother Donnchad.

Wailing followed the screams. *Keeva!*

"Get away from here!" Enya cried.

They allowed her to pass. She found the cottage door wide open. The children crying.

"Keeva! Branna!" She burst in. Branna sat on the floor cradling someone.

"What happened?"

"My leg hurts," her Keeva whimpered.

"They were looking for the men. Said they were hired to herd them like sheep," Branna said as she peeled away one of Keeva's shoes. "She was coming in from the herb garden and they just stomped right over her. Wild boars!"

The leg was red and oddly misshaped. Enya lifted the girl to take her to the bed. "Fetch cold spring water," she ordered the maid. "And rags."

Fe was right when he'd said she should stay with the children. If she had brought Keeva inside herself ... Now she understood the reason God had not provided her a way to depart.

As Enya cared for her daughter she mumbled under her breath. Gormley? Donnchad? Malachi? Who else was among this perverse band of marauders? Surely her father as well.

Chapter Twenty

Many have become my enemies without cause; those
who hate me without reason are numerous. —
Psalm 38:19 NIV

Because the road was so highly traveled, Michael would have no trouble finding rovers to see him on his journey. "Take care, Colum. Your mother's clan may start trouble for you. Whether or not they succeed may depend on your prayers."

"I do not understand what has caused this. Has she not been separated from them for a very long time?"

Michael placed his hand on Colum's shoulder. "They gave her no mind until the prophecy. Word of it traveled to them, probably by the hand of Malachi, and they decided that rather than uphold the peace her marriage with your father was to bring, they'd try to destroy what was foreseen."

261

"You mean the dream my mother had when she was expecting me? The one about the beautiful cloak?"

"Aye, the one that proclaimed you to be the light of Jesu that will spread far and wide." Michael brushed his hair from his eyes. It was the color of the iron gall ink Colum had tried to mix, dark but not black. "At least *we* know that was the prophecy. They see it differently."

"How is that?" Colum truly wanted to understand.

They strolled together toward the almonry where Michael sought to meet up with folks traveling north. The day was fair with blue sky peeking around mounds of white clouds. A good day to begin a journey. For them both.

"Recall the story of Jesu's birth," Michael began. "King Herod did not properly understand the prophecy. He thought of Jesu's reign as being an earthly institution, to usurp him, did he not?"

"He did. 'But you, Bethlehem, in the land of Judah, are by no means least among the rulers of Judah; for out of you will come a ruler who will shepherd my people Israel.' That was the word from God, but Herod thought Jesu would threaten his position so he sought to be rid of him by murdering male infants."

"Indeed. And so, the Mac Noes believe the prophecy means you will one day rule all of Éire, and they were hoping to have that for themselves."

"But they don't have the strength. Not against the Sons of Néill, or even the Cenél Conaill who make up only one piece of the dynasty."

Michael wagged his head sadly. "Oh, but such is man's delusion. He thinks himself more important than he is, and so who can persuade him? But know this: a fellow who feels emboldened comes like a thief in the night. Unexpected, and possibly more dangerous than the fiercest army of warriors due to his ignorance. Be on guard."

Colum tapped the weapon strapped to his leg.

Once Michael found traveling companions, they said farewell, and Colum paused to watch his friend go north to the land Colum knew was populated with angels. Pondering, he wondered if he should ask his teacher if all angels are supernatural or if some show up fully human.

Later, after checking in at the chapter house and being told that he must build his own shelter because "you won't find a common dormitory here," he gathered stones for a foundation. That was where Ciarán found him.

His old colleague took the heaviest stone from him and nodded to an open spot. "Over here. How are you, my friend?"

"I am well. Happy to be here with you."

"You can share shelter with me until you get yours built. We have an uncommitted hour currently. 'Tis a warm day." He looked longingly toward the river. "These days are few, my friend!" He glanced toward another lad. "Come on, Donál!" They both ran as though their feet had sprouted wings.

Colum dropped his traveling bag and rushed after, shedding his outer garments on the bank. Donál splashed water in Colum's eyes so he responded in like. They laughed and gasped at the unexpected pleasure. After his third immersion into the chilly waters, Colum lifted his head and shook water drops from his eyes, sensing someone watching him.

Later, as they sat in the scriptorium listening to a teacher, Colum whispered to his old friend. "I think someone was observing when I was in the river."

Ciarán gave him half a smile. "There are thousands of monks here, lad," he whispered. "Of course someone was watching."

Colum opened his mouth to respond, but snapped his lips shut when he saw the teacher looking at him. He picked up his stylus and began to scribble on the margins of his practice parchment.

After a week of lessons, prayers, and periods of silence for contemplation, Colum decided he must have been wrong to be concerned. Nothing seemed amiss. A few days later, captivated by his rigorous training, he forgot all about it, until a crash resounded outside the scriptorium during a lecture by Abbot Finnian. Colum instantly sensed danger and believed his presence at the abbey was the cause.

"What is this about?" The abbot tamped his crozier on the cobblestone floor.

Everyone scurried like mice save for Ciarán and Donál, who stood faithfully by Colum. Shouting and the clamber of running feet came from outside. Colum retrieved his knife.

"What are you doing?" Ciarán asked, eyes wide.

"Get behind me!" Colum stomped toward the door, making sure the monks were between him and the abbot. Shoving open the heavy scriptorium door, he could barely see the adjacent buildings for the masses of men running to and fro, shouting. They were not all monks, however. Strangers in a rainbow of colors he had not seen since leaving his parents' clan advanced from the open monastery gates, chasing the monks in all directions. Colum held his weapon over his head. Drawing in a deep breath, he sent forth a shriek as powerful as his lungs could manage.

The crowd, most of whom had no weapons, not even the interlopers, stopped and scattered. Not content, he ran after the men who had attempted to threaten the abbey, chasing them down the cloister and back through the iron gates.

A great cheer rang out, but Colum felt no pride, just anger. Justified as it might have been, he would seek absolution from the abbot as soon as he could.

"Well done," Donál said, giving Colum's shoulders a sound shaking.

When everyone settled down, Ciarán pulled him aside. "What were you thinking, my friend?

You didn't know what awaited you outside that door. You'll not be so foolish next time."

Colum put his long dagger away and attempted to flatten his crumpled tunic. "What do you mean? There will be a next time?"

"There will. Those were warlike monks who live in the valley and worship in the wee church there. We are always fighting off one group or another jealous of our successful enrollment and our hordes of pilgrims. If not them 'twill be the Mac Noes."

Colum urged his friend to step away from the others. They gave Colum nods of appreciation as they returned to their desks.

"What do you know of those Mac Noes, Ciarán?"

"I am one, don't you know."

Colum had forgotten. His friend was not warlike in the least. It had been easy to forget. "We are distant cousins, then, on my mother's side."

"I suppose we are, although we belong to the church now. Where we were born and to whom is of no consequence. We are brothers, sons of the Most High God. That is all that matters."

"You speak justly."

267

Ciarán looped his arm around Colum's neck and spoke into his ear as they walked back to their places. "But truly, I'm afraid they're coming from the south with violent intentions. A few advance men have been about, causing a ruckus. I am no help. They won't talk to me. My father was a mere tradesman with no say among them." He raised his fair brows. "Might you know something about this, my friend?"

The abbot called the students to attention.

"We will talk later," Colum said. But he didn't relish having the conversation. He shared his warlike relations' angry outbursts, and he did not wish to corrupt the abbey or risk being cast out. His display of vengeance just now had been as much a surprise to him as to anyone.

For weeks after, Colum refused to talk about the incident, except to the abbot who had agreed to be Colum's confessor.

"We must consider the fact that the Mac Noes may attack simply because you now live among us."

Colum was stunned. "I should leave then."

"God has not given us a spirit of fear, my son. You are part of us now. God planned for you to be here, so here you shall be. We've taken measures. The king of Mide, whose people descended from another son of Néill Noigiallach, has provided warriors to protect the monastery school. There have been no disturbances since."

"Is that all that needs be done?" Colum felt troubled deep in his soul.

"For now. The brothers who have been longest with me will pray and we will consult, and if God directs more action, we shall listen."

The plan sounded satisfactory, but still Colum sensed something wrong. After they spoke, he ordered his own action. The abbot hadn't required it of him, but Colum spent his praying hours strolling the perimeter of the community repeating the Psalms. Seventy-five verses in one direction and then seventy-five verses on the way back. He found he could complete this before the early morning prayers if he did not tarry.

Blessed are those whose ways are blameless, who walk according to the law of the Lord.

Despite his attempts to focus on the Psalms, thoughts plagued him, especially on the morning he knew the abbot was discussing the situation with his group of elders. Perhaps if Colum gave himself up to the Mac Noe, he could save the community. If his mother's clan believed he was

269

destined to rule, as Michael had said, going to them might satisfy their wrath. Of course, he would never become High King of Éire, or even the clan's king. He had always known his purpose was to be in the church to serve Jesu. But like Michael had said, these men did not understand the prophecy because they thought Colum was meant to become a ruler of men.

He tapped his fists against his temple. He didn't want to leave. The monastery was supposed to provide him wisdom and knowledge. The path had been set up for him, hadn't it? These kinds of doubts kept him awake at night and now invaded his time of meditation.

He gazed at the sky, hoping to find answers there. The orange and pink-blushed heavens told him night would soon fall. If he did give himself up for the good of the monastery, it would best be done in the daylight. While the abbot's advisors met, Colum must pray. He hurried to the church.

Donál met him on the path. "Are you quite all right, Colum?"

"Not knowing if a decision has been made about the Mac Noe is troubling me."

"I could inquire."

"You wouldn't mind?"

He grinned. "If it would ease your mind, I'd be happy to. I am on my way to the chapter house and 'tis on the way."

They parted and Colum made his way to the church.

Once inside a swell of emotions made him stumble. He quickly grabbed a bench and lowered himself onto it. *Why is this happening to me?* A red-hot fire in his chest caused him to clutch the front of his cowl and cry out so loud his voice resounded off the ceiling beams and returned to him.

A few men rushed out the door, but he barely noticed. The psalmist said, "Evening, morning and noon I cry out in distress, and he hears my voice." Colum was there to talk to God. This stature assigned to him by men—not God—was unjust and God was going to hear him. After several minutes of heartfelt prayers, a booming voice called out from the rear of the church.

"Just like yer mother, are ya? Heard she did the same thing in the church."

Colum turned slowly toward the voice, the words of his guardian ringing in his ears. *Be on guard!*

271

Chapter Twenty-One

An angry man stirs up strife, and a furious man
abounds in transgression.
—Proverbs 29:99 NKJV

Colum turned toward the voice. A tall man with a face like bleached leather glared at him. His clothes were the color of wet stones and the long white hair of his beard had been carefully groomed and plaited. He held a spear in his right hand, the point pressed downward to the floor. The fact that he was alone lessened the threat this stranger posed.

Colum rose to his feet. "What do you know about my mother?"

The man huffed. "I hear she was in a church like this one before you were born." He turned his head and looked about as though there was something to see on the unadorned walls. His gaze settled on the altar, where a jeweled cross loomed over the golden chalice and paten. If he was after treasure it was best he take it and spare lives. He surely had men outside the door. Where were the abbot's soldiers?

When the man sighed and sat on a bench in the way of a storyteller about to impart an old saga, Colum realized his intent was not to plunder. "Your mother, Enya, she wailed and cried out like a banshee that day. The priest thought she was a drunkard."

Colum stepped toward him. The old man lifted his palm. "Steady, lad. I'm not saying she was, just that the fire in her sparked up a bit, you know. Like you just now. You are your mother's son, aye?"

"State your business."

The stranger nodded. "Indeed you are. I had to send her away. She's a bit mad. Might have pierced me with my own spear while I slept." He chuckled. "Hiding here in this monastery, are you?"

"I'm not hiding." Could this man be not only a Mac Noe, but someone close to his mother? Colum should have asked more questions when he visited. His parents should have told him things. Not knowing, possessing outright ignorance, was a disadvantage he should not have to suffer. "Who do you think I am?"

"Please, sit with me."

Colum didn't move.

"You were named Crimthann, aye?"

"I was."

"But this church, these people, they gave you another name." He tapped a wrinkled finger to his forehead. "Columcille, that it?"

"Again, stranger, I ask that you state your business."

He shrugged. "Dove of the Church." He caught Colum with his stare. "But you are no dove, are you?" He laughed without merriment. "None of us are. We are hard in spirit and in deeds. Tough enough to survive for thousands of years. Only the fiercest fighters live to tell of the battle, lad." He smiled. "You are one of the tough. One of the Mac Noe."

So he was here to take Colum away. "Your business?"

"To return my daughter's son to his people. You don't belong here."

This was his grandfather, his seanathair. Colum sat two bench rows in front of the man and turned to face him fully. "Shall we be honest with each other, Seanathair?"

"Of course. I come with the truth."

"But not the whole truth. You want to get me away so that I do not threaten you with kingship. My father's clan is most powerful. I am as much a part of that clan by blood as yours. You know this. For all I know, you plan to kill me, not embrace me as a long lost son."

The old man's demeanor shifted. His eyes turned black. "I will have the last word, not that lass." He tossed his spear away.

The door to the church opened. Two men with lime-spiked hair and blue marks streaked across their faces entered. His seanathair turned to them. "You have the abbot?"

"We do," one answered.

Colum jumped to his feet. "He has nothing to do with this dispute."

His grandfather ignored him. "Remove his head and put it on my spear. Take it to the monastery gates where everyone will see it."

"What?" Colum dashed for the door.

The two men locked their arms through his, rendering him defenseless. Beyond the open door he could see more intruders, some of which shuffled away to complete this brutal man's decree. "Why would you kill the abbot? He is a man of God!"

The old man groaned. "We do not fear your God, but your refusal to come with me has necessitated a … display of will."

Colum struggled until someone clubbed him over the head, sending shocks of pain through his body.

When he awoke in the infirmary, Ciarán stood over him. Colum's brain throbbed with the beating of a thousand drums. "The abbot's dead?" he asked.

"The abbot is not dead."

"What happened?"

Ciarán scooted a wooden stool to the side of Colum's cot and sat. "The king of Mide's army arrived. The men who threatened you and the abbot, unfortunately, escaped in the battle."

Colum brought a hand to his head. "You were right, my friend. 'Twas the Mac Noe. My own grandfather, 'twas."

There was no relief on Ciarán's face.

"They did not kill the abbot, you said?"

Ciarán shook his head. "A volunteer was sought to be an impostor before the men came for him. 'Tis his head that stands at the gate, the substitute."

277

Colum's heart ached. He had hoped the whole monastery had escaped bloodshed. "Do we know who?"

"We do." Tears rimmed Ciarán's eyes. "Donál, 'twas." He made the sign of the cross on his chest.

"Nay!" Colum sat up despite the throbbing. "I sent him. I did not mean for him to do this!"

"Of course you did not." Ciarán wiped his eyes with his thumbs.

"How did my grandfather get in, let alone make his way to the church? How did they know where the abbot would be?"

"Someone has betrayed us," Ciarán said. "We have hiding places, but the men, few in number, found us."

"What are you doing?" Ciarán tried to prevent him from leaving.

Colum was taller and stronger. He pushed past him. Blood meant nothing to the Mac Noe. His muscles tensed and his headache grew with every step he took.

At the gate men were removing Donál's head and placing it in a burial sack. "Be careful!" He grabbed one man's arm, feeling the bones in his arm give way. Then the unmistakable sound of

Donal's head hitting the hard packed ground. A surprised monk had dropped it. A fury ran from Colum's heart, down his arm, and through his wrists and fingers as he was unable to let go. The man let out a scream that startled Colum and made him release his grip. The man's disjointed limb was grotesquely disfigured. Colum tried to apologize, but his words seemed inadequate.

Later, Colum sat on the floor of the abbot's house listening to the man's scathing reprimand.

"Your desire for revenge has cost this servant the use of his arm for some time."

"Those men should never have gotten inside the monastery."

Finnian rubbed his arms in the chilly, fireless cell. "It was not your place to enact any kind of punishment, Colum. And even if it was, this man was not to blame."

"Indeed he was not."

"You will think about this for the rest of the day. No meals. Only contemplation. Seek God's wisdom. He will show you what you have done. When you have been enlightened, return with the terms of your penitence."

"You want me to enact my own punishment?"

"I believe once your anger assuages, you'll understand what you have done. Colum, your guilt will be so vast that only you will know how to abate it. Only you and Jesu."

At a late hour Colum sat at the outdoor baptismal. The moon cast a white shadow across his feet. For hours he had thought only of Donál and grown more and more angry. Not at the abbot for allowing a substitute, for such things had to be done for the protection of the community, but with himself. Colum had sent Donál to the place where he had met his resurrection far earlier than he should have. He alone was to blame no matter how those men had gained entry. Perhaps his punishment should be to turn himself over to his grandfather and live among those who shared his shame, his curse, his temper.

Chapter Twenty-Two

There's nothing so bad that it can't be worse.
—Irish proverb

Keeva's leg had healed but she now walked with an obvious limp. She couldn't move more than a few paces without sitting down to rest. Enya watched her once graceful dancer as she ground dried herbs at the table board. She ran a hand through the girl's sunset-colored hair.

"How are you fairing today, darlin'?"

Keeva smiled her response. "I think I can get out to the garden now."

"Let's not be rushing things."

"But Maither!"

"Finish up here and then I'll help you to sit outside the door, all right?"

Keeva nodded. One so young should not be an invalid. There had been no other attacks, causing Fe to speculate that their family had been targeted. Today he was out with several men searching for evidence of where the attackers had gone.

While Enya and Branna were feeding the children a supper of mutton sausages with onions and carrots Fe returned. He tossed his walking stick to the corner and plopped down in his chair.

"They've gone off to meet the others, those Mac Noes."

Enya set down the platter of food and went to him. "'Tis my clan, as I feared, then?"

"'Tis indeed. We squeezed the information out of that weasel priest over in the church."

Enya groaned and sat on the floor at her husband's side. "I was so afraid of this. My family is cursed with horrible tempers. You should have realized this before marrying me."

"Now, now. I married you, Enya, because you are my love. You are not to blame for this. As bad as they all are, I did not suppose they would harm a wee child. If anyone is to blame, 'tis me for that reason."

She brushed a tear away. He did not understand.

Fe slammed a fist on his knee. "Those cowards. Keeva was in their path that night, and they didn't care. And now they are after our son."

"What?" She sat up to catch his gaze.

"At daybreak we're off to Clonard, but they'll be there already."

She scrambled to collect her traveling bag. Fe tried to stop her. "There is nothing you can do, Enya. 'Tis a vast place, lots of men. I didn't mean to alarm you. They'll not easily snatch him."

She glanced over at the children who ate without disruption. The gracious Branna was skilled at distracting them when necessary. "Are the rest safe here, Fe?"

He tipped his head toward the window. She hurried over and noticed several men outside gathered in groups.

"Most of the men from the clan are staying here for protection," he said. "Will be no snaring of children at play and no invasions of cottages. We were negligent, but no more. If King Brody will not send an army down from the castle, we'll form our own."

"That does reassure me."

He nodded, stroking his beard.

She was as despondent as she'd been the day she pleaded to God for a child. How was she to know then how much having children would break her heart? She couldn't protect them herself, and yet as a mother that was what she so desperately wanted, needed to do. "My fears have followed me from the land of my birth, but I don't know why. I've never known what made my father behave as he does."

Fe took her into his arms. "The lust for power. The primal craving to control and dictate to others. They want to keep our son—who has been foreseen as destined to have great influence over all Éire—far away from the place of high kingship."

"Is he not far from that now?" She was glad she had not been able to convince him to come home after all.

"They do not think so. That fool Malachi believes his cousin will become the leader of our kingdom and grab all the power for himself."

"Brody?"

Fe laughed. "'Tis as obvious as the nose on my face that man's no leader. The clan will vote for a new king to replace him before too long due to Brody's inadequacies."

"If that happens Gormley will become unbearable. Perhaps they will leave."

Fe shrugged.

"But you think our son is safe now?"

284

"I will make sure of it, even if I have to travel to your father."

She gasped. The youngest began to cry. "Take them to their beds, please, Branna."

The servant nodded, gathered them, and herded the wee lambs to the new rear room Fe had recently built to expand their cottage.

"You believe they will kidnap him?" Enya whispered.

He touched her cheek. "I do not believe they can, my love."

"The monastery has soldiers?"

He cupped her chin with his hand. "I do not know. But God has willed our son to be at the monastery and there is nothing mere men can do to change that."

She so desperately wanted to believe him, but she knew a father could have no true understanding of a mother's heart. "May I write him a letter for you to deliver?"

"A brilliant idea."

She gathered writing materials and sat in front of the fire. The children returned and padded over to her. Wee Sheela's glossy hair held the scent of heather, having been rinsed in the basin of spring water Kyna kept full. Enya kissed each one, contemplating how much she'd miss them when she sneaked out to follow Fe. She bid Keeva to linger a moment. "You are getting better each day, my sweet lass."

"I am."

"You listen to Branna, and always do what she says."

"I do, Mamaí." She stuck out her lower lip.

"I am not saying you haven't been obedient. You have. You are a very good daughter."

Keeva's face brightened.

"Continue to heed your nanny's words always."

"Aye, Mamaí."

Enya squeezed her as tightly as she dared, keeping in mind the girl's injury. At least they all were safe here under the wings of the mighty Cenél Conaill.

When they were off to bed she turned again to her writing. This note would precede her arrival. She wanted Colum to know why she had to come. Perhaps if it became necessary her son could explain this to his father. She knew Fe would not like her coming after him, but he had never been truly angry for all her disobedience. He would forgive her even if he couldn't under-

stand her reasoning. Having her thoughts recorded could only help them all.

My dear son,

I understand now just how important the
schools are to you. God has given you a desire to
learn so that you may in turn teach others about
Jesu. What I wish you to understand about me is
that I come from a long line of men who thirst for
revenge and power and unleash their fiery tempers against even their own offspring. My father
showed me no kindness, no mercy, when I was
under his roof. The monastery was my only escape, as it is now yours even more so. I am
grateful God has given you such a gentle loving
father, even though you are rarely in his company. 'Tis his blood that runs in your veins, and I
pray to God every day that nothing of my clan
lives in you.

You may see me from time to time, perhaps
only from a distance. A mother must see with her
own eyes that her grown child is doing well. I
vow not to disturb your studies. You must not feel
obligated to show me any hospitality at all. I only
seek a glimpse. When you are ready and all
threats from warring clans are abolished, you will
come home to visit, and we will welcome you

with all that we have to offer. For now, study diligently. Give no thought to us while you are focusing on learning. That is how I wish it to be.

Remain vigilant. Let no one, especially the Mac Noes, distract you in any way.

Your loving mother Enya.

When she was satisfied and the ink had dried, she rolled her message, tied it with a leather thong, and placed it with fresh clothing for Fe to pack. She would wait half a day before following her husband, and as soon as she'd seen Colum was safe, she'd hurry back ahead of the party of men. It was a risky plan, but she truly felt she had no other choice. God would watch over her and her children while she was away from them.

The next afternoon she told her servants as little as possible, hugged her children, and set off toward the hoof prints left in the sodden ground to the east.

A few hours later, the sound of a chariot on the road behind her made her stop. Deciding it would be best to venture off a bit into the woods until it passed, she steered her mount past a wee stand of oaks to wait. That was when she realized her mistake.

Chapter Twenty-Three

Do not hold against us the sins of past generations;
may your mercy come quickly to meet us, for we are
in desperate need.
—*Psalm 79:8 NIV*

Finnian would not be convinced. "This is too hasty. I have known you to be devout, always seeking God's voice." The abbot slid his fingers past his tonsure and down the length of his graying hair. "Perhaps the absence of Michael has brought this about."

Colum clinched his fists under his robe as he spoke. "I am sure of this, Father Abbot."

Finnian shook his head. "I believe you believe so. But your assurance is ill placed. God would never have you leave Clonard and join your mother's murderous clan." He was still thinking of Donál. "Your willingness to sacrifice yourself could be viewed by some as commendable, perhaps, but this could not be God's will."

Colum sighed, not knowing if he was expected to respond. The abbot's judgments were meant to be final.

A voice called out from beyond the abbot's door. "I have urgent news, Father Abbot."

Finnian invited the messenger in. When the young man saw Colum sitting on the floor, he stammered. "I … didn't know. I am not sure if … you may wish to hear this news alone."

"Tell me quickly," Finnian ordered.

"It concerns Columcille's mother."

Colum got to his feet, bending low to keep his head from hitting the roof. He had grown and now stood taller than most anyone else in the monastery, and apparently he was now too large for these dwellings. Annoyed at the awkwardness of trying to lift himself upright, he spat out, "I must hear it!"

The messenger stepped backward toward the door.

"Go on," Finnian said.

The fellow gripped his hands together as he spoke. "Well, it seems Brother Columcille's father was traveling to Clonard. Unbeknownst to him"—he nodded toward Colum—"your mother

291

followed. I am sorry to say the Mac Noe have taken her away."

Colum barreled past the monk like a bull escaping its pen. But there was no one outside. He marched back in. "Where are they?"

The monk's expression resembled a startled woodland deer. "Who?"

Colum stood nearly touching his chin to the fellow's forehead. "My father, who else?"

"Well, I mean, I am only carrying a message that was passed on from the guards at the gate."

Colum rushed out again, the sounds of the abbot calling for him to be sensible falling in his wake. He would have kept running until he found his father's party, who undoubtedly were searching for Enya and her kidnappers. He would have exchanged his life for hers without compulsion. He would have—if he hadn't stumbled and fallen hard on the monastery path, holding his knee in agony as bolts of pain shot through his right leg.

Ciarán caught up to him there. "I knew these courageous outbursts would come to no good end."

Colum groaned. "Help me up."

Ciarán wrapped one of Colum's arms around his neck and boosted him up by pressing his shoulder firmly against Colum's chest.

"Let's go after them!" Colum said, wincing.

"We're going to the infirmary."

Colum motioned to the monk messenger who was still staring dumbfounded. "Let him take me. You go."

"Me?"

"Of course, man. You are a Mac Noe."

"But I've told you, I hold no influence."

"You know them. You know the place. Please, Ciarán, go in my stead. See if my father needs assistance."

Colum's friend twisted his lips the way he always did when considering something. As he helped the other monk take hold of Colum, Ciarán kept his voice low. "I will do it. I am always hearing how my low standing makes me an inferior student. This will show the lads." He winked.

Colum waved his hand. "No substituting yourself as our poor brother did for the abbot. Promise me."

"Do not be troubled. I intend to behave as a Roman ambassador." He made the sign of the cross and then rushed off.

"Easy," Colum warned the fellow assisting him. "Don't be carting me off like a sack of hazelnuts."

After he was delivered into the care of the brothers attending the ill, Colum lay on his cot and gazed at the willow branch weaving on the ceiling. If he could not complete this duty to his clan, at least his good friend would take his place. All he could do now was concentrate on the pain in his leg and the hollowness in his spirit that came from not knowing if his mother was strong enough against to stand up to her aggressors. In many ways, she was a stranger to him.

Father Malachi was the last person Enya expected to see on the road. She should have been more cautious. He'd snuck up on her from behind while she had been focused on what lay ahead of her. As she sat tied up in the back of his chariot, she imagined the tongue-thrashing Fe

was going to give her. The old man who had cap-
tured her wanted nothing more than to ensure
the position of his relative. When he learned that
Enya's son had no intention of challenging Brody
for kingship, he'd let her go. Most likely he'd deliver her to her husband, and such a spectacle
would be humiliating to Fe.

Early in their marriage she had feared her impulsive notions would drive her husband to
anger. She no longer worried about the rising of
an irate spirit because she knew none existed in
Fe. Now it grieved her to realize how much she
would be disappointing him. She kicked the back
of the rig, miffed at getting herself into this trouble.

Suddenly the rig halted. Sitting as she was,
facing backward, she could not see what had
stopped them. Twisting in an effort to look to the
front caused the ropes to rub painfully on her
wrists, so instead she shouted. "Only a few hours
to your church, Father. Why stop now? If you
must lug me there, let's get on with it."

"Oh, we'll be getting on with it, daughter."

The shock of hearing the voice from her past
that she could never forget made her gut tighten.
A swooning feeling filled her head.

He moved around the chariot to face her. Same tall frame and hard face. His hair had turned white since she'd last seen him but it was his demeanor more than his looks that proved he was her father. She struggled to appear more composed than she felt. "Oran Mac Noe, what right have you to detain me?"

"Right?" He lifted his chin and cackled. "You are merely a game piece, child." He pressed his fingers to his thumb as he spoke. "A tool to bring us all what we want. Have you forgotten the prophecy?"

She grunted as her struggling against the restraints did nothing to free herself. "They misunderstand my son. He will not rule man. He will shine the light on the path to their salvation."

Oran leaned against the rig and pressed his face into her hair. "'Tis not your son's prophecy that I refer to, daughter. 'Tis yours."

Ignoring the chill running down her back, she spat out her reply. "You did not value me as a good luck talisman when you sent me away to be married."

He backed away from her and gazed up toward the sky. "You see those magpies up there?"

She glanced toward a flock gathering in the tree branches.

He kept his head close to hers as he spoke. "Matters not where they go during the day, nor in what numbers. What is important to them is that they return. At dusk, you know, they all come back." He put his hand under her chin and forced her to look at him. "And I knew it would be so with you. You'd return. Either of your own free will because your husband had tired of you or we'd be bringing you back." He sighed as though bored with the conversation. "I care not what you do or where you go when we're done with you. Perhaps your husband will take you back." He huffed. "But likely not. Not after the lads at home take a turn with you."

How could a father say such a thing to his own daughter? Her hands grew icy. She reminded herself that he used the power of intimidation, and she must not let him be victorious any longer. "My husband will wage war for my return."

Oran lifted his spear and pumped it in the air. "Let him." The whiteness of his knuckles gripping the weapon. The redness flushing his face. The baring of his gritted teeth. He was as venomous as ever. Fe must stay away because her father would kill him.

"'Tis futile," she said, looking away. "You want me in exchange for my son, no matter what you say. But he won't come. You do not understand. He is married to the church."

Oran returned to his horse and mounted easily as though he were a much younger man. "What is logical bears no consequence." He huffed. "You were never a worthwhile daughter to me, always running off here and there."

She had been clever. Wise enough to avoid him. And in his anger over being outsmarted, he'd let her go.

The sound of hoof beats resounded down the road. "My men." Oran turned his horse to face the sound. "They have already been to the monastery where your son resides."

Malachi had left the reins to tighten her restraints as though she were a sheep ready for market. He kept his gaze from meeting hers.

"You did this!" she sneered, wishing she could get her hands around his measly neck. "You sent trouble to my son. Why? You said you were some kind of spiritual father to me. Your father was my son's foster father. Have you no loyalty? No dignity?"

When he finally lifted his head to look at her, an object sprung free from his clothing and dangled into the air in front of her. Round metal with spikes protruding on one side. She recognized it from the time Gormley had tried to school Enya in her pagan ways. This was an amulet worn only by the one who ordered human sacrifices. All others had to bend to this one's will. She stared at him in disbelief, remembering what his father had told her, that his son had not embraced the Christian way. He was a priest now. She had thought … But nay. The amulet meant Malachi was a druid, and also the *cúiseoir*, the Accuser.

He grasped the amulet with one hand, stuffed it back beneath the neck of his tunic, and returned to his place at the front of the chariot. But they didn't move. They waited for the approaching horsemen.

A cloud of dust flew into her face as the men halted their mounts in front of Oran's horse. Her father's voice bellowed. "Has the sacrifice been made?"

An acid taste formed on her tongue. How had the God she vowed to trust allowed this to happen? She turned her head and spit the dirt from her mouth, but the appalling dread remained.

"Aye, a young monk," one man said.

"No!" Sobs rose from the depths of her soul.

Oran shouted. "Not your son, woman. Contain yourself!"

She gasped and watched as he turned toward the man who had spoken. "It was ordered to be the abbot," Oran said. "What is this about?"

A slow, widening grin spread across the man's face. "We thought it better to take one whom young Columcille was fond of. He takes personal responsibility for this one's fate and is overwhelmed by guilt."

"I see," Oran said. "I hope you are correct. If not, you will take personal responsibility." He drew out a long knife and placed it under the man's chin. With the jerk of his chin he indicated toward Malachi. Enya could not see what Malachi was doing. "He will decide," her father said, "as is fitting the druid."

The man trembled.

Enya looked away. She'd seen her father kill a man before, and she did not wish to see it again.

The chariot lurched, taking her away to be the captive of an insane man who thought she could bring him favor by being a fifth daughter of a fifth daughter, which she could never do.

On the way back they were delayed by a destroyed bridge. This angered her father so much he beat some of his servants with a hazel rod. When he was finally able to convince the others to build something they could cross, it took two more days. She was given only gruel and sips of water and her weakness eliminated any thoughts of escaping.

When they reached the place of her birth, she had no time to consider whether anything had changed or if any of the monks who had taught her to read were still there. A melee erupted from near the central fire. People shouted and argued, flinging their arms in the air. As they got closer she saw a young man dressed in the garb of a monk, standing on a wooden box. He appeared to be trying to out shout the crowd. She only saw him as Malachi turned the rig around to park it. Now she faced the opposite direction while all eyes seemed to be focused on the disturbance.

A movement in the shadows of some willows caught her attention. There seemed to be several figures crouched there. One turned toward her. When the person emerged with a finger to his lips, a rush of excitement pounded against her heart. Fe!

A couple of his men crept behind him as others kept watch. She bit her lip as he slid his knife under the ropes and freed her. The noise from the center of the crowd drowned out any sound their footsteps might have made. They rushed through the woods without speaking. If Oran caught them, they'd all be killed.

When they finally reached the spot where the men had hidden their horses, she stopped. How could she get on that horse and ride away? Oran would not cease his pursuit.

"You should hurry," she said to Fe. "He'll kill you if he finds you here."

"He won't find us. Come along."

"I cannot go just yet."

"Do not worry about our distraction. 'Twas a plan we worked out together. That fellow is our son's good friend. They may treat him ill but they won't harm him. He is one of theirs and 'twas their own riches that paid for his schooling at the monastery. They will want him to return. And as you see, he seems to be holding his own."

"I don't know what you are talking about. Fe, listen to me. I cannot go because the Mac Noe have the cúiseoir."

He touched her face. "I do not know what you are worried about, my love. Your people, their ancient superstitions, none of it is of consequence. You should not have followed me and caused all this trouble, but since you are here, let us go on and see our son."

"Fe, the cúiseoir. 'Tis Malachi. Gormley told me what the Accuser does. Don't you see? He wants to sacrifice our son to his gods."

"Gormley? Malachi? I pay no heed and you should not either."

"But you should, Fe!" She felt helpless once again as he lifted her up to sit with him on his horse. "Listen to me!"

"You may have your say when we are away from this place."

Her thoughts steamed as they rushed in the direction of the River Boyne. She had learned something vital, and he would not listen. If it came from one of his men, he would have. He thought her hysterical and filled with pagan notions. His steadfast refusal to hear of anything of the pagan people would cause him to neglect crucial information. The Mac Noe believed Malachi had the authority to order a sacrifice and their belief would compel them to comply despite what any Christian might tell them. Even warning the residents of Clonard would do little. What must happen is a change in Malachi's status, and confronting him would be necessary.

She sighed as she stared at the back of Fe's sweat-stained tunic. They were racing away from the druid. They were going toward Colum. *Dear God, let them hear me.*

Chapter Twenty - Four

He who vindicates me is near. Who then will bring
charges against me? Let us face each other!
Who is my Accuser?
—Isaiah 5:8 NIV

His study for the day came from the book of Isaiah, the great prophet of old. Colum could see many parallels. Israel would not turn from their wicked ways. His mother's clan would not either. He prayed diligently that his mother would escape the peril she had been plunged into, either with Ciarán's help or by some other divine intervention.

Once the pain in his knee had lessened, Colum returned to his own cell and to his normal routines. He could not yet walk for long periods of time, but he kept up the practice for as long as he could manage. It had been the only thing that kept him from worrying about what Ciarán was up to.

At Clonard, the day's working and prayers began in darkness. Colum had grown accustomed to the practice since his days at Loch Cuan, but in the midlands, the time before sunrise seemed wrought with holy mystery. Here the shadowy trees seemed to cleave to the breath of God momentarily before releasing it like a flock of sparrows.

Colum tried to force his thoughts back to the scripture he had memorized. *He who vindicates me is near* ... He covered his mouth with his cowl to block the smoke of the blacksmith's forge, and then spotted the messenger monk scurrying toward him, waving his arms. When the monk got close he paused with his hands on his knees, gasping for air.

Colum shook his head. "You really must learn to do this job with more efficiency. How in the name of heaven can you expect to communicate with this level of exertion? Now, speak, lad."

The monk lifted his head but remained bent over as though he'd just raced a horse and won. "Your mother has escaped. She and your father are approaching Clonard. They should be here within the hour."

Colum patted the monk on the back, perhaps a wee bit too roughly, for he'd pushed him off his stance. The lad regained his balance and held up a hand. "Please, do not touch me."

Colum chuckled. "Aye, I won't again. Do forgive me."

The messenger nodded. "There is more. Not all is excellent."

When is it ever? "Go on."

"The Mac Noe, they have … that is to say, they believe they have the … uh …"

Colum coughed and turned away. Not because the smoke from the blacksmith's fire irritated him, but because the messenger had. Colum feared the lad's hesitation was stirring up his anger. Why couldn't he just say what he meant?

"We have an army," Colum said, moving slowly down the path. "There is nothing to fear from the Mac Noe." Although they had already murdered an innocent monk, Colum would not give in to fear. "Do you have news of Ciarán?"

The lad hurried to keep up with Colum's long strides. "I do. This is the best news. Would you like to hear it alongside the abbot? He is in the church."

They weren't far away. "Let's go, then."

When they entered, Father Finnian gazed up from his place behind the altar where he had been blessing the communion bread for the morning's worship. The night's dampness still spread itself on floorboards and benches. The messenger's enthusiasm seemed to provide the warmth the place needed.

The messenger regained his vigor. "Father Abbot! I have news about our brother Ciarán."

The abbot nodded, raised his right hand over the bread, crossed himself, and then moved toward them. The three of them proceeded silently down the center of the building and exited the door. Then Finnian turned to the lad. "Wait."

They turned toward an open field. The sun was about to make an appearance. This miracle of God's handiwork was an opportunity for worship. The monks never missed it and many gathered nearby to watch.

A white line of fog hugged the grass. The low chant of the monks added a fitting prelude to the eminent rising of the sun. In the distance, the fog curtain lifted, exposing a dolmen, a reminder that men and women had realized the sacredness of the site for many generations. As he listened to the mixing of the monks' voices, and added his own, Colum felt lifted from care. Certainly, the news that his parents had escaped safely and that his friend had done well helped to send his spirit soaring.

The distant horizon began to pink. A chilling breeze teased the hem of his cloak. The smell of charred wood was now only faintly detectable. The approaching sunrise diluted anything un-pleasant. A few moments later the fog appeared lighter, lace-like.

And then it began. In the eastern orange sky, a round glowing light rose from a bed of black trees. Streams of sunbeams streaked out like stretching arms after a long sleep. The clouds be-hind the sun gleamed like polished brass. The sun-touched vegetation began to reveal its true colors. Larger and larger the sun grew, warming Colum's face. The hand of God seemed quite near.

Finnian turned to the lad. "Tell me quickly. No time for a long story."

The messenger's face revealed disappoint-ment. He swallowed hard, seemingly contemplating how to condense his missive. "Brother Ciarán appealed to the king, who in

309

turn consulted a neighboring ruler, and they agreed that Clonard's God should not be angered by the capture of Colum's parents. And they let them go. Our brother negotiated quite nicely, it seems."

"Excellent." The abbot tapped his crozier and they moved back to the church.

Colum raised his hands as they walked. *Praise be to God for his great mercy.*

Immediately after the taking of the sacrament, the messenger departed the church. The sounds of voices outside the building raised a dilemma for Colum. Stay, do what God and the abbot expected of him. Or, go to his parents. Colum did not move and instead thought about all that had happened. He'd had no vision. Had God chosen not to reveal things to him as he had done in the past? Was the disobedience of straying thoughts the reason?

He stayed behind after the brothers left the church. He had chores to complete, but he felt compelled to remain. He prayed fervently, asking God to forgive him. With his head bent and his eyes closed, he once again began to feel the presence of God.

He felt pulled into a whirlwind. White lights swirled around him. Then suddenly from the bottom of the whirlwind, a face emerged. He recognized it as Malachi, the troublesome son of Colum's foster father. The face blurred and in its place appeared a symbol of some type. It was round, but only smooth on one side. Sharp spikes lined the other half. Then the whole caught fire and burned red, then yellow, then blue—the hottest fire he could imagine.

Someone touched him on the shoulder, shattering his vision. He was still trying to decipher it when he looked into the face of his earthly father. They embraced.

"Where is Maither?"

"She is well. Trying to convince the abbot that this business is not yet finished."

Colum stood. He had grown several inches taller than his father. "'Tis not finished?"

Fe laughed. "Let's go, lad. They are preparing a meal for us. 'Tis finished, all right. You know how your mother gets these foolish ideas into her head."

He did not know. "Have you seen my friend Ciarán?"

311

Fe scratched his red beard. "Is that the fellow they are talking about? The one who avoided a war by using mere words?" He laughed again. "Let us go to the table now. There is plenty of craic to be had about these adventures."

Colum's mother kissed him, quickly embraced him and then pulled back to stroke his cheek. After a moment she returned to her chair beside Finnian. Colum heard about how Malachi had surprised Enya, restrained her in his chariot, and drove her back to the place of her people only to discover Ciarán was already there proclaiming the misdeed that had been committed.

"You should have seen him," one Fe's men said. "Standing on a box, so eloquent he was. Had them eating out of his hand like pigeons."

Another man chimed in. "Before they knew it we stole Fe's woman away and arrived back here."

Colum noted his mother cringing. She wasn't enjoying this retelling.

The man continued. "Word came that Brother Ciarán had been granted land for his troubles. He is one of them, don't ye know. He's to build a monastery on the River Shannon."

The abbot looked as surprised as Colum felt. His young friend was not a priest or a bishop. Perhaps he would give this land to Finnian.

"I am happy you are safe, Maither. He nodded to Fe and then to all the men seated near him. "I rejoice in the safe return of you all."

His mother slammed her plate on the table and stood. "'Tis not over, you fools. The Mac Noe have the Accuser, and he has set my son as his next victim."

The Father Abbot tugged on Enya's sleeve until she reluctantly sat down. He cleared his throat. "I think not, my good woman. This is a pagan practice that we will not submit to."

"But you do not under—"

Colum's father reached across the table and grabbed Enya's wrist. "Say no more."

Enya's face turned pink and then scarlet. As soon as Fe released her she defied him by standing up again. "Who among you knows the mark of the Accuser?"

No one spoke. Colum was embarrassed for his mother. She must not understand that Christians do not follow such superstitions. She reached for a vat of gravy and a knife. Dipping some out on the tabletop, she drew with it as though it were ink. A round circle. Then with quick flicks of the soupy liquid she made three more marks on one side. She drawn the shape he'd seen in his vision right after he'd seen Malachi's face.

Chapter Twenty-Five

Why, what could she have done, being what she is?

Was there another Troy for her to burn?

—*W. B. Yeats, No Second Troy*

Enya was desperate for someone to listen to her. They thought she was suggesting they follow the pagan beliefs, and since they had that notion already she was unable to convince them otherwise. Drawing on the table with the food the abbot had so graciously provided was, of course, ungrateful and disrespectful. She saw the horror on her husband's face. But what else could she do to shock them into seeing what she truly meant?

By the grace of God her son broke through the chaos she had created.

"I have seen it!" he bellowed.

Because of his size and his exploding voice, he demanded attention. Mugs plunked down on the table. Knives dropped. The whole party stared at

Colum. He seemed surprised by this, as though he had no idea his words would silence the room.

The abbot stamped his crozier on the floor. Colum sat back down. Was her son being silenced simply because he confessed to knowing what the symbol of the Accuser looked like?

"This will not do." She went to Colum and urged him to stand up. He was reluctant but finally complied. "My son and I will return momentarily," she announced before directing him outside.

As soon as the door to the refectory closed behind them, Colum raised both arms in the air in surrender. "Maither, do you not understand that here I am not your son? I am a brother, and under the authority of the abbot. You may have just gotten me expelled from Clonard."

Worry washed over Colum's handsome face.

"If they'd banish you for supporting your mother, then so be it." She was weary of all those men, even Fe.

"You don't mean that. After all you've sacrificed to have me here, I would have supposed you'd do all you could to keep that from happening."

She gripped his large hand. "I will, son. I promise you. But first, tell me that you understand that the Accuser is a grim threat to you, and to all in this place. Help me convince the abbot, and your father, that the Accuser must be commanded to face you, within the presence of an army, of course, for your safety. 'Tis the only way to dismiss this pagan practice."

He tilted his head to one side.

"You do not understand me, do you?"

"I don't."

"But you recognized the symbol. When I made that mess on the table, you said you had seen it."

"I had a vision, Maither. Not long before you arrived, God showed me the face of Malachi, and then that peculiar amulet. But I don't know what it means. I did not yet have the opportunity to allow the abbot to interpret."

"The abbot?" She slammed a fist atop a stack of water buckets leaning against the refectory wall. "You don't need him for this."

Colum's startled look surprised her. Was he, a strong, tall lad, afraid of her? "Listen, son. Surely God sent you that vision so you would know what I'm saying. Malachi is the Accuser. In the pagan

317

ways, he is the one to choose the next sacrifice. Your foster father, the abbots, all your teachers? Have they not told you what those in darkness do?"

"I know, Maither." He stared at the ground.

"I do not tell you this to bring grief, although we must know the darkness in order to confront it."

"I agree." He looked up at her.

Enya took a deep breath. "The Mac Noe believe they must obey him or risk angering the gods."

"Ridiculous." He rubbed his thick hand over his chin. "There is only one God, and he does not require murder."

"We know that. They do not. Of course, your understanding is why you are becoming a great Christian leader. You will show them." As though a thick fog had lifted from her mind, she believed what she'd said. Her son was God's servant, an influence akin to the great saint of old, Patrick.

He sat on the ground and leaned against the wall. "Such things are not easy, Maither. I am still a student. There is an order to be followed. A necessary discipline. I cannot go about doing things just because I believe them to be right. When one trusts only one's own judgment—without the consultation of what we call a soul friend—trouble results. Aye, I know God showed me the mark of the Accuser. Let me ponder this under the guidance of the abbot."

Fury lit her head like a torch. "There is no time for pondering."

"There is always time to do right. Haste results in error, sometimes grave error. I know. My haste likely caused the death of one of the brothers. I will not repeat my blunder."

"But Colum, they won't listen to me in there. They think me a hysterical woman. You can convince them. You know I'm right."

"I will tell the abbot everything, but please allow me to do this in the proper order."

The door squeaked open. Father Finnian emerged, motioned to Colum, and the two of them wandered down the path away from her.

Shortly after, Fe came out. "Enya, we are guests here. What were you thinking?"

Her frustration began to subside. At least her son had listened. "I had to, Fe. The abbot would not hear me."

"We should leave. I've told the abbot we would deliver some grain to Ciarán for him, at the place near the River Shannon. We'll go there before we head home. We owe him at least that."

Enya wanted to make sure they understood, but she must trust her son. God had given him a message. And he had shown her that even when humans would not attend to her, God heard. "I miss my babies," she admitted, curling herself into her husband's arms. "Let's be off."

Fe consulted the army protecting Clonard before joining her in their rig. "Our son is in good hands, my sweet."

She acknowledged the presence of watchmen, numerous hounds, locks on doors and gates. If the time to confront the Accuser had to be postponed, at least her son was well guarded.

Now her prime task would be convincing Fe she was not adhering to pagan beliefs. True, there had been a time when she waivered, but Kyna had been a great influence. Enya wished she did not have to convince her husband of this. It was infuriating. Perhaps Kyna would have some advice for this. Perhaps Enya should learn from her son and do things in the proper order.

"Are you angry with me, Fe?"

They rode off through a green pasture before he answered. She allowed him this time. She would not insist he answer. No reply was confirmation. If that was how he felt, she would try to make up to him.

He didn't speak until after they found the Slí Mór, the great road that would take them to the place where Brother Ciarán was to set up his center of learning.

Fe let out a long, slow breath, and leaned against her shoulder. "I cannot stay miffed at you for long, my Enya. You know that?" He smiled and patted her leg.

"Fe, please believe me. I am not following the old ways. I just … I know what the old ways are and because of that, I feel I must—"

He put a finger to her lips. "No need, Enya. You have allowed our son to handle things. I am proud of that."

Proud? She snuggled as close as she could without interfering with his driving. "We won't linger at this place they call the Meadow of the Sons of Noes, will we?"

"Not at all, but you mustn't worry. The Mac Noe are nowhere near there."

321

"I wasn't thinking so, or the abbot would not have sent us there. I just must see my babies soon."

"I promise no longer than necessary."

A few days later, as they approached the wide expanse of the blue river called Shannon, they spotted smoke on the horizon.

"I fear we may be too late," Fe said.

"How could we be? He was granted this land by the king of this territory. There should be no dispute."

"What should be is often not what is."

"We should not accept this without investigation." She thought about Colum's misery over the killing of one of the brothers. "We must do what we can if young Ciarán is in trouble."

He nodded. She probably did not need to say that. Her husband was kind and compassionate. She bit her lip, remembering to be as observant of his intentions as she wished him to be of hers. *Forgive me.*

But as they neared the flames and smelled the putrid odor of burning flesh, she too feared they might be too late.

Chapter Twenty-Six

*Christ has our host surrounded
With clouds of martyrs bright,
Who wave their palms in triumph
And fire us for the fight.*
—*From the hymn "Christ Is the World's Redeem-
er," words attributed to St. Columba;
translator: Duncan MacGregor (1897)*

When Colum finished describing his vision to the Father Abbot, he bent his head toward his knees and settled in for a long wait. The abbot would reflect on what he said, pray about it, and perhaps leave to consult another brother. Even so, Colum's confessor had to be thinking back to when Enya drew the shape on the table with the gravy.

After a few moments Finnian excused himself, as Colum thought he would. If there indeed was danger coming, as Colum's mother believed, the brothers might not be afforded the luxury of time.

He moved toward the front of the church where he and the abbot had met so that Colum could explain himself. He was alone, save for God, so he spoke aloud. "Why do you torment me, Lord, with these visions? I have no power to act on them."

"Why assume that the need to act is yours?"

Colum turned toward the voice. "Michael! I did not think to see you here again." He started to move toward his friend and mentor when Michael held up a hand to stop him.

"You do not see me here in the flesh," he said.

"Of course I do. You would not have me to believe this is another vision. I do not feel as though my thoughts have been carried to another realm." Even as he said this, he sensed something out of place. Michael stood before him as he had many times before, but a tingling in the air, like the foreboding of rain, seemed to whirl through the building.

"Not a vision," Michael said. "I am coming to you as though on a cloud. Do not doubt it, though you cannot conceive how it is possible. I am God's messenger to you and you must take heed. Tell me you are listening."

Colum sat on a bench, keeping his eyes on Michael. "I am."

"Good. Our Father God wants you to know that the vision you received about the amulet was meant to warn the abbot that trouble is coming. Not just from Malachi, but from other forces. He must prepare for your sake. The trouble will not come to Clonard but rather to the next place on your journey. God will tell Finnian this as well, but when you advise him you have already been told, he will understand."

"I don't understand," Colum admitted.

"That is not necessary. What is required is faithfulness."

A mist formed, something Colum had never before seen inside a building. When it cleared, Michael was gone. Or the idea of Michael. He wasn't really there, but the message had been delivered nonetheless.

Colum leaned his head down between his knees and locked his hands together behind his neck. He could not imagine what all this meant. His fervent prayers were not being answered. All he could do was wait for Finnian to return.

After he had recited half of the hundred Psalms he had memorized, the abbot returned. "Follow me to my cell," he ordered.

A brisk gale pushed them along, sending a shower to dampen Colum's mood. As they scurried along the path, Colum began to wonder if the abbot was going to dismiss him from the community. It made sense. If he left, Malachi would follow, thus saving the others from harm. He made up his mind to volunteer to go. Finnian would not be able to stop him if he was no longer under his supervision. God must have other plans for Colum, something other than the prophecy his mother believed in.

Once they were snug indoors, the abbot would not allow Colum to speak, though he tried to interrupt many times.

"God has spoken clearly to me, lad. I have no doubt. There is a threat."

Colum used the power of his voice this time to interject because Michael had told him to. "And the threat is not from Malachi and not to Clonard."

The abbot's countenance paled. "I was just about to say those words exactly."

"You were. And while we must deal promptly with the one they call the Accuser, there is something else that must happen."

327

"Indeed. I will ordain you a priest and then send you off to the monastery of Mobhi Clarainech."

Colum blinked and slapped a hand over his mouth. Surely he must leave, but this was not what he expected. He mumbled. "Michael said nothing about …"

He could not complete his thought. Horns blasted and the monastery bells sent alarm through the entire settlement. They rushed outside and were halted by a group of brothers. "The one the people call the Accuser has arrived, and not in peace, Father Abbot."

Colum wanted to tell them all to forget it. There was no need for all of this. But before he could say anything he and the abbot were escorted to the refectory where soldiers with spears stood guarding the doors. Colum was stunned to discover they were not being shielded from Malachi, but rather they'd been brought in to face him. Where were the soldiers ordered to protect them?

The stubby man sat in the place normally reserved for the abbot. He wore crimson robes, no hat, and licked his fat fingers as he leaned over a plate of partridge bones nearly picked clean. The amulet Colum had seen in his vision hung from a cord around Malachi's wrinkled neck and rested on his chest.

The abbot pounded his crozier on the floor. "What is the meaning of this?"

Malachi stuck his fingers into a wee bowl of water, dried them on a towel, and then met the abbot's stare. "I am a man much like you, Finnian. A man of the church, a follower of Patrick's. And as such I must commend you and your brothers for such fine hospitality." He chuckled. "Even if I did have to coerce your students a bit."

Colum noted the brothers who worked as cooks standing against the wall, clearly shaken from their encounter with Malachi. How much time had gone by between his arrival and the ringing of the bells? Malachi had snuck in while Colum and Finnian contemplated the matter. They should have listened to his mother after all.

Colum stepped forward, ignoring the admonishment from Finnian. "Anyone who would kidnap a lone woman cannot call himself a follower of Patrick's God."

Malachi stood. "Who is this who addresses me? The child, the foundling who was raised by

329

the church out of mercy for his pitiable circum-
stances?"

Colum dug his fingers into his palm. The man
was doing it again, trying to raise his ire, stoking
his anger as he'd done ever since Colum was a
lad. He reminded himself that in God's eyes no
status can prove a man worthier than another.

The abbot spoke finally. "You will leave Clonard immediately. We will show no further
hospitality to you. Be on your way."

Malachi did not move but his companions,
rough-looking fellows with yellow teeth and unkempt beards, raised their spears. The men
protecting the monastery finally showed up and
matched their stance, each side waiting for their
leader to allow them to strike.

Malachi sighed and tossed his napkin on the
table. "I am finished here. But hear me, Finnian.
I cannot leave without Colum. Send him with
me, back to his people, and we will all depart
from your most pleasant and well-appointed
monastery."

"I will go," Colum said to the abbot.

Malachi nodded and pushed himself away
from the table board.

The abbot thumped his crozier. "It shall not be."

Malachi shrugged his shoulders. "He said he would go."

"He won't." Finnian pointed his crozier toward Malachi. The soldiers supporting him aimed their spears at the throats of the others.

"You leave me no choice," Malachi said, fingering his amulet. A red cloud bloomed on his face. He bellowed as though he had authority, which of course Colum knew he did not. "Therefore, as the one the pagans call the Accuser, I order Colum as the next sacrifice."

The soldiers and the burly men began to scuffle. Colum slipped out the door. His intention was to escape Finnian. If God willed him to live to teach many, as the prophecy seemed to say, then Malachi could not kill him even if he did go. No one can alter God's plan. His mother might think she could, but Colum recalled the words of the Psalmist: only the Lord God ordered his steps.

Steps away from the scuffle, someone called to him. "Order your steps over here." Michael's voice again.

331

The sound seemed to come from somewhere in front of him. He crept forward until he detected a parting in the ivy covering a stone wall. As he entered he realized he was inside one of the hidden shelters the underground tunnels emptied into, a system of escape that had been built into the monastery. He'd only seen them once before and that had been when he'd first arrived and Ciarán showed him around.

"This way," the voice beckoned.

Turning first right and then left around the walls, he came upon an opening. He descended the damp steps believing he was being led outside. All he needed to do then was make his way to the stables or wherever Malachi and his men had left their horses. He wasn't sure what he'd do after that. Perhaps visit these distant relatives and gain their trust. Convert them and bring peace. Once he explained that Christ was the only sacrifice needed, somehow this Malachi situation would be resolved. Clonard certainly did not need to become entangled in it.

Colum rubbed his hand along the subterranean wall as he walked, bidding the place a farewell that felt both necessary and risky. No, more than risky. Leaving here felt wrong. But he knew no other way. God would show him the way out, and he chided himself for giving in momentarily to fear. *The Lord will order my steps.*

The passageway continued to lead downward. How far would he have to go to get beyond the monastery's rampart?

The Lord will order my steps.

A faint light at the end of the corridor encouraged him to make haste, despite the welling dread in his stomach. He rushed forward. Best to get on with it. The passageway led to a room. At the far end several people huddled.

"Thank the Good Lord!" Finnian reached both arms toward him.

Colum leaned against one wall. The dampness seeped through the back of his tunic. "How am I to help if we're all hiding underground?"

Michael's voice spoke again, but Colum realized it was only within his head. "Where is your accuser? Has he left as well?"

The abbot stared at him, obviously with no intention of answering Colum's question so he voiced the one he'd heard Michael ask. "Where has Malachi gone?"

Finnian waved his arms above his head. "Gone? I don't know, lad. We are leaving these affairs to soldiers."

As if he'd been beckoned, the messenger monk descended a stairwell opposite the one Colum had come down. He bowed respectfully toward the abbot. Tenting his fingers, he inhaled, let out a breath, and then spoke. "The interlopers have been taken to the king's tower. We have been assured that it is safe to return to our cells."

There was a collective exhale.

Finnian turned to Colum. "There is no accuser who casts any blame that is beyond the safety of our savior's arms."

The next day Colum was ordered to prepare to remove to Glas Naoidhen, the monastery founded by Mobhi Clarainech. Obviously, Colum's plans the day before had been his own, and not God's. After what he'd told his mother about proper discernment, he should have known better. Colum dug his fingers deep into the folds of his cloak and found the wee rope cross his mother had given him long ago. He always kept it in a pocket and thought of her now as he rubbed it with his thumb. He must face his accuser before he left.

A king's guard directed Colum to the tower, where a humpbacked man led him to Malachi's chamber. The imprisoned man who had thought he was an influential druid sat staring up at a small window high on the wall.

Colum shouted to avoid misunderstanding. "I have come so that you can accuse me. You have wanted to all my life. Let me hear what you have against me."

Malachi turned slowly. With one hand he gripped the peculiar ornament around his neck and with the other he braced himself against the floor. "You have been chosen to drive out darkness. And the darkness will not easily depart."

Without warning Malachi yanked the metal piece from his neck and flung it toward Colum. The spiked side pierced Colum's skin at the top of his shoulder, just missing his neck. Searing pain knocked him off his feet as he gasped for air. Blood spurted down the front of his cloak. Willing himself to stay conscious, he saw Malachi's pleased expression moments before he collapsed against the guards, who carried him out of the tower.

Chapter Twenty - Seven

Play on, invisible harps, unto Love,
Whose way in heaven is aglow
—James Joyce, "At That Hour"

Enya counted three floating biers. The funeral fires were burning high, the reason for the stench they'd detected on their way toward the river. Fe stopped the rig when a couple passing in the opposite direction approached. "What goes on here?" he called out.

"A terrible plague," the man answered.

"Do you know," Fe asked, "if a young monk called Ciarán has arrived?"

The man looked at the woman with him, then back at Fe. "No monks around here at all. Fishermen, we are."

Enya wanted to tell him that would soon change due to the decision of their king, but the fisher folk here would discover that soon enough.

The woman held up a finger. "Ciarán, you say? That was the name?"

337

"'Twas," Fe acknowledged.

"A monk you, say?"

Fe dismounted and approached the couple. "You have heard of him?"

The man snapped his fingers. "Now that you mention it ..." He turned to his wife. "That the fellow who's meant to build on the riverbank?"

The woman nodded.

The man bobbed his head. "That fellow was diverted to a place called Glas Naoidhen, both sides of a river, I heard. Never been there myself." He cocked his head to one side. "Sent there, they say, seeing as we've had no much sickness. A riddle, though. Wouldn't you think a man of God, that being Patrick's God, would come here in the time of our need?"

The man looked so miserable that Fe leaned out to hug him and offer a blessing. That was her Fe. He rejoined Enya and promised to inquire. "Our condolences for all your trouble here."

She spoke once they had turned away from the settlement. "Fe, how will we fulfill the abbot's request?"

"Don't see how we can now. Don't know where that place is, both sides of some river."

"We are released then."

"Seems so." They fell silent as they rode past a forest of newly dug graves. They'd seen nothing like this around Clonard.

"We must escape this pestilence, Enya. Our young ones need us." He dropped one rein and used his free hand to wipe his brow. "God forbid the plague has gone north."

Her arms ached to hold the children. They'd been away too long. Tugging her shawl over her chilly shoulders, she watched a cluster of mourners, felt sorrow emanating from their hooded black figures. She felt guilty for being glad she wasn't one of them. A sense of dread descended like a sudden downpour, causing her to wonder if something had happened, or was about to.

The sounds of wailing came from the crest of a wee hill. A row of people snaked down toward the burial ground. Enya smacked a hand over her mouth when she saw the casket they carried. It was small, so very tiny.

"Aye, Fe, let us hurry home. You are most correct."

CINDY THOMSON

After a few nights of sleeping under their rig, they found a home to take them in on what they estimated to be the night before their last day of travel. Fe rewarded the family for their hospitality by giving them the bags of grain the abbot had intended for Ciarán.

"I will repay Finnian from our own stores. For now, these folks need it. Besides we won't have to lug it any farther now."

The woman served them a lovely creamed clam stew and razorbill eggs she roasted in the coals of her fire. The people of the cliffs ate a diet different from what she was used to, but quite delicious. Sadly, it reminded her of her mother's demise, although they'd gathered a different type of egg. Enya ate as much as she could to be polite, but unease flustered her stomach. When everyone, including Fe, had drifted off to sleep, Enya rose from their blankets near the hearth and went outside to watch the moon.

Who is it, Lord? Who among my children is in danger?

She searched her mind for the scripture Colum was so fond of. He'd scrawled the verse across the bottom of many of his letters to her over the years. Something about the Lord deciding the path of a good man. Even if he stumbles, the Lord is there to hold him up. Not those words exactly, but close. She thought of the old saying she'd heard most of her life: If life leads you down a stony path, 'tis best you wear sturdy shoes. Which was right? Depend on God or take care yourself? This was the question she constantly debated.

A cloud partially shadowed the nearly full moon. A wolf cried in the distance. She wished she could find answers out in the wild landscape, like Gormley had always claimed to do. But she couldn't. The only help and comfort she'd ever been able to experience had come from within herself. If God dwelled in her, as the old priest claimed God did for all believers, then was this compulsion to take action so wrong? Still, who was deciding her path? She wanted it to be God but was afraid to chance that alone.

She lowered her head to pray, to plead, to cry out silently so as not to wake the household. *Shelter my children from all harm, God. Keep peace within them and peril without.*

She stood and turned toward the house. No church nearby. She longed for the peace she so often felt within the building referred to as God's house. What were these poor cliff dwellers to do without a church?

The moon rose over the top of the house, bright now without the hindrance of clouds. A breeze, surprisingly warm, touched her cheeks. *I am here.*

She knew it was so. Whatever awaited them, she needed God to strengthen her.

The next day Fe said little as they traveled. They were weary, to be sure, but when Enya thought she could bear it no longer, she reminded him that she had agreed that he was right and they needed to come home.

"'Tis not that, Enya." He kept his eyes on the path ahead.

"What then?"

He drew in a long breath and released it with a heavy sigh. "I am concerned. I left our family under superior defense, but something like what we've seen? An illness that comes without warning? What if one of our own is suffering? We must be there."

She swallowed hard. She was not alone in her worry. "We will be soon."

At last the rolling hills of home stretched out before them. They passed familiar pastures and a few of the tenants' houses. Enya drew in an expansive breath. The scent of dew on the grass, cattle dung, peat fires. "The sickness has not come here," she told Fe.

Creases still burrowed across his ruddy brow. He stared straight ahead. She clasped her hand over his. "All will be well, my love. Here anyway. Our Colum—"

He violently shook her hand away. "Put your focus where it belongs, woman. You have children who are not at the age of maturity."

Tears clouded her vision. "I do miss them. Why do you think me such a horrible mother?"

"I do not!" He said it just as forcefully.

"What is happening to us, Fe?" A sob escaped her chest.

He grunted, gave her a half smile. "We do not understand what each of us holds in our hearts."

She wiped her face on her shawl. The gelid morning air stung her cheeks.

Her wounded feelings faded when her children appeared outside their cottage. Fe pulled the rig right up to the door rather than stopping at the barn. Keeva came out first, rosy cheeked and healthy-looking despite her limp. Enya wrapped her arms around the girl's waist while Keeva hugged her neck. "I have missed you, my sweet."

"I have been good, Maither."

"You do not have to tell me. You are goodness itself."

Meredit and Egan latched on to her next. Nothing felt better than holding them.

"Ma!" Wee Sheela wiggled down from Branna's arms and tottered to Enya, chubby arms extended.

Enya scooped her up. "Let's get inside and have tea." She turned around and saw the older children frolicking with their father. Love for children was not confined to a mother, not in this family. Other men might shun affection but not Fe. She was glad of it. None of her children would suffer a father like she'd had.

"Forgive my long complaining?" she whispered to Fe as they crossed the threshold.

He winked at her. Nothing soothed worry more than seeing that your family was well. There was a place in her heart, however, that still felt dark as midnight. *Oh, Colum, be well!*

Chapter Twenty-Eight

However long the day, night must fall.
—Irish proverb

Colum was nauseous while concentrating on the pain from the wound in his neck. He lifted a hand toward it only to have it pushed back to his side.

"Lie still, lad, and let me do my work."

He studied the shape above him, willing his eyes to focus. Finally, he discerned that Brother Bart, the physician at Clonard, was the one leaning over him. "What happened?"

Another voice. Familiar. A friend. "Feisty as ever!"

"Ciarán?"

"'Tis himself!"

His friend moved into Colum's line of vision. Colum lifted his other hand toward Ciarán. "What? Why?"

"An act of ill will. But do not worry. Old Brother Bart will have you good as new. I'm here to travel with you. We are going to Glas Naoidhen. I'm to move on, but for a few months we'll both be—"

"Silence!" Brother Bart barked.

The sound of metal. Pouring water. The room was hot. Windows flung open. "What is happening?" Colum thought he might gag. From pain? From the blazing heat of a fire?

"He is going to stitch you up, friend. After he pours—"

Colum screamed as liquid landed on his neck. Arms pinned him to the bed as he struggled like a lamb on a butcher's table.

Moments later he collapsed, exhausted, surrendered. Darkness fell.

When Colum awoke Ciarán was still at his side. Ciarán's sand-colored curls needed trimming. They hung so low they nearly brushed against what seemed to be a rather large bandage at Colum's neck.

"You should see the barber," Colum told him.

His friend laughed, blue eyes gleaming. "You don't look so fine yourself."

Colum groaned and tried to roll to the side that was not injured.

"Easy now, lad." Ciarán helped him to shift a bit. "If you lay still you'll heal faster, so says Ol' Bart. And the faster you heal the sooner we can start our adventure."

"Adventure? Have you been into the communion wine?"

"Well, friend, I can see you are better already. As soon as you can actually move without assistance, we're to be off to Glas Naoidhen."

"What has happened to my assailant?"

"Malachi? He was sure he had killed you. We allowed him to keep his folly."

"He is still in the tower? You don't think they will execute him?" The man infuriated him, but he did not wish him nor any living being dead.

"I don't think so. The church won't take him back, though."

"Well, that's a relief."

Ciarán chuckled. "The church has some wisdom anyway."

"Don't let the abbot hear you—"

"The abbot is here, brothers!" A messenger darted into the room. Finnian hadn't overheard, thankfully.

A few moments the later the sound of the abbot's robes came swishing through the threshold. "I am most pleased to see that our prayers were answered."

"'Tis only a minor flesh wound," Colum said, his head aching.

Finnian leaned over him, smelling like sacred incense. "That is not what Brother Bart said. One foot in the grave, said he. But look at you now. The blush of roses has returned to your face, young man."

"Then there is no need to send me away. Malachi is no threat. I will heal and get back to the scriptorium."

The abbot and Ciarán exchanged glances.

"'Twas not a punishment," Ciarán said. "'Tis a great honor."

"So they are always saying," Colum murmured under his breath. He motioned for his friend to come closer, despite the annoying shimmy of his loose locks. "I am keeping you from your appointment. Do not volunteer for this. You are to build on the land granted to you."

"Later, perhaps. There is a great plague in that land so my delay is not because of you.

However, it is fortuitous." He flashed a familiar mischievous grin.

They did enjoy each other's company. Colum was not looking forward to saying good-bye. He glanced back at the abbot who was tenting his fingers impatiently. "I understand, Father Abbot. Thank you. And thank everyone for their prayers."

"May God continue to bless you, Columcille." The man nodded, turned, and quickly departed.

Colum winked at his friend. "I suppose we are to be off, then."

Ciarán started to give Colum a playful punch in the forearm, but then thought better of it. "Aye, we are."

A few weeks later, while they were traveling, Colum realized he should have written his parents to tell them of the relocation. Studying for his ordination at Clonard had occupied all his time. They would learn, however, if they tried to correspond with him at Clonard.

When they arrived for their orientation they discovered that Mobhi was quite old and feeble. The community was expansive, perhaps even bigger than Clonard. There was plenty to do, many manuscripts to copy, even if they were of the old Irish tales and not scripture. Colum could add to them because of his tenure with Gemman, but that was not his desire. He wanted more of the Holy Scriptures. There was precious little of it unless an abbot was able to travel to Rome or Tours and get a book. This abbot, however, was not able at all.

Abbot Mobhi spoke slowly, as though his cheeks were padded with bandages. Perhaps they were. "You, Columcille, will take your lessons in the morning with Brother Paul and myself to further prepare for priesthood. Although you are ordained in the priesthood, you shall learn our order before carrying out duties. In the afternoon, you will go to the scriptorium. Except on Sundays when our usual disciplines and worship take place."

For that he was pleased. Spending so much time in the scriptorium meant he could better assess the monastery's collection.

The abbot inclined his white bearded chin toward Ciarán. "You, son, will direct your own disciplines."

Ciarán's brows lifted. "Father?"

The abbot dismissed him with a wave of his hand. "You are to found a new community. 'Tis reasonable that you begin here what you will do there." He coughed. "There are plenty of people both inside these gates and beyond that need your prayers."

"I'm to be a hermit, then?"

For the genial Ciarán, this would a test of endurance.

"God will instruct. Pardon me. I have caught a sudden chill and will retire to my bed. God be with you all."

Colum and his friend exchanged concerned glances before parting.

In the following weeks Colum enjoyed his firm but intellectual instruction from Brother Paul, a man of about thirty years who surely had the entire Latin Bible inscribed in his memory.

"If only I could read all the books," Colum complained one morning.

Dapples of sunlight sprinkled across the table between the two men. Colum's instructor allowed the silence to linger a moment, a teaching technique Colum had come to recognize as customary for Brother Paul.

The man steepled his fingers and leaned on his elbows. "Would the books not then become ordinary? Would their words cease to stir you if you did not have to strive for them?"

Colum paused even though he knew what he wanted to say. He'd learned to tamper his impulsiveness. He held up an index finger. "I would read without compulsion. At times I would do so kneeling, as the Spirit led. I would pray over the text. I would know the words I am reading are sent from God in Heaven. This, teacher, I am convinced would be good for my soul."

Paul smiled. "You are learning quickly, young Columcille. 'Tis a good thing you are heading to the books right now." He patted Colum on the arm as he stood. "God's blessing on you."

Colum stood as he had many times during the weeks he'd been at Glas Naoidhen, staring at rows of pocket bags hung on dozens of wooden pegs. Some held parchment scrolls, some bound books, all filled with possibility. He glanced down at his ink-stained hands. He was a scribe and had been given only one of these to copy, a psalter. There was no harm, indeed much good, in reminding himself of the verses he had memorized. Perhaps that was why Brother Paul had given him this task. He would perform it well and look forward to the next assignment. Perhaps the Book of Matthew if it was here.

His pen had just lifted off the end of page he'd completed when someone whispered in his ear, telling him Ciarán wished to see him at the stables.

His friend stood beside a black mare that had been loaded with sacks, a wee wagon hitched in back. "You look fine for a hermit," Colum said.

They slapped each other on the back affably.

"I am well." He cocked his head toward Colum, examining his shoulder. "I must say the blooms are back in your cheeks, friend. Are you enjoying your training?"

"I am. Brother Paul is loath to allow me all the books I would like, but he is fair and full of wisdom. Are you off to the River Shannon?"

"In time. First I am going to the Isle of the Saints."

"Saint Enda, is it? You are traveling to an ancient place. I have read about it."

"I was there when I first felt the call to the monastery. Enda was a great help to a young man from a common upbringing who had no idea what this compulsion to learn more about Jesu meant. And now a new adventure awaits. Father Enda has much wisdom to impart and will surely one day be called saint. There are souls to be saved, don't you know? And Mobhi wants me there to study, as you are here, to become priest before I head to the land that was granted to me." He blushed. "Well, given to the church through me."

Colum smiled. He would miss his friend, but what a joy for men like them to be doing what God willed. "You will increase the kingdom mightily."

Ciarán winked. "Not me, young priest, but God alone."

"Amen. Allow me to say a blessing over you?"

His friend nodded.

"May your roof shelter only friends. May your enemies flee. May God's angels take you to heaven hours before the devil knows you're dead."

Ciarán laughed and playfully punched a fist toward Colum's jaw. "Don't let old Mobhi hear your incredulous teasing, friend."

Colum sobered. "He is not well. Nor are some others. 'Tis good you'll be leaving here and not contract whatever fever is about the place."

"He will be in my prayers. You take care as well, friend."

They embraced briefly and then Colum watched as he trotted off beyond the tall sanctuary boundaries, a pathway of shadows. He called out, causing Ciarán to turn and wave. "I hope to visit your establishment, Ciarán. On the river. Look for me there."

A month of Sundays later there was no one but Colum well enough to say mass. He was able, having been ordained at Clonard, but despite knowing exactly what to do he felt uneasy. This was not his community. He was surely at least eight monks behind the abbot in order of authority. Less than a hundred men attended, some of those shading their eyes from the light of the dim candles and shivering so that their misery seemed to echo off the stone walls.

As he walked toward the refectory, someone called out that no meal would be served. Colum headed to his cell, noting the lack of ringing bells, the dearth of usual chatter. A few men who passed him bore strange welts on their faces. He couldn't imagine what was happening but he would pray in earnest alone in his dwelling.

A few days later rumors emerged that King Diarmait was packing up and preparing to leave Tara. Some said he would head north because the pestilence had not reached in that direction. Colum could not pretend he was not relieved for his birth family who lived almost as far north as one could go on this island.

Late in the day Colum labored in the scriptorium. Two Sundays prior Brother Paul had ceased his lessons because, as he put it, "I've no more to share. Prepare to teach others."

But there was no one to teach, so many had died or lay sick in bed. Only a handful of monks joined Colum in scratching out the transcriptions the abbot had ordered them to do.

He rose from his desk and went to a cabinet on the other side of the room where the ink was kept. The monks who worked at illumination had left to take on more critical duties. He wanted to try the rare, red ink. He'd sketch something on the back of the parchment he was working on.

Once he'd found the desired ink and brought it to his desk, his stylus hovered above the page. What to draw? A cat? The flaming globe of the sun?

The door burst open, sending a cold breeze that rattled his parchment and caused him to drop his instrument. Red ink ran in a jagged line across his work. He returned the stylus to the ink pot and turned around, furious at the interruption.

A monk stood there, eyes bulging as though he'd seen a banshee. "Pack your things. The abbot has ordered every able person to leave the monastery immediately."

"Why? Go where?" one of the scribes asked.

Brother Paul entered behind the other man. "If you have homes—mothers and fathers, brothers and sisters—go there. The Father Abbot wishes no more lives to be lost in this place."

"Where is Father Mobhi?" Colum asked.

Brother Paul approached him, keeping his voice lowered. "He has the sickness. Heaven will soon accept another saint."

"I will stay," Colum offered. "At least while he lives."

They both glanced to the other scribes who were gathering up pocket bags preparing to leave. "There will be no one left to write of his passing," Colum said.

Brother Paul nodded. "But then go. We all will."

The next morning Colum sought out the chronicle the monks referred to as the annals. In its pages were written the celebration of feast days, the progression of kings, and the dates and events surrounding the deaths of priests, bishops, and abbots. It was now Colum's solemn duty to record the death of Mobhi. He owed at least this to the man who created the center of learning that had taught Colum much.

When the ink dried, he shut the book and returned it to the proper storage shelf. He gathered the pocket bag he had been given that contained a few parchments and his stylus. Brother Paul had also allowed him to keep one of the older psalters. The one Colum had made would remain in the scriptorium. After the pestilence passed, the hope was the school would reopen.

"Where will you go?" one of the younger monks asked him as they both walked toward the boundary crosses.

He could follow Ciarán. There had to be more books somewhere, and why not at Enda's school? But he might be interfering. His friend was the one meant to receive instruction there, and everyone said Father Enda, a temperamental man, preferred to keep his establishment small. Colum did not want to upset a delicate balance and cause his friend trouble.

He turned to the young fellow. "I suppose I will travel to my beloved Daire, the place where angels dwell. How about you?"

"Loch nEachach, where my mother is."

Colum offered the lad an apple from his pack. "'Tis a fine plan, to go north, they say. I'll travel with you part of the way."

Much later, as he alone approached the land of his father's people, he spotted Michael in a pasture with some horses. Ah, angels indeed.

359

Two others joined him amongst a couple of foals. Could his sisters have grown so tall? He saw Michael bend down and whisper to one of them.

"My brother," she shouted. "Maither, Da, our Colum is home!" She took her sister's hand and rushed to the cottage.

Exhausted from his journey, Colum joined Michael and reclined in the grass.

"Look at your feet, lad. You walked from Glas Naoidhen?"

Colum held out his legs, wrapped in the rags that used to be his shoes. Dried blood crusted his toes. "Mostly. A few farmers allowed me passage on their hay wagons and pony carts. I shall have to make new shoes."

"I am happy you arrived well. There is a terrible illness in the south."

"You heard?"

"I did."

"And you know Mobhi is with God now?"

He nodded.

Colum rubbed his unshaven tonsure. "You did not turn around as I approached. You did not lay eyes on me, yet you told my siblings I was here."

He laughed softly. "You have visions, and yet you do not understand this?"

"Sometimes I think you are my guardian angel, Michael."

"Do you, now?"

Shouting from the cottage caught their attention. Enya emerged with Fe behind her. He carried the youngest children.

"Colum! We've had no word from you. What a glorious surprise!"

Leave it to his mother to greet him with a chastisement. He glanced behind her and saw Keeva come toward him with much difficulty. She was nearly a woman now. Why had he imagined she would still be a child? He bent low to scoop her up in his arms. "What happened to you, lassie? Do not tell me you fell off that horse."

She frowned.

He glanced to his parents whose faces were also crestfallen.

Enya smiled tightlipped. "'Tis over and done with. She is much better. Have you seen her herb garden?"

Keeva blushed as Colum released her. "I have been learning about the healing and culinary properties of plants."

"'Tis true," Fe said. "Our neighbors come to consult with our Keeva. One young man is especially keen to trade his leatherwork for her herbs." He winked at her.

Keeva cupped a hand to her mouth as though she was only speaking to Colum. "Wants to marry me off, our Da does."

Colum offered his arm to her as they made their way back to the cottage. "I will have to meet this young man myself." Obviously, life had gone on here without him.

Later, after a meal of salted pork and stewed apples, Colum accepted Michael's offer to stroll through the fields. "To see what you might help with," he explained.

Colum's father had planted six new fields since Colum last visited. "Feeds the community well, I suppose."

"Your father feeds the body, but you feed the soul. God has a plan for us all."

"They are well here. I am glad for it. But what happened to Keeva? They do not seem to want to talk about it."

"She was hurt in an attack, Colum. Do you see the sentries over there?"

Colum squinted in the setting sun toward a neighboring cottage. Three dark figures paced, spears at their sides. "I had not noticed. What is this about?"

"Seems your grandfather and his men were here, a threat this place had not seen before."

"After they tried to take my mother?"

"Before."

"They tried to make war? They hurt my wee sister?" His anger, the curse that he'd worked so hard to bury burst forth with force.

"'Twas long ago. I expect your father will dismiss those men, or I should say convince Brody to do so. He's the king, though 'tis easy to forget. He is not much of a leader."

"Some thought I should have been king."

"You were in line, true. But God had other plans."

"Do they still threaten? Should we do something about it? Father's uncles have vast armies we could call upon."

"True, your people have much power in the north of the island. But do not concern yourself with that. Those Mac Noe have crawled back to the pit from which they came."

"And Malachi won't be helping them now." Colum began to relax.

"You have forgotten how to focus, how to be still and sense what God is telling you, Colum."

He grasped Michael's forearm. "'Tis fitting we are back together then, my friend. Here in the land of angels."

But when he turned to see slender Keeva sweeping the threshold of the cottage, leaning heavily on the broom because of her lameness, his heart ached. How could God allow an innocent to be harmed?

Chapter Twenty-Nine

'Tis a long road that has no turning. —Irish Proverb

Enya was delighted that her son had returned, but this time she did not expect him to stay. He was a grown man with an education and a calling. Still, she was glad for the time to visit.

After weeks of merriment, feasts with the neighbors, bringing in the harvest, and engaging in long talks over mugs of ale by the turf fire, Enya sensed her eldest son growing restless.

Colum played a game with stones and sticks that she had never seen before. He was showing his younger brother, but Egan was having a hard time understanding the rules.

"Nay, lad. As I said, turn the stick north and south." Colum's booming voice caused the whole household to fall silent.

Egan's face turned pale as seashells.

"Let me help," Enya said, guiding her younger son's hand.

They played a bit longer, but the joy of it seemed lost.

"I have chores to do," Egan announced. He jumped to his feet and scrambled outside.

"I was too critical," Colum said, collecting the pieces from the floor. "I suppose the strictness of a monastery has no place in a home."

"Outside." Enya shooed the children. "There are still tasks to be accomplished even though your brother is here."

Branna doled out the children's boots. "We will weed the herb garden while Keeva is off at the neighbors. She'll appreciate that."

"Wonderful idea, Branna. Thank you." Enya shut the door behind them.

"Keeva seems to adore that fellow, the leather worker," Colum said.

"She does. A fine young man that Sean, even though he is Nola's son."

"A Murtagh, is he?"

She nodded.

"I am surprised you allow it."

She waved dismissively. "The feuds of long ago. We must forget. I was young and foolish."

"We all must outgrow the foolishness of youth, it seems." He plopped down into Fe's chair by the fire.

She pulled up a stool to join him. "How wise my son has grown. I am so proud."

"Not wise enough most times. I dare to hope that I have learned from my mistakes."

She pointed to the game pieces he'd gathered into a brown sack. "I see your temper gets the best of you at times."

His pale face reddened. "I … 'tis just this house, being here."

"What do you mean?" Enya instantly thought about her own escape from her family, her bid to outrun the fury. Was her son thinking the same now?

"I am sorry, Maither. I am away from the routines of my spiritual disciplines and have become tetchy. Perhaps I should go."

She shook her head and reached for his hand. "Stay as long as you'd like. I do not have the gentlest of manners myself, but I see that you are humble and remorseful. Your brother will understand."

"Thank you. I will apologize to him."

367

Apologizing was not a part of the family trait that Enya recognized. "I know you'll be moving on after the sickness in the south has passed."

"I fear that will not pass quickly."

"Then build your own school here."

He arched his red brows. "Here?"

"Sure, and why not?"

He seemed to consider it. "I am not very good at being idle."

"Like your mother." She reached out and placed her hand against his handsome cheek. "And your father."

"Do you think the king—Brody—will grant me land to this?"

"He owes us, I do think."

"Let me pray about this decision." A thought seemed to come to him. "Oileán Thúr Rí."

"Nay, son. Not that island. I am speaking about land here, under our feet."

But Colum seemed enthused by the idea. "Sure, and that's fine, for later, but listen. I have heard that the island has a wee colony of Christ followers. A good place to start using my calling from God. And later, a community here. Seems like a natural progression, wouldn't you say, Maither?"

"I would say." As soon as she could she would speak to Fe about this. They could begin construction while Colum was away.

Sailing to the island north of his homeland did not take long. It could be seen from the shore. Colum was met by a man who shared a name with Colum's guardian.

"Welcome, holy man," this Michael said, helping him out of the boat that had been sent to ferry him to his fellow Christians.

In the days that followed, Colum began to understand why the small group of people had chosen the island, this Tower of the King. The name came from centuries earlier when, it was said, a one-eyed king ruled here. A tower, now long gone, may have stood there. Or perhaps the sharp cliffs that guarded the island from anyone trying to invade by surprise were referred to as a tower. From where they'd built the community the beach could be plainly seen. In fact, the island was so small water could be glimpsed from everywhere, giving the residents a humbling awareness of how finite they were.

This island was a suitable refuge. Quiet, no fishermen calling out about the day's catch, and no farmers guiding a plough. No tradesmen clanging anvils or chopping down trees. No cattle or sheep bells to interrupt the music of the sea or the cadence of the wind. It was not necessary to have a monastery bell there since there were so few people to call to prayer or worship. Necessities were bargained for on the mainland and brought over. In this serene place, the voice of God could be more easily ascertained. Colum loved the island despite its lack of a scriptorium or collection of books. That, however, he was already beginning to remedy.

Friends he'd met at the schools he attended were slowly finding him, bringing manuscripts. One monk, an expert at preparing vellum, brought over a boatload of skins and planned to stay on to teach his trade. Colum spent many hours instructing four men the skill of a scribe as they copied from borrowed manuscripts.

After four full moons, Colum knew he'd need to leave the island. He hadn't thought to depart so soon, but his own desires should not prevail.

"We have a direction now, and you must obey. Certainly, you'll return from time to time," Michael told him one sunny spring day when he visited.

Colum sat alone on the beach after his conversation with Michael. The squeaking gate sound of the corncrake birds and the waves licking the rocky shore seemed to compete with the voices quarreling in his head. Stay? Go?

He brushed the salty spray from his lips and glanced around at the rocks on the beach. An infinite number even after they had taken many for huts and walls. No matter how many communities he helped build, there would be a need for more. Michael was correct. He had to move on. There much more to do. He looked forward to fellowship with his guardian Michael just as soon as the boat brought him home.

He wandered to a pile of particularly round stones. The residents of the island had collected them. Some called them prayer rocks, others cursing stones. Either way, they had come to represent the power available to all Christ followers—an ability to commune with God. He touched the top of one ivory rock, incredibly smooth from the constant action of the ocean's waves. The power of God. The faithfulness of the Redeemer. *May this place speak to the hearts of all who come seeking truth.*

Not long after Colum sat with Michael, his long-time spiritual guide, and faced the valley. Tuffs of fluffy angel-like clouds loomed overhead. "Focus, now," Michael instructed. "Close your eyes. Think about what you smell and what you hear."

Dew and cattle and the laughter of children. Soon he was no longer aware of the brightness of day touching his eyelids. He saw Ciarán lying in a bed, a towel folded over his forehead. He inhaled with difficulty and put his hands against his torso. Opening his eyes, Colum felt a pain in his own chest. "He needs me."

"I believe he does, or will before long," Michael replied.

Colum did not question how Michael knew what he meant or to whom he referred. Details did not matter. Far away on a windswept island his friend was ill. Or perhaps he was already at the place near the River Shannon. It would be a great journey, but Colum had been at his parents' home for a complete cycle of the seasons and that was long enough. There was nothing for him to do there, they'd have to agree. A school would be built one day perhaps, but because the time had not yet come, his days had been mostly idle. Such lack of activity after returning from the island had been difficult. To finally have a purpose was invigorating, even though troublesome concerning his friend.

Michael put his hands on Colum's shoulders. "Go to Ciarán and know that while you pray at his side, God will show you your next step. You should not delay."

Colum had thought the islands would be safe from the plague. Therefore, Ciarán must have gone on to the Shannon. He would have traveled quite a distance up that great river. He could have gotten the sickness along on the way, if that was what had happened. "I am not sure of his location, Michael."

"It has not been revealed, so go to the island in the west. There will be direction there for you even if your friend has left."

His mother was distraught. "You could catch it too. We saw so many people being buried. There is much death there. 'Tis why we left." She began to wail like a banshee then. Thankfully they were alone in the stables. She'd frighten the children in the house.

"I have been around it before, Maither. God will protect me."

Tears streaked down her face, but she began to compose herself. "We promised Abbot Finnian we would send word of Ciarán, but we were never able. We came home. We had to. We were concerned for the children." Her knees nearly gave way and he helped her to her feet. "Perhaps that is why you should go." The words seem to choke her. She steadied herself against a horse's stall. "You will satisfy our obligation to the abbot."

"Do not worry, Maither. I will do this. And I will return as soon as I am able and build a school in Daire."

She sniffed, wiped her face on her apron, and hugged him. "That will be fine. We will all help."

She pulled back to look at him. "We will prepare while you are away. Such things take time and labor."

"Bless you." He put a fingertip to her fore-head.

She wept again, but this time more gently.

He had already bade farewell to the rest of the family before meeting his mother in the stables. He'd promised to bring the children nets from the fishermen who labored in the bay that feeds the Shannon. No one tied such sturdy, well-made ropes as they, he'd told them. When you live in a large monastery you meet traders. Colum had admired their nets. One of these sailors was to meet Colum at the coast where a farmer promised to keep the horse Colum borrowed until Fe could come back for it. Then they would sail for an island Colum had never been to before and thus begin the journey to find Ciarán.

Michael's words echoed off the trees as Colum trotted away on the back of Fe's mighty horse. *"God will show you your next step."* Had Colum been hasty with his declaration to his mother? His heart yearned to return, but what if Ciarán died? God forbid that Colum would need to stay in the land where the people had sent Malachi to kill him.

PART THREE

Chapter Thirty

The man who offered to take Colum in his curragh to the island had a kind face weathered from the sun. His kin had taken in Fe's horse. "Where are you going, if I may ask?"

Colum explained about his ill friend at the Isle of the Saints. "He may have moved on to a place along the great riverbank, but I do not know. Therefore, I will make that great island my first destination."

The fellow filled a leather pouch with amber liquid as he spoke. "If that is where you're going, lad, you have many islands to visit on the way, like stepping stones."

"Aye, I expect so. Safe ports, points to rest, make repairs, and prepare for further travel, is that not so?"

The man pulled a fat, folded garment from an oiled leather satchel. "'Tis so, and you'll be needing better clothing to meet the ocean. She saves up her fury for the fledgling sailor."

Colum gratefully accepted the outer garment.

The man nodded in his direction. "You, being a holy man quite so, may have heard of my final destination. From this place you will find another to take you onward."

Colum knew there were establishments in the west, like the community of Enda. "I am not familiar all of the communities. Are we headed to one?"

The sailor, who'd said his name was Bairre, continued to load his craft while he spoke. Colum handed him a crate to be stowed. "Molaise's community at the place folks call the Sacred Island."

He had heard of it. "I am looking forward to going there. You say you'll be staying there? I'd like to repay you in some way."

The man looked at him a moment, his blue eyes contrasting with his sun-stroked face. He winked and nodded his head, then turned his attention to his floating craft still tethered to a post. "Why do you think I welcomed you, lad? I'm a

379

good fellow, for sure, but a seaman like myself desires a blessing, don't you know. 'Tis no greater prayer for protection than that of a whole island of consecrated men."

After they climbed in and rowed away from the inlet, Colum said a prayer for their journey. "God hears," he told Bairre.

"Sure, 'tis true. Trust God, but do not dance in the curragh." He laughed at his own joke. After a few moments, in which Colum took the opportunity to pray silently, the man spoke again, his voice rising over the water sloshing against the leather sides of the craft. "Of course," the sailor said, "'twill be many days before we get there. First we will stop at Árainn Uí Dhomhnaill."

"I thought you said we are going to the Sacred Island?" Colum felt deceived.

"Oh we are, but we cannot get there in a day, my friend. We must stop at Árainn Uí Dhomhnaill. As you said earlier, there are ports to rest and restore our strength. We cannot go on without pausing there."

"I suppose I am at a disadvantage. I do not know the sea."

Bairre blinked as he rustled through a bag. He pulled out his pouch of ale and breathed a long, satisfied sigh. Perhaps he'd feared he'd left it behind. "You will know the sea soon enough, lad."

"Are they friendly, the Uí Dhomhnaill?"

"They won't bother you so long as you do not mention that you are of the Cenél Conaill."

Perhaps he had indeed been tricked. "They sometimes war, 'tis true. But they descend from a common ancestor. Will we need to explain?"

Bairre chewed on a piece of straw. "We will not, so long as we keep to ourselves. Follow me, do not speak to anyone. All will be well. We have God on our side because of your prayers, aye?"

Much later, as they neared the island very late at night under the light of a half-moon, bonfire lights dotted the horizon. The sounds of brass trumpets called out to the lonely sea. At first the sound was mournful and muted, but suddenly the blasts came rapidly, like an alarm. "They have seen us?" he asked his companion.

Bairre pulled his oar from the water. "This is why I brought you, lad. Now is the time to call upon God."

Enya paced outside the stone hut that encased one of the wells. Kyna had insisted Fe be brought there when Enya called for her a few hours ago. Fe had been moaning in his sleep and now was wracked with fever.

The door opened and the old cook stepped out, closing it behind her. "I will send the stable lad for straw to put under his bedding."

"Let him come back to his bed. He will be more comfortable."

"You know that is not wise. He may have the plague. Return to the house and try to sleep now, child."

True, if Fe had contracted the yellow fever— the disease that turned the skin to a ghastly pallor and caused the neck to swell with lumps, all the while sending the afflicted one into a ranting world of demons—the children had to be protected. "No one else has this illness. It cannot be." But she knew it could be because Fe had traveled to trade.

She humbly agreed to leave him be and made her way through the damp grass, her stomach turning with fear. Her soul split as she longed to be with her husband but also her children. *Why,*

God, are you always tormenting me by dividing my heart in two?

Inside the dark cottage she reached for the poker. Stirring the ashes to find a reassuring spark, her thoughts darkened as she realized Fe could die, taking half her heart with him. And the disease might not stop there.

She sat in his chair and rubbed chilly fingers over her face. Colum had gotten away in time. Should she also send the others? Where would they go? Where on this green island was safe? The caves in the cliffs over the ocean? One of the islands perhaps?

An ache bloomed in her chest as she realized no plan her mind could conceive was adequate. There was nothing she could do, and that realization was the most painful feeling she'd ever experienced.

Glancing to her mending basket, she recalled the days before the children were born. How foolish she had been thinking those times were the worst. She'd been desperate enough back then to think of tying her wish to the branch of a fairy tree, hoping it might give her what she wanted. 'Twas God who had opened her womb after that. Only he could grant life. If only saving

Fe could be as simple as tying a ribbon to a stick. Now that she believed in the God of Patrick, such simple hopes of the country people gave no solace. God was not always listening, it seemed, and she doubted she could petition him whenever she chose.

But she could try.

She had called out in desperation once before in the church. She could not get there now, but she had always believed the true church of God existed around her rather than in a structure man built. The stars traced out the rafters, the trees became the walls, and the grass the floorboards.

She snatched a blanket from her bed, wrapped it around her, and left the cottage.

She stepped quietly around Keeva's garden, nodding to the dark stems and leaves that grew there seemingly only because of Keeva's love for them. She headed toward a grove of towering pines, their scent sweetly stroking the breeze around her. A fallen tree created a bench where she sat and inhaled deeply. Enya longed for the sense of peace she had many years ago inside Father Cruithneachia's church. She'd never forgotten it. She wondered, hoped, that it could be found there under the pines.

After a few moments, she found she could not unhitch her thoughts from Fe. There could be no peace with her husband lying so ill in the well house, could there? She squeezed her eyes shut. Her son always seemed to be able to calm his spirit, even his anger. There must a way.

She listened to her breathing.

In.

Out.

The smell of pines.

The darkness she could feel even with her eyes closed.

In.

Out.

Oh, God. Can you hear me?

I do, child.

She lifted her heavy eyelids. She had not actually heard the words with her ears. Somewhere deep inside, she'd felt them. Like sitting in a boat on a calm lough and sensing that the water is deep, even when the view is clouded. You understand somehow that you can't touch the bottom with your oar. You don't have to try.

Enya knew. God heard.

A tingling wiggled from her fingertips through her forearms. Peace. All would be well.

385

She turned to the west toward the well house. Lantern light bobbed in rhythm with her now steady heartbeat. Standing up gently as though any rapid movement might cause her peace to spill down into the forest floor, Enya moved toward the light.

All will be well.

Today or tomorrow or in a season, all will be well.

When she approached the bearer of the lantern, Enya was stunned to see it was not Kyna but Gormley. "Why are you here?"

"Your nurse has sent for me. Didn't you know?"

"Kyna would never—"

"Not that old woman. Your children's nurse, Branna."

"But why?" Enya placed an open palm against the well house door.

Gormley shook her head. "There is nothing your prayers to your God can do about this."

Enya withdrew her hand and placed it over the cross around her neck. "How dare you say such a thing!"

"'Tis true. Only a tincture of yarrow and elderberries will lessen the fever. Branna knew this.

Kyna does too, I imagine, though her pride would not allow her to call for me. I have more of these herbs than anyone." She jiggled her chin. "No worries, I will address Kyna inside. I should not tarry."

Enya moved to block the woman's entry. "You should remember how Fe reacted to you being in my house the night my eldest son was born. He will not want you here."

Gormley shrugged, causing the tightly woven wrap around her shoulders to fall toward her elbows. She cradled a reed basket bulging with clay jars. "'Tis your own husband's life you risk. I will do as you wish."

Elderberries and yarrow? Enya glanced toward her daughter's dark garden. She did not know what she had planted there. But she did know Gormley was never hospitable. If she wanted to help, there had to be a reason other than charity. "Does the king know you are wandering about on a dark night?"

Gormley would not meet her gaze. "He is sleeping. Do not concern yourself with my husband."

"Oh, is that the way of it? Have you not concerned yourself with mine?"

387

Gormley sighed. "Branna asked for me to come. She is concerned."

When Enya left the cottage, her children's nurse had been sleeping beside wee Sheela. "If she was so worried, why did she not consult me, her employer?"

Gormley turned to leave. "I do not know. Perhaps she finds her employer petulant." She removed a jar from her basket and set it beside the door. "I do not mind bringing my tinctures to a very ill man. I have brought it for him, not you. Your husband is a great help to all who live in this glen. The king wishes to see him well, perhaps even more than you do."

What right did Gormley have to offend her? Enya hurried to stand in front of her. "The fact that your husband is king does not entitle you to insult a woman at her own home in the middle of the night when her husband is ill."

Gormley's stare matched the intensity of Enya's. "The fact that you follow the new religion also gives you no such right."

"What do you mean?"

Gormley's basket of jar clanked as she crossed her arms. "I come here in peace and with good charity. But you reject me because I follow the old ways. What does that say about the good will of your God, Enya?"

The peace. Where did it go?

Enya squeezed her eyes shut and balled her hands in fists, willing her anger to dissipate. She wished to hear the wind through the pines once again. When she opened her eyes, Gormley was gone. The jar still stood in front of the well house door. She picked it up, pried off the wooden lid, and dumped the contents under the willow behind the building.

When she returned to Fe she found Kyna dozing in a corner. Enya bent low to dip a rag into the spring water and then tapped the cloth on Fe's forehead. He still burned with fever while he slept.

What if Gormley was right? What if that mixture she had brought could have cured him? She shook her head. She couldn't trust her. What had it been? Elderberries and yarrow. Even in the darkness the liquid had appeared watery, not dark like it should have been from the berries.

Weariness made her long for sleep, but instead she nudged the cook awake. "Go on, now. I will care for him for a few hours. Go to your bed."

Kyna put a hand to her back as she rose. Caring for a man with a fever was no task for someone as fragile as she.

"Send Branna out in the morning. You rest. You've done all you can."

Kyna tilted her head upward and sniffed. "What is that I smell?"

"I don't smell anything." Could she detect Gormley's potion? It was outside and soaked into the ground. Enya hadn't noticed an odor when she'd dumped it. But the old woman had many years of experience with herbs and cooking spices.

"I have sniffed that before. The bark of elderberry. Has someone come to poison us?"

Enya had been right not to trust that woman. "Gormley. I dumped what she brought in the willow grove. She claimed it would help Fe's fever, elderberries and yarrow, she said. I did not trust her."

Kyna held up a finger. "Good you did not. She lifted her nose and sniffed. The berries perhaps, but I smell something else." Her glassy eyes grew serious. "If you brew the bark or the leaves, you'll get not a cure but a poison." She glanced to Fe's sleeping form on the floor. "Don't you worry. Either of you. I will handle this."

"Nay, Kyna. You must go to your bed. You're exhausted."

"In time." She hobbled out the door and called over her shoulder. "As they say, I can sleep when I'm dead. While I'm among the living I'll do what I must."

Chapter Thirty-One

The captain went to him and said, "How can you sleep? Get up and call on your god! Maybe he will take notice of us so that we will not perish."
—*Jonah 1:6 NIV*

No sooner had Bairre asked Colum to pray than a hard rain began to pelt them. Soft rain on the hills never bothered Colum, but this lashing, together with the crashing ocean waves made him fear for his life.

"At least the trumpets have ceased!" Bairre shouted. He grabbed some rope and tied it to his waist, ordering Colum to do the same.

"Can we wait it out?" Colum asked. He hoped they might pass the island by. Going there seemed unwise.

"Only on the bottom of the sea." Bairre handed him an ore. "We'll head for that cove, a wee sheltered spot I've been to before in a storm. "Don't worry. Keep praying. 'Tis working."

How could he think spinning about in curragh during a storm was God answering prayers? Colum's stomach felt like he'd swallowed a school of flapping fish. Salt water splashed into his mouth. Still, he did as the captain said and beat back the waves with his ore and prayed for calm shelter.

The storm raged like a provoked rabid wolf. They would surely capsize. Colum didn't know if he could swim. His only experience had been in the river back at Clonard. Even while he was on the island close to home he had not ventured into the water.

Bairre turned to him and said something, but with the roar of the waves in his ears, Colum couldn't make it out.

Deliver us, O God.

He felt himself being pulled to his right and lifted up and out of the curragh, but then after a wave subsided, he crashed back to the floor of the leather craft. His oar was gone, but the rope had done its job.

Bairre slapped the back of his oiled overcoat and shouted into his ear. "Easy lad. *Afna*, a tempest, surely, but 'tis no cyclone. We are almost there."

When at last they moored under a rocky outcrop, Colum drew in great gasps of air. Never had he been so sure he would perish. Now that they were safe, he felt every discomfort head to toe. His lungs hurt. The muscles in his arms trembled. Cuts on his hands and face stung from the saltwater.

When Colum left the boat, his legs would not support him. He collapsed on a patch of purple dulse. Bairre stood over him, laughing. He did not look like the experience had injured him at all. "Whatever do you find humorous?"

"I warned you the sea would initiate you, lad. But look, you've fared well. When you untie your coat, you'll find your shirt dry."

Colum doubted that. He sat up and dabbed at the stinging on his cheek. Bairre had a wee cut above one eye. "How did this happen?"

"Ah, the waves kick up the shells and all sorts of debris. Look like an old sailor now, you do." He returned to the curragh and before Colum could offer to help, he'd dragged it to a safe spot behind a boulder. "Are you able to walk yet, lad? We should get on to that cave I told you about."

It was still raining. Thunder rolled in the distance and the waves, while lessened a bit, still crashed with intensity. At least no one would be searching for them yet.

Once they were inside the shelter Bairre found, Colum removed his outer coat. The man had been right. He was fairly dry underneath. Unfortunately, he could not say the same for his feet. He removed his shoes and leggings while Bairre worked to kindle a fire. When flames began to lick at the wood, Bairre removed to the back of the cave. Colum warmed his numbed fingers over the fire.

Bairre returned carrying dry blankets and woven mats. Colum leapt to his feet to assist. "Where did you find these? This is no inn, is it?"

Bairre's blue eyes gleamed in the firelight. "'Tis my own personal wayside, I'd say, though a few sailors share it with me. Come here every time I pass this way. Occasionally bring a few folks with me, so I have stored plenty of bedding."

"What a blessing." Colum rolled out the mat and lay down. Never had a bed felt so good. "How soon can we leave for the the Sacred Isle?" He was still concerned about the natives.

"Patience, lad. We've only just arrived. In the morning, after we catch our breakfast, we'll go to the settlement and make some trades. 'Tis why I've come, you see. They desire my special brew. I take in trade their salted fish."

"Brew? That's what's in the crates?"

"'Tis, indeed. My little pot. I'm a merchant, not just a carrier of monks, lad."

"I see. How long will that take?"

"A few days. And we'll be wanting to refresh ourselves before we depart." He winked.

Colum turned away, not wanting his distaste to show on his face. "I thought you said we'd be best to stay to ourselves here."

"I may have said that, aye. I meant you. You, because of your bloodline, should stay behind. Thanks for reminding me."

Gladly. "I will stay here and pray for your soul, Bairre."

He chuckled. "Ah, and that's a good thing. A very fine idea."

Colum was not a stranger to austere cave dwelling. He did not mind Bairre's absence, but he was eager to arrive on the island where Ciarán had gone. On his third day alone, while cooking a dinner of dulse and clams, the sound of several male voices startled him. The chatter came from the shore. He crept to the cave's opening and peered out. Below him stood three men with stiff limed hair carrying spears. In the span between two Sundays now he'd been scared witless twice.

Enya would have gone after Kyna if that wouldn't have meant leaving Fe alone. Gormley was not worth the altercation. Enya had seen through her evil plan, after all. Now Enya had two people to worry over, her husband and her cook.

Peace, she pleaded in her mind.

At daybreak, Fe roused.

"How are you, my love?"

He blinked. She felt his forehead. Cooler. He parted dry lips and she brought him a cool rag to suck on.

"Where?" He turned his head to the side to look around.

"You were quite ill last night. Kyna thought it best to keep you away from the children. And with your fever, the cool well house served you soundly."

397

He let out a breath, and then a cough, rolling over to his side. "I'm better."

"I will get you some broth, but you should stay here until we are certain." She believed he was better. One does not recover from the plague so quickly, so he must not have it.

When she returned, he was asleep. His fever peaked once again. Tears welled in her eyes. So drained was she due to distress and lack of sleep, she wondered if Gormley might have snuck in and succeeded in poisoning him. The well house was too small for any sneaking about, however.

A tapping came from outside the door. Keeva arrived holding a basket. Dark circles loomed under her eyes from a lack of sleep. Enya stepped out into the morning light, shutting the door behind her. "What have you brought, darlin'?"

"Elderberry tea made with berries. For his fever."

Enya embraced her with such force that the lass winced. "What's wrong, Maither?"

"Oh, nothing. He's improved." Enya realized she'd frightened her. "Tell me, daughter, what else have you learned about healing herbs and berries?"

Keeva nodded toward the garden. "I've been growing different kinds in case we needed them. But the elderberries I scavenged."

"Just the berries, you said. Not leaves or bark?"

"Oh, nay. Only the berries can be used. I'm very careful."

"Of course, my sweet. You are so very clever to know what your da needed. I will give it to him and come to the cottage as soon as Branna arrives to relieve me."

"Branna? She isn't coming."

"Why? Did Kyna not come for her?"

"She did. And they left together. I thought you knew. They asked me to come to the well house."

"What are they up to?"

"An errand, it might have been. They did not think to tell me."

"Of course. I will stay with your father. You will be my messenger." Enya took the basket from her. "We do not yet know if the fever is catching. They should have known better than to send you."

"But the children."

"Won't take long. Your brother can manage while you're gone."

399

"I am able to care for Da. Please—"

"You are, but I do not want to endanger—" She stopped herself before blurting out that Fe's illness might be fatal. It wasn't, of course. She refused to consider it … but she still needed to be cautious. "Listen, I need you to go see Brody."

"The king?" Keeva pulled her shoulders back.

"Sure and he might be our appointed ruler, but he is Gormley's husband just the same. One of the tenants of this land. He is not to be feared. I beg you to think of him as only a common man. We require his help." She smiled trying to appear reassuring. "Neighbors help each other. Like the Murtaghs do."

Keeva smiled at the name of her beau's clan.

"I would ask your father's brother for help but he is out at sea collecting seal skins for the winter."

"Shall we ask the Murtaghs, then?"

Most drank too heavily to be of help, and young Sean alone would not be enough. "Trust me when I say we need Brody. The others are too busy minding their own … employment."

"Not your uncle either?"

Enya let out a breath. Fe trusted Ernán, but Enya could not. "Nay, they are off hunting too.

'Tis the season to make sure our barns and cooking pits are well-stocked."

Keeva bit her lip and nodded.

"Fetch my parchments and writing utensils. Do not forget the ink pot, and tell your brother he must mind the wee ones."

"Aye, Maither." She faced the cottage.

"Keeva?"

She turned.

"You will not have to say anything when you go to Brody, only give him my letter."

Keeva's long eyelashes brushed her cheeks as she turned to go. She would do this, Enya knew, only because her mother asked.

Fe slept a bit more peacefully as Enya wrote the letter. Keeva waited patiently outside the door.

Greetings King Brody,

Please accept my apologies for not coming to you in person. My husband is too ill for me to leave him.

Enya lifted her pen. She knew she could not say everything in this note. She could not even accuse Gormley because she had no proof of what she'd tried to do. Not knowing whether Kyna had spoken to him already, she had to try. She rubbed her fingers between her eyes. She wanted to hate Gormley. Indeed, there was reason. She had tried to take Enya's loved ones away from her, even murder them if she could.

And yet revenge would not solve anything. Brody must already know Gormley's ways. He surely acknowledged her wayward beliefs about the spiritual realm. Brody did not share them, though, or he would not have been elected king. Despite the desperate acts of the current priest, this was certainly so. Enya wondered if Malachi and Gormley's plan to seize power, with Brody being king and Malachi leading the church, had been thwarted because Brody converted. Perhaps this had pushed Gormley to drastic actions such as poisoning people like Fe. Appealing to Brody might the only way to stop Gormley's treacherous acts and put an end to her attack on Enya's family.

She watched the rise and fall of Fe's chest as he breathed uncomfortably in his sleep. Why had she not cared enough to ask Fe about Brody before? She had been so jealous that her son was not able or willing to become king that she had not cared to know anything about the one appointed. Now that it was important, Fe could not tell her.

It seemed proper that she petition the king. Perhaps God was guiding her to do so. She prayed her intuition was correct. Every king kept a learned man among his advisors to read missives from the priest. Someone would read this to Brody.

Enya lifted her gaze to the wee domed ceiling and watched the shadows cast by a burning torch Kyna had propped against the stone wall. What must she say to this man she barely knew? There was more at stake than she'd first thought. Gormley's old ways were destructive. Her beliefs might cost lives if she was not stopped. And those who tied their hope-filled wishes to the branches of the thorn bush? God did not wish those people to be lost to him. Enya had to choose her words carefully. The most powerful, life-changing words must be written right now. What were they?

Through the crack at the bottom of the door she noticed a shadow waxing and waning while Keeva paced.

403

Fe was still resting. Their daughter's tea had helped. Praise Jesu.

Enya dipped her stylus into the ink pot and continued.

Now is the time, in the face of pestilence, despite the eyes of hatred, despite all manner of corruption and ill-gotten gains, to look to the Maker of Heaven. I have chosen thus, and will not condemn someone who is unversed in the ways of Jesu. Unless that person seeks to cause harm in the name of unsound beliefs. Therefore, I humbly ask you to examine the actions Gormley has tried to take against my family. While she must be stopped, she must foremost be helped. The priest is corrupt. Fe is unable to do anything at present. Brendan is away. You, king, must speak out and help those who wander as though lost in a spiritual desert.

She wanted to say that he should grant land for a monastery, but there was no time to write more. She could do that later. Fe was stirring, and she could not keep Keeva waiting any longer. She met her daughter outside and chastened her not to roll the parchment until the ink was dry. "Take your father's fastest horse."

"Is he going to help Da?"

"Only God can truly heal."

"Then why—"

"'Tis my hope Brody will see with the eyes of a righteous king." Enya had hoped the men of Fe's clan would stamp out the war-like acts taken against the clan, but she now understood that waiting for another to do what you yourself are capable of doing was wrong.

Keeva pointed her long, pale arm toward the well house. "But Da!"

Keeva had never been defiant before. "I will tend to him. Please, you must go now."

She did not move. "Why do we care what King Brody does about his nosey wife? 'Tis Da who is in danger from illness. Will you ask the king to send his physicians?"

Enya embraced her daughter. Such a tender heart should not be subjected to grief so young. "Your tea is helping." But they could not know what the future held. She decided to tell Keeva the truth. "Yesterday Gormley sought to poison your father."

She gasped. "That is why he is ill and no one else?"

"Nay, I stopped her. For now. She must be prevented from doing anything further."

With drooping eyes Keeva looked at the well house door. "But Da!"

"I am afraid he may have contracted an illness from traveling. The physicians and healers here know nothing of it. And indeed, there was no cure for those we saw. That is why you all must stay away. For now. Until we determine the fever's course. Pray. Trust. And be strong. That is what we all must do."

She sniffed and nodded, and then held out the parchment. "May I read it? Before I give it to the king?"

"You may. 'Tis my intention to help everyone. Anyone who opposes or questions what I've said may fall victim to the schemers, and therefore you must hurry. Speak to no one on the road. Tell no one of your mission. This should come to his attention before Gormley has chance to learn of it. And after you see it safely into his hands, depart immediately. If you see that woman any-where around—"

"Do not worry, Maither. Kyna and Branna are going to see that she is not in this kingdom for some time."

"What do you mean?" Enya gripped her daughter's wrist. "You said you knew nothing of their plans."

"I said they did not tell me. I overheard a wee bit. I did not understand until now." She took a step backward as though Enya's words were a slap.

"Do not take offense, darlin'. I did not mean to accuse you. Tell me. What else?"

"Only that they intend to send Gormley on an errand to Emain Macha. They planned to tell her of a ritual happening there. They thought she would go straight away."

"I do not know why they would think she would believe them."

"They planned for her to think she is listening in."

Kyna was clever. This was surely the plan. With Gormley away there was a better chance of talking sense to her husband. "Thank you for telling me this, Keeva. Now you must go. We cannot know if Gormley will turn back."

The girl nodded and scurried toward the stables.

Enya went back to Fe. He had earlier been riding a wave of hope and healing. But now as she gazed on his twisted, moaning body, he fought the tempest of what she was beginning to believe was the dreaded plague.

Chapter Thirty-Two

Here's to a fellow who smiles
When life runs along like a song.
And here's to the lad who can smile
When everything goes dead wrong.
—Irish saying

Colum watched the men as they wandered about, seeming to look for something or someone. Then their attention shifted toward the shore. He could not see the edge of the ocean from the cave, but someone must have arrived in a boat.

His heart pounded like a ceremonial drum as he crept back into the cave. Should he run out? He did not wish to be cornered in the darkest reaches of the cavern. But if he left, where would he go? As he was contemplating his choices, he heard his name called. Peering out again, he noticed the warriors rolling away barrels, the cargo Bairre had brought over. All of it. Bairre beckoned him from the direction of the shore, but a spear-shaped rock formation blocked Colum's view. While he considered whether the sailor might be warning him away or bidding him to come forth, he heard Bairre's voice again.

"Can't leave the boat. Come on, lad! The danger's passed."

Colum scrambled to collect his traveling bag and then tossed the mats and blankets toward the back of the cave. Taking the path they'd used on the way up, he half slid, half trotted his way down to the rocky shoreline. He found Bairre waving his arms. "We're to be off now," he shouted.

The boat was remarkably lighter. It took no time at all to reach the open sea. When the island was a small dark hump on the horizon, Colum dared to speak his thoughts. "You brought nothing with you."

Bairre let out a heavy sign and laid his oar across his lap. "Brought myself, my whole self. Suppose that's good enough." He glanced at Colum, measuring him from head to toe with his eyes. "Got yourself too. That's something. Did you put anything to eat in that bag of yours?"

He thought of his uneaten supper back in the cave. "When would I have time for that, the way you were shrieking?"

The sailor shrugged. "We'll catch fish."

"And cook it how?"

Again, a shrug.

"Get into some trouble there, did you?"

The sailor grinned. "A wee bit of trouble with someone's wife."

Colum groaned. Bairre likely paid them off with all of his little pots of brew. He should have assessed the man's character before setting sail with him. If he had an oar he would have snapped it across his knees just then. He bit back words and reached inside his mind for the scriptures he'd memorized. *Cease from anger, and forsake wrath: fret not thyself in any wise to do evil.* He repeated this over and over until the heat in his head began to subside.

"Are we headed in the right direction, Bairre?"

Another shrug.

Colum could tolerate no more. "What kind of sailor are you? Are we to starve out here on the ocean? You must know if we'll make it to the Sacred Isle or not!"

"Steady there, lad! We'll not starve. You're right to be angry with me, but we must both keep

411

our heads. I'm an old sailor. I know how to get us out of here."

"Why didn't you say so, then?"

Bairre huffed and rubbed chafed knuckles across the front of his shirt. "Thought you'd save us with your prayers, I did. But perhaps you are not as righteous as I had thought. Putting all your faith into one poor fellow and his wee boat, now that's far more frightening than losing all your food, your oars, and all your small pots, I'd say."

Colum gritted his teeth as he stared out at the disappearing island. The man was right. He was not nearly as righteous as he wished to be. He was fallible, weak, and still prone to lose his temper. He ignored Bairre's blathering as he searched his mind for more scripture. If only he had it written down. Then he could find the exact words he needed at the time he needed them. As soon as he returned to the land of his father's ancestors he would see about building a scriptorium. Perhaps more than one. And each with more than enough room for books.

Bairre stared out at the watery expanse. "We'll just catch a channel here that will push us along. We're close."

They spoke no more as they glided on the waves. When the clouds spilled their storehouses of rain, both men donned their waterproof garments. At least they were not without proper clothing. They could go without eating for a few days because thankfully their fresh water store was still onboard.

Colum welcomed the silence. The sailor had prattled on far too much so far. Now Colum had time to pray, and to plead to God. For their safety. For Ciarán's health. For all mankind.

But all he did was stare at the waves. His prayers had come to naught thus far. He wasn't sure God accepted prayers from such a belligerent man.

The hours passed. They shared sips from jars dipped into the water barrels, but no conversation passed between them. It was not until the following day that Bairre mentioned the stars that told him which way to navigate. "One more night and we will catch sight of the island we seek."

Colum thanked him and rolled to his side, hoping sleep would come.

He must have dozed off. When he next opened his eyes a faint pink glow tinted the horizon. Sitting up, he began his morning routine of prayers and contemplation, what he'd done every morning except for the previous day, and for that he implored Jesu's forgiveness. When he finished his prayers, he turned to Bairre's end of the boat. The sailor held tight to one end of a rope. The other end seemed to be attached to a weight plunged into the water.

"I beg your forgiveness," Colum began.

"No need. You've cause to be angry. I acted foolishly." Bairre's blond eyelashes brushed the top of his cheeks as he aimed his voice toward his feet. "I did not mean what I said. I am sure as a man of God your prayers are worthy. No one should make assumptions about another's soul as I did."

Colum could not argue. "'Tis all forgotten. I, too, must ask that you forgive my outbursts."

Bairre nodded and turned his attention to what he'd been doing.

"What have you got there?"

Bairre tugged until a wooden bucket with brass fasteners rose out of the water. Once the saltwater rushed out the slotted sides, Colum could see that it was filled with shells and snapping creatures too large to be sieved out. "Is there something edible in there?"

Bairre blinked his sapphire eyes. "Could be." He pointed his free hand outward. "And within sight is Molaise's community, the Sacred Island."

Colum squinted out toward the horizon. "And no horns welcome us."

Bairre chuckled. "No, indeed. But welcome us they will. 'Tis a quiet place, save for the stonemasons."

"Molaise's monks are stone carvers, then."

"You haven't seen the likes of it, I'd say. They are fair at brewing, as well."

Colum gave the man a grave look.

"Don't you worry. I'll not be bringing any back to the last place. They won't need it, having mine, and I've no notion to visit there again anytime soon." He straightened his back and stuck his thumbs under the collar of his coat. "I've come here for prayers, as I told you."

When they got closer, Bairre gave Colum orders about where they would land. "The best port is not near the monastery. We'll walk a bit but 'twill be good to get our land legs again."

After they landed and hauled the craft up on the rocks, they set off up a boulder-lined path and through a meadow where two goats eyed them suspiciously. Colum did feel wobbly. He was thankful he could steady himself before meeting Father Molaise. There were no cliffs here to ascend. The walking was leisurely. Colum measured his steps in psalms. *Open my eyes so I can see your wonder.*

Later, when they were settled into a small guesthouse in the community—it was tiny compared to those he had seen thus far—Colum had questions. Bairre had not hidden his eagerness to be away from the place, although he'd been eager at first to come. "'Tis time you explained yourself. You said this was your final destination and yet you seem prepared to leave with me. You know of the trades produced here, yet you knew nothing of the size of this abbey."

Bairre shrugged. "I did not know what it was like here. I'd been told things, tales that were apparently embellished. I had thought I might … well, never mind." Bairre pulled a wool throw up to his chin. "No need to find yourself another curragh, Colum. I will be taking you to the Isle of the Saints now."

"Will you? I am not sure I should trust you."

"Oh, is that the way of it? Who got us here with only drinking water and his wits about him? You are fine and fit, now aren't you?"

"You have not been honest with me."

Bairre stood, holding his cover under his arm. "I do not see that I need to explain myself, young monk. I have given you safe passage and asked for nothing in return but prayers."

"Where are you going?"

Colum could see in the man's eyes that he had no plan. The island did not have any homes in which he could seek shelter and no caves or high boulders.

"I suppose nowhere." He lowered himself back to the floor. "I desperately seek prayers. I fear God is not pleased with me."

"I am happy to pray for you, Bairre. Where will you go after you deliver me to my destination?"

"Perhaps I will stay there. This does not seem to be the right place."

Colum stopped asking questions. The old sailor was on a spiritual quest it seemed, and Colum did not want to interfere with God's plan for the man. And he was relieved to know he had transportation to the place where he hoped to find his old friend.

That night Colum dreamed, not about Ciarán, but about his father. Fe stood in the middle of one of his fields. A bull raced toward him, but he did not move or try to save himself. Colum attempted to run toward him, but his feet were sucked down by bog mud. As the animal closed in on Fe, there was nothing Colum could do but watch. He woke up sweating and wondered if he had contracted the illness now that he was further south. A fever can cause wild dreams. He wiped a hand across his forehead and realized he could not lift his tired legs from his bed, though he longed to open the door and let in the night air. The dream was gone, but the paralysis was real. He lay in agony for hours before drifting off to sleep again.

Colum awoke at dawn to the soft murmurs of prayers. He was not sick at all and his legs once again obeyed him. He joined the other monks in prayer.

Later, the abbot beckoned Colum to his cell for what he'd been told was to be a chat. The room was surprisingly well appointed, as though Molaise expected to be living there permanently.

The floor was covered in fresh rushes, still green. His woven sleeping mat was secured to stakes in the floor. A wee fire glowed from a central pit.

Father Molaise tipped his chin. "You are your companion are comfortable, I trust?"

"You are very kind. We do not expect special treatment, just shelter."

The abbot interrupted him. "Hospitality should never be assumed, but as a monk you know it must always be given, as Jesu would do."

Colum nodded and sat by the fire at the abbot's invitation.

"You may have also believed that we, hermits on a lonely island, live uncomfortably."

Colum thought it best not to reply. He had already been admonished not to make assumptions.

"We afford ourselves whatever comfort or discomfort comes our way." He clicked his tongue and shook his head. "I am not concerned with these things. Others may judge us, but it does not matter. We live here in communion with God and he alone is our judge. Now, the reason I asked you to come here to speak privately is because I am aware you are troubled."

"You are?"

"I have heard news of you, my son. That might surprise you, this being a windswept island off the mainland mostly forgotten. But others have rested here as you have in route to the community of Father Enda. After contemplating all you have shared thus far, I realized that this monk others speak of is you."

"I do not know why anyone is talking about me in this manner, Father Abbot."

He laughed. "Do not be troubled. I can see your studies have kept you away from such chatter, but one day you will have many pilgrims visit you, and you must be prepared."

Colum wasn't sure this was his calling. He wanted to study books and to establish many schools, not a single hermitage where he'd wait for spiritual wanderers to land on his doorstep.

"'Tis said you will be a great leader and save many souls. You have heard this yourself, I am sure. It has been said of you since you were a foster son."

"It has, you are correct. I only wish to study hard, transcribe as many books as I can, and build more communities in the north."

Molaise bobbed his head while staring intently at him. "God speaks to you in visions and dreams, aye?"

"He does." Colum wondered how he knew because he'd told no one but Michael. "Do you know a man called Michael?"

"An angel, you mean?"

Colum's throat grew parched. While Michael acted as Colum thought an angel might, Colum had never once told anyone how he sometimes pondered whether Michael might actually be a celestial being.

Molaise bobbed his head. "I have visions and dreams as well. Such gifts must be carefully nurtured and contemplated. You will learn."

Colum had to swallow with difficulty before he could speak. "Michael has been here?"

Molaise waved his hand dismissively. "This is not what we need to discuss. I feel that your traveling companion will not want to stay on the island long, so I must speak now before you are compelled to depart. You have had a dream that your father is ill, haven't you?"

"I have. And then I thought it was I who was infirm when I awoke, but not so. I am fine."

"Hmm. I see. You have been visited by a bad spirit, one that sought to immobilize you when you awoke."

What a mighty prophet Molaise must be to know so much. "I believe so."

"God instructed you to go to Ciarán, aye?"

"That is correct."

"You must not go back to Daire until you have completed this mission. No matter if your father is on his deathbed. Do you understand?"

"Is he? On his deathbed?" Dread threatened to choke him. What would his mother do without his father? Colum was the eldest and his brother was not yet grown enough to care for her.

Chapter Thirty - Three

Wisdom is what makes a poor man a king,
a weak person powerful,
a good generation of a bad one,
a foolish man reasonable.
—Old Irish saying

K eeva stood at the well house door, her legs wobbly from her long ride. "Is Da ... is he ..."

Enya joined her outside and closed the door. "He is sleeping. You took the message to Brody?"

"I did as you asked. He was none too happy to read it."

Enya steered her daughter to a low stone wall where she could rest while she explained. Putting an arm around her, Enya drew in a breath to calm herself. She had asked Keeva not to stay and watch the man read it. "You should not have tarried."

"I did not. A messenger caught up with me on the road. I would not have spoken to him because you ordered me not to converse with anyone on my travels, but I recognized him and knew he was from the castle. Was him that said the king is angry."

"With me? Not you, certainly."

"Neither of us, Maither. He wanted to know where Gormley had gone. I think he will deal with her, as you hoped he would."

"You told him, then?"

"I told him what I had overheard but did not swear it was so."

The sound of horse hooves sent the stable lad running past them. In the distance Enya spotted two hooded figures she recognized. "The women have returned. Hurry back to the house. I checked a moment ago and your brother was playing with the wee ones. After you refresh yourself, get supper for all of you. You have done well, my daughter."

"And Da. You said he's better?"

"Go on. Don't keep the children waiting." She would postpone telling her that Fe would not be returning to the house this night. She hurried to the stables.

"What is the meaning of you two leaving like this? Why was I not told?" The look on their faces froze her in her tracks. "What has happened?"

Kyna allowed the lad to assist her. Her legs trembled even after steadying herself on the grass. Branna hopped down with the ease of youth, but her expression matched that of the old cook's.

"Trouble has returned." Kyna took Enya's arm as the three of them walked toward the house.

Enya was eager to learn what had happened. "Keeva overheard you talking. You led Gormley away, did you? To the ancient place?"

"We did," Branna answered. "Was the best way to catch Brody's ear."

"And she went?"

"She did," Branna said. "That is not the trouble."

"Tea," Kyna groaned.

"Look at you," Enya scolded. "At your age taking a trip on horseback. What were you thinking, woman?" She glared at Branna. "You should have refused her."

"I tried to convince her to send me alone. I told her I'd find a lass to help me complete the deception and send Gormley away."

425

Kyna waved her free hand in the young woman's direction. "We trust no one else. Not now."

They entered the house and were immediately met with cheering children.

"Missed you," Sheela called out, first embracing Enya and then Branna.

Meredit and Egan, both on the cusp of adulthood, interrogated Keeva on her trip to see Brody. They were in awe of their sister gaining an audience in the castle, and the three of them chatted happily. Too soon her children would know the harsh consequences life could bring merely because of a trip Fe had made. She would allow them this merriment for now.

The young nanny took up the serving of the meal, allowing Keeva to sit down to eat with the others. Kyna huddled by the fire wrapped in the blanket Enya brought her.

The laughing children. The golden glow of the fire. The coziness of the cottage as the day's sunlight began to fade. Enya would like nothing more than to rest there, but she could not. "Tell me what is wrong," Enya insisted. "I must get back to Fe."

Kyna raised watery eyes to look at her. "There can be nothing right. Not while Malachi breathes. But I fear 'twill be me, not him, who departs the earth first."

"Nay. You just need to rest." Enya's hands shook as she reached up to pull the blanket tighter around Kyna's shoulders. "Malachi is in the tower. You remember."

"He's not," Branna said, looking up from ladling broth into a bowl.

Enya stood. "What do you mean?"

Branna left the children and put both hands on Enya's forearms. "We thought Emain Macha would be a fine place to send Gormley. How could we know she'd reunite with that evil priest there?"

"This cannot be. Does the king know?" She glanced at Keeva but could not send her back to the castle at this hour. With Branna returned, Enya could go.

"He knows," Branna said as she jostled Enya's hands up and down. "We went there, arriving soon after Keeva left, they told us."

A heavy sigh came from the chair by the fire. "Your heart was in that letter you wrote Brody, but I fear it will do no good. Our king will not stand against his vile cousin. His wife, perhaps, but not Malachi."

"What will they do?" Enya whispered to the two women.

Kyna spoke with a trembling voice. "Close our church. Forbid our prayers. Banish your son from this kingdom." She began to cry and quoted a verse that Enya remembered from when they could get practice manuscripts from the monks. *"Per diem incurrent tenebras et quasi in nocte sic palpabunt in meridie."*

"What is she saying?" Branna asked.

Enya answered as she stared at the crumpled form of the woman sitting by the fire. "They find it is dark in the daytime, and they grope at noon as if it were night." Enya left her servant and collapsed at Kyna's feet. "What will we do? If only Fe could—Oh, I must go to him."

The door opened and Keeva entered. Enya hadn't seen her go out. "Oh, Maither, I fear it may be too late."

Enya rushed past her, scurried across the damp grass and lunged at the well house door. Once inside she threw herself on Fe's chest. He groaned, thankfully still breathing. She sat up and used her hair to wipe perspiration from his face. Her dark strands were an ominous contrast to the pallor of his cheeks. "Come back to me, Fe."

428

Two days later they held a wake. Not for Fe, but for Kyna. With grief covering her like dense fog, Enya waded through the days focusing only on Fe. He was conscious now only minutes a day.

"He's healing," Branna told her when she came into the house for fresh linens. "That is why he sleeps so much. You'll see."

"We must believe, Maither," Keeva said. The two of them were chopping root vegetables at the table board. "I have more tinctures for you to take." She rose and brought down a clay jar from a shelf. She managed her limp now as though she'd always had it.

Enya could barely whisper her thanks. Kyna had done things like this before, and now it was Enya's daughter's turn. Fe would be so proud of her. *Fe, come back to us.*

She was changing the sheet her semiconscious husband was lying on when the stable lad came in. "Forgive me," he mumbled. "A summons from the king has arrived. He requests your presence straight away."

"I've no business with the king." She smoothed a fresh covering over her husband's large form and rose to dip spring water from the well.

"I beg your pardon."

She gazed at the lad who stood stick-straight, turning his felt hat over in his hands. "I will not come."

"'Tis urgent, they say."

"Who says?" She detected the sound of horses snorting right outside the well house. More than one horse. She opened the door.

Three of the king's soldiers sat on charcoal stallions. They wore leather helmets, dark clothing, and high boots the color of pitch. Because of her melancholy their presence failed to intimidate her.

"What do you want?"

"To escort you, Enya of the Cenél Conaill, to see King Brody at once. At his order."

"There has been a death here. You cannot command me—"

"We insist. King Brody insists."

Her first thought was to send them on their way. They had no right to insist, and if Fe had been alert enough to speak to them he would have ... but, she had never known Brody to push his way. Something had happened and it probably involved Malachi. If it weren't for her worry over Colum, and the fact that the ghastly pagan priest had wanted him dead, she wouldn't obey. However, deep down she thought Brody could muster the courage to rule as he should. She hoped so. She prayed so. Feeling exhausted, gloomy, and impatient, Enya had no will to confront Gormley on her own.

The horses stamped and whinnied.

"Go get Branna and tell her she must attend to my husband," she ordered the lad.

Brody paced the vast hall. He paused and pointed a finger at Enya. "He has renounced his position as priest. He knows he has no power over me. He's trying something else now, this Accuser business."

"Why does this bother you?"

"'Twas what he said to me. How he said it." The man's face was bleached with trepidation.

"He said, 'I am inside you. You know that. Even now you hear my voice inside your head.'"

She recalled him saying something similar to her once, something about being her spiritual father. "He attempts to intimidate you. Pay no heed."

Brody rubbed his chin. "Perhaps. Chilled me to the bone, though. How does Fe fare?"

She rubbed a hand over her face. "My husband is not well. He needs me at home."

"Any word from Brendan, then?"

"He has not returned."

Brody's shoulders sagged. Had the king no advisors?

"Why did you send for me? I don't know that I can do anything."

"Fe is missed," he said, shaking his head. "Your letter. You showed great wisdom on this matter. I believed you wanted to consult me on this issue, so I have chosen to include you."

He said so, but she knew the real reason was because Fe was incapacitated and no other with any gumption was nearby. Her husband had handled more matters than she probably knew. Better get on with it so she could leave. "What is the urgency? Please, tell me now."

He rubbed the knuckles on one hand as he spoke. "I can banish Malachi. My wife doesn't want me to—"

She would not sweeten her words. There was no time. "How much longer will you defer to her? Are you not king? If you think it best for the people, then do it, man. I know what my husband would tell you. He would say take care of your own household or you will never rule with authority."

She turned and ran down a corridor toward the stables, feeling time slipping away like drops of waters through her fingers. As she rode back home in the king's chariot, his driver told her what Malachi's banishment would mean. "He'll be in the south now, never to cross the Bluestack Mountains. I hear he plans to travel by the River Shannon if the king banishes him. We'll not be seeing that mad dog again."

The Shannon? Oh, Colum.

Molaise had no answer for Colum about his father. "We cannot control what visions we are given. 'Tis God's judgment to reveal what he wills. The challenge is to obey."

Colum knew in his heart the wise abbot was right. He had to trust that God would care for his mother whatever she faced. When he left the island, Bairre announced that he intended to return there.

"Here? You're to be a monk, then?" Colum was surprised, but delighted.

"We are to figure that out, Molaise and me. I want to learn more about this grace that your God—our God, I mean—is freely giving."

Colum slapped him on the shoulder. "And you shall, my man. You shall."

The voyage to the Isle of the Saints was not as perilous as the previous journeys even though it took longer. They were able to navigate within sight of land and enjoy the shelter that provided. God's grace was already evident. As they sailed closer to the island where Colum hoped to find his good friend, the wonder of the beauty of it nearly left him speechless. There were actually three islands. They were headed to the largest and the first within their sights. Vivid blue skies met their arrival and the sun, for once, was warm on their backs. The easy landing also made for a favorable impression. "Are you sure you would not rather live here?" he joked with his sailor friend.

Two brown-robed monks met them at the shore. "God's blessing on you," the tallest one said when they disembarked. "Have you come to see Enda?"

Colum accepted a hand from one of them and stepped out of the boat. "May God give you peace, brothers. I would like to see your teacher as soon as it can be arranged." He cleared his throat. "I am, I regret to say, quite anxious to have a word with him."

"Patience," the shorter man said as he helped Bairre empty the boat. "Most travelers are pilgrims come to see Father Enda. He is on the mainland at present. We cannot know when he will return."

"I can tell you." Colum was confident God had spoken. "He will return at the next full moon."

The tall monk raised an eyebrow. "Are you the one called Columcille, then?"

"I am." Perhaps God had given this man the gift of discernment.

"Your reputation is renowned among the Christian fathers. A great prophecy has been spoken regarding you."

Columcille was beginning to dread this reputation others said he had. What man can know what the future holds for another man? Does not each one possess a free will to decide his own path, even to choose not to take the one the Lord God has marked out? He was trying with all his being to be devout, but who could know whether he would succeed? "Only those coming after us can judge the worthiness of such a prophecy."

The monk shook his head. His long brown locks whirled in several directions, caught by the ocean breezes. If it were not for the man's tonsure, his vision would be veiled like a horse with an unkempt mane. "We have sensed God's intention for our people," the island monk said. "This gives the brothers great hope. I pray you have not come to dissuade them."

Colum reached to grip the man's hand. "I bring good tidings without despair. I am looking for my friend Ciarán. He came to Enda by instruction from Mobhi. Is he here? God has sent me to attend to him."

436

The expression on the two monks' faces twisted from delight to dismay. "'Tis good the Father Abbot is coming. He will instruct you in regard to your friend."

Enda would be protective of his student. Colum must be patient.

The tall one took Colum's traveling bag and motioned with it to a grassy path leading toward the center of the island. "I am Brother Cormac and this is Brother Maol."

Colum introduced the sailor.

Bairre bowed. "I thank you for your hospitality. I will rest one night and then I must depart."

They nodded and then led the way to the guest house. Once they delivered them to one of the larger round buildings, the monks backed away toward the door.

"'Tis nearly terce. Please excuse us as we go to the church."

"I will come also," Colum said. He would ignore his growling stomach. Whatever the monks were not telling him was probably worthy of prayers and fasting.

Standing in the midst of about a hundred monks, Colum had thought he would find solace. He required such discipline. But his mind returned to Ciarán. Instead of repeating the psalms and the prayers of confession, he pleaded with God to reveal Ciarán's fate. If his friend was dead, why wouldn't God tell him? Why had his gift of visions vanished nearly as soon as he stepped on this island? The last time he felt God's spirit stirring within him was when he'd announced the abbot's whereabouts. Nothing since. However, simple logic told him Ciarán was not here on the island.

He was about to leave to find Bairre and tell him they must leave, when Brother Cormac gripped his arm. The monk squeezed so tightly Colum feared he might cry out and disturb the prayers of the faithful. "Outside," the man whispered.

A low ray of sun temporarily blinded Colum outside the church. His legs were weak from having not eaten, and his disappointment in not finding his friend after having traveled so long by sea prompted him to rush past the monk and seek out the curragh tied somewhere along the shore. Unable to find it or Bairre, he began smashing small stones against larger boulders. As his anger boiled up like a soup pot, Colum released the stone he held and covered his ears with cupped palms. Why? Why had none of the things he thought would happen taken place? Not one. He had not completed building his schools. He had not found Ciarán. He had not become the holy leader the rumors predicted he would be. And now, no angels and no visions. God had abandoned him.

Flinging himself down to the rocky ground, he noticed how bloodied his hands had become from smashing rocks. His mother had spoken about some kind of family curse. Perhaps he had it. Dropping him off at a church when he was a lad hadn't cured him of it.

"Why did you leave the church?"

He turned and blinked in the sunlight. Brother Cormac moved to block the sun with his body.

Colum drew in a breath to steady himself. "Why do you ask me this? Did you not ask me to leave?"

Cormac knelt down to meet Colum's gaze. "Certainly not. You are most welcome."

Even though his words expressed hospitality, Colum detected no warmth in them. He much preferred the company of Molaise. Why would this monk ask him to leave and then deny it?

"You did not grip my arm here?" He clasped his bloodied fingers around his left forearm.

Cormac's eyes bulged as he saw blood staining Colum's sleeve like a spilt bottle of ink. "I did not. What has happened to you?"

Colum stood, realization dawning. "Please excuse me, Brother, but I must depart. I thank you and wish you God's peace."

"Wait," the man moved in front of Colum's path. "The monk you seek, the one Father Enda escorted to the flatlands of the River Shannon, is very ill. Perhaps you must go there."

"Perhaps I must." God had spoken after all, despite Colum's failure to repudiate all worldly inducements.

Chapter Thirty - Four

I am certain that God, who began the good work
within you, will continue his work until it is finally
finished on the day when Christ Jesus returns.
—Philippians 1:6 NLT

"I will stay with you as long as you need me."

Bairre hoisted a sail as he and Colum departed for the mainland.

"You are kind, my friend." Colum said a prayer for their journey. He felt sure he would find Ciarán alive, but perhaps not for long. The sorrow of losing his friend was only eased because of the hope of heaven. And that was enough. It had to be. There was some other reason God wanted Colum to arrive at the River Shannon. He could not imagine what that might be, but he would be faithful. The journey of the Christian faith was nothing if not wild and mysterious.

A sudden thought jolted him so much he nearly fell into the water.

"What's wrong?" Bairre tied off the sail and came toward him.

Colum lifted his hand. "I have seen my father in my mind. A tall, strong man, he is now feeble and his thoughts are garbled. Please, a moment of silence. I must pray for him."

"Then I shall too." Bairre sat in the bottom of the boat and bowed his head.

Enya was stunned to see the abbot standing at her door. "You are welcome here," she managed to blurt out. "Tea," she ordered Branna while offering Father Finnian Fe's chair. "I am afraid my son Colum is not here."

"Oh, I thought he was gathering students at a new school." He jostled the book he held between his thigh and the side of the chair.

"He was. Then he got a calling … uh, that's what 'tis, aye? A message from God to depart?"

The abbot nodded as he rubbed his bare fore-head. "Where, may I ask?"

She shot Branna a nervous look as the girl scooped herbs into a pot. Branna tipped her head, understanding that she must hurry to make the abbot comfortable. Enya pressed her palms together in front of her chest. "He is looking for his friend, a monk called Ciarán. Somewhere south." She felt foolish. Of course he went south. There was not much north.

"I see."

"Father, I am concerned about my son. Might you be able to get a message to him?"

"Since the plague, communication has been difficult. I know location of Ciarán's assignment. For the mother of Columcille, I will do what I can. What is this message?"

She told him about Malachi, but to her surprise he did not seem alarmed. "I will send your message with the carpenters who will go there for the building," he said.

She wasn't sure it would be delivered with the urgency she hoped, but it seemed the best she could do. There was more troubling her.

"My husband, he is quite ill. Might I implore you to pray for him, Father Finnian?"

Another nod. An uncomfortable silence ensued as they waited for the tea to brew. "Something to eat, Father Abbot?" she finally said. Why had she not thought to offer before? Why did this man's presence unnerve her?

"A bit of bread only," he replied.

She had forgotten about the austere habits of these men.

Moments later Branna served the man while Enya waited. The man's lips moved silently before he took the bread and cup from the servant. Was that it? Did he not need to stand over Fe? She should have paid closer attention to Colum's lifestyle. *Oh, God, instruct me in your ways.*

Much later Finnian lifted the book he'd brought. "Do you know what this is?"

"I have seen many of the manuscripts the monks create, Father Abbot. I was fortunate to have been taught by monks when I was a child."

He smiled. Finally.

"What a blessed childhood you must have had."

"Oh, no, 'twasn't."

His dark brows lifted.

"I mean, that part, the brothers teaching me, that was indeed. The rest. My family. Well—"

Finnian lifted a finger. "I see. And God found you in that sad place and touched you with the gift of learning."

She had never thought of it that way. Her delight must have shown in her face because he smiled again.

"This book is nothing like those you have seen. I had hoped to show it to your son. I am recently returned from Rome and have been given this." He patted the leather cover as though he held a newborn baby. "A psalter, but unlike what you may have seen, and more besides. The Holy Scriptures, most of what we have that the brothers labor to translate, are written in Greek—they refer to that as the Septuagint. That language is unfamiliar to most men today. Comprehending the language is a great struggle. We obtain some manuscripts in other languages and some are easier to read than others, however the accuracy of these is uncertain."

He glanced up at her, possibly detecting her confusion. She blinked and dipped her head hoping to convince him to continue.

"Ah, well, there are other copies written in the language of the church. These manuscripts are known as the Vulgate, a word that means commonly known, so that all ears may hear." He stroked the book in his lap again. "That is what I have here. The translation of Saint Jerome. What

445

is most significant to our understanding is the translation of the old Hebrew texts. Jerome has given us that. Have you heard the story of Abraham and Isaac?"

"Please forgive me, Father Finnian. I understand that these words are so very important. But so are your prayers. My husband—"

"Say no more." He tucked the treasured book into his robe and followed her out the door.

Fe was sleeping. Finnian stretched out his hand and asked God to heal him and to bring him back to the family who needed him. And then he said something that touched Enya deep inside. "Because of your great and abiding love for this woman, you will not abandon her in her hour of need. This, I believe."

Then he left, taking his treasured book with him. She would tell Colum all that happened, and tell him about this book. Perhaps that would help make up for him not being able to see it.

She sat at Fe's side and dabbed his face with spring water. His cheeks appeared smooth again and his dry lips were once again pink. He opened his eyes. A clearness in them revealed recognition and departure from the sleep of the plague.

Several weeks later as Fe sat at the table board across from her, sipping an herbal concoction Keeva had brewed for him, Enya remembered that she intended to write Colum a note. Now would be a good time for that. Fe was not his old self, his wit and wisdom had not yet returned to him, but he was alive and helping with the harvest. God had spared him by answering the holy man's prayer. Colum needed to know that. She supposed her son's final destination would be the new dwelling near the Shannon. Colum would be interested to know about this book, this Vulgate translation bearing the interpretation of a long-dead saint of the church. As luck would have it, there were tinkers visiting who offered their services delivering messages. They used that great river to transport their goods. God provides.

Colum stood over Ciarán's grave, recalling his friend's last words. "This is my day of resurrection, Colum, but 'tis not yours. Not for a long time. Continue on. For me. For Jesu."

He glanced up at the stone structures dotting the riverbank as he fingered his mother's rope cross in his pocket. He had thought to leave it on his friend's grave, but somehow, he thought it should be returned to Enya. When the time was right. Not, he hoped, to be put on his father's grave.

Several men in hooded robes scurried along a path between the buildings. Ciarán had begun a school and it flourished despite the death of its founder.

A breeze rattled the long hair touching his shoulders. A gray cloud floating in and flung fat raindrops at his feet. "Rest well, my friend. You have been a bright burning lamp to many." He stared at the darkening wet mound of dirt. "One day a church will be built here over your grave and you will forever be surrounded by the prayers of the faithful."

As the deluge continued Colum rushed into the common house to escape it. He had not even crossed the threshold before the sun came out again, bathing his damp shoulders in light. He sat at a transcription table to record Ciarán's death in the monastery's annuals. A monk approached him with a folded piece of parchment. He knew before he accepted it, it was from his mother. The quality of the vellum was not equal to that used in monasteries. "God bless you," he said to the messenger, taking it from the man's hand.

An amulet dangled down from the man's neck. Malachi!

"I told the lad I knew who you were and would give it to you. You don't mind, surely, as we are old acquaintances."

"What are you doing here?"

He pulled up a stool, uninvited. "I did not care for the Sons of Néill. I suppose you did not either. That's why you've come here."

"Do not suppose anything at all. You are a pagan. A lying criminal who once disguised himself as a priest in Jesu's church. Why did they allow you to enter?"

He chuckled. "Very inhospitable of you, the one they call Dove of the Church."

Malachi was wearing the weapon that had pierced Colum's flesh. It should never have been given back to him. Colum's heart raced and his palms perspired despite his efforts to calm himself. A Psalm! He must draw on God's Word.

"Do not fear me, son. I am a spiritual father to many, even if you do reject me."

"You tried to kill me."

"You mean that matter with this?" He held up the sharp metal instrument of the Accuser. "Just a wee misunderstanding, lad. A slip of the fingers. I do not accuse you." He let the amulet fall back to his chest and waved his fingers dismissively. "No matter. Read your note. 'Tis from your mother."

"Where did you get it? Have you harmed my family?"

Malachi huffed. "I am offended you would say this. I was sent away unjustly and gained passage with some traveling men. When I learned their trade was delivering all sorts of messages, I inquired of a few of them and learned they'd come from Fe's estate. Sure enough Enya had done some writing. They were more than happy to be relieved of coming to this place. I did everyone a favor, and you do not thank me."

"You've read it." Colum clinched his fingernails into his palm.

Malachi shrugged. "I suppose I have." He grinned with graying teeth. "You will find the part about the book most interesting. It seems your old abbot, Finnian of Magh Bile, has acquired a copy of Saint Jerome's Vulgate. Not that your mother says so, but you will infer as I did.

You enjoy those kinds of writings, aye? I imagine you'd like to see it. Your mother certainly recommended you do so."

"This was private." Colum's thoughts turned from anger to curiosity. If Finnian had the Vulgate, he had to go see.

"Are you not sitting among a community, Columcille? Is not everything here shared?"

"Not with you. I will speak to the—" He couldn't. The abbot was dead.

Colum would not debate this man. He would be leaving soon anyway. First, he needed to speak to Bairre. "You will be on your way, man. Do not disturb these true believers."

"I have no intention of bothering anyone here. And as you said, I am to move on. Until we meet again."

"We should not."

Malachi's nefarious grin rubbed raw against Colum's best judgment. He'd better leave before Colum hauled him out to the road.

The stubby man took a few steps toward the door and then turned around. "No one knows where I go, Columcille. There is no one to hinder me. I am a free man."

"You escaped the tower, I suppose."

451

"Nay, I was released."

Colum's father would never have allowed that, but Brody was king and Fe was ill, he supposed. Malachi's release made sense in that light. Even so, why had Malachi come down here to haunt Colum like some banshee?

Malachi moved away again. He spoke over his shoulder. "I was just about to leave anyway."

Colum watched as the hunched, black-robed man walked out.

"Let me come with you," Bairre pleaded, his round eyes appearing larger than usual.

"Go to Molaise," he told him. "That is your path. Mine leads me to Magh Bile."

The gritty sailor continued stuffing his sensible seafaring clothing into his bag as the two of them spoke in the guesthouse. "As you wish." He paused and looked up. "I will miss you, Colum, and your strength, even that fiery temper of yours."

Colum cringed but tried not to show it. "I will pray for you, my friend. Perhaps we will meet again." He moved toward the door and then thought to warn him. "Should you encounter a man called Malachi—older, round and fat, with an evil stare and the amulet of the Accuser around his neck—stay far away."

"Shouldn't be hard with that description. Not a friend of yours, then?"

"An enemy of God."

Colum's clan had sent him off with more than enough ornamental metal baubles to pay Bairre and borrow a mare to take to Magh Bile. The owner would retrieve it there later. Apparently, the monks often worked out arrangements like this.

When he left he was alone on the road, perfect for contemplating his mother's letter. Praise Jesu, his father had survived the same illness that had claimed Mobhi and Ciarán. His siblings were doing well. The new community was in good hands with the men he'd put in charge. And now, if Finnian allowed it, he'd have a copy of Saint Jerome's scripture with which to teach them. No copy he knew of had arrived on the island before this one. It would be infinitely better than the assortment of material he'd had access to thus far. Jerome had been ordained by God to put to ink and parchment the true intent of the ancient writers. His text, the Vulgate, was for everyday people. Every man and woman could be taught from it the true messages, insightful inspiration, and instruction for living a faithful life. The thought of it thrilled him. Finally, the fulfillment of his mission was in sight. All things had worked together for good.

Be a bright flame before me, O God,
A guiding star above me.
—Attributed to St. Columcille

"I am happy to allow you a look," Finnian said, guiding Colum to his church at Magh Bile. "That is why I traveled to your homeland. I believe our Heavenly Father wills for you to study it."

"Would you like for me to take it to Daire for a time?"

Finnian looked horrified. "Study it here, of course. It is not to leave my possession. You must understand, I endured a journey of great peril to bring this to Éire. Rome is not as it once was. War. Plague. Rat-infested streets where men haunt in shadows like demons and use long blades to strike down Christian pilgrims. God alone protected me in order for me to bring this book to our island. I cannot allow it go anywhere I do not."

You did this for yourself, Colum wanted to say. *For the wealth of your own community.* Why did Finnian not trust his own student? Colum held his tongue and agreed. He was eager to read it and would waste no time with arguments. The church was dim, but Finnian brought candles. He placed them in brass holders on the altar and then brought the scriptures out from underneath. He placed the book on the wooden table but not close enough for the flames to cast much light on the writing. Colum had to squint to read the Latin words.

Finnian sat with him for at least an hour. Colum would have read longer had the bell for prayers not rung. Reluctantly, he passed the book to the Father Abbot, who returned it to a shelf under the altar.

Colum had to ask for forgiveness several times during prayers as his mind wandered to the great book. He would ask Finnian to allow him to copy it. More candles could be brought to the church, along with ink and parchment. He would spend as many hours as he needed to. His followers should have access to these words.

After prayers the brothers consumed a light meal of bread and hazelnuts. Most would go to their beds after, but not Colum. God had impressed upon him that he must make a copy, even if it meant making an untidy reproduction so that he could finish as quickly as possible.

He stopped his former teacher as he walked to his cell along the monastery path. "Father Finnian, my people should also read Jerome's text. May I spend time in the church to copy it?"

"Copy it? Certainly not."

"You can depend on me to be careful and diligent. Did you not once say I was the best scribe you ever had at Magh Bile?"

"'Tis true, but this cannot be done."

"Why?"

Finnian held up this hand and then calmly walked away. Colum had not realized his former teacher would be so selfish.

"He does not wish the pilgrims to go elsewhere. If they did, his monastery would cease to prosper. He does not value you nor trust you. Never has."

Colum spun around. That voice. Malachi! But no one was there. He glanced around at every shadow along the path but saw no one. He banged a fist against his temple. Ever since he was a boy that man's voice stirred up Colum's anger. Malachi had never had anything good to say about Colum. Despite the praise of almost every other person he met, all he heard was condemnation from Malachi. That foul man truly was the Accuser and now he haunted Colum's thoughts without even being present.

Colum went to his bed with his supper turning in his stomach.

The next day he tried again but was only met with the blank stare that he had known from his days as a student in Magh Bile. The look meant he was foolish to even ask. Colum made up his mind to cast Malachi's condemnations away and focus instead on Ciarán's words. "Continue on." He had to. For his friend. For the sacrifices of his other teachers, his foster father, his parents. For the many hours Michael had spent teaching him to lean not on his own understanding but to lift his thoughts to heaven. Aye, he must.

After night vigils, which were made in each monk's private cell, he made his way to the church. The clear sky gave way to a blanket of ice-colored stars, but no moon. He was quite sure no one had seen him as he slipped inside. It was so dark he wasn't sure how he'd copy anything, but he had brought his tools just in case. Finnian had all the candles.

The book was in its place. He pulled it out and when he opened to the first leaf a beam of moonlight shot through the side window. Suddenly all the text was visible. He rapidly set up his ink and parchments and began in earnest, not knowing how long the light would last.

He copied until he could no longer fight the boulder-like pressure on his eyelids. He had gotten much done and would return again at the same hour.

A twang of guilt tugged at him as he let himself back into the guesthouse. One of the visitors stirred a bit, opened his eyes, then rolled to his side. Hopefully he had assumed Colum had gone to relieve himself. He stashed his writing supplies under his cot and willed himself to fall asleep quickly.

The next morning he was groggy. Another monk eyed him suspiciously. "Bad dreams," Colum said, and the man turned from him. He didn't care if these men liked him or not. He would do what he had to for the rest of Éire.

For fourteen days he kept up his stealth. No one was the wiser. As former student, Colum was welcome to stay as long as he wished, so he spent his free hours in the scriptorium exploring the monastery's collection, something he'd meant to do for a long time anyway. He had about dozen pages left to copy. The light had visited him every night. A miracle.

One night a frosty sheet on the pathway to the church caused him to slip and fall. He grunted at the impact. With his size he could not stumble quietly. Getting to his feet, he glanced around. All was quiet so he continued on. With his hand on the church's door latch, a sudden sound made him turn around. Was it the snapping of a twig? Was someone watching? He counted to ten and stared out into the inky night. Finally, when he was about to blame his imagination for the sound, a cat came trotting out of a nearby yew. Colum let out a breath. "You startled me, kitty." The creature wove its way toward him, left, right, and left again, as though it did not wish to be seen as too eager for attention. Colum rubbed his knuckle across the wee cat's ginger head. The animal sniffed and trotted off as if it was Colum who had done the disturbing.

He entered the church, careful to close the door without a sound. After about a quarter of an hour, he glanced back to the door for no reason he could think of. The church entry bore a large keyhole, although the door was never locked. He thought he detected a bit of movement there. He rose and walked toward it. When he was about twelve paces away, he bent down for a look.

An eye!

Someone watched him. He scrambled to the door and flung it open. A dark figure rushed past the yew, carrying what he thought was that blasted cat.

Enya finished her morning devotions and returned the page she'd been reading to the stack Kyna had used. A stab of grief overcame her for a moment, and she steadied herself against the windowsill, lightly tipping some of the herb pots Keeva had put there.

"Are you all right, Maither?" Keeva hurried to her side.

"Do not worry about me. 'Tis your brother."

Why had she said that? Had she not just been thinking of the old cook?

"Have you gotten a message, then? I did not see the tinkers."

Enya reached out and pushed aside a golden lock of her daughter's hair. "I have not. Sometimes I have ... feelings about things."

"About him especially."

"I do not love him more than the rest of you. Please know that."

"I do know. That is not why I said that. You fear the prophecy, do you not? Because of your birth order and he is the eldest? Something like that?" Keeva stared off through the window panes as though remembering the chapters of their lives.

The lass had only recently began speaking so frankly to Enya. She was a grown woman now. She had carried so much responsibility since Fe's illness. "I do not fear, I worry. Too much, I know."

Keeva put her hand on her mother's shoulder. "These feelings you have, you have needed them in the past, aye? Because he has been away so much."

Enya laughed. "Your father always said I was impulsive. My spirit has gotten me into some predicaments. I think your father is right. I should think longer before I act." She sighed. "Must be obvious. Even old Ninnidh once said that to me."

"But, Maither, could it not be that God is guiding you this way?"

"Perhaps so." Enya smiled at her. So much like Kyna, this one. "The evil priest, the man who was not really a priest, I worry he will find Colum." Enya stroked her daughter's silky hair again. "As I did worry for you, my sweet lass." Her heart ached that Sean had not yet asked to marry Keeva. Perhaps because of her imperfection.

"Worry does nothing to help."

"You are correct, daughter. All we have left is to pray."

"Then we shall." Keeva gripped Enya's hands and the two of them asked for God's protection as a sunbeam shone through the window and warmed their faces.

Father Cruithneachia had been right all those years ago when he said God would grant her request. God had blessed her and taken away her barrenness, which turned out to mean more than bearing children. It meant she had a family now, one that loved her and one that she cherished with all her heart.

After Keeva left to gather eggs, Enya pondered what she'd said. If God had given her this sense of foreboding, what was she to do with it? Aye, pray, and they'd done that but the feeling niggled at her still. Another message?

She thought about Abbot Finnian's visit. That book. The story of Abraham and Isaac. She knew that Abraham was the father of all the believers yet to be born. But she did not know this story the abbot spoke of, and he hadn't told it to her. She hadn't allowed time for it, of course, but who could blame her with Fe so ill?

Blame her? She'd felt blamed all her life. True, she now was blessed, but these feelings? Where did they come from? She wished to rid herself of this belief that she was cursed by way of her bloodline. She had not passed it on. That she could see. But Enya herself? How to become blameless in the eyes of God?

She wished she could read that book the abbot carried around. Perhaps she could visit Magh Bile and ask to see it.

Chapter Thirty-Six

There are no unmixed blessings in life.
—Irish proverb

Colum was caught. The wandering monk looking for his cat had seen Colum and woken Finnian. Now they stood in the church with Finnian's candles burning brightly from the altar, exposing Colum's transgression.

"This in no way harms your book," Colum protested.

"You did not have permission to do this." The man's face grew crimson.

"You did not grant it, but you should have. You know how much people will learn from this."

"You wanted wealth for your own kin, the Sons of Néill."

This was about power, then. Colum had not figured on that. And it should not be. It should be about bringing Jesu's light to the people. All the people.

"I wanted only wealth of knowledge, Father Abbot. What you taught me."

His plea had no effect. Before he could object further the abbot gathered up both the book and its copy and rushed out.

"That is mine," Colum called out. "My labor. My own parchments and inks. You don't think you can ..."

But his words went unheeded.

He tried several times over the next few days. Finnian simply would not listen. Colum's followers were so few. He needed an army to get his copy back. He paced in front of the guesthouse. There had to be a way.

The ginger cat scampered past him. Colum looked up to see the snitch following behind. The man paused as though he thought Colum would assault him. He would have liked to, but perhaps this man could help. "Tell me, who rules in this part of the island?"

"King Diarmait, of course. High king, he is."

"And where is this king?"

"Suppose at the castle."

The cat moved silently until he was at the man's feet. He picked it up and tucked the cat's head under his arm as though fearful Colum might harm it. Colum would never do such a thing and was at first offended, but then recognized that the man was simple-minded. Of course the king was in his house. But where?

"How might I find this castle?"

Finally, the man told him what he wanted to know. He would leave today, taking the main road north and then following the second dirt path on the left up a hill and past a field of nettles until he came to the castle at the top.

He'd never gone to a castle before. He'd been told these castles were nothing but oversized huts. Those who had traveled far reported that in the Byzantium Empire those with power and standing lived in opulent dwellings referred to as palaces, buildings painted with gold and dripping with jewels. He shook his head at the thought. His countrymen were too busy to bother building something that would eventually return to dust. The brothers built round huts from stones that were sturdy and snug. Even the churches dedicated to Jesu could not boast such comfort, although comfort was not the purpose. Keeping the rain off one's head and shutting out nighttime noises were most important. Whether a king lived in a palace or a castle or a wee hut, the ruler needed wisdom above all else. And that comes only from God.

He abandoned his musing when he reached the palisade.

Saying he was one of Finnian's monks brought Colum the audience he sought. He was shown inside and taken to a room to wait. This building was more spacious than any he'd ever seen. The ceiling rose to a height at least twice that of his stature and about twenty men could stand comfortably side-by-side without touching the walls. He was pondering the unpleasant idea that perhaps one day Éire would boast of Byzantium-style structures when King Diarmait entered.

"I am most pleased to have the prayers of the Father Abbot falling on my fields and streams," Diarmait said. "What is it you have come about?"

Colum explained the situation. "I am due my own property," he pleaded.

The king stroked his beard, the faded yellow color of an older man. He was about Fe's age and build, and hopefully he would display wisdom. Finally, the ruler agreed to consider the case.

Colum was escorted to meet with a scribe. "Sign your name here."

He did so.

"This will be delivered to Father Finnian and then the king will summon you both back here when he has made a decision."

"How long?"

The man stared at Colum over his long, pointy nose. "The king will decide, not me."

Colum returned to the monastery, determined to wait as long as necessary. When he entered the guest house he was met by the attendant. "Someone is waiting to see you at the women's house. Shall I have her meet you in the rectory?"

There was only one woman who would want to see him. Why had she come so far?

"Colum!" Enya kissed him. "Did you receive the letter I sent to the monastery at the River Shannon? And the message before that. Carpenters were supposed to … you must not have." She twisted her smile into a worry.

"I did. I was there. What has happened and why have you come?"

"I didn't know you'd be at Magh Bile. I came because of Father Finnian's visit to me. I am pleased to see you, all the same."

"But, Maither, if you thought I was at the community of Ciarán, why would you come here? True, the abbot has a wondrous book, but I do not see why—"

She put her fingers to his lips. "I cannot say why. I felt compelled to come. 'Twas God's urging. Let us not waste time on that. You did not get the warning about Malachi. I am delighted you are safe and sound here."

"Oh, I saw him. Sent him on his way. But I don't know what you mean by your warning."

She huffed. "Well, 'tis been said the plague disrupted communication. Malachi was banished, and I heard he was headed to the River Shannon. I knew that was where your friend was. He is the Accuser, and there is no one he holds ill will against more than you, my precious son."

"I know that." He wouldn't tell her about his altercation with that amulet, if she didn't already know. Banishment of that man was proper, at least for those in the north. "Let us join the brothers for a meal now."

He was allowed a corner away from the others to sit with his mother. She chatted on about the book, and he was loath to tell her about the dispute. She suddenly stopped and grabbed his hand as he was about to taste his food.

"There is something wrong. I cannot say exactly what. I thought it was Malachi, but you say he has not bothered you. There is an unsettled feeling in my gut, son."

He returned his utensil to his bowl. "All right. I will tell you."

As he was explaining how selfish the abbot had been and why he had to go to the king, he could see on her face she did not agree.

"'Tis always best for the community to settle its own disputes."

"He won't even talk about it, Maither. I used my own supplies and my own labor. I did not neglect my chores here in all that time. That copy is mine."

Her eyes flashed with anger. "Malachi. Gormley. They set this up."

"Oh, Maither. There would be no reason. I knew you'd worry over this. I did not want to tell you for that reason. Understand, though, that

King Diarmait seems to me to possess wisdom. He will see it my way."

"And if he does not? Will you forget all this and come home?"

"I will come home."

She seemed satisfied with his answer, but he had already been thinking about his alternatives should he need them. He could not let Finnian prevail. He would find help if the king ruled against him. He hoped his father's clan would defend him, but if not or if their army was small … Well, he hoped it wouldn't come to that, but if it did he would seek aid from all the branches of his kinsmen. They needed his copy of that great text. When she saw it, when she read it, she would understand.

"Colum, does that book contain a story about Abraham and Isaac?"

"It does, in the Book of Genesis."

"That is the one Finnian thought I should hear. I came to see it for myself."

How could he argue with such a request for spiritual knowledge? Was that not what he thirsted after as well? "Indeed you should. You see, this is why our people need a copy. How can we allow one man to control access to such knowledge and inspiration?"

"Lower your voice, son. You are a guest here, as am I."

Word came the next day. King Diarmait would render a ruling.

"A quarter of an hour and the business will be finished," Colum told his mother, trying to convince her to go to the church to read the precious book.

"I want to come. How often is it that your own mother can be by your side when a king speaks to you?"

Aye, his own mother. Why indeed must she follow him like that poor monk trails his pesky ginger cat? But he could think of no more excuses.

This time the cavernous hall was packed to the rafters. Nearly every one of Finnian's men had come. Standing about were groups of families who rented pastures from the king and all the craftsmen and their apprentices. The king's champion and many of his soldiers had come. The bakers, cooks, and servants rimmed the outer edges of the crowd. Only Colum and his mother represented his side of the argument.

The king stood on a platform that afforded the crowd a view. He stamped his scepter three times and the crowd's shouting dissolved to a weak murmur.

"My good people," Diarmait began.

Colum feared he was about to give a long discourse. "Get on with it," he whispered.

His mother squeezed his hand.

The king waved his arms outward, summoning more cheering. Then he lowered his hands and the people were silent. "To every cow, her calf. To every book..." He paused, sending Colum's heart thumping.

"...its copy."

The crowd roared joyfully.

"Nay," Colum shouted. This could not be. He was ordering Colum's copy to remain with Finnian. "That's unjust!" But his normally powerful voice was caught by the crowd's roar and sent back to him in wee, shattered pieces. He tried again, but to no avail. Dropping his mother's hand, he pushed through the crowd. When he

474

finally managed to get close to the king's platform, he found it empty. "Wait," he shouted, waving his arms at a guard standing near the curtain where Diarmait must have just exited. "I must speak to the king."

When he got closer, the guard tugged on his cloak so that Colum's ear met the man's lips. "You've already done that. The ruling is final. Leave or see the inside of the dungeon, man."

Colum stumbled outside with the celebratory crowd. There had been no one to support him. The king had ruled what these people had wanted to hear, what Finnian wanted. Diarmait had said he cherished the prayers of the Father Abbot. He had obviously not wanted to rule in such a way as to anger Finnian. He kicked at the soil with his boot. Superstitions! Even kings who were baptized in Jesu's name thought favor was gained by pleasing the monks to whom they'd granted land. He should have realized that.

After searching for his mother for an hour, he encountered the simple-minded monk. "Gone to the church, she has."

"I don't suppose she'll see that Vulgate now."

"Oh, she is. With the Father Abbot, she is."

The ginger cat had been circling the man's legs. The animal looked up at Colum and blinked one amber eye. He was beginning to hate cats.

True to what the man said, his mother was bent over the altar with the abbot at her side. They both turned when he entered.

"Son, I have read the story. The one I came to hear."

"We must depart right away." He could not make himself look at his former teacher.

"Just because King Diarmait ruled against you, Columcille, does not mean people like your mother cannot come here and read this."

Ruled against you. The words burned in his mind like hot coals. "Maither!" he shouted. Doves roosting in the thatched roof flapped about at the sound of Colum's voice.

Enya bowed toward the abbot and left with Colum.

His mother traded a length of finely woven cloth to a man who allowed them to travel in the back of his cart. "Going nearly the whole way," he said. "I am most happy to take you."

Colum gritted his teeth. Most happy so long as you are paid, he thought. No one does what is right. Not one person.

He left his mother near Eochu's Lough, the great body of water away from the sea. "I have meetings to attend to. Go ahead of me. I will come home shortly after," he promised.

Her eyes watered as she said good-bye.

He looked away.

She touched his jaw. "I still think something is amiss. Please be careful. Heed your mother's warnings."

"I hear you, Maither."

Finally, she was gone. He waited until he could no longer hear the cart's wheels. Turning quickly back to the shoreline, he picked his way along, looking for the path that led to a hut where an anchorite lived. He and Ciarán had talked about him. He lived along this lake somewhere. And what a vast lake this was.

Chapter Thirty-Seven

Now I know that you fear God, because you have not withheld from me your son ...
—Genesis 22:12 NIV

Enya did not understand what all the fuss had been about. She did not need a copy of the story of Abraham and his son Isaac to hold in her hands. The message had embedded itself in her heart. How long Abraham and his wife Sarah had wanted a child. They'd waited longer than she had. Enya had already known that part of the story. In fact, before Fe had taken her to Cruith-neachia's church, Enya had felt as though she were Sarah. But she hadn't understood there was more to the story. God had wanted the boy back. Or, rather, God had tested Abraham to see if he was faithful.

She stared out at the gathering clouds as she pondered this in the back of the rumbling cart. She would be home soon, and so would Colum. She had not done well with this test over the

478

years, but now she finally understood. She was eager to tell Fe. She prayed his mind would be clear enough to comprehend.

This revelation brought her joy, and yet, a dark premonition still stalked her, as it had since she first arrived at Finnian's monastery. *What is it, Lord?*

A few hours later she began to recognize the landscape. Her driver stopped at a cottage where she was able to board a wagon heading toward home.

A man and his wife, relatives of the Murtagh clan, were off for a visit and she was welcomed to join them. "The Cenél Conaill, is it?" the husband asked.

"'Tis."

"Been visiting your son, is it?"

"I have." She scooted down under a blanket, hoping to avoid any more questions.

"Tired, are ya?"

"I am." Never had she known such a chatty man. The wife uttered not a word, but then, when could she have?

"I suppose ya are, all that traveling. Our cousin Sean. Wasn't he to marry your daughter?"

"They are friendly. He has not asked." Those Murtaghs. So nosey.

"I suppose he will soon enough. How is your man? Fe, is it? A big fellow, as I remember." He glanced over his shoulder to look at her in the wagon bed. "I thought he'd be king by now, I did. But, ah, we've been away for some time."

The wife gave him a look, but he did not stop.

"'Tis peaceful now, so there is nothing to worry about."

Finally, the woman spoke up. "Who's doing any worrying? Leave the poor thing alone, Mac. Can't ya see she needs to sleep?"

"I suppose." He tossed his voice over his shoulder again. "Thought you'd like to know, though. An army's been gathered, mostly from Fe's clan. For your son."

She sat up straight and threw off the blanket. "What are you talking about?"

"Oh, so you didn't know, then. Well, it seems an urgent message was sent. We got it at our cottage as well, but we don't have any sons."

"What message?"

The wife punched the man's arm. "See what you've done, Mac? Got her all upset and she hasn't even gotten home yet."

"Tell me," Enya demanded.

"Something about a book. King Diarmait? Your son did not like his judgment and requested assistance. I suppose there will be a war when 'tis all decided."

"A war? Are you sure this is about my son Colum? They call him Columcille. I just left him a few days ago."

"That's right. All came about quite quickly, I hear."

She didn't want to believe it, but who else would Diarmait make a judgment about a book for? Her stomach tightened. Colum was angry. The curse. Her bloodline's curse.

You have not withheld from me your son. The story she'd read came back to her. But, God, not this!

On the western shoreline, the stories said, lived a man whose home had been an ancient sight of pagan worship. Many believed the area to still be holy, although none of the monks Colum had met had ever been there. Now that he had done this thing, the events played over in Colum's mind.

As he had searched, pulling back brambles and reeds, Colum wished Michael had been with him. His prayers had seemed empty. Perhaps that was because he focused on the search.

He paused, lifted his head and closed his eyes the way he had done many times when he'd felt God's presence. The air had a wet grass scent. A few birds squawked nearby. Badgers scurrying to their shelters. He stood still and listened.

He nearly fell face first into the lake when someone spoke behind him.

"What are you doing here? I tolerate no students and no gawkers!"

Why had Colum not heard him approach when he'd been listening so carefully? No matter. The hermit he sought had found him.

"I have come to evoke the right of testimony." He'd remembered the phrase from some scribbles he and Ciarán had found on the backside of a manuscript they had been copying. The tale of this hermit had been a secular story not sanctioned by the abbot, but velum was too precious to throw away so they'd discovered it. Ciarán had told him then to forget about the hermit's tale, but the dispute over the book's copy had driven Colum to try anything.

The hermit, covered by an untrimmed beard and baggy clothing, sat on a rock and leaned against his walking stick. "From the Sons of Néill, are you?"

"I am. My father is of the Cenél Conaill." Colum sat on the grass in front of the rock so as to not tower over the man. "How do you know this?"

The old man's eyes had lit with a twinkle. "That phrase, the right of testimony. I heard a scribe had recorded it in some monastery. And I heard a blessed member of that clan was being educated in the church." He winked. "Don't be thinking hermits don't hear gossip." He chuckled. "Wondered how long it would take for someone to claim testimony."

"I was robbed of what was lawfully mine, a valuable copy of a book, and ruled against by King Diarmait."

The man laughed. "I never expected to be put to task because of a book. Ah, so be it."

"You can do it, then?"

"Summon the Cenél nEogain, Dál Riata, and all of your kin to come to your aid, you mean?"

Colum nodded.

"The Mac Noe as well," the hermit said.

"I don't think that's a good idea."

"Oh, 'tis. They are also of the Sons of Néill. If their leader does not participate, the other clans will destroy him. You do not want that held against you."

"True, he did not wish eternal harm on anyone."

The man continued. "You have claimed the right of testimony. This is an old law that many have forgotten save the rulers. They know it must be done. It shall be done. And in return you will swear never to visit me again nor speak of me and this place to any living being?"

Colum had clasped the man's hand to show his agreement.

Now he wasn't sure what he'd set in motion. He could not summon the clans without the Mac Noe, it seemed.

"What is taking Colum so long? He should be here by now." Enya stood near the stables and watched her son Egan fasten a gold torque to his upper arm. At least the other warriors would know her son was from a royal bloodline and be honor bound to protect him.

"He'll be here if he was truly the one who called for an army." Fe rubbed his temples as he spoke. He'd wanted to go too but he was still too weak.

Armies, weapons, golden torques … Enya could scarcely believe what she was seeing. Brody approached, riding atop a black stallion. At least he'd found the courage to lead his army. She turned to her husband. "This is not about a book, is it?"

Fe moved his fingers to his neck, trying to rub out his discomfort. "To Colum, aye. But no kings fight over such things. This is … territory. The Uí Néills of the north driving down the Uí Néills of the south. 'Tis the only reason King Diarmait . . ." He huffed. "High King, he thinks he is, but nothing but a representative of the southerners. Never before has our kingdom been so strong. Victory is assured."

"Must Egan go? He is so young."

Her son glanced at her with dark eyes. He wanted to be a man and to fight was a matter of honor, at least to him.

Fe turned toward her, blocking her view of the lad. "I have thought of that. Something ... to save ... honor. Do not worry, my heart."

Fe had trouble stringing his words together sometimes. Enya hoped that in time this would improve but she was overjoyed to hear him use such a tender form of the endearment he'd chosen for her long ago. However, how could she not worry? Was she to sacrifice another son? This time it could be for eternity. How could she survive that?

Someone rode behind Brody. Not a warrior. Someone with an uncovered head. Someone with a tonsure. Colum!

She ran toward him.

"Maither, I beg your forgiveness. My business took longer than I thought."

"Come see your father, Colum. He has waited a long time."

Fe limped toward him, the soles of his feet seeming to give him pain. "My son, come down off that ... horse, will you?"

486

Colum jumped to the ground and embraced his father. "You are well, Da. You are very well."

He would see soon enough, Enya thought. That is, if he also did not go to war.

When they were all seated around the hearth, Fe turned to Colum and placed his large hand on his eldest child's shoulder. "Have you called for assistance from the … the warriors … true?"

"'Tis, Da."

"That book means …'tis that important?"

"More vital than any other manmade object."

Fe nodded as though he understood. Enya could not imagine anything more important than the lives of her children. Men might debate about how being in control of waterways and charcoal mines and grazing pastures ensured the survival of their children, but Enya would never agree those things needed to be taken by force. God provides.

Egan spoke up. "The lads, Colum, they wonder how you did it. How did you convince the Cenél nEogain and the Dàl Raita to join us? Especially in such a short time."

Colum's face reddened and he bent his head low. However he did it, it seemed he would not be telling them. Finally he looked up. "'Tis what's right, brother. We need that book."

"Nay, we do not."

They all glanced up at Enya, mouths drooping.

"Well, I mean, we can memorize the scripture. Is that not what you did at school, Colum? That's what you teach your novices to do, I would think."

Colum resumed studying the floorboards. "Not the same. Not at all. This is the Vulgate, written for the common people." He stood. "I cannot explain all that now. Let us go, Egan."

Fe went outside with them. Hopefully he really did have a plan to save their sons.

Chapter Thirty-Eight

Isaac spoke up and said to his father Abraham,
"Father?"
"Yes, my son?" Abraham replied.
"The fire and wood are here," Isaac said, "but
where is the lamb for the burnt offering?"
—*Genesis 22: 7 NIV*

"Save your breath, Da. I know what we are doing." Colum led his brother and father inside the gates of his monastery. There would sanctuary here. It was right to bring Egan. He was too young. And Fe could not fight.

Egan protested. "They will say I am a coward!"

"Let them," Fe said. "This is not your fight. You own no cattle. You pay no tribute to the king. Let the men with a stake in this fight. Your time will come."

They encountered one of the Murtagh clan, Sean, a lad Colum had been told would one day marry Keeva. They were still too young. Many young people had been sent to this sanctuary for safe keeping, and that was proper. Egan would not be alone. "'Tis good to stay here," he told both young men. "The clan must have a generation held back in case … Well, know that you have a role here."

As Colum prepared to leave them with the monks, his father followed him out. "Nay, Da, you cannot come."

"As well as you can, son. You have no weapons."

Egan was settled in and could not overhear, so Colum spoke sincerely. "Your health is not good enough. You are recovering from a plague. Stay here."

"And leave your sisters and your mother in the cottage alone?"

His argument was sound. "Come on, then."

When they returned home, Brody and the others had left.

Branna met them at the door. "Said they were going to the shore, to cut off Diarmait from the sea. They said if he had to march his army inland he'd be weaker."

That made sense, although Colum would never catch up to them now. They'd gotten a great lead.

Using one of his father's best horses, Colum headed west toward the distinctive mountain Binn-Gulbain. He tried to ignore his mother's pleading looks. It hadn't calmed her when he'd told her he wasn't going to fight. He just needed to know the outcome. He'd stay far back.

"Something dark and menacing is about to happen," she'd said.

What war is not that? If Finnian had not been so stubborn …

During the long days of travel, Colum began to plan what he'd accomplish at the schools he'd build. They would grow and produce new teachers who would then teach countless others. Getting this book back would help that cause. He was right. He knew it.

After a day of travel a sinking feeling overcame him. He thought it was probably the same sense of doom his mother had described.

The next day as he descended the path down toward the shoreline, smoke clouded the distant horizon. What he would normally assume was fog carried a bitter smell.

Death.

As he continued on he began encountering men walking in the opposite direction.

"You, there. Have you come from battle?"

He got no answer from the first dozen he approached. Their faces bore bits of battle lime nearly covered with soot. Some led horses who had red streaks across their flanks. Of course these were warriors. But whose?

Finally he encountered the battlefield. The stench and presence of vultures told him the battle had occurred days earlier. A few stout men with shovels worked to bury slain fighters.

"Who prevailed at this battle?" he continued to ask.

No one answered. Leaving his horse, he walked about. Thousands lay dead. This had not been a fair fight. One side was slaughtered.

He tripped over a disembodied leg and landed on his hands and knees. Regaining his composure, he realized he was on top of a body. Unseeing eyes met his. A trickle of blood had dried on the dead man's cheeks. Horrified, he sprung to his feet and had to step on arms, shoulders, and even heads to find a vacant spot to stand. He held a hand over his mouth, trying not to vomit.

"Disease sets in now."

He spun around, almost expecting the voice to come from one of the bodies. A man wearing common clothing glared at him. He held a torch. Another man behind him was digging a grave.

"What happened here?" Colum was finally able to choke out.

"I hear a priest ordered the Uí Néills of the north to fight a war. And them the most powerful on the island, they lost but one man in the battle."

Colum spread his arms out over the dead he could see. He would pray for these souls. "And how many lost on the other side?"

"Three thousand."

Colum lowered his arms. "So many? How can you be sure?"

"Well, the clans, they know how many each sent. Doing the calculations, heard it was three thousand. What are you doing here, Father?" He narrowed his eyes. "Might you be that priest, then?"

Colum put his hand over his heart. What had he done? "King Diarmait, is he among the dead?"

"Ah, he is not. Left this morning. Said he was going to the priest's new school, up north, to make him pay for this."

Colum's family! He could do nothing more here. Fe might not be able to protect them. "Thank you, kind one, for telling me what happened. I will pray for the departed, and also for all of you." He turned and left. His prayers would have to be said as he rode. His horse was too tired. There seemed to be many abandoned beasts with which to trade.

Colum was able to return in less time than it took to get to the battlefield. He had been dreading what he'd find where the fight occurred, now he feared what he might find at home if he were too late. When he paused to water his horse, he encountered another soldier. "Where is the rest of the army, the ones who were victorious?" The words almost choked him with guilt.

"All directions, I suppose, although most headed toward Tara for a victory feast."

"Not you?"

"I've no stomach for it. This was a battle like I've never seen. Our forces were more numerous, our weapons far superior. 'Twas not a fight." He poured water over his head without blinking. "This was butchery. I do not know that I will ever sleep again without waking in terror." Tears mixed with the spring water streaking down his face. "How can I face my wife and children after what I've done? I should never have gone."

Colum embraced the man and allowed him to weep into his shoulder. None of them should have gone. He wasn't sure he'd ever sleep again either.

When he finally arrived at his parents' cottage, wails of grief sailed out from the walls. Something dire had happened. Why hadn't he listened to his mother's premonitions? He pulled open the door, knowing he had to face whatever it was.

Diarmait stood in the center of the room. Of all the horrors Colum had seen on the battlefield, this was the worst. A severed head dangled from the king's hand, dripping dark spots on his mother's carefully swept floor. "A wee payment," he yelled, shoving the head in Colum's direction.

Please, God, don't let that be Fe or Egan.

With all the blood it was impossible to tell.

The man bolted out the door, taking the head with him. Keeva and her sisters huddled together in one corner of the cottage. Enya crouched on the floor, crying out as though her heart would break. Fe was not there. He went to his mother and tried to get her to look at him. "Where's Da?"

The door crashed open and in walked Fe. "Diarmait thought that was your brother. Was not."

Enya gasped.

Colum pointed to the door. "Should we go after him?"

"The king? Risk another war? We will have to let it rest."

"What happened?" Colum stood, legs trembling.

"I believe you do know what happened, son. Or did you not reach your destination?" Colum's father appeared stronger than he had earlier.

Strife builds endurance. That's what the monastery schools taught.

"I did. A terrible thing." He stooped down to gather his crumpled mother into his arms. "I am sorry. Very sorry."

She lifted her head to look at Fe. "Not Egan? He's all right?"

"Still at the monastery. Safe, but perhaps not sound. Has been a terrible shock for them all. That brute killed a Murtagh."

Colum closed his eyes.

Keeva wailed. His mother left him to embrace her.

"Was it Sean?" Keeva asked.

Colum dared to look at his father. Fe nodded.

Colum grieved inside but not even his temper could emerge from the guilt he felt. "I must go to the brothers."

No one, not even his mother tried to convince him to stay. He would walk. He would not burden his family again by taking their horses or carts.

The cold air stung the salty streaks on his face. The depth of his sin was inconceivable. God should punish him. Colum was willing.

497

When he'd gone a little way, he realized he was near the hill where he'd spent time with Michael, learning to trust the visions God had given him. That was gone now. God could not trust him with any gifts now. He decided to climb, though it was quite dark and the angel-like clouds now loomed in the sky like menacing demons. When he reached the top, he lay down and wept bitterly.

A few moments later he was aware of a presence. He opened his eyes. "Michael. When did you get here?"

"I am always here, Colum."

"You know what I've done?"

Michael stared at the demon clouds, but they did not seem to disturb him as they had Colum. "I know."

Colum sat up and pounded his fists on the ground. "Finnian was wrong to keep my copy. Diarmait was wrong to cross the boundaries of sanctuary and murder that lad."

"I cannot argue."

Colum breathed in the night air. For the first time he listened to the sounds. Wind stirred dry leaves. His own beating heart echoed in his ears. His heart still ached for all the lost lives, but here in this place of angels he was able to breathe deeply once again.

"What about you, Colum? What were you wrong about?"

"I … I should not have called for war. I don't know what else I could have done, but there had to be another way."

"It did not go well for the Mac Noes. With their inferior battle skills, they made many military mistakes. They gave up, abandoned your armies in the middle of the fight and headed home. Diarmait did not only kill an innocent monk, he also has the head of your grandfather."

Colum gasped. "The one life lost?"

"Aye."

"Does my mother know?"

"Diarmait went to the cottage to tell her himself."

"Oran Mac Noe was a cruel man. He treated my mother poorly."

"That is so, but it does not change the pain she felt hearing the news." Michael turned toward Colum, hands on knees. "We always hope for more, even when the other person has no intention of giving it. A lost soul is a terrible thing to mourn."

"What should I do? What kind of penance?"

"I suggest you travel back to Molaise. Work out your penance with him."

It was a good suggestion. Molaise was a wise man and Colum trusted him. Travel weary as he was, he knew he must do this. "What about the brothers I was going to see? Shouldn't I at least—"

"Leave the comforting to me."

Truly Michael was better at that. Fe would be best at comforting Enya and Keeva. So Colum left Michael and strode back down the hill and toward the sea. The feeling of dread was gone, replaced with shame and enough sadness to carry for the rest of his life. And he was still a young man.

Chapter Thirty-Nine

Although I am imperfect in many ways,
I want my brothers and relations to know
what I'm really like,
so that they can see
what it is that inspires my life.
—*St. Patrick (from St. Patrick's Confessio)*

Colum sat in Molaise's hut waiting for a reaction to the story he'd just told. Who wouldn't blame him? He had ignored good sense, had failed to pray about his decisions before acting, and had ignored the stabbing dread both he and his mother had sensed. He could have prevented those three thousand deaths. And that of Sean and Oran Mac Noe's. And years ago he was to blame for Donál's death.

Molaise closed his eyes. Colum didn't dare do the same, although he was so very tired. He wanted to be ready when the abbot father spoke. Many minutes passed.

Colum searched his mind for his familiar psalms. The Lord is a refuge for the oppressed, a stronghold in times of trouble. Those who know your name trust in you…"

"For you, Lord, have never forsaken those who seek you," Molaise finished. He drew in a breath and then waved a hand toward Colum.

"Sing the praises of the Lord," Colum continued, "enthroned in Zion; proclaim among the nations what he has done. For he who avenges blood remembers; he does not ignore the cries of the afflicted."

Molaise nodded as though satisfied. "He has not forsaken you, Colum."

Colum swallowed hard. "Praise be to God."

"But he does require penance. I see that you are remorseful."

"What do you assign me, Father Abbot? I will follow your instruction."

He sighed. "Are you not a priest now, son?"

"I am."

"Do you not have brothers to teach?"

"I do."

"Tell me, what is your greatest pleasure?"

He did not have to consider this. "Sitting on a hill in my beloved Daire, with angels all around me."

"Then that is what you must do without."

"Leave Éire?"

"Far enough that you cannot glimpse it."

"Where should I go?"

"I think you, as a priest, should establish the guidelines of your banishment, Columcille."

Banished. Like Malachi. Except that he had to decide to where.

"Sleep, and in the morning you will know."

He thanked the abbot and lay down with a rock as a pillow, hoping the discomfort would bring clarity.

And in the morning, he knew.

Bairre set the sail despite being confused about the destination. "You know, Colum, I am happy to take you anywhere, but we'll be sailing right past your home. Shouldn't you visit, one last time?"

"Nay." He stared at the green coastline, taking in every memory of Éire he could. "If I did, I would violate the penance I've accepted."

"But you're the one who set it. Surely you could—"

"I cannot. This time I will not fail Jesu nor any person."

Bairre finished his work with the sail. They caught a gentle wind and since the weather was fair, Bairre was able to sit and share an apple and bit of soft cheese.

"Speaking of people," the sailor monk said.

"Are you lonely on that island? A change from the life you're used to, aye?"

"A change for the better. I have not been lonely since I began to walk with Jesu."

"Ah, fine, that is."

"Remember that fellow you told me to watch out for?"

"You don't mean Malachi? You've seen him? That man, growing old and lame, seems to pop up everywhere. Like a weed."

"That's the one I mean, only I did not see him." He hesitated.

"Go on, man. What do you mean?"

"The Father Abbot, he asked me to tell you this once we were safely on our way."

Anger turned over in Colum's stomach like a bad meal. "What has that man done?"

"Nothing. Well, I mean he probably has, I do not know." He tossed the apple core into the water. "What I mean to say is, the Father Abbot has had a message from him. I'm to give it to you."

"A message? I cannot think of what that man has to say that should concern me."

Bairre's expression turned to wrinkled worry. "Those that hurt us in the past cannot do so any longer. Do you not believe this as a follower of Jesu?"

Colum handed him a water-filled sheep's bladder. "Your training has taught you much, Bairre. I am grateful for the reminder. What is this message?"

"Malachi asks, begs, that you allow him to come to Innis nan Druineach and become one of your followers. He says he is remorseful and seeks mercy from you and from Jesu."

"Come with me?" He tried to shake the suggestion from his mind. "He tried to kill me. He says he is the Accuser. He was somehow allowed to keep that amulet, the weapon he used on me.

My own grandfather, God rest his soul, believed him."

"And that's the way of it, isn't it? To save those lost like your own grandfather?"

Lost. Colum would never forget those three thousand and one lost souls. Was this perhaps the beginning of restitution? "What does Molaise think of this?"

"Only said that the way will be difficult for you but not for God."

Colum stared at some seals frolicking on rocks near the mainland. "Though I walk through the valley of death, I will fear no evil."

Bairre continued the psalm. "For God is with me."

"Send word that he may come." Colum's penance had begun.

"Banished to Innis nan Druineach? Why there?" Enya stared at her husband in disbelief. She'd known Colum would have a price to pay within the church even though the laws of the clan did not condemn him.

"The Dál Raita offered it after the battle."

"But why? He has his own island monastery just off the coast. There are no Christians in the Dál Raita place."

"That is just the reason, my heart. Molaise sends word that Colum made the decision. He shall work to save as many souls as were lost."

"But he can do that from his own community."

"What is a punishment if it does not provide sacrifice? Try to understand. He chose not to be close to his home as a punishment."

She checked on the pot over the fire. There was not much cooking to be done now that there was only the two of them and Keeva living in the cottage. The others had their own families now. Just last week Egan had married into the Murtagh clan. It had felt like another loss while also feeling like a healing. Her youngest son was happy.

"Why must we always lose something, someone, Fe?" She fought back tears.

"'Tis a full circle. Do you not see? Long ago I asked if I were not enough for you. And here we are again." He kissed her, reminding her once again how much she loved this man.

"You are more than enough, I'd say," she teased, patting his belly.

Keeva came in from the garden carrying an armload of parsley and a basket of berries. "Let me help you, darlin'." Enya took the basket.

"I heard the news from Nola. Our Colum's not to come home again."

"Och, that woman. Is there nothing she won't blather about?"

Keeva set the green parsley on the chopping board. "'Tis not only her. Gormley …"

"You'll not be speaking that woman's name in this house."

Fe went to the cupboard to retrieve his cup. "Now, Enya, has the woman not repented? Does she not spend all her days minding her grand-children inside that drafty castle?"

Enya set the basket on the table board and then braced herself against it. She drew in a long breath, telling herself not to speak before uttering a prayer. "She has." She remembered her father and the terrible night that king brought news of his death to this very cottage. "Jesu wills that not even one be lost."

Keeva began to hum as she set about her work. She filled wee jars with oil and placed herbs inside. She had become the clan's healer with her concoctions and more importantly, with her heartfelt prayers. Even Fe agreed such a combination was beneficial for the people. Our plans may never come to fruition, but God still uses our gifts to accomplish his purposes.

"Maither, I hear there are some rare plants on an island."

"Oh, where? We must go there."

She turned and winked at her father.

"What are you two up to?"

Keeva wrapped cloth around the top of one bottle and tied it with string. "The island is called Hinba. 'Tis far away. Somewhere near Innis nan Druineach. Isn't that right, Da?"

"That is where it is, I believe. I hear 'tis a wee place where the monks might go for occasional quiet contemplation, away from their daily duties at the monastery Colum's to build." He wrapped his arms around Enya, still holding his cup in one hand. "I expect you will do the same on occasion. Go there for a glimpse of your son."

She blinked back tears. "I would not interfere with his mission."

"You never have, my heart. You have only wanted to love him."

She thought again about Abraham and Isaac. God knew how much Abraham loved his son. The test was to show Abraham that God loved him the same way. And now she knew. All that she had been through, all that she had sacrificed, had not kept her from loving her children. What it had done was reveal the depth of God's love for her. Fe was right. They had come full circle. What God had given her was not hers to keep forever. It was like the cloth in her dream, something she could hold on to for a fleeting moment. And yet, when she shared it with the world, she gained more than she could have ever imagined. So many things in this life were inadequate. But God's love? That was abundant, more than enough to confirm her worth and heal her soul.

She turned to Keeva. "When shall we make our first journey to Hinda?"

"Tomorrow."

Colum had eleven men come to help him set up his new monastery. The twelfth, Malachi, had not yet arrived. Perhaps he would not come. One

510

of the first things Colum did was build his cell at the top of a wee rise in the landscape, away from the others. Inside he placed a stone. He would always rest his head there to remind himself that to allow personal comfort would be to forget. And he would never forget the pain he had caused others.

To his surprise, the wee cell did offer comfort. God met him there every day and filled his soul with joy. This comes, Molaise had told him, from following God. And there were angels above that island. He sensed their guiding presence just as strongly as he had in Daire. Today, he had a vision. Go to one of the wee lonely islands just off the shore and bestow forgiveness. He did not understand. No one lived there. But he would be faithful.

He took a curragh and set off alone. The wind was strong in this place, the land just distant enough that even on a clear day he could not glimpse his beloved Éire. He no longer mourned that loss. There was more to come.

Pulling the craft up on the sandy shore, he prayed for guidance. Voices in the distance startled him. Female voices. Laughter. As he climbed the steep hill the voices grew louder. He was surprised to find his mother and sister picking flowers. "What are you two doing?"

They turned to him. "Scavenging for my tinctures, of course," Keeva said, as though he'd just come upon them in the cottage garden.

"We won't bother you," Enya said, embracing him. She turned in the direction of his curragh.

From that vantage point Colum could see the exact spot where his monks were busy building. His mother could see for herself that he was fine without disruption. God provides.

"Why have you come over today?" Keeva asked.

"God sent me. To offer forgiveness."

They stared at him blankly. He shared their confusion.

Another voice shouted from the shore. "Hello! I see your boat. I am looking for Columcille."

They hurried to the edge of the hill and looked down. "Isn't that—?"

"Oh, no. We've no weapons," Enya said, pushing Keeva behind her.

When Colum had allowed Malachi to come he had never imagined his mother and sister would also be there. "He is an old man. He will not hurt us. Stay here and let me speak to him."

He scrambled down the hill.

"Oh, thank goodness," Malachi said. "I thought I was on the wrong island." The man wore a plain colorless garment. Gone was the ominous amulet of the Accuser.

"You are." Colum pointed toward Innis nan Druineach.

"Well, what are we doing here?"

Colum turned around. His mother and sister had not obeyed. They had come down to the shore.

"You have no power here," Enya said, pointing her finger at the man.

"You ask what are we doing here," Colum said. "I see. God has brought us here. For forgiveness."

Enya's cheeks reddened. "The Accuser seeks no forgiveness, only seeks to condemn."

"No longer." Malachi spread his arms open in surrender.

"He never had the power to accuse anyone," Colum said. "Unless we gave it to him. We accuse ourselves. I will no longer do that. I choose love." He pulled the rope cross from his pocket and placed it Enya's hand, curling her fingers over it. "This time, something for you to remember me."

Enya and Keeva stood on the shore and watched as her son and his former enemy rowed back to the island where they would build a sacred place. Soon Bairre would return for her and Keeva and they would tend to their own sacred garden where Fe awaited. And who knew about her daughter? The lad who assisted Bairre had stared at Keeva the whole trip. Perhaps a romance would bloom.

She glanced up at the sky where billowing white clouds floated on the bright parchment sky. When she shaded her eyes from the sun, she saw the cloth from her dream, the one she'd had before Colum was born. It stretched from above her head to far beyond the island where Colum was headed. Shades of green, blue, purple, and red, were so vivid she gasped. Little pinpricks shown through the cloth. It was as though with the sun shielded she could see the previously hidden stars. A voice resounded in her head. *Because you have been faithful, I will bless the earth with as many saved souls as the stars in the sky and as the sand on the sea-shore. These followers will take over the lands of their enemies, and through your offspring all nations on earth will be blessed. Because you have obeyed me.*

Acknowledgments

I acknowledge that presenting a novel to readers is a great privilege. I also know that I could not have done so without readers who are waiting for it, prayers from my prayer group, the patience and support of my husband, Tom, and the grace of God. Thank you!

There were a few others who helped out as well. Thanks to Jim McVeigh for helping with the pronunciation guide. Thanks to Daria Blackwell of coastalboating.net for her advice and resources on sailing the islands off Ireland's Atlantic coast. Thanks to early readers and critique partners Donna Wyland, Erin MacLellan, and Tamera Kraft. You read parts of *Enya's Son* so long ago you probably thought I had given up on it! But your feedback stayed with me and helped make the story stronger. Thanks again to the wonderful John Pierce for proofreading. Your support means so much and your willingness to help with short notice is very much appreciated. I'm extremely thankful I had the opportunity to work with a fabulous editor, Jamie Chavez, who is also a dear friend. That came about because of a generous cultural grant awarded to me by the Milwaukee Irish Festival's Scholarship and Grant Committee, for which I am so very thrilled and grateful. Thank you for your desire to see *Enya's Son* reach readers and for working to see that Irish stories are passed on.

Author's Notes

Most of what is known about St. Columba (Columcille) comes from the account written by the abbot of Iona about a century after the saint's death, *Vita Columbae* by Adomnán. Columcille lived from approximately 521 to 597. Where his mother Eithne (Enya) was born is not known. One theory is the Fanad Peninsula, County Donegal. Another is somewhere in Fermanagh. I chose the latter without pinpointing a location. The names of Columcille's siblings are recorded in ancient writings, however I have tried to simplify their names, as I did with Enya, for today's English-speaking readers.

Ciarán, who founded Clonmacnoise in 544, was known to Columba, although they met at Clonard rather than at Loch Cuan. Whether he came from Eithne's clan or not is unknown. Since Eithne's father was known as "son of a ship," in the Irish, Mac-naue, and Clonmacnoise means meadow of the Mac Noes, I chose to make that connection.

The battle of Cúl Dreimhne, or Battle of the Book, took place around 555. For those keeping track of such things, I have condensed the time-line for the sake of the story. The battle was fought over a psalter Columcille copied and wanted to keep. King Diarmait's ruling, "To every cow, her calf. To every book, its copy," is sometimes called the world's first copyright case. An ancient book called the Cathach or Battler, could be that very book. It dates to the appropriate era and is a transcription of St. Jerome's Vulgate. It is now housed at the Royal Irish Academy in Dublin.

Many of the place names I've used were taken from *Irish Place Names* by P. W. Joyce, originally published in 1870 under the title *Irish Local Names Explained*. I recommend all of Joyce's books for those wanting to know more about ancient Ireland. They have served as the primary reference for all of my Daughter of Ireland novels. I have kept to the ancient spellings as much as possible, although the place names over the years have become somewhat anglicized so it's uncertain whether the people in Columcille's day would have used these.

Medieval monasteries were a major advancement over the tiny, hermit-like isolated homes that some monks lived in previously. They included a church, refectory, sometimes a dormitory and scriptorium, and all the necessary functions of a city, such as blacksmith forges, agricultural fields, barns, and hospitals. They truly were the centers of trade and learning in ancient times.

It was said Columcille used a rock for a pillow. Why he did so in my story comes from my imagination. Tales have been told that his pillow rock was the actual one that Jacob used according to the Bible or that he brought Jacob's pillar stone with him, having taken it from Tara where it had been used as a coronation stone. The legend further proposes that this became the Lia Fail (Stone of Destiny) or Stone of Scone, now in Westminster Abbey. There are other legends about the Stone of Scone, tales that fire the imagination!

A note about the "Right of Testimony" that Columcille evokes in *Enya's Son*: that came strictly from my imagination. There was, however, some summoning of the clans that took place since a great army fought in his behalf.

Two good online sources for those wanting to know more about the historical Columcille include:

http://www.colmcille.org/colmcille/birth-early-life/

http://www.stcolumbaheritagetrail.org/who-was-st-columba/

Place names:

Éire is Ireland.

Fir-monach, meaning the men of Monach, is the Irish word for Fermanagh, a present-day county in Ireland. This may have been the region where Enya was from.

Loch Cuan is the Irish name for Strangford Lough.

Daire, as used in *Enya's Son*, is the northern reaches of Ireland, and would likely have been located in County Donegal and County Londonderry/Derry.

Magh Bile is the monastic site of Movilla Abbey founded about 540 by St. Finnian (different from Finnian of Clonard.) It is located in County Down, Northern Ireland.

Laighen is the Irish word for Leinster, a province in Ireland today consisting of twelve eastern counties.

Cill Dara, Church of the Oak, was St. Brigid's foundation, modern-day Kildare.

Meadow of the Mac Noes is Clonmacnoise.

Innis nan Druineach is present day Iona, Scotland. In ancient times known as Isle of the Druids.

Hinba is an island thought to be off the coast of Scotland and used by Columcille's monks, although its exact location is unknown. Legend is that this island might have been Eileach An Naoimh, where lies the supposed grave of Columcille's mother. Scholars have differing opinions on this, however.

Tower of the King is modern day Tory Island.

Árainn Uí Dhomhnaill is Arranmore off the coast of County Donegal.

The location of Cruithneachia's church is unknown so I have made an educated guess.

The Sacred Isle is Inishmurray, an uninhabited island off the coast of County Sligo where St. Molaise founded a monastery in the sixth century.

Eochu's Lough is today's Lough Neagh, the largest freshwater lake in the UK and Ireland. Speaking of lakes in general, I have used both spellings, loch and lough, but they are pronounced the same.

Emain Macha is also known as Navan Fort, an ancient ceremonial monument near Armagh, Northern Ireland.

Clonard Abbey was an ancient monastery on the River Boyne in modern day County Meath. It was founded around 520 by St. Finnian. The Twelve Apostles of Ireland were educated there. For more about that, please see my book *The Roots of Irish Wisdom: Learning From Ancient Voices*.

Binn-Gulbain is Ben Bulben or Benbulbin, a distinctive mountain in County Sligo, an area often referred to as Yeats Country. When I visited, Ben Bulben appeared in the background of nearly every photograph I took. It was near this mountain that the historic battle over the book Columcille copied took place.

Glas Naoidhen is Glasnevin, near Dublin, most recognized today for its nineteenth-century cemetery where many Irish notable figures are buried.

The Isle of the Saints refers to the Aran Islands where St. Enda lived.

Slí Mór is the Great Road or the Pilgrim's Road, formed by an esker or a ridge created after the melting of a glacier. It ran from east to west, cutting the country in half, and brought travelers to Clonmacnoise where they could then travel north and south on the River Shannon.

For readers who would like to read more about St. Columba, I suggest Tim Clarkson's book, *Columba*. There are many others as well.

Please stay in touch by signing up for my newsletter,
http://cindyswriting.com/newsletter-signup/

You can also contact me here:
http://cindyswriting.com/contact/